T0365918

SHADOW
BALLET

SHADOW BALLET

A Novel of Mystery and Intrigue

DAN RAGON

 iUniverse

SHADOW BALLET
A NOVEL OF MYSTERY AND INTRIGUE

iUniverse books may be ordered through booksellers or by contacting:

iUniverse
1663 Liberty Drive
Bloomington, IN 47403
www.iuniverse.com
1-800-Authors (1-800-288-4677)

ISBN: 978-1-4917-7076-4 (sc)
ISBN: 978-1-4917-7077-1 (e)

Library of Congress Control Number: 2015912312

Print information available on the last page.

iUniverse rev. date: 8/28/2015

ACKNOWLEDGMENTS

No story is the work of a lone writer, sequestered in an icy garret, scratching thoughts on a growing stack of ink stained pages. The story begins with a vision, then materializes as the collected sum of conversations, discussions, arguments, jokes, plaudits, and criticisms of friends, family and acquaintances interested enough to offer an opinion on the efforts of the author to express the vision coherently. This story is a work of fiction, set in a real place and real towns, which have fallen victim to the views, memories, and fanciful liberties of the author. The characters, plot, and events portrayed are fictional. I apologize for using names which may duplicate those of persons living or dead. The places I have described are plucked from my memory of California, Humboldt County, Big Lagoon Park, Patrick's Point State Park, and the characteristic weather patterns of California's rugged north coast.

This story is dedicated to the memory of Gale Silva, whose love and support encouraged me to pursue the dream of a lifetime. Gale left us in 1993 before this story was more than a few pages of disjointed dialogue and characterizations, but her memory will forever guide my fragile craft through the turbulent waters of time.

In the writing and development of this story I have many people to thank. My parents, Glenn Ragon, Humboldt County Deputy Sheriff (retired), who lived and worked as a detective where this story is set and taught me to appreciate the awesome majesty and beauty of nature and the north coast; Dariel Ragon, who taught me to understand people and to recognize a conflicting view as a window to a broader perspective. Thanks to Katie Finnigan for prodding me for the next pages as soon as she finished reading the latest pieces of the first draft. Sincere appreciation to Austin Green, for reading, editing, and helping me to focus the story line and dialogue. My love to Damon and Colleen Nicoli, who carried on my business interests while I pounded the keys. A special thanks and nod of appreciation goes to my brother Jim, for being a harsh critic, a good reader, a strong supporter, and for helping me to complete the presentation of this story. Importantly, this story would never have found the way to publication without the talented and diligent efforts of my friend and agent, Chaz Raymond.

Dan Ragon

This book is dedicated to the memory of

Gale Silva
1945-1993

A bright candle whose shadow will forever
flicker on the path of my life

Truth concealed in a kaleidoscope
of shadow and light.
Gossamer fabric woven of triumph and tragedy,
of hope and despair,
of wisdom and foolishness,
of fantasy and reality.
Balancing observed fantasy
within masked reality
makes us each the same,
each unique.
—Dan Ragon

PROLOGUE

A ghostly image amid the steady rain, he silently drifted along the lane of sleeping cottages shuttered and curtained against the cold wet darkness. Storm winds ripped the curtain of night, muffling the rumble of nearby surf. *A miserable night for man or beast*, he thought, *perfect conditions*. Encapsulated in nature's camouflage, he drifted among the shadows to the fence separating the yard from the cabins facing the beach.

The drumming of the rain drowned the sound of his passage among the vines and tall weeds surrounding the small shed built against the fence. Concealed by the structure, he slithered into the next yard.

A sculpture of shadow, he flattened himself against the fence, watching and listening for any sign of detection. Satisfied he had avoided notice, he dashed for the nearest cabin and dived under the rear corner. Carefully identifying and disregarding the sounds of the storm, he strained to hear if he was still alone. Ignoring physical discomfort, he focused on the job at hand.

A half hour elapsed, marked only by the chatter of falling rain. Nothing moved but his chest and his eyes. Silent as a spider, he crawled beneath the cabin until he was directly across the grassy driveway from the neighboring cabin. Fifteen feet separated him from his target. He paused, eyes and ears alert while the rain rode the wind and pelted the ground. He only needed a few minutes to set the bugs and escape along the beach, where the surf would erase his footprints. A vague uneasiness invaded his thoughts, a nagging doubt he might not have detected a clever pursuer. The splatter of raindrops and rattling downspouts created a wall of noise loud enough to cover the approach of even the clumsiest oaf. It was like trying to hear a pin drop in a boiler factory. *Relax. You're dodging raindrops and seeing bogey men.* He edged into the open space between the cabins. Movement darted across the corner of his vision followed by a heavy thud. Silent darkness swallowed him.

1.

PAUL ARRIVED AT THE CABIN BENEATH A CRYSTAL
clear summer sky. The screen door came unhinged as it opened
and caught against the weathered planks, tilting drunkenly
toward the front door. "Well, there's a happy greeting," he
mumbled and dropped his suitcase. He pulled the screen
open far enough to disconnect the rusty spring and propped
it open with a red clay pot containing the skeletal remains of a
flowering plant. The happiness of his arrival took another hit
when he saw crusty surface of the lock. "With my luck, the
lock will be full of salt and won't work," he grumbled as he
fished the key from his pocket. To his delighted surprise, the
key smoothly released the dead bolt with a satisfying clunk.
He picked up his suitcase and reached for the knob.

"Hi there! Are you the new owner?"

Paul turned to discover a woman standing at the edge of
the street. She was about five feet four, with brown hair, and
what looked like a trim figure disguised by a baggy jogging
suit, her face partially concealed by large sunglasses and a visor.
He thought she made a compactly attractive package.

"Sorry, no. I didn't buy the place. I'm just renting it for a
few months."

"Oh," she sighed. "I noticed the For Sale sign was gone a
couple weeks ago and I thought... well... it doesn't matter."
A bright smile spread across her face and her voice took on

a happy lilt. "Well, let me be the first to say welcome to the neighborhood, for however long you're going to stay."

"Thanks. I take it you live here?"

"Yeah, I'm the cabin at the end of the street." She pointed to where the gravel surface ended a short distance to the south.

"So, are you the Welcome Wagon lady come to offer baskets of free samples of local products and two for one coupons at the finest restaurants?"

She laughed. "No, nothing official or formal, just a neighbor. There are only twenty-five cabins in the subdivision so everybody sort of watches what everyone else is doing. It's only fair to warn you some of the neighbors are real busybodies. Poking around in everyone else's business is more exciting than watching soap operas and it gives us something to gossip about. In the city the police try to get folks involved in Neighborhood Watch to discourage burglaries. Here, watching the neighbors doesn't require any encouragement at all."

"So I shouldn't go outside unless I'm properly dressed?"

"Absolutely. And don't leave your curtains open unless you enjoy an audience." She flashed a brilliant smile. "By the way, I'm Jean Parker, and, uh, like I said, I live in the last cabin," again pointing down the weedy gravel road that separated the cabins from the edge of the bluff which dropped fifty feet to the beach below.

Paul was a little surprised to be greeted before he could open his door, but found himself enjoying the encounter. *You may have to be here for a while, so you might as well just go with the flow.* "I'm Paul McAfee. Nice to meet you, Jean." He realized meeting her had released the tensions of a long trip into an uncertain future.

"Nice to meet you, too." Jean smiled brightly. " Just ask if you need help finding anything. I'm usually somewhere close."

"Thanks. I guess we'll be seeing more of each other."

He admired her shape as she walked away. *Not too tough on the eyes. Might be fun getting to know her.* He didn't realize he was being discreetly observed from behind the curtains of the cabin next door while they talked.

The cabin was about fifty years old, and quaintly representative of the timber industry which dominated the region from the years of the Gold Rush until the early nineteen-sixties. Built in a compact L shape, the utilitarian floor plan provided a surprising amount of livable space. Paul paused to admire the open beamed living room with a stone fireplace, varnished Douglas fir flooring, and a panoramic view to the west. In contrast to the rough-hewn elegance of the room, the furniture was summer cabin kitsch. A mixture of scarred chairs, an end table, and a small couch, all apparently retired after they had expended the best years of their life, populated the space. In a vacation cabin where wet swimsuits and sandy feet were expected, the eclectic gathering of fading dowagers was appropriate. The one remarkable piece of furniture was a bentwood rocker with the finish rubbed off the arms. The caning sagged in the center and was pulling away from the edges, but the rocker was good quality. Given a fresh coat of lacquer and re-caning it would be a welcome guest in any home. He found a soothing comfort in the aging furniture desperately clinging to the last precious hours of service.

The kitchen, off the living room to the right, was large enough for one person to work in at a time. On the left was a small pantry, an apartment size gas range, and an ancient Crosley refrigerator with the door closed, unplugged, in the corner. On the right was a counter beneath an ocean view window flanked by two cupboards. The aged sink, whose patina of nicks and stains told of years of use and intermittent periods of neglect, was centered below the window. The counter-top on each side of the sink sported a scarred and cracked linoleum surface worn to the backing in places, leaving the geometric pattern over a yellow background a fading memory in the corners. Dreading what he would find inside, he held his breath and opened the refrigerator to find it host to a variety of different colored molds and the fetid odor of a drying swamp. "Yuck! Add some serious cleaning supplies to the shopping list and don't forget a large box of industrial strength baking soda!" He chuckled. "Look at the bright side. Cleaning and stocking this old girl will make me feel at home."

Geez, this place reminds me of the little shack Tim and I rented when we were in college. About the same age as this one, but with two bedrooms. It was a great party pad. It's amazing either of us managed to find time to study, let alone graduate. We've sure come a long way since those easy days with no responsibilities; all the way from youthful freedom to doing our best to escape the repercussions of what we took on so eagerly. Smiling at fond memories, he strolled through the living room into the bedroom. An aging double bed and chest of drawers filled the room to near capacity. A small closet was tucked to the right of the door. The cozy bathroom shared a common wall with the kitchen. A shower, washbasin and toilet took up all but a small walkway. He laughed when he noticed the toilet paper supply was a single sheet hanging crookedly from the cardboard roll. The walk through completed, he started for the car to get the rest of his things.

He paused on the front porch to admire the coast and ocean for the first time. The sights and sounds engulfed his senses like a light being switched on in a dark room. The cool breeze off the ocean was rich with the smells of the living sea and the beach. He crossed the gravel street to stand at the edge of the bluff. From where he stood at about its mid-point, the beach stretched north and south in an unbroken expanse nearly five miles long, terminated by a tree studded rocky prominence at each end. To the south, the bluff rose gradually to a height of nearly three hundred feet and arced back away from the gravel beach. Cut away by eons of wind, rain and surf, the layers of raw earth were a subtle rainbow of brown, yellow, and red. To the north, a sand bar cluttered with driftwood, scattered clumps of grass, and flowering vines separated the surf from a lagoon fringed on the north and east by towering coastal redwoods growing to the water's edge. Accustomed to navigating the concrete canyons of the south, he was awestruck by the unsoiled natural majesty spread out before him. Filling his lungs with fresh air he surrendered himself to the primeval taste of the planet giving birth to itself. His mind stirred with visions of early man drifting south beyond the edge of the great sheets of ice and leaving the first footprints in the shifting surface of the beach below him. The travails that brought him here forgotten, he stood on the edge of the continent discovering a thirst he had never known and drank deeply from a fountain of inner peace.

Paul reluctantly dragged himself back to the present. As much as he'd like to forget his responsibilities, years of discipline won the battle. He needed to get settled and stock the place with groceries and basics like toilet paper and something to sanitize the refrigerator and eradicate it's incredible smell before what was already a long day was done. The day began when his car coughed up its transmission as he was crossing the river at the south end of the county. He had studied a map of his destination while he waited to complete arrangements for a rental car. Over a lackluster breakfast he'd pushed aside his frustrations and tried to learn something about where he was going to live for the next few months. The freeway bypassed most of the towns along his route, but in places the old highway was marked as a scenic route, particularly a section near the forks of the Eel River labeled The Avenue of the Giants. As he carried in his luggage, his mind retreated to the spectacle of the road snaking like an ebony river through the leafy green canyon of tall trees. After a lifetime where big trees were sixty feet tall, he felt dwarfed by the massive giant in Founder's Grove which for many years held the distinction of being the tallest tree on the planet. Like so many before him, he was struck speechless by the majesty of a tree that began growing more than a thousand years before Rome became an empire. Reaching nearly four hundred feet into the sky, the towering presence was mute testimony to the power of nature and the endurance of the plants that provide the oxygen required for man's survival.

He dropped his bags in the bedroom and focused on the task at hand. The map showed a town a few miles up the highway where he expected to find a supermarket, or at least a general store. The short drive was scenic in a way he never imagined. Elk filled every grassy space, wandering fearlessly into the traffic lanes, their antlers towering above the cars. Paul stopped to watch the animals, marveling at their proud stature. Two more lagoons crowded against the ocean as he drove north. The first a brackish lake, the second a narrow body of fresh water separated from the ocean by an isthmus of sand crowned by the highway. Too curious to ignore the significance of this phenomenon, he stopped to read the historical marker and to taste the water. To his amazement, with the surf crashing behind him and marine spray drifting over him, the water in the lagoon was cold, sweet, and fresh.

Orick had never been large, but it served as the community

center for the region. It offered a supermarket, gas stations, a clothing store, and a building supply along with the remains of extinct lumber mills that had once flourished. Most of the town looked relatively new or recently refurbished. Major floods had destroyed the town twice in the past forty years, but with old west stubbornness, the residents rebuilt their homes and businesses.

He parked next to the supermarket and paused to watch the people on the street. Some were obviously tourists. Their clothing and behavior set them apart from the people who fit in with the rustic character of the town. He knew he looked equally as out of place as the tourists he was watching. His pinstriped dress shirt, gray wool slacks, and tan windbreaker, the mark of an urban businessman, were a badge of non-conformity here. He decided to make the clothing store his first stop.

He noticed the cars in the lot weren't locked. The windows were down and the keys hung in the ignition of the car next to his. Avoiding a habit built on years of city life, he dropped the keys in his pocket and walked away without locking the car.

It was 3:00 pm when he put his new clothes in the car and he still had a lot to do before the end of the day. Resolving to complete his chores regardless of the hour, he walked toward the Supermarket without noticing the man watching from a battered Ford pickup.

The sun was still high in the western sky when he returned to the cabin. At this latitude, June meant long days, the sky only darkening for about eight hours. The unplugged refrigerator waited like a silent curse. "If I'm going to use you, I've got to clean you, so I might as well get started," he advised the silent appliance. "You smell good too, old girl. How do you feel about a bath and some fresh perfume?"

He changed clothes and attacked the ancient refrigerator like a man on a mission. The chrome shelves and the crisper drawers he set outside, leaving a box the size of a steamer trunk to scrub and sanitize. An hour and a half later, with sweat running down his face and the afternoon sun streaming through the windows, the task was complete. The old Crosley hummed contentedly as it began chilling its interior. The quality of the porcelain surfaces was apparent as the interior came clean and sparkling, ready to accept the foodstuffs and three boxes of baking soda. The tiny stove was even worse than the refrigerator, it just wasn't growing. Evidence of old spills had cooked hard in the burner wells. The rest of the exterior was an easy clean up of accumulated dust. Years of blackened cooking residue would not be expelled from the oven by a dose or two of oven cleaner, but he applied the product and expended half a roll of paper towels wiping the surfaces. "A hammer and chisel might help, but the paint would probably come off with the grease," he sighed. "At least the surface of the dirt will be clean and anything still alive won't survive the heat." Another hour, another gallon of sweat and elbow grease, and the small kitchen looked and smelled like somewhere you would want to prepare food. *The last time I had to work this hard to clean a kitchen was the place in Sunland Tim and I bought as a fixer upper after he came home from the Army. What a difference a place in the desert makes. Here there's so much moisture and life in the air the problem is fighting back the growth. There, the challenge was trying to pour on enough water to keep everything from cooking in the heat. At least I haven't seen an army of cockroaches like the one we found there. We must have spent a thousand dollars on bug spray and roach motels the first year. I miss those simple times when the future stretched out in front of us like a candy store filled with our dreams. I wonder what decisions we would have made if we knew then what we know now.*

He opened a beer and walked out to stand at the top of the bluff. The play of early evening light altered the colors and the shadows. The ocean surface glittered with shifting patterns of reflected light and sky, and the breeze brushed against him with a cool edge. Looking north toward the sand bar separating the lagoon from the ocean, he saw the foot of a trail at the base of the bluff. "Right now a walk on the beach is just what the doctor ordered," he muttered.

The path was clearly visible as a track where the growth was shorter than the wind blown areas on either side. It led to a point where the bluff curled to the east and sloped down to the lagoon and beach. The trail itself was a picturesque journey, winding down the bluff along the natural terrain until it spilled onto the beach in an alluvium of footprints across the gravel shingle. Walking south along the beach through the driftwood logs and drying kelp, he studied the cliffs rising from the beach to the redwood trees above. For years, intrepid climbers had scaled the walls to carve their names, initials, and fraternity icons for the benefit of posterity. Surprisingly, even with the continuous assault of wind and rain on the sandy surface of the cliff, the etched graffiti was incredibly enduring. Some of the work was more than one hundred feet above the beach on the nearly vertical wall, offering mute testimony to the ability of the artists to suspend gravity long enough to leave their mark.

He was surprised at the unique nature of the shingle. Instead of sand, the beach was made up of polished gravel in a wide variety of colors. Most of the stones were rounded and flat, no more than three inches in diameter. When he knelt for a closer look, he discovered quartz in several shades of white and pink, iron red chert, and even agates and obsidian. "This place is a rock hound's paradise," he said in awed appreciation. To the north he could see the gray sand separating the lagoon from the ocean, but there was no clear dividing line where the gravel turned to sand, the size of the gravel just got smaller and blended in an invisible transition. Although it was after 8:00 pm, the sun remained above the horizon, the phenomenon of latitude which a few hundred miles north means the summer sun never drops below the curve of the earth. LA and the business felt like another planet in another life. His spiritual interlude was disrupted by his growling stomach.

Although he surveyed everything as he climbed the bluff trail, he failed to notice the figure seated beside a driftwood log or the wizened face in the window of the neighbor cabin. "I think I'm going to like this place," he mused. "So what's not to like?"

2.

JEAN PARKER CONSIDERED HERSELF A REFUGEE.
Her resume listed a University of California degree, two failed
marriages, escape from an unsatisfying career, and a fading
faith in the ideals of her youth. She had played the game
properly, kissed all the politically correct backsides, flattered all
the right clients, said all the right words at all the right times
to all the right people. Carefully molding her aggressiveness,
she rose steadily to the level of financial stability and security
to which she had aspired only to discover she had reached
the wrong destination. Dissatisfied with her career and her
marriage, she cashed in her chips and fled from everything
she had worked to achieve, seeking refuge at the edge of the
continent, ready to focus on what she really wanted to do when
she grew up. She had learned money was a poor substitute for
being at peace with yourself. If you weren't at peace, money
was just another responsibility impeding your contentment.
Jean decided to live the dream that could never materialize if
she devoted her time and creativity to clawing her way up a
corporate ladder.

She studied herself in the mirror as she stripped off the
soggy jogging suit. She had never considered her figure the
stuff men would admire in a Playboy center-fold, but she liked
what she saw. What began as walks on the beach had become a
regimen of running and walking. She had never been willowy.
Even in her youth her shape was soft and curvy, but the result

of the months of exercise was pleasing. She was proud to see her mature body glow with good health. Strong, smooth muscles rippled beneath clear skin, another benefit of not needing to paint herself for work each day. She smiled at her image, including the crow's feet at the corners of her eyes and the soft dimples at the corners of her smile. After years of dressing for success, she felt better about herself now than ever.

Steam was rising from the shower when she stepped under the needle spray. The hot water rinsed away the residue of her run. A run on the beach always left her feeling slightly stretched... physically, mentally, and emotionally exhilarated... a natural high. She thought about her new neighbor as she shampooed her hair. She didn't realize she had begun to feel lonely until she saw him. Her thoughts drifted and she found herself revisiting what brought her here. Strident years of discord and disagreement had boiled down to one brief and final blow out.

"You know, Jean, you should do the whole world a favor and go off to be a starving artist," Gil, her second husband, told her. "Go someplace where the last thing you need to do is interact with anyone on a personal level! You're so damned unhappy with me, with your job, with our home, with our marriage, with everything else you ever talk about, why don't you just move to the cabin you bought in the north woods and disappear from the real world! Whatever it takes to make you happy, stop whining and complaining and do something about it, because I'm sick and tired of listening to you and watching you mope around here with your chin on the floor!"

"Well, if you're so damn sick and tired of me, why don't you just gather up your crap and move out!" She shouted at him.

"That's your answer to everything, isn't it? If you're

unhappy and somebody else doesn't like it they should just remove themselves from your life so you can enjoy your misery. I don't have a clue what you think you really want, but I resent you taking your frustrations out on me!"

"What you really resent is that I make more money than you do! I'm successful and you can't handle it! You don't listen to yourself and your self-serving excuses for why you didn't get the last promotion or the one before it! I know what it takes to succeed in a large organization, but you refuse to play by the rules! You always fight the system! You always have to show up your boss and prove he's an idiot! So what if he's an idiot? He's the idiot who controls your future! In the last ten years you've worked for four different companies and left every one because you said your boss was a brainless jackass who wouldn't promote you! Wake up and smell the coffee! Everyone else can't always be wrong! I've had enough! I don't want to talk about it any more! If you aren't leaving, then I am! Let's sell the house, get a divorce, and get the hell away from each other!"

"Fine! I'm outta here! I'll come back when you're at work and get the rest of my stuff. At least I won't have to put up with any more of your bullshit!" He stomped out the door and slammed it behind him, a physical exclamation point at the end of his parting sentence. Six weeks later they met at the courthouse to sign and file the papers to terminate the marriage. Six months later the house had been sold, the assets divided, her resignation accepted, her stock in the company sold back. She moved at the beginning of the new year to heal the wounds of an unsatisfying life. Two weeks later the final decree arrived in the mail, a final punctuation mark on the first four decades of her life.

The finality of her second failure in the marriage arena poured over her in an avalanche of emotions. Anger, fear, desperation, rage, and depression all attacked at once. She found herself sitting alone on the beach with the papers crumpled in her hands while sobs racked her body and tears coursed down her cheeks. "What's wrong with me?" she cried out to the surf. "Why can't I find a way to be happy or at least satisfied with the way things are? What do I want and why do I keep looking for it in all the wrong places?" Her heart in tatters, her soul shredded, her hopes dashed, she surrendered herself to grief and sorrow, weeping until her tears ran dry. The catharsis of letting go was like a butterfly emerging from its cocoon. She would never forget what she had been and done, but instead of the triumphs and traumas caging her, they became a promontory offering her a perspective she previously lacked. "All right Jeannie," she said to herself as she watched the shorebirds chase up and down the sand in the ebb and flow of the surf, "life's been a bitch and you've done your best to be one too. Today is a new day and the only person you need to make happy is you. So decide what you want to do and get on with it. Stop worrying about making plans and start doing what you love to do and see where it takes you." She straightened her back and left her tears and her past soaking into the sand while she walked down the beach with a smile on her face and the vision of a painting forming in her mind's eye.

Jean was sitting on her porch soaking up the warmth of the late day sun when Paul crested the trail. She watched him gaze at the ocean and beach while he walked to his cabin. He looked relaxed, but a troubled wrinkle between his eyebrows remained. *At first glance you look like Mr. All American Average, but looks are usually deceiving. I wonder what your real story is.* His pace was unhurried, his movements smooth and athletic. She guessed his age at about forty. He was in good physical condition with a strong chest, a fit torso, and powerful legs. The steep trail from the beach didn't seem to cause any strain. He seemed like a nice guy, but there was something about the way he looked, or acted, or carried himself... something... ominous. He wasn't looking in her direction, but she felt like she was being watched, and not just by the resident snoop at the end of the street. A sense of foreboding seeped into her bones. She looked around without moving from her chair, but failed to discover anyone watching her. Goose bumps rose on her arms and she shivered with a chill that had nothing to do with the weather or her lightweight blouse. It was like a voice was screaming at her to run for cover. She walked into her house and bolted the door behind her, something she had never done since moving here.

She felt a pervading sense of wrongness, as if a cruel harbinger of unpleasant events had walked through the door behind her. Uneasiness hung in the room like the shadow of an unwelcome guest. Pulling on a sweater, she looked around her cozy quarters as her feelings of safety and security evaporated.

3.

THE ENGINES HUMMED SOFTLY AS PSA FLIGHT 473
leveled off at cruising altitude. The flight attendants worked the
beverage service cart while the broken landscape of California's
San Andreas Fault paralleled the flight path like a jagged scar
scratched in the ground by a giant astride a broomstick horse.
Summer sun shining through the windows lent a festive air.
Sounds of conversation ebbed and flowed, and laughter tinkled
when a joke was shared between the newlyweds seated next
to the emergency hatch. Suddenly, the floor erupted in a ball
of flame, sending burning fragments of the aircraft and it's
precious cargo plunging five miles to the earth below.

Paul bolted upright, the echoes of his scream ringing
his ears. Chest heaving, pulse pounding, sweat dripping
from every pore, his eyes frantically searched the room. The
unfamiliar surroundings gradually settled into focus, dimly
illuminated by the filtered gray light of morning. He closed
his eyes and breathed deep. The surge of adrenaline from
the nightmare gradually began to recede. He threw back the
tangled covers and put his feet on the cold floor, the chill
sensation completing his transition to reality. Last night, he
had blissfully surrendered to sleep as soon as his head hit the
pillow. Now, in the cold gray light of day, his mouth tasted
like the bottom of a birdcage and drying sweat chilled his skin.
Wide awake in the retreating shadows of his dream, sleep was
no longer an option.

He stumbled to the bathroom and turned on the shower. He wandered into the living room to look at the new day while he brushed his teeth. To his surprise, yesterday's sparkling clear view had been replaced by a misty gray curtain of fog. He could hear the surf, but the edge of the bluff was indistinct in the low gray cloud. He could see clear blue sky through the fog, but at ground level the world was blanketed in a soft moist shroud.

"I think I'll take a run on the beach first," he said and went to turn off the steaming shower. "Timing is everything. It's ready and I'm not."

The beach trail was damp and sandy soil clung to his shoes. He paused to look both ways at the bottom and decided the gravel would be an easier running surface than the sand. He set out at the rhythmic pace he had developed years earlier. The footing along the damp edge of the surf was soft enough for each step to sink into the surface and give slightly as he pushed off. *Be careful you don't pull a muscle, dummy. The way this moves under your feet you could hamstring yourself with no effort at all. Make this first day an easy one to stretch out the kinks, warm up your muscles, and get a feel for things.* After a half-mile he slowed to a rapid walk to allow his breathing to stabilize and to prevent his muscles from cramping. A quarter mile later he turned back to the north and increased his pace. The muscles in his thighs began to tighten after a half-mile, announcing the need for more training before he was ready to handle the distances he managed easily on a firm, level surface. He slowed to a fast walk and maintained a vigorous pace to keep the blood flowing and his breathing deep. *The good news is I managed to run the fear out of my system. I wonder how long it will be before I stop having the same damn dream. It's been two years since I had a peaceful night's sleep. Maybe I'll find an answer among the driftwood and skeletons of past lives washing onto the beach to dry in the sun.*

He would have missed the trail if not for the pattern of footprints leading to it. Keeping his pace steady as he climbed the bluff, he walked briskly to his cabin. *Now a shower will really feel good.* He left his shoes and socks on the porch and padded barefoot to the bathroom and turned on the shower. He sighed with pleasure and gratefully surrendered the last vestiges of his unwelcome wake up call to the healing waters.

The insistent buzz of the alarm dragged the sentinel into groggy consciousness. It took three fumbling tries to silence the annoying creature. He was shocked he had overslept and wondered how long the damn clock had been yammering in his ear. Suddenly alert, heart racing, he checked the clock to verify the time then grabbed his watch in disbelief. Both said 5:45 am and it was full daylight. "Jesus Christ, what time does the sun come up in this country?" he growled.

Realizing he might already be too late, he pulled back the tent flap. Fog filled the air with misty vapor that collected on the needles of the redwood trees and rained gently onto the ground like a spring shower. *Shit! The whole fucking world could be going by a hundred yards away and I wouldn't be able to see it! How the hell am I supposed to maintain a decent surveillance if I can't see what I'm supposed to be watching? Christ! I need radar to find anything in this soup.* He rubbed his eyes to push away the residue of sleep. "All right, if plan A doesn't work, then redesign the project to suit the conditions. Time for plan B!"

Refreshed and invigorated, Paul dressed in blue jeans and cotton shirt and took a moment to make the bed. His mother's voice echoed in his mind, telling him it was less effort to keep things clean than clean them up. Housekeeping handled, he headed for the kitchen to make breakfast. As he walked through the living room, he picked up his watch from the end table and skidded to a stop when he saw the time. At 6:35 am it was bright daylight. *Back home, the sun would just be peaking over the top of the hill. And the fog. We get fog in the valley, but nothing like this. So thick it clings to your clothes like a layer of fur, but you can see blue sky through it. It's chilly, but not really cold. I'm sure I'll get used to it after a while. I guess you can get used to almost anything. Some things are just easier than others. Some things you just have to accept.* He dropped the watch on the table. "Who cares what time it is!"

The kitchen was supplied with all the basic utensils, including a cast iron frying pan, a couple of small kettles, and a battered aluminum percolator that looked like it had lost a war but contained the necessary parts for a few more battles. "Ah yes, all the comforts of home. My kingdom for a Mr. Coffee. God hates a coward. Fill it with water, put some grounds in the basket, and add heat. If it turns out good, I'll drink it. If it doesn't, I'll drink it anyway."

Accustomed to modern appliances and non stick pans, Paul was a bit daunted by the grim looking frying pan, but when the greasy black layer covering it inside and out didn't wash off he decided eating what was cooked in it probably wouldn't inflict serious injury. In minutes he had bacon sizzling aromatically and coffee merrily percolating. His head was inside the refrigerator when he heard a knock at the door. Uncertain what he had heard, he paused to listen. He heard three sharp raps on the front door.

"Who the heck is beating on my door at this time of the morning?" he muttered. He looked through the window and saw Jean Parker at his front door. Shaking his head in amazement, but admittedly happy to see her, he opened the door.

"Good morning! I see you're an early riser."

"Good morning. Uh, Jean isn't it?"

"Very good. Got it right on the first try. I was going to take a walk on the beach, but I smelled coffee and bacon and thought I'd say hello. You know, be neighborly, boldly go where I hadn't gone before. Maybe ask you to go for a walk with me," she said breezily. Sparkling brown eyes looking directly into Paul's made something catch in his chest. Her cheeks turned pink and her voice took on an embarrassed quality. "I've never done anything like this before, but I wanted to get to know you and I didn't want to wait. What do you think? Too pushy?"

Paul chuckled. "I'll admit this is new territory for me too. I don't know if I'm supposed to feel like you're being pushy or be flattered by the attention. It sounds like you had to work up some courage to try this and I hate to eat alone. Would you like to join me for breakfast?

"I was hoping you'd ask." Jean stepped into the cabin and turned toward the kitchen and the source of the delicious odors now filling the small dwelling.

Paul squeezed past her into the tiny kitchen. "The space is a bit tight for two, but I need to turn the bacon or instead of crisp it'll be burnt,"

"Cozy, would be a more polite description."

"If by cozy, you mean so small you need to step outside to change your mind, then it's definitely cozy. I was going to scramble some eggs to go with this. You have any special requests?"

"It would be totally out of character for a pushy broad who comes to your door in the morning not to make a special request, but you probably don't have the ingredients for a California omelet with fresh mushrooms, salsa and cheese. How about the basics, but please don't cook them in the bacon fat."

"We share similar tastes. It sounds like you've eaten at El Torito in North Hollywood. The omelet you described is their specialty. I like my eggs gently cooked in butter. If you want to help, why don't you set the table. The plates are in the right hand cabinet above the sink. I'll try to keep the place from going up in flames."

"I can do that! I'll try to keep out of the way while the chef is at work."

"Do you like your eggs wet or dry?"

"I prefer them moist. Is that a good enough description or do you want me to lean over your shoulder to make sure you don't over cook them?"

"I could just scramble yours in a bowl and let you eat them with a spoon or you can take your chances with El Gourmet Jefe who is diligently preparing a marvelous example of bachelor cuisine."

"I'll take my chances as long as there's enough coffee to wash it down," she said as she opened the cupboard and took down some battered Melmac plates. "Aha! Gold may be where you find it, but whoever chose these dishes must have discovered it after they bought this stuff. Just to be safe, I think I'll wash off the top layer of dust before we use them. Then again, being a bachelor, maybe you like mouse droppings as a garnish with your bacon and eggs."

"Please wash them! Dish soap is under the sink. My god! Who would have chosen that pattern? Those are borderline nauseating."

"Pretty bad aren't they. Probably something they got for

DAN RAGON

free with ten gallons of gas. Not just a plate at a time, either. Fill your tank and take away a set of dishes only a blind person could stand to look at. Then again, these look like they've gone a lot of miles so someone may actually have chosen them. The glasses are vintage Welsh's, a slice of Americana."

"The rent is pretty user friendly. Most of the furnishings in this 'Furnished Ocean View Cabin' look like retrievals from the dumpster behind the Salvation Army. Except for the bentwood rocker and the bed. The bed is quite comfortable and the mattress is almost new. A good indication of what the owners consider important."

"You're renting the location, the ambiance, the neighborhood, which includes, at no additional charge, the lady who lives three doors down and likes to barge in uninvited at breakfast time," Jean said with twinkling eyes and a lopsided grin.

"The agent mentioned all those things when I rented the place, except for the neighbor lady who insists on making sure neither of us is lonely. If he had told me about you I might have taken a cabin on the other side of the lagoon."

"If he'd mentioned me he could have rented it for much more. You didn't really come here to be alone did you?" she asked as she dried the dishes and set them on the small table in the corner of the living room.

He looked into two sparkling eyes crinkling at the corners with laughter. Her innocent question had struck a deep and very painful chord. Paul stared wordlessly into her eyes. *How can I tell her I came here to be alone. Especially when I feel so incredibly happy to see her and have her standing just a few feet away. She's like a bright ray of sunshine pushing aside the clouds. Maybe I didn't come here just to get away and be alone. Maybe I came here because we both need each other. Try to relax and*

22

don't color anything she says with facts and details she can't possibly know. Oh, man, look at the change in her face. She thinks she's really screwed up.

"I'm sorry Paul, I didn't mean to step on your feelings," she stammered. "I was just trying to be funny. I'm sorry." She set the dishes on the table and reached for the coat she had hung on the back of a chair. "I guess I let my mouth run on without thinking. Maybe I should gather up my big mouth and leave before I make things any worse. I'm sorry about the extra food. I'll try to make it up to you sometime."

He stared at her hardly hearing what she said. When he realized she was about to leave he held up his hand. "Wait. Don't leave. I want you to stay. I'm really glad you're here. I tripped over some old baggage and had to catch my balance. You had no way of knowing. Besides, these eggs are done. Everything's ready. Can you bring me the plates?"

"Sure." She needed a moment before her hands stopped shaking enough bring the plates for him to fill with eggs and bacon.

"This really looks good." She set the plates on the table. "Go sit down, I'll get the coffee."

Paul watched Jean fill the two chipped mugs, remembering Lisa doing the same thing at a small beach house in Baja. Pain gripped his heart and his eyes blurred with unshed tears. He bowed his head and breathed deep. He only became aware of Jean sitting next to him when she placed her hand on top of his. "I'm so sorry. I've managed to get both feet in my mouth and the teeth marks feel pretty permanent. I'm truly sorry."

Paul looked at her with deep sadness in his eyes. He formed a tiny smile with his mouth and squeezed her hand. "You couldn't know. You didn't mean to dredge up old ghosts and I need to remember I can't live in the past. I'm okay now.

Let's eat before these eggs turn into fossils. Do you need salt and pepper?"

"No, this is fine."

"Well, mine definitely need help. I may need to eat a bland diet someday, but I'm still young enough to enjoy food with character. Salt and pepper might make it almost edible."

"While you're up, do you have any cream and sugar?"

"I do. I gathered up all the necessities yesterday. Sorry I didn't ask. I've been a bit distracted by my surprise guest."

"Please don't think of me as a guest. I'd rather be your friend from down the street who hates to eat alone. I'm sorry if you feel like I've pounced on you, but since I'm already here it's a little late to worry about first impressions, especially since you haven't tossed me out on my ear."

"I have to admit I'm enjoying the attention."

"When you arrived I felt like I'd just been released from prison. I didn't realize how lonely I was after living alone for the last six months. Seeing a nice looking man show up had a rather strange effect on me, but I'm not going to apologize for being forward. Whatever made me approach you, I don't want to change it. I want to be your friend and I hope we can discover some common ground and common interests to share. Maybe it's loneliness, maybe it's something else, but you seem like a decent guy who's weathered some personal tragedies and could use a friend."

"You don't even know me. How do you know you're safe with me? I could be a mass murderer."

"Are you?"

"I don't think so, but if I was, would I admit it?"

Jean shrugged. "True enough, but I've always trusted my instincts about people. On the other hand, I married two guys I shouldn't have, so maybe my judgment isn't perfect, but I'm too old to stop trusting myself. I almost did. I almost lost faith in my ability to make good choices. Then one day I decided the choices were mine and I was going to make them with confidence and let the chips fall where they may. So I think I'll just sit here, enjoy my coffee, and try not to drown in the mysterious depths of your eyes."

Paul smiled and took a sip of his coffee. "Ugh! Maybe if you added enough sugar and cream to this witch's brew you could manage to choke it down. This stuff is dreadful! It tastes like I burned it."

Jean took a careful sip of her coffee. "Yep. It tastes like you had the heat a little too high, let it percolate a little too hard for a little too long, and left it warming on a burner a little too hot. No giant errors in proportions, just enough small mistakes to produce an unpalatable result. Let me guess. At home your Mr. Coffee does it all for you."

"You got it. I even buy coffee in those neat little packs for a perfect cup of coffee."

"You're a real pioneer aren't you?"

"Oh yeah, a regular Daniel Boone. Truth be told, I've never really been out of a city. If I'm not home, I'm usually in a hotel with room service."

"Culture shock. I should have figured as much. New clothes, new shoes on the porch, new car in the driveway, and," raising her cup in salute, "a new man in the neighborhood."

He laughed joyously. "Thanks, I needed that. There hasn't been much laughter in my life lately."

"Mine's been pretty drab too. Do you want to talk about it?"

"Some day, but not right now. Right now I feel pretty good and I'd like to take a walk on the beach with the rather nice, pushy, brazen hussy from down the street."

"Hussy? Nice talk!"

"Well, if the shoe fits, wear it proudly!"

"You make it sound like I stopped by to see if you were seducible."

"Well? What's your conclusion? Am I?"

"I think everyone is. It's all a matter of time, place, and circumstance. If all the elements are there, it can either mean falling into bed or falling in love or both. Sometimes the order changes. What I want to know is if you want to be seduced... or fall in love... or either... or both?"

"I think I'll take that under advisement." He took the dishes to the kitchen.

"Are you an attorney?"

"No way. I just like to mimic their trite phrases at generally inappropriate times. Are you ready to finish the walk you were allegedly taking this morning before you conveniently detoured onto my doorstep?"

"What do mean, allegedly taking a walk?"

"You were taking a walk from your cabin to mine. If I wasn't up you were going back to your cabin to wait a half hour and try again until you found me up and about."

"I'm pretty transparent, huh?"

"Yep."

"Are you mad at me?"

"Furious. Let's hit the beach."

They didn't take notice of the sentinel when he passed them at the bottom of the trail or of the observer in the end cabin who logged the time and date in her journal and added notes on what they were wearing and her observations regarding their behavior. Engrossed in conversation, they turned north onto the soft sand.

The sentinel continued south, pausing frequently to kneel and study the beach stones, surreptitiously watching Paul and Jean as they walked along the surf's edge in the lifting fog. The air glowed softly in the patches of brightening light, tiny snatches of rainbows haloing the drift on the beach.

"We have a serious problem. I can't see his cabin from my campsite like I thought I could. This place had a fog bank to rival London this morning. I couldn't see a hundred feet. I'm too far away to maintain surveillance. Can you get me into one of the cabins on the bluff?"

"Not an option. I don't want him to get suspicious. The place next door has been vacant for a long time, but he would immediately know you were there and so would the neighbors. It's too risky. You need to manage from the campground. You can come and go from there and no one will get suspicious."

"I understand right alongside is too close, but what about the one next to the artist's place? I hear the owner is only around for a few days at a time and gone for months in between. It's risky, but I'd at least be close enough to see what's going on."

"Maybe so, but the old broad at the end of the street would be suspicious about another stranger. Besides, the owner never rents it out. We tried already and were politely told to take our offers and requests elsewhere. He doesn't want anyone in his house when he's gone and has an arrangement with the Sheriff's Department to check the place regularly. Where are you now?"

"I'm at the lagoon store. I'm watching McAfee and the artist walking on the beach. I lost him for a little while yesterday when he switched cars at the south end of the county and it took me most of the day to reestablish contact. The artist was having breakfast with him this morning and I had to wait for him to make a move. That's why I couldn't call earlier."

"Our friend is a fast worker. Arrived yesterday and already managed to hook up with the only unmarried woman in the neighborhood under the age of sixty."

"Well, whether he works fast or not, I've gotta find a better location. There's no place to hide and watch here. I have to take advantage of the open spaces and keep my distance so I don't attract his attention. It's even tougher now because she could spot me too."

"You didn't really expect this to be easy did you?"

"You can't blame me for hoping."

"Do the best you can with what you've got unless you find a better option. We don't want him to know you're there, but you've got to stay as tight on him as you can."

"I understand, sir. Never let him see the sun reflect off the lenses."

"You got it. Stay in touch."

"Thank you, sir."

The sentinel watched the couple from his campsite. They started at a brisk pace and slowed as they approached the north end of the lagoon. *What are you two talking about? Do you have any idea who you're with, lady? If you knew, would you still be with him?* While he continued his observation his thoughts wandered in search of a solution to the problem of remaining undetected. *Planting a locator on his new wheels shouldn't be a problem. His cabin is the challenge. It'll be easy enough to compromise if I can get in and out without being seen, but the damned old lady next door's got her nose pressed against the window all the time.* A small smile lifted the corners of his mouth. *Even she can't see through the pea soup that blanketed everything this morning or in the dark, especially if it's pea soup and dark... or storming.*

He began to relax as a plan formed in his mind. The sun filtering through the trees fell in a bright patch on his shoulders, warming his back and easing the tension. The panic gripping him earlier fell away. *It's still the same game. Waiting, watching, and adjusting to Mr. Murphy's antics. Blame me for letting myself think this was going to be easy and not granting proper respect to the job. Same game, same rules, same cardinal rule: never underestimate your opponent. Time to take another look at the target.*

He saw the widow watching him through the sheer curtains in his peripheral vision as he passed her house. Her eyes felt her like a laser on the back of his head. *No matter what I do, the damned nosy old broad"'s going to see me. Even darkness and fog might not be enough cover. No telling what hours she keeps. Senior citizens are notorious for wandering around in the middle of the night with the ghosts who haunt their memories.* Concentrating on maintaining the appearance of a tourist, he studied the way the lots were laid out. A cold smile tugged the corners of his eyes when he realized he could reach Paul's cabin from the property in the rear. *Once I'm done I can go down to the beach and double back along the edge of the lagoon. The old broad will never know I was here and neither will Mr. Paul McAfee. With a little luck the property in the rear will be vacant, or in use by weekenders who aren't inclined to be standing guard like a damn watchdog day and night.*

The sentinel whistled softly as he retraced his steps, making it a point to closely study Alma Jacobsen's yard and house. After all, no self respecting visitor would be able to ignore it, perched like a sparkling tiara on the brow of the bluff, the beds of pansies smiling brightly at all who might pass.

As he approached, he saw the little old lady tending to her flowerbeds. He wasn't certain whether to walk by or stop and try to talk with her. It was going to be tough to get past her without being noticed. He decided the best thing to do was play it openly like any other curious visitor.

Alma heard the stranger approaching and was on guard. She'd committed his face and features to memory. He would probably stop to talk. She didn't want to talk, but she did want a closer look at him. She instinctively knew he wasn't some tourist looking at quaint cottages. She worried about his real agenda.

She used her peripheral vision to observe the stranger without demonstrating her attention. Even from her awkward location she was able to confirm what she had already cataloged. He was about six feet tall, with dark hair, olive complexion, and a fit athletic build. He looked like a coiled spring, ready to instantly respond to any threat.

4.

"A PENNY FOR YOUR THOUGHTS," JEAN SAID.

"I was just trying to put things in perspective," he waved his arm in a sweeping motion. "You know, the ocean, the lagoon, the beach, the trees, the foggy mornings, the sunny afternoons, the starry evenings, the unexpected rain, and the absence of man made noises."

"Feeling a little overwhelmed?"

"In a way. I've lived in LA all my life and I've always been surprised when visitors are awestruck by the sprawl of the city and speed of the traffic. It just seemed normal to me. I was born and raised there and only left for business. Some friends have been trying for years to get me to come up here, but until now it wasn't something I wanted to do. They kept telling me how unbelievably beautiful it was and I kept saying I didn't have the time. They told me I should take a vacation. I said I didn't need one. Now I can't figure out why I resisted for so long. I feel like I'm on a different planet."

"We all tend to stay inside our comfort zone, our own personal rut, as it were, but it's our rut, and we cling to it like a barnacle until something comes along and blows our ship so far off course we have to crawl out into the light and look around. Sometimes you discover there's a whole world you never knew existed. It's not anything new, it's just something you've chosen to ignore. It's human nature. Marketing demographics show most people live, work, and play within a radius of about thirty-five miles. It's sort of like having a leash tied to your ankle with the other end staked to the ground. You just keep going back and forth and around and around inside the same circle."

Paul chuckled at the mental picture of his leg caught in a trap with a thirty-five mile long chain stretched to the limit as he marched around in a circle. "God, you make my life sound so depressing."

"Hey, I'm guilty of the same syndrome. I married the same guy twice. Different name and face, but the same guy. Same attitudes, same ambitions, or lack of them. I stayed in the same job for fifteen years fighting to out cheat, out maneuver, and out brown nose my way up the corporate ladder. You want to talk about a rut, now that was a rut. Everything I did was choreographed by somebody I was trying to impress and there was a whole chorus line of people just like me doing their best to stand out from the crowd. It was a real drag."

"So why'd you stay with it for so long?"

"Ambition, greed, habit, responsibility. There's a lot of explanations, but mostly cowardice. Afraid to cut the umbilical of a secure job and trek out into unfamiliar territory and risk not succeeding."

"Were you successful?"

"I worked my way up the food chain only to discover it wasn't worth it."

"Why not?"

"All I got for my effort was my name on an office door, a good sized pay check, and someone constantly trying to dislodge me by pointing out how long it had been since I had done something really stupendous. Dog eat dog."

"Job was a real bitch, huh?"

"Cute," she smiled. "I'm glad to be out of the fight pit and in hibernation here."

"It's a great place to hibernate, isn't it."

They sat down by a driftwood log and leaned against it facing the surf. Several minutes passed without conversation while they looked at the sea.

"So how does an ambitious yuppie just toss it in and go off to do nothing?" he asked.

"It was surprisingly easy once I made up my mind. It helped to know I was going to do what I'd always dreamed of doing. The worst part was getting everything sold or stored or left in someone's care, the rest was easy. I always wanted to spend my time drawing and painting what I wanted to draw and paint. In advertising, I used my creativity to satisfy someone else's idea of how they wanted things to look or sound. It sure wasn't art! It's purely commercial art and that's not an unintentional pun. Commercials are commercials whether the medium is print or air. It's lucrative enough, but after fifteen years it got very old, very tired, and extremely unsatisfying. I could feel my creativity drying up and blowing away like dandelion fluff on the winds of commerce. I felt like part of me was dying with every piece of commercial drivel I manufactured and then convinced the client was the answer to public recognition of their latest product.

"Now, I paint and draw for me! I don't care if no one ever expresses an interest in owning my work. I paint because it makes me feel good. I love the solitude, but my art makes me feel alive in a way I've never felt before. Not even when I was in college. Back then my projects were pointed at satisfying my professor's idea of what art should be. I was doing what my teachers wanted because I wanted to get a good grade. Without good grades I wouldn't be able to compete for a job where I could do what someone else wanted. If I didn't do what the client wanted, I couldn't get paid. You want to talk about a chain tied to your ankle and staked to the ground, that's what my art had turned into." She paused. "Good lord, I do go on don't I?" His face erupted in a huge smile and he laughed. She punched him playfully on the shoulder. "It's your fault for taking a lonely divorcee for a walk on the beach and getting her to start talking about herself." She laughed quietly and smiled.

"You should smile more often, it spreads your beauty across your face like sunlight dancing on the water." The color rose from her throat and became a full blush. "Sorry. I didn't mean to make you uncomfortable. I figured you knew how you look to other people."

"I've never heard anyone call me beautiful. I don't think of myself as beautiful. I've always thought my face was pleasant enough to attract a man if I wasn't too choosy about finding some gorgeous hunk."

"Maybe you set your expectations too low."

"Well, if my marriage record is any indicator, I certainly set my sights on relationships doomed to failure."

"Life turns in strange ways. Our reactions to those changes affect the people who touch our lives as much as they do ourselves. What's the line of poetry? 'No man is an island unto himself'."

"Or quoting Shakespeare, 'All the world's a stage, and all the men and women merely players," Jean responded.

"Fate is a hunter," He said with a smile.

Jean laughed. "The game's afoot!"

"Tallyho! The fox!" Paul shouted.

They leaned against each other and cast their laughter into the thunder of the surf and the calls of sea birds. The pain and disappointments of the past washed away in unfettered joy.

As her laughter drained away, Jean looked out of the corner of her eye at the man to whom she found herself being drawn. *Who are you, Paul McAfee? I don't know anything about you, but you've broken the dam inside me and managed to bring real laughter to my life for the first time in years. I feel safe with you. I only know you've come here to try to come to terms with your past. I wonder when you'll tell me about it. You will or you won't in your own time. Either way, I'm going to enjoy our time together.*

"Paul?"

"Hmm?"

"I thought I'd call you back to the real world."

"I was just thinking."

"It has a way of making you do that doesn't it?"

"It does. I was comparing the beaches in LA with the beach here. They're worlds apart and not just in miles. Here the beach is natural. Driftwood, kelp, the occasional dead fish, crab shells, clam shells, all the stuff native to an ocean. People have to share the beach with Mother Nature. Even the smell is different. In the south it smells like salt water. Here it smells like a living creature."

"And the beaches in the south are a lot warmer."

"Warmer, yes, but that's not the most important difference. Southern California beaches are so sterile. There's no driftwood or kelp or dead critters. They drag the sand every night to smooth it out and remove all the evidence anyone has been there. It's a janitorial service to get rid of the footprints, knock down the sand castles, pick up the empty cans and bottles and forgotten towels to get everything ready for the next day. Everything looking new, or at least freshly washed. I never thought about it before. Everything is so smooth it looks and smells unnatural, like it's man made. Heaven forbid a child should cut a foot on a clam shell or find a dead fish. No driftwood fires for roasting hot dogs and marshmallows. Here, there's so much evidence of life and death and the smell of it all is like... like... uh... I don't know quite how to describe it."

"You mean its like Mother Nature has BO and you like the smell of it?"

Paul laughed. "You have a lyrical way of expressing images."

"Maybe you're a typical male who likes the smell of a woman, even old Ma Natcheral?"

"There you go! Only a man could love the smell of," Paul looked at Jean without finishing the sentence.

"Pussy?" she said with a playful smile

"Yeah! Pussy! Even if it's Mother Nature!"

"It sure didn't take us very long to dissolve a rather intellectual conversation into the earthy elements, did it?"

"Doesn't look like it!"

"In my case, it's probably because a life of celibacy may be getting tiresome, but you're a good looking single guy with no ring on his finger. What's your excuse?" She smiled gleefully. Her mood shifted as she watched the mirth drain from his face to be replaced by a powerful vision of sadness. Paul looked out to sea, then slowly raised his knees, hooked his arms around them and leaned his head down on top of them.

Jean was stunned. *What have you done? You really stepped in it this time, stupid. He doesn't have to explain why he's here or why he says and does what he does. I'll bet he's lost someone he loves, he's at a loss about how to deal with it, and with all the sensitivity of a porcupine you bash him over the head with a really stupid question, stripping him to the bones of his pain. What are you gonna do next? Offer him your body to help him to get over it? Heck, be real understanding, offer to sell him your body so he doesn't think he's supposed to care whether you enjoy it or not. At least you won't be offended if he turns you down. This is a really nice hole you've dug for yourself! Got any good ideas how to climb out of it or do you think with a little effort you can dig it even deeper and pull it in on top of yourself? Whatever you do, try to keep your foot out of your stupid mouth!*

Unsure what to do, Jean watched him withdraw as if he was shrinking, like a balloon slowly deflating. His breathing gradually slowed. She didn't know how long they sat this way, he silently lost in a world of pain and misery, she fighting back tears and wondering if she had burned a bridge she could never restore. Uncertainty impeded her overwhelming desire to hold him until his pain subsided.

Time passed, the surf crashed on the shore, shore birds plucked morsels from the sand, the breeze drifted across the lagoon, the planet continued in its orbit, but Paul didn't move. She saw him engulfed in his pain, drowning in personal sorrows, his heart breaking, shut off from the outside world, and immersed in an autism of grief.

You started this, it's up to you to finish it, one way or another. Do what feels right. Follow your heart and trust it to lead you where you should go. She slipped her arms around him and gently hugged him. Thinking only of the human need to be comforted, she opened her heart to this man she barely knew. She rested her cheek against the top of his windblown head and waited. *Take your time. Take as much time as you need. I have nowhere to go and you have to find your own way back. I won't leave unless you tell me to. I started this fiasco, and I'm here until it's over or you send me away… whichever happens.*

Paul sat almost catatonic in a prenatal position as sorrow flooded forth from what seemed like a bottomless reservoir in his soul. There were no tears, no sobs, nothing to bring a relief, just an incredible emotional agony with the power to swallow him up and encapsulate him inside its bitter walls. He let it all flow out and surround him. His emotions were like a swarm of harpies orbiting and pouring venom on him along with their harridan shrieking, blotting out the world around him. The sound of the ocean and the smell of the beach disappeared as he relived the terrible moment when he learned the terrible news. Once again he felt the air seep from his lungs, feeling like he had been punched in the gut. Lisa and Tim's flight had gone down a hundred miles south of San Francisco. There were no survivors. Life as he had known it was over. He had wandered through the months of investigations and questions and sympathetic expressions like a sleepwalker unable to awake from an unending nightmare. There was no waking. There was no Lisa arriving home. There was no baby to coo over and cuddle. There was only the terrible lonely emptiness to steal his laughter, flatten his smile, and darken his days.

Gradually, he realized he was not alone. An arctic blanket of pain and sorrow lay over him, inviting him to escape into self-pity, but calling him back from the edge of the chasm of pain was another heart beating next to his. Drawing himself up out of the swamp of depression he felt arms enfolding him and a woman's breast pressed against his arm. Along with the warmth and tenderness of the embrace, her scent brushed against his senses. Gently scented by a hint of perfumed soap and her own distinct fragrance, the air about him crackled with life. He instinctively slipped his arms around her and pulled her tightly against him.

Gradually, Paul realized he was clinging in quiet desperation to a woman, but the woman wasn't Lisa. It couldn't be Lisa. Lisa had been dead for two years. Slowly, he raised his head and looked into Jean's soft, gentle eyes. He looked warily for any hint of accusation or disgust and discovered only kindness and understanding. The sounds and smells of the beach flooded over him helping to wash away the residue of his latest encounter with grief.

"Sorry," he said quietly, pulling away and stretching his legs out in front of him.

"For what?"

"I guess I owe you an explanation."

"I disagree. Life never runs smoothly down the path we hope it will. Everyone has experiences that tax their ability to maintain their equilibrium. I'm not here to judge you. I'm just a friend who would like to help if I can. No payment is expected for offering a shoulder to lean on. Besides, you made me breakfast, so we're even."

"Thank you for making it easy."

"You're welcome."

Jean stood and brushed off the sand. "Come on.," She held out her hands. "There's a half mile of beach between here and the cabins. Let's finish our walk and enjoy the morning sun."

Paul allowed her to pull him to his feet. He felt exhausted, but his emotional pain was easing, like healing had finally begun. "You're a nice lady, Jean Parker."

"How very perceptive of you to notice."

They continued down the beach, hand in hand.

5.

THE WEATHER HAD CHANGED. THE PREVIOUS DAY
began in a cool misty cloud, then burned away to reveal a
warm, clear afternoon; an idyllic summer day. The wind shifted
to the southwest during the night, bringing a gray sky sagging
in tattered streamers of chilly rain. Paul watched from his front
porch as the rain marched like a brigade of soldiers across the
face of the bluff. The porch was barely large enough to shelter
him from the rain and occasional splatters blew against him.
*Those sheets of rain are like the passing of time, each day following
the one preceding it in an endless panorama of missed opportunities.*
He tilted his chair back against the wall and let his thoughts
drift back to those exciting days when it all began…

"C'mon Paul, get your butt in gear!" Tim yelled.

"I'm coming, I'm coming, keep your shirt on!"

"Tempus is fugiting my man, if we don't make this
appointment we're both in danger of losing our shirts whether
we have them on or not."

"Yeah, and if I don't have this damn stuff in order we're
not going to get the money either!"

"You spent all night on the business plan. I thought you
had it done."

"It is done! I'm just double checking. It has to be right or
they'll just smile politely, usher us to the door and tell us they'll
get back to us, someday. Someday isn't on the calendar. I don't
want a someday answer. I want a today answer."

"Gordon and McAfee is going to happen! If this gaggle of money changers can't see the promise of our business we'll just take our little dog and pony show down the road until we find somebody with real vision. Now c'mon, let's go!"

"All right, all right, I'm coming." Paul closed his brief case. "If it ain't ready by now, it ain't gonna be!"

"There you go. Now let's go dazzle 'em with brilliance."

"Or baffle 'em with bullshit, right?"

"You got it. We've got the greatest team act going and it's time for the men with the money to show their appreciation!"

Their team act began on the baseball practice field with Bryan McAfee hitting fungoes and flies to the boys and drilling them until their reactions and moves became second nature. He gradually increased the intensity to the maximum speed he could hit the ball, making the balls they fielded during a Little League game seem like slow motion. Bryan was fifty-five years old when Paul was a high school freshman, but in spite of arthritis and age he coached and encouraged them and never missed a game. All the hard work paid off in baseball scholarships to USC for Tim and UCLA for Paul. Both played well in college, but neither had aspirations to play professionally and both escaped the notice of the scouts. The game opened doors to an educational opportunity they used to their best advantage, graduating with high grades, high hopes, and glittering dreams of one day building their own company.

The meeting with the bankers was a masterful performance. He arrived prepared to present convincing evidence of the viability of their business plan to a bunch of suits whose sole purpose in life was to torch the dreams of innovators. Instead, Tim had taken control of the meeting like a conductor leading a symphony orchestra and called on Paul to support him by handing out the carefully prepared business plan. Paul entered the meeting nervously confident. Tim entered the room like a rock star taking charge of an audience. Paul witnessed what five years experience in sales for a major corporation had taught his best friend. Tim's natural exuberance and charm were so infectious even the most staid banker couldn't resist. Their dream became reality. Gormac, Incorporated was born.

The business flourished with Paul handling the administration and Tim knocking on doors for products to sell and customers to serve. Computer chip manufacturers pressed them to distribute their products, assemblers took products from their warehouse as fast as they could import them, and money flooded into their bank account. For ten years the dream carried them on its wings, soaring higher than they dared to imagine, only to become a nightmare spreading terror and tragedy across the landscape of their lives.

"Paul?"

"Paul?" Jean placed her hand on Paul's.

"Huh?" Paul saw Jean kneeling next to his chair, her brow creased in concern.

"I'm sorry if I'm intruding, but I spoke and you didn't respond. It was like you were looking right through me, staring into the distance at nothing. You were barely breathing. Are you okay?"

Jesus Christ! I came here for seclusion and she's always in my face! She warned me she was a busy body. Truth be told, I'm really glad to see her. Paul studied Jean's face for a moment. Close up, her features were distinctly pretty, but in her eyes he saw something beautiful. "Yes, I'm okay. I was just thinking about good times and good friends. I guess I zoned out. It's one of those annoying habits I need to work on."

"Dueling with the demons of the past?"

"A lot more accurate than you might imagine. I came here to get away from the pressures and stresses, but it's not so easy to get away from myself. It's like the guy who never gets lost. Everywhere I go, there I am."

"I'll be glad to listen if you want to talk. If you'd rather I keep my distance and let you roam those dark places on your own, I will. I've already made the journey you're on. I'll give you whatever time and space you need. Just tell me what you want me to do."

"Thank you. I appreciate your offer, but I'm fine. I'll try to limit my forays into the dark waters of catatonia to those times when I'm not sitting on the front porch for the whole world to witness my insanity. That way I won't keep upsetting my nosy neighbors. Fair enough?"

"Fair enough! I'm on my way to Alexander's store. Can I pick up anything for you? Milk, eggs, coffee?"

"I think I have everything I need at the moment, but thanks for the offer."

Jean stepped off the porch. "I'll see you later," she said over her shoulder as she began to walk away. Then she turned back. "Will you have dinner with me tonight?"

"Huh?".

"Watch my lips." She pointed at her mouth. "Will you have dinner with me tonight?"

Paul grinned. "Sure, what time?"

"I'll stop on the way back and we can decide."

Paul watched Jean walk down the street with a spring in her step, her umbrella balanced against the wind and rain.

Jean returned to Paul's cabin when late afternoon was creeping toward evening. A curtain of drizzling rain blocked much of the sunlight. She joyfully inhaled the soft marine air and stepped into the shelter of the porch. *Okay, honey, you haven't had dinner or spent time with a man for a year, so don't be a jerk. This guy is walking wounded. Keep it light, keep it friendly, and have a nice evening.* She set the bag of groceries on the chair, shook out her umbrella and reached out to knock on the door. It swung open to reveal Paul smiling at her.

"If you're from Avon, I already have everything I need."

"At least you could have waited for me to knock!"

"I saw you and was waiting for you to knock. For a minute I thought you hadn't stopped, but when you shook out your umbrella it was as good as a door bell. Would you like to come in out of the rain?"

"I really need to go home and get things started. Do you want to come with me so we can talk while I fix dinner or would you rather wait until later?"

"Which would you prefer?"

"If you come with me I can interrogate you about what you do or don't like to eat. Helps avoid mistakes and you can have more time to bask in the glow of my sparkling personality."

"Then I shall escort you home to protect you from the bogeymen and any other nefarious creatures who might have unpleasant designs upon you. Is there anything I can bring in the way of food or drink?"

"Nope. I think I have it covered."

"I'll grab a jacket."

"You can carry the groceries and I'll carry the umbrella. Don't forget to turn on your porch light. It will be a homing beacon for you later."

"Can't. I put in a new bulb and it still doesn't work. I'll just have to find my way home by Braille."

"Ready to brave the elements?"

He picked up the groceries. "I was born ready."

They tucked under her umbrella and stepped into the elements. "Hard to believe it's summer, isn't it?" Paul said.

"The weather here is a bit unreliable unless you're relying on it to change. It's part of the character of the place."

"Character. An interesting term. Sounds like you're describing a fine wine, a cheap beer, or an eccentric."

"Too many years in advertising. Those terms just filter into your vocabulary when you use them all day to invite people to buy something."

"So do you write ads for magazines and television?"

"Past tense. Very, very past tense."

"Oops! My turn to suffer foot in mouth disease. I didn't mean to remind you of a bad experience."

"Not your fault. It's a long story."

"We have a long evening."

Paul's smile made her realize how happy she was to have the evening stretching out in front of them.

Jean's cabin shared the same weathered appearance as the others on the street. Wind, rain, and sun had eroded the soft areas of the wood siding, leaving the harder growth lines of the planking standing out like a free form sculpture. She had planned to paint the cabin, but she came to appreciate the silvery look of the weathered redwood. Although built about the same time as the other cabins on the bluff, the architecture was different. A veranda across the front provided a wide covered area from which to enjoy the spectacle of the setting sun. A hip roof with Dutch gables sheltered porthole windows north and south, a west facing dormer looked out over the kicked out roof of the veranda. The yard was a simple combination of mowed grass surrounded by native azaleas and rhododendrons. The cottage could be planted on almost any coast. It simply looked how a seaside cabin ought to look.

"It looks like a fan of Andrew Wyeth designed your house."

"I fell in love with it as soon as I saw it."

"I think I understand why."

"I considered screening the porch, but I can't bring myself to sacrifice the unrestricted view of the ocean. I mean, look at this!" She swept her arm across the horizon. "Screens would keep out the insects, but they'd put a dimmer on the visual glory. Even when it's rainy and gray and the changing light plays peek-a-boo in the clouds and rain, it's, oh, it's hard to put into words. The best I can do is to say it's a natural force that stirs my soul."

"I like the uninhibited animation in your face and voice when you talk about the world you see from your front porch. Once in a while, a person finds a special place that unlocks feelings they didn't know they had. It sounds like you've found yours. It's an enviable accomplishment."

Jean studied his face for a moment, hoping to discover the real person inside the stranger. She saw only the mask people show the world in order to defend themselves against the judgment of others. She resigned herself to learning what he wanted her to know when he wanted her to know it and opened the door. "C'mon inside, it's too chilly to stand out here gazing at the horizon."

The cabin was a well planned use of a square. The front half was devoted to a combination living room and dining area with a vaulted ceiling and a loft lighted by the porthole windows in the Dutch gables. On the left, the rectangular kitchen ran most of the length of the cabin to a small service porch at the rear. Two bedrooms were separated by a bathroom, which opened onto both rooms. Jean had converted the south bedroom into an art studio, taking advantage of the two windows for natural light, plus a skylight she added to further brighten the space.

The fireplace on the south wall of the living room was a small brick affair with a mantelpiece of native redwood supported by carved sconces at each end. Jean had furnished the room with a six-foot sofa facing the fireplace and a classic leather chair perpendicular to the couch. The latter faced the front windows across a coffee table created by a local craftsman from a slab of redwood root. The room had a warm, comfortable feel, but Paul's immediate attention was drawn to the painting above the fireplace.

The artist had captured more than the sweeping grandeur of the lagoon and the mountains, more than the surf and ocean spray attempting to leap the isthmus of sand dividing it from the lagoon. The style was not of the classic artist whose draftsmanship attempts to capture the exact appearance of the subject, nor was it the ethereal style of the impressionists. The style resisted categorization, but somehow managed to cross and bridge them all to make a bold statement, drawing the viewer inside amidst the clouds, the spray, the birds, and the rainbowed light of the sun shimmering through the moist air. Paul stopped two steps inside the room and gazed at the painting with a dumbfounded stare.

"Do you like it?"

Paul simply nodded and walked toward the fireplace to get a closer look.

Jean watched Paul approach the painting and reach out to touch the frame as his gaze swept across the painting. Jean took the bag of groceries from him. "I'll just go put these away."

"Yeah, sure," Paul mumbled. Suddenly he tore his gaze away from the painting. "This is spectacular! It seems to reach out and draw you inside, like you're walking into the painting. Where did you find it?"

"Right outside. I painted it."

Paul spun around and looked again at the painting. The impact was just as powerful, just as hypnotic, just as startling. "This is your work?"

"Sure is. I think it's the best I've ever done. It just sort of appeared on the canvas from all the different ways I've seen the lagoon. I had it framed a couple weeks ago. I love to sit and look at it."

Paul stared in wonder. "I've never seen anything like it. I have some appreciation of art and I own a few pieces, but this one is like falling into another dimension. It isn't passive, it, it, embraces you!"

"The frame shop owner liked it too. He offered to buy it, but I like it too much to sell it. Someday maybe, but it's the first really successful piece I've done. Painting it was like having someone else's hand guiding the brush. Every time I see it I remember the incredible experience of creating it."

"Total expression of the feelings you explore from the front porch?"

"Maybe, but I don't try to analyze it. I just enjoy it without questioning the how or the why."

"I don't know what to say. I'm incredibly impressed. I really can't find the words to tell you how special I think it is."

"You don't need to say anything. I can see it speaks to you by the way you respond to it."

"Stunned silence speaks volumes?"

"It does for me. Want a drink?"

"Sure. What do you have?"

"Well, I have a cheeky little red wine to go with dinner, your basic Milwaukee suds, or if you're into something with a bit more punch, some of Jack's finest Tennessee sour mash."

"Nice selection of inebriates. Beer sounds fine. I don't want to dull my senses, unless you suggest being drunk would make me less aware of the food and company."

"Oh, you're going to pay for that. I may not be Julia Childs, but I can cook. How about a glass of water? It'll wash the cobwebs off your taste buds and it won't dull your senses."

"Ooh, the lady has teeth."

"The better to bite you with," Jean said with a leer as she took a bottle of Budweiser from the refrigerator.

"You told me you had a Milwaukee brew, and you offer me south St. Louis. Haven't you heard about truth in advertising?"

"So you're more of a connoisseur of frothy brews than I am. Do you want to drink it or debate the quality of the vintage?"

"Oh, I think I can force myself to swallow a Bud."

"How magnanimous of you. The kitchen is small. You can either lean against the doorway or drag up a chair and relax while I make some magic with dinner."

"You do take charge, don't you?"

"Sorry. I'm accustomed to being responsible. Sometimes I forget not everyone appreciates being managed."

"You are who and what you are. Don't apologize for what you worked hard to learn and achieve."

"Are you really as nice as you seem?"

"Like Popeye says, 'I yam what I yam and that's all that I yam.'" He raised the beer bottle in salute.

She laughed. It felt good to be with someone who could make her laugh. It felt better to be with a man who recognized her independence without feeling threatened by it. "I'd better get out of this coat and get cooking."

Jean wore a simple cotton blouse and blue jeans. The curve of her hips and the swell of her breasts were as apparent as the fact she was trimly athletic. She enjoyed seeing Paul smile as he watched her move about her kitchen.

The wind complained as it buffeted the cottage, driving the rain into a tinkling song against the windows while the cozy house sheltered its occupants in a warm embrace.

The drizzling rain was a blessing and a curse for the sentinel. His reconnaissance had revealed how to reach the McAfee cabin under cover of darkness. He only needed a few minutes to set the bugs. It shouldn't be difficult, but he was uneasy. A sense of lurking danger prickled the hairs on the back of his neck, but the source remained an enigma. He knew how to avoid being detected by the old woman on the corner. The artist was a known commodity, she kept to herself for the most part, at least until McAfee appeared. *What was he missing? Who was he missing? Where and when was Mr. Murphy going to jump up and spoil his planning? Who would be his courier?*

The problem tugged relentlessly at his mind as he strolled along the beach. His employer was breathing down his neck to get the devices in place regardless of the risks. A feral smile slowly stole across his face. "And sometimes you just get shithouse lucky," he said softly. With the satisfaction of a hunter seeing his prey walk into an ambush he watched Paul and Jean walk to the end cabin and disappear inside. "Enjoy yourself my friend. You and your libido just made my job easier." With a lighter step he strolled toward his camp and the implementation of his plan. As day drifted into early twilight, the lowering skies surrendered more of their burden in an effort to climb the rising slope of the land. *Perfect conditions. Maybe this won't be so tough after all.*

6.

"FORTYSIX-TWO, HUMBOLDT."

The crackle of the dispatcher's voice was definitely not what he wanted to hear. The shift had barely started and Detective John Ragsdale faced an already full schedule. He needed the day to play catch up and it sounded like his schedule was about to be tossed out the window.

"Go ahead"

"We have a floater at Big Lagoon"

"A floater! Shit!" John growled and slammed his fist against the steering wheel. Floaters were his private nightmare. The last major flood had swept the river valleys clean of structures and for months his primary detail was to retrieve and identify the bodies deposited in the detritus of the receding waters. He had been the newest detective in the squad and the nastiest details always went to the new guy. In the course of the detail he had garnered several nicknames: digger, grave robber, ghoul, and his favorite, stiff stroker. The gallows humor of the cop fraternity is often misunderstood by the uninitiated, but without the laughter and jokes the stress of the daily diet of inhumanity conspires to drive even the strongest mind into cynicism. Decade old memories of the sight and smell of a decomposing corpse caught in the limbs of an uprooted tree with pennants of dead plants streaming from the body still haunted him, sometimes waking him in the middle of the night and disbursing all chance of going back to sleep.

"Another floater! Couldn't someone else catch the damn call?" He keyed the mike. "Do you have a more specific location?"

"Affirmative. The body washed up on the north end of the beach. Fortysix-nine is on location."

"ETA to the lagoon thirty minutes. Is fortysix-nine Tom Schroeder?"

"Affirmative. I suggest you wear your walking shoes, take your umbrella, and don't forget your sunscreen."

"Ha-ha. Enjoy the sunny beach, right?"

"If the sun's shining, you might as well enjoy it. Coroner is rolling."

"Me too."

John focused his attention on the beauty of the north coast as he drove, letting the rugged grandeur wash over his soul and calm him in preparation for the gruesome task ahead. Murders and unexplained deaths were the primary purview of a senior detective. Over the years he had studied hundreds of cases to sharpen his skills, but experience and study didn't immunize him against the horror of man's inhumanity to man. As he drove he mentally listed questions he would need answered to unravel the circumstances and events that had cast a lifeless body ashore with the flotsam. "Maybe I'll get lucky. Maybe it's the fisherman reported missing last week."

He arrived under a low hanging sky, the air cool and damp in the wake of a recent shower. He changed into the work boots and down jacket he carried in the trunk. He only needed to ruin one pair of shoes and catch a nasty cold to learn to stock his car with a variety of gear to suit almost any circumstance. He was a compactly muscular man with a physical build requiring him to shop among the larger sizes on the clothing racks. At five feet nine inches, his carriage and demeanor projected the aura of a much larger man, an intimidation factor he was adept at using. Thickening around the middle at forty-eight years old, he maintained good physical condition and stamina by walking and doing hard physical labor on his days off. Gyms and workout machines never attracted him. He loved to walk through the mountains and for a workout he preferred to split wood, help a rancher friend bring in his hay crop, or any kind of physical labor producing the satisfaction of a finished job in exchange for sweat and sore muscles.

He shouldered the pack with his crime scene tools and set out across the sand to where a small crowd of onlookers served as a homing beacon. Tom Schroeder was diligently protecting the scene and collecting identification information from everyone in the crowd.

John was glad Tom was first on the scene. Tom wasn't a detective, but he understood the critical need to preserve a crime scene and how the most insignificant remark might be the key. Tom was a good observer and topped the list of deputies he would choose to handle a crime scene.

"Morning, Tommy, how you doing?"

"Hey, John, trying to keep things pristine."

"Who found the body?"

"The kid over there with his dad"

"Whose tracks do we have here?"

"The boy's are the small ones. His father's lead to the head. Dad did a good job of taking care of things until I got here. He sent the boy to call us and kept everyone else away until I arrived. No one else got close before I arrived. Not a track of any kind. I looked for signs of a struggle, but I didn't find anything. I think he died somewhere else and floated ashore here."

"Did you take pictures before you covered him up?"

"Three rolls."

"Good job. Just put them in my pack."

"Usual place?"

"Yeah. Did you get names, addresses and phone numbers from everyone here?"

"Got 'em right here." He patted his pocket.

"Excellent." John spoke to the crowd of bystanders. "I'm detective John Ragsdale. I may need to talk to each of you before you leave. I only have a few questions and I'll try to finish as quickly as I can."

He turned his attention to the father and son standing at the front of the crowd. "Would you and your father come with me, please?" He led them about twenty feet away to a driftwood log.

"My name is John, why don't you come sit with me," he said to the boy as he patted log. "What's your name?"

"Nick," the boy said quietly.

"Nice to meet you, Nick. The deputy tells me you found the body. I bet it was pretty scary."

Nick nodded slowly, staring at the sand on his shoes, a child on the edge of puberty caught in a situation beyond his experience, requiring maturity beyond his years.

"Not like TV or the movies is it? I know how I felt the first time I saw a dead man. It's pretty difficult to handle. Right now it's really important for me to learn everything I can about what you saw. I really need your help. Do you think you can help me?

Nick looked up at his father, who nodded encouragement, then faced John and nodded.

"Good. You and your dad have worked hard to do the right thing this morning and you've already helped a lot, so let's get down to the tough part and get it over with. Okay?"

"Okay," Nick said softly, "I'll tell you what I can."

"Great. Just tell me what happened this morning. Don't worry about how you tell it, just tell me the story like you would to one of your buddies."

"Okay, well, uh, we got here last night and it was raining so we couldn't do anything but sit inside and play cards. I like playing cards, but it's really bogus to come all the way here and not be able to go outside. So this morning we came out to walk on the beach before breakfast. I still haven't had breakfast. Is this going to take very long?"

"No, it won't take very long. How old are you?"

"I'm almost eleven."

"Going into sixth grade, huh? I bet your friends wish their dads would take them on a trip like this. So what happened next?"

"Well, we were walking down the beach and I saw something laying on the sand. I told Dad it was a seal, but he didn't think so. He said seals are a different color. So, I ran up here to see what it was and, and, it was, it was,"

"Pretty bad, huh?"

Large eyes, threatening to overflow with tears looked directly at John, but Nick's voice was strong and firm. "It was really gross!"

"Then what did you do?"

"I called my dad."

"More like screamed at me," his father said.

"Yeah, well I don't blame you. It's enough to make anybody scream."

"It was nasty! There were flies crawling all over him. I ran back to my dad. I was scared."

"It's okay, Nick. You did fine. Do you remember anything else about the man?"

"Not really. Dad told me to run to the store and call nine-one-one. The lady at the store helped me. When I came back Dad wouldn't let me get close again. He said I might make a mess of things and make it harder for you to find out what happened, so I just helped him keep everyone else away." Nick grinned. "It was really fun telling all those grownups what to do."

"Your dad was right. You guys did a great job of protecting things for us. I appreciate everything you did." John spoke to the father. "Well, so far I know you're the proud father of this young man, but for the sake of the proprieties could you tell me your name and why you're here?"

"Angelo Manetti. I grew up in Blue Lake and graduated from Arcata High, but never moved back after I left for college. My folks moved to Arizona when Dad retired and I don't have any family here anymore, but there's something about the place I can't get out of my system. Something about taking the boy out of the country, but not taking the country out of the boy, I suppose. My wife is from San Francisco and we've lived there ever since we got married. She's not real excited about the great north woods as she calls it, but Nick and I love it. We come here once a year. Just Nick and I, to get away from the city and breathe some unprocessed air."

"The place just creeps into your bones doesn't it," John said. "When I was in the service all I could think about was coming home. I came back and never left. I still love it. What happened after you sent Nick to the phone?"

"I stayed here to keep people from walking around the body. Nick's scream was a real crowd magnet. Everybody on the beach had to come see what all the excitement was about. I did my best to make them keep their distance. I knew you guys would want the scene to be as undisturbed as possible."

"Deputy Schroeder said you checked the body."

"Yes, I did. I wanted to see if he was breathing or had a pulse even if the guy looked dead."

"Are you a doctor?"

"No, but I've had CPR training and was taught to check for a pulse and breathing because a person can look dead when they might be able to be saved. I had to at least check for life signs. You know what I mean?"

"Sure. You did the right thing. Do you recognize the man?"

"No. Like Nick says, we just got here last night, and it was raining, so we stayed in the motor home and played cards. We were both feeling kind of cooped up when we got up this morning so we decided to walk first and eat later. We were hoping to discover something new and exciting, but this sure isn't what we had in mind."

"Yeah, it's a rough start on the day for all of us, especially our friend over there. Are you staying at the lagoon campground?"

"Yeah, we have a standing reservation every year when school gets out for our annual guys only get away. Nick has two sisters and sometimes we both feel like we need a little time away from a house full of women."

"How long are you planning to be here?"

"We've always stayed a week, but after this, well, . . ?"

"I understand. This has been pretty traumatic and I'm sure it's put a damper on the fun, but I have to ask you to stay at least one more day in case I need to talk to you again. Sometimes we think of questions later and need to come back and talk to witnesses again."

"Dad, I don't want to go home yet," Nick pleaded. "This is our time. I want to go fishing, and swimming, and hike in the trees. I don't want to go home yet. We just got here."

Angelo put his arm around his son's shoulders. "I guess

we'll be here for a while. Nick has spoken. This is a time I let him decide what we do and have things his way. The rest of the year he's expected to be a good follower, but this is our week for him to be the boss. It's fun for me too, I don't have to worry about entertaining him. He calls the shots and I'm the chauffeur."

"Sounds great. Times like this are important for both of you. I think that's all I need from you. Here's my card in case you think of something, even if doesn't seem important. If it comes to mind it could be very important, so please give me a call."

"Can we go now?" Nick asked.

"Absolutely. Go and have a great time. You'll have to go back to your sisters soon enough."

Suddenly all thought of the dead body seemed to flee Nick's mind, releasing his youthful exuberance. "I don't even want to think about them. This is our time to have fun. C'mon Dad, I'm hungry! Let's go make pancakes!"

John watched them walk away together. He admired their relationship. He walked back to the crowd of bystanders.

"Were any of you here before Angelo and Nick?"

"He was the only one here when I got here and he wasn't letting anyone get near the guy. I've seen guard dogs who were less troublesome," said a gray haired man in a hat festooned with fishing flies. "He said this was a crime scene and we weren't going to get close enough to clutter it up with a bunch of unrelated tracks and confuse things."

"Thank you for cooperating with him. He was right about a bunch of tracks cluttering up the scene. I appreciate you waiting. Do any of you know the victim?"

"He looks like the guy with the pickup and camper in the campground," an elderly woman said.

"What is your name ma'am?"

"Evelyn Woodbine. My husband and I come here to look for agates and driftwood. We always stay in the campground because it's so pretty and we can afford it on our social security."

"And you think you may have seen the victim there?"

"I think so. My eyes aren't as good as they used to be, but he sure looks like the guy with the beat up pickup and camper."

"Is it in the campground over there?" John pointed across the lagoon.

She shaded her eyes against the brightness of the morning sky reflecting off the water. "It's hard for me to see, but it looks like it's still there. Yes, there it is," she pointed. "The one with the tent next to it. Now, why would anybody sleep in a tent if they have a camper? Do you know what I'm saying? It doesn't make any sense. Nice soft bed in the camper and he'd rather sleep on the ground or on a cold cot. It just doesn't make sense!"

John smiled, reminded of his grandmother and her attitudes about the comforts, or lack of them, when camping. She never thought sleeping on the ground was much of a treat either. Her favorite description of camping came from an article in *Outdoor Life* entitled *The Misery Kit*. "Are you sure this is the man you saw over there with the camper?"

"I think so. I never got a real good look at him, but I'm pretty sure it's him. He always had clothes on when I saw him and he wasn't very sociable. Always kept to himself, but I suppose a fellow has a right to his privacy, even in a public campground."

"Thank you, Mrs. Woodbine, I appreciate your help. Does anyone else think they may have seen the victim?"

The chorus of shaking heads was enough to satisfy him nothing more was going to be learned by talking to each person individually. Most of the people were acting restless to be away from the gruesome scene. "Thank you for waiting. You're all free to go."

John lifted the plastic sheet and examined the nude body that lay twisted and partly on its right side. Dead eyes stared vacantly through a thin coating of sand. Even with flies and ants busy going about their business there was no smell of decaying tissues.

"Terrific." John muttered. "No ID."

"The closest thing we got is the old lady maybe recognizing him as the owner of a camper." Tom said.

"I don't see evidence of a fatal injury, but we can't see the back of the head or the other side of the body. So we have a body washed up on the beach with no apparent cause of death and of course, just to make it interesting, no jewelry, no watch, and no wallet. Nothing to tell us who this guy is."

"Looks like we have to do things the old fashioned way. Talk to everybody in the area and anybody else we happen to bump into." Tom said.

"Yeah, unless we can find a fingerprint record on him someplace. If he's never been arrested or licensed for a regulated industry, it's a long shot." John saw the coroner approaching. "Looks like the body squad's here. Maybe they'll find an answer or two. Personally, I don't think this one's a floater."

"Educate me. What do you see that I don't?"

"It's not what you don't see, it's what you don't recognize as significant. Once you've seen a few bodies that have been in the water, you recognize the signs. Floaters, particularly those found in the ocean and coming through the surf have certain characteristics this guy ain't got. I don't think he's been dead more than a few hours either. He's dirty and there's some insect activity, but those critters show up in the first half hour, so it doesn't mean much. The fact there isn't much damage from them is. No stink either. The body's fresh." John frowned. "This whole thing looks hinkey. I may be wrong, but I think he was supposed to be carried out with the tide and the killer missed his timing. The body never got into the under tow and sure as hell didn't wash up on the beach after a day or two in the ocean."

"You can see all that without a turning him over and taking a closer look?"

"Yep! Hang around while I discuss things with Denny. After we've finished we'll take questions from the peanut gallery."

Coroner Dennis O'Malley was a stocky local native of Irish lineage in his early forties. His ruddy complexioned face, creased with laugh lines and topped by a shock of wild red hair beginning to gray at the temples, never seemed far from a smile. His current assistant, a gangling solemn faced youth of strictly business demeanor, carried a large equipment bag.

"Dennis, me laddy, 'tis a fine soft marnin' fer an Irish feller to be oot un aboot, dontcha think?" John spoke in an Irish brogue.

"Top o' the marnin' to you, John. You wouldna have a wee bit of the Irish whiskey to liven up me coffee now, would ya?"

"Sorry, but we both bein' on duty means clear heads must prevail."

"Aye, 'tis a point well taken, but I was thinkin' of the fragrance of the morning when we lift back the cover from our friend restin' so peaceful there and disturb his slumbers with our pokin' and proddin' about."

"Well, you can put such thoughts aside, my friend. This one hasn't been cold very long and his swim looks to have been rather brief. This one's so fresh the last of his Right Guard is still with him."

"Dispatch reported a floater."

"It looks like he came out of the ocean, but I doubt he was in the water more than a few hours. He's so fresh his belly hasn't started to swell and the eyes and lips are still intact. Even the gulls haven't shown up for breakfast yet. I think this is a dump job. I think it was supposed to drift out to sea, but came right back in."

Experience had taught Dennis to listen attentively to John's observations. The Irish jokes between them began at a department picnic when they discovered both their great grandfathers had come to America from County Cork to work on the transcontinental railroad. Dennis considered John's observations at a crime scene as good as gold. Still, he made it a point to be moderately contentious to keep the investigation objective.

"Everything you say sounds well and good, but I'll take a bit of a look for myself and let you know if you tripped over something obvious." Smiling like a mischievous leprechaun, he removed the plastic blanket from the body. "You ready Fred?" he asked his assistant, who was standing nearby with a video recorder.

"Already recording."

"We have lights and camera so here goes some action." He began with a description of the body, noting the position of the arms and legs and the paucity of post-mortem scuffs and scratches.

"Help me turn him over, John. There has to be something to show how he got dead and naked. Natural causes usually beat the crap out of the victim when they remove the clothing."

They rolled the body onto its back. "Well, look what we

have here. Cause of death appears to be a loss of continuity of the cranial cavity as the result of blunt force trauma."

"You mean somebody busted his melon?"

"Somebody or something. It sure looks like his final headache was a real head splitter."

"Any idea what sort of weapon was used?"

"The legendary blunt instrument."

"Not much blood for a head wound is there?"

"No. There's not much blood in the sand either. I think you're right about this being a dump job. I also think you're right about time of death. Rigor hasn't set in and the lividity indicates the body was face down when the blood settled. Pretty good assessment, with a little effort you might even make a semi-incompetent assistant one day."

"Well, damn me with faint praise. I appreciate your kind offer, but I think I'll stick to chasing bad guys and let you carve up the victims."

"Oh, now that's just rude. How many times have I found the evidence you needed to nail one of those bad guys? Huh?"

"Probably not as many as you'd like to take credit for, but I'll admit you do good work, just not very much of it."

"And the horse you rode up on. So much for examination at the scene. It doesn't look like this one got dead here so there's no point in chasing our tails looking for evidence. For what it's worth, I agree with you about time in the water. It looks like he got tossed in nearby and floated up on the tide shortly thereafter. All right Fred, let's get him bagged and dragged so we can get down to the real work."

The coroner's car disappeared into the trees as John and Tom walked to their cars. "Hard to imagine a murder happening in a place this beautiful isn't it, Tom?"

"Like the man says, shit happens. I keep thinking I'll reach a point where it doesn't bother me to see what people do to each other. How long did it take you to get used to it?"

"I never have. I learned to build a wall around my feelings while I'm working a case because I have to be objective. Not getting comfortable with it keeps the fires burning bright for me. I can set my lunch bag on a corpse and eat a sandwich while I examine the body, but that's just the face I paint on for the world to see. It's not how I really feel. I use my anger and sadness to fuel my determination. I've never gotten used to it and I don't want to."

"Good advice. So what's next? Do I help you follow up or get back on the beat?"

John took a moment to reflect on this offer while appraising the young deputy. At six feet tall and two hundred pounds with broad shoulders, flashing blue eyes, and light brown hair, Tom was a study in eagerness, bursting with youthful energy. "Good idea, I could use another pair of eyes, ears, and legs." John reached into his car and picked up the radio mike. "Humboldt, fortysix-two."

"Go ahead."

"Request Tom Shroeder be attached to me for the rest of the shift. I need his help to cover the ground before the trail gets cold."

"I'll notify the lieutenant."

"We'll be away from the radio for a while."

"Stand by a couple while I clear this with the lieutenant."

John grinned. "She doesn't want to take the heat if someone hollers about me grabbing you off your beat."

"Fortysix-two, Humboldt."

"Go ahead."

"Fortysix-nine is assigned to you for the remainder of the shift."

"Thanks." He hung up the mike. "Okay, kid, you ready to get down to the hard work?"

"You bet. You lead and I'll follow."

"Good. First thing you need to do is check out the pickup and camper Mrs. Woodbine told us about. Don't try to make entry, just take note of everything in the campsite, take pictures and run the plates. Check and see if anyone is missing from any of the campsites. Oh, yeah, check with the park ranger to see if he remembers the guy with the pickup and camper, see if he can describe him. Ask again if anyone remembers the guy or remembers seeing him. It's probably a blind alley, but it's the only alley we've got. Be careful to keep the campsite as pristine as you can. I'll catch up with you in a little while."

"I've seen this look before. What are you thinking?"

"There's a trail to the beach from the cabins on the bluff. The body had to come from somewhere close and it seems like a logical place to start looking. Unfortunately, it rained all night and probably washed out any blood evidence. Between the weather and the tide and the sand it's going to be tough to find anything, but I've got to go look before any more of mother nature's clean up crew shows up."

"I've had the north county beat for the last two years and it ain't the busiest place in the world, so I've spent some time getting to know the area and the people who live here. I might notice if something is out of place."

"I appreciate what you're saying and I want you to tell me if anything looks out of place, but we've got a lot of ground to cover and only two of us to cover it. I need you to work the campground. I'm going to take a walk on the beach. Maybe one of us will get lucky."

John knew the lagoon and the beach well. It had been had been a favorite for family picnics and fishing when he was growing up. Even though it was familiar territory, searching the shifting beach surfaces was a challenge, surf and tide could have washed away any trail. Looking at the bluff below the cabins, he thought about how the victim might have reached the beach. *Could the victim have fallen from the top and hit his head when he landed on the beach? It's as good a place to start as any. I don't believe for a minute he fell off the cliff, bashed in his head, took off his clothes and went for a swim. Even if he was pushed off the cliff and dragged into the surf, it doesn't explain the missing clothes. Had the victim been near the surf when he was attacked? If he was attacked. There has to be something here. It's probably right under my nose if I could only recognize it. C'mon old beach, talk to me! Tell me what happened last night.*

An hour later, he had covered the distance of the bluff face south as far as the end of the street and back to the north, but he found nothing to indicate someone had fallen to the beach. There were tracks in the gravel from people walking to and from the beach, but nothing offered an explanation for a nude, lifeless body lying just above the surf half a mile up the beach.

The beach trail was the obvious access point for someone carrying a body from the cabins, but there was nothing extraordinary in the delta of footprints at the base of the trail. It was as though the body had appeared out of thin air. He scanned the beach from a vantage point half way up the trail, hoping to see some anomaly not visible from beach. He silently sifted what he knew so far. *Think of it as a challenge. We haven't found very many pieces of the puzzle and the ones we've found don't tell us much. Somewhere, somehow, they always screw up and leave a trail. Whoever did this covered their tracks well. It almost looks professional. Professional? Seems unlikely, but not impossible. Last night the conditions were perfect for trying to dispose of a body. Everyone huddled up to keep warm with the drapes closed and a fire going. One of those nights when even the dogs don't bark. It doesn't matter. I'm gonna find you. You just hide and watch. You ain't gonna get away. I'm going to find you!*

The radio crackled to life as he neared his car. "John, can you hear me?"

He spotted Tom near an older Ford pick up and camper. He waved in response.

"If you've finished your morning constitutional there's something you should see." John increased his pace. Right now anything would be welcome.

The pickup looked like it had seen better days. The body was battered and rusting in patches, the doors and fenders were wrinkled and dented, and the window glass was beginning to fog in the corners. It looked like a tired old heap running out its last years as a weekend beater. A perfect choice for an outdoors-man who didn't want to worry about scratching the paint or denting a fender when he got off the pavement in search of a good fishing or hunting spot.

"Did you get anything off the plates?"

"Registered to George Nathan at a P O Box in Sylmar."

"Sylmar? Where's Sylmar?"

"LA I think, but I'm not sure without a map."

"Did you run Mr. Nathan for a drivers license?"

"I sure did. Guess what came back."

"A real address perhaps? God knows he doesn't live in a Post Office box."

"Nothing."

"Nothing? Nothing at all?"

"Nada. I've got the office on the phone with the DMV trying to get a line on the guy. I haven't taken a close look the camper yet, but I did talk to everyone in the campground. No one saw much of this guy. Everybody remembers seeing him around, but nobody got a good look at him. They say he kept to himself and they respected his privacy. Trying to find out anything about him is like chasing a butterfly's shadow."

"Kind of like the way he landed on the beach. This case is definitely bent. The plates cold?"

"Yep. No wants and the registration is current. Comes back to a seventy-two Ford pick up. I didn't try to verify the VIN because I didn't want to step on anything before you got here. We don't really know if this belongs to the guy on the beach do we?"

"Uh-uh. Just the old lady's guess. At this point about all we can do is look it over. No probable cause to open the doors, but we can look through the windows. The ruling says the eye cannot commit a trespass. Let's hope we see reasonable cause for a warrant. As luck would have it, the curtains are drawn in the camper so all we can do is look in the cab."

"Don't give up yet. I noticed a couple things about this heap while I was waiting for you to finish your little hike."

"Talk to me."

"Look at the tires."

"Uh huh?"

"This is a beat up ol' stump jumper, right?"

"So?"

"The tires are the best you can buy."

"Maybe he likes the best where the rubber meets the road."

"Maybe, but I took a look under the truck too."

"And?"

"Look for yourself, a flashlight helps," Tom handed him a five-cell unit.

John did not expect what he saw. The outer shell of the truck was battered and worn, dirty enough to avoid attracting attention from a casual glance, but the undercarriage was first class, high-performance equipment. The exhaust system was obviously custom made to enhance the performance of the engine without giving away its identity. "Excellent observation. Conclusion?"

"All things are not what they seem."

"Very clever, grasshopper. It could prove to be the theme song for this little adventure."

"Fortysix-nine, Humboldt."

"Maybe they found something to identify our friend."

"Hope springs eternal."

"Right. Humboldt, fortysix-nine, go ahead."

"All we have on George Nathan is the vehicle registration. No California drivers license, no social security number, no other address, no wants, no warrants, nothing."

"Thank you."

Tom looked at John with a puzzled expression. "Borrowing a line from Alice in Wonderland, curiouser and curiouser."

"Welcome to the other side of the looking glass. I'm not sure what we've stumbled onto, but I think the body wasn't supposed to be found and if this truck belongs to the victim, it was probably supposed to do a disappearing act as well. Even if the body turned into a floater, the chances are it wouldn't have floated back in for a couple days. If ever. By then it might have been totally unidentifiable. The truck would be gone, the campers who were here would be gone, and we'd have a different sort of investigation. It looks like we've arrived in the middle of the game without a program and no announcer to tell us the names of the teams or the players."

"What do we do next?"

"Are you sure you talked to everyone in the campground?"

"Everyone accounted for in all the campsites. This is the only one I haven't found a camper or campers to go with."

"What about the park officer?"

"He never saw the guy from this camp. He has four campgrounds to cover and as long as he gets an envelope with the campsite number and the fees he doesn't spend much time looking to see who is where or what they're doing unless there's a problem or a complaint."

"Nobody complained about our missing camper did they?"

"Nope. Like I said, it's like trying to catch a shadow. Everybody remembers him, but no one got a good look at him. He's also the only visitor we can't locate."

"Damn. We need a search warrant to get inside this truck. Whatever we find is inadmissible when we get to court without a warrant, presuming we ever get to court."

"Judge Thomas sits up here when court's in session. He might be able to help. He lives here and he's semi-retired, but he's sharp and doesn't get reversed. He might think we have enough to establish probable cause in terms of identifying the owner. Besides, we both think there's something weird about the truck."

"Weird doesn't constitute probable cause for a search warrant. There's no law says you can't rebuild an old vehicle using new parts and technology as long as everything fits inside the required parameters and this isn't the work of some shade tree mechanic. This was done by a pro and I'd bet a month's pay all the mods on this beast are right down the middle of the regulations."

"I agree, but it can't hurt to ask. At least he'll tell me what he needs to give us a warrant."

"I guess it's worth a shot. I'm going to go over to the cabins and start interviewing people. You chase down the judge and see if you can talk him into giving you a search warrant."

"How do we keep the pickup secure while I'm talking to the judge and you're interviewing the neighbors?"

"We gotta take our chances. There's no one we can ask to cover things and the longer it takes to talk to people the colder the trail gets. We've got to just hope for the best."

"I'll be back as soon as I can."

"Don't let any grass grow under your feet. I need you back here fifteen minutes ago. Don't waste any time trying to convince him. Get a clear set of guidelines, thank him politely and boogie."

The entire length of the sand bar separating the lagoon from the ocean was visible from where John parked across from Alma Jacobsen's cabin. The site where the body was found was clearly visible, but would require a powerful set of binoculars to see any detail. He looked at the cottage behind the white picket fence, hedge and flowerbeds. The windows were about six feet above where he was sitting, offering an even better view of the beach. The cottage was a perfect lookout. He considered who might choose to live there. *Someone who wants to be able to see everything would buy a place like this. Someone who loves to watch, or is on the run and wants plenty of notice if trouble is on the way. Either way, I bet it's somebody interesting.*

Alma watched the unmarked car stop across from her cabin. The activities of the morning hadn't escaped her attention, but she continued with her daily ritual of tending to her garden. She liked her garden tidy, neatly pruned and weed free. She enjoyed the work and especially enjoyed the prim appearance of her yard.

She knew the detective still hadn't seen her when he stepped from his car. She could see through the foliage from her vantage point on her knees behind the hedge without being seen from the other side. When he paused at the front gate to glance at the beach, she slipped out of sight behind her cabin.

John admired the yard as he closed the gate. *Someone spends a lot of time and love on this place. A weed wouldn't stand a chance. It would be evicted as soon as it reared its ugly head. Whoever lives here loves to work in the garden. I feel like the place is trying to talk to me. I wish I could understand what it's saying.*

Getting no response to his knock, he moved on. *It's early in an investigation already filled with dead ends. Not even dead ends. More like shadows of a ghost,* he mused. As he walked back to the gate, a jogger topped the beach trail. John mentally tallied the physical characteristics of the jogger. *Maybe six feet tall, about one hundred ninety-five pounds, brown hair showing some gray at the temples, probably forty-ish, in decent shape, runs like an athlete, would definitely be strong enough to carry a body down to the beach and dump it in the ocean. Interesting.*

"Good morning," the jogger greeted him as he trotted past.

"Good morning," John replied. *Definitely in decent shape, he's run long enough to work up a sweat, but his breathing is strong, not labored. He probably runs every day.* The jogger ran to the next cabin and went inside. *Looks like I should be able to talk to him this morning. I'll give him a little time to shower before I beat on his door.* He walked down the street, noticing the difference in the condition of the yard of the jogger's cabin. It was recently mowed and tidy, but lacked the fussy neatness of the corner lot. A bar code sticker on the window of the car parked behind the cabin indicated the jogger was probably a visitor.

The next cabin was obviously unoccupied. Leaves and detritus on the porch had blown there over an extended period, a mixture of old and new material. The yard needed attention, but was not overgrown.

There was no need to try the next cabin. It had obviously been empty for a while. Berry vines were trying to swallow the rear of the cabin, the front steps were in need of repair, and the screen door had fallen victim to the ravages of time. John's thoughts animated the property. *You look sad. You miss the sound of people and laughter inside you. I'll give you a closer look later. You might be the perfect hiding place for whoever has been making trouble around here. I'll get the office to run the records on who owns the place if Tom doesn't already have it close at hand. Can't forget to use what he's learned.*

John admired the well kept cottage at the end of the street as he approached it. A curl of smoke drifted from the chimney on the gentle breeze. The light through the sheer drape over the window indicated occupancy.

His knock bore fruit this time.

"I'll be right there." The voice was female.

He appreciated the view from the porch. No matter how many times he visited the lagoon he was always awestruck by the sweep of the view. He glanced toward the sky where patches of brilliant blue were peaking through the overcast. The door opened behind him.

"Hello?" Jean spoke through the screen door. "Can I help you?"

John found himself facing an attractive woman. "I hope so. I'm detective John Ragsdale." He offered his badge and ID for her inspection.

"Have I done something wrong?"

"I don't think so. I'm investigating an incident that occurred on the beach last night."

"What kind of incident?"

"A body was found on the beach this morning. I'm trying to learn who it is and how it got there."

"I wondered what was going on down there this morning when I saw the crowd."

"Yeah, that sort of thing usually attracts attention. I didn't see you among the crowd. Weren't you curious what all the excitement was about?"

"I used my field glasses to look from here. I saw a cop and didn't want to get in the way. I didn't think you needed any more footprints in the sand."

"I appreciate your discretion. Could I have your name?"

"I'm Jean Parker."

"Your middle name?"

"Katherine."

"Is that with a 'C' or a 'K'?"

"A 'K'."

"Your address?"

"I have a post office box at Alexander's store, but this is where I live."

"How long have you lived here?"

"I moved here in January."

"You live alone?"

"Yes."

"Where were you last night?"

"I was home. Right here. All night."

"Did you see or hear anything unusual last night?"

"What do you mean by unusual?"

"Whatever might have attracted your attention. Like the way the gathering on the beach got your attention this morning."

"No."

"Just for the sake of clarity in my investigation, can anyone verify you were home last night?"

"Yes. Paul McAfee, the man three cabins down, had dinner with me last night."

"How late did he stay?"

"Isn't that a little personal?"

"Yes, it is, but a man died last night. He may have been murdered. Murder's a very personal crime. Your personal life would ordinarily be none of my business, but I need to eliminate anyone not involved. It's important for me to know how late he stayed."

"I didn't look at the clock when he left. We spent the evening talking and enjoying each other's company. You know, sometimes people just sit and talk!" Jean said sharply.

"I meant no offense and I didn't mean to imply anything improper. I apologize if my questions make you to feel like your privacy has been invaded. Unfortunately, it can be an unpleasant side effect of my job. Once again, my apologies for the inconvenience and thank you for your help." He noted how Jean's eyes flared with the heated intensity of her last response.

"Aren't you going to give me a business card and ask me to call you if I think of anything?" Jean's voice dripped with salty sarcasm.

"Sure." He handed her his card. "My home number is there in case you need to reach me when I'm off duty."

Jean read the business card. "Thanks. This way I have your phone number if I ever need a detective."

John was neither surprised nor upset by Jean's reaction to his questions. He was prepared for resentment when he asked good people invasive questions. The identification of people with solid alibis was critical. He turned his attention to the jogger's cabin. The jogger now had a name. He already had an alibi for part of the previous evening, but she hadn't said what time he left, leaving him a whole handful of qualifications as a suspect.

John thought about what might have happened the previous night while they were doing their mating dance. There were five cabins along the top of the bluff. Presuming these two were together and the resident at the other end of the street was home, there were still two empty cottages where mischief could occur without being noticed, indicating a possible location for the murder. If it was a murder. He still wasn't certain the death wasn't accidental. There were any number of ways for the injury to have occurred and just as many to explain the lack of clothing, but it just didn't feel like an accident. He believed it was a murder. He also believed the murder occurred close to these cabins. It was only a hunch, but hunches are a response to observations the mind subconsciously correlates, whether or not the conscious mind recognizes the relationship. When he reached the jogger's cabin the smell of fresh coffee drifted from the kitchen window.

Paul stepped outside as John put his foot on the bottom step. "Good morning again, officer. What can I do for you?"

John smiled. "Good morning, I'm John Ragsdale." He presented his ID and badge. "Have we met?"

"Only a few minutes ago. Call it intuition. Something about the way you look or walk. I would have been surprised if you weren't a cop."

"I guess it shows after all these years. Occupational hazard. I was hoping you might be able to help me. An incident occurred last night and I'm trying to sort it out."

"I saw a bunch of people up toward the end of the lagoon this morning. Is it something to do with that?"

"The body of a man was found there this morning.

We're investigating the circumstances. It may have been an accident, but until we know for certain, we're handling it as a homicide."

"Wow! A murder? Here? I thought the most excitement around here was deciding whether to go fishing or watch the cars rust."

"Ordinarily true, but once in a while an unfortunate incident intrudes on the boredom."

"How was he killed?"

"The coroner hasn't determined the cause of death yet. I'm trying find out where everyone was last night. We're not sure if the death occurred last night or some time earlier, but the more possibilities we can eliminate, the closer we'll be to the real story. I noticed you have a rental car parked in back. Are you a visitor?"

"Guilty as charged. I'm taking a long overdue vacation."

"Where do you call home?"

"Granada Hills. It's a neighborhood of Los Angeles on the north side of the San Fernando Valley."

"I didn't get your name. Do you have your driver's license?"

Paul fished out his wallet and removed his drivers license. "Am I a suspect?"

"I don't think so. I asked for identification because you aren't a resident." He wrote Paul's vital statistics in his notebook and handed the license back. "How long do you plan to stay?"

"I leased the cabin for six months."

"I hope you enjoy your visit. It sounds like you'll be here long enough to experience the full symphonic range of the weather. Did you stay in last night or were you out braving the storm?"

"I braved the storm long enough to walk to the end of the street. I had dinner with the lady in the last cabin. We spent the evening in front of the fire drinking wine and getting to know each other. So I guess the answer is yes and yes."

"Stayed in but not at home, huh? Could you tell me her name?"

"Jean Parker."

"What time did you come home?"

"I don't know for sure. I wasn't wearing a watch. I'm still not wearing a watch. I took it off when I arrived and don't intend to put it back on until I have to go back to the real world."

"Did you happen to look at a clock when you got home?"

"I honestly wasn't paying attention. We'd had a lovely evening together and I wasn't worried about the time. The rain had stopped and I stood on the bluff for a while looking at the ocean and the beach."

"Wasn't it a little tough to see with the cloud cover?"

"Not really. The moonlight was shining through the clouds. It was a spectacular sight, especially the waves. It was like they were filled with stars, but the light was purple and blue. I've never seen anything like it. I wondered what was in the water. I was going ask Jean to come out and watch with me, but she'd already turned out her lights."

"What you saw is bio-luminescent plankton."

"It glows in the dark?"

"Yeah. Mother nature's way of making sure they can see in the dark. So you had a nice evening with Ms. Parker?"

"Very nice. She's a lovely lady and an incredibly talented artist. I hated to leave."

"But she didn't invite you to stay?"

"Don't let your imagination run away with you, detective."

"Imagination is my stock in trade. It's the only way I know of figuring out the things people do to each other. Even so, there are times when my wildest flights of fancy fall short of what I see. But getting back to my original question, what time do you think you came home?"

"The moon seemed to be about a hand's width above the horizon. You could probably consult the almanac for a translation, but I would guess about an hour or two before moonset. Close enough?"

"Yes. Actually an excellent reference. Tell me, while you were standing up here looking at the surf, did you see anyone on the beach?"

Paul looked carefully at the detective before he answered. "No. I couldn't see much detail or very far, but the lights in the surf went as far as I could see in either direction."

"How long have you been here?"

"I got here a couple days ago."

"What do you do for a living? I may change jobs. A six month vacation sounds pretty nice."

"My partner and I have a small import business."

"What do you import?"

"Electronic components for the computer industry."

"What's the name of your company?"

"Gormac."

"Gormac? How do you spell that?"

"G, O, R, M, A, C. My partner and I used our last names to create the name. We liked the one word handle better than Gordon and McAfee. We talked about changing it after the company was established, but decided to stay with what was working."

"Name recognition is important and it's an easy one to remember. Are you married?"

"Widowed." Paul said quietly, looking away and gazing at the horizon.

"I'm sorry for your loss. I can see it's difficult for you. Time is supposed to heal all wounds, but I'm not sure they actually heal. Some things you never really get over, you only learn to live with the pain."

"I'm working on it. It's part of the reason I'm here. I'm hoping to find a way to move on with my life. It was a double loss for me. My partner and my wife both died at the same time."

John saw Paul from a different perspective. "Wow. A double hit. Absolutely devastating. I'm sincerely sorry for your loss. I presume they were in an accident?"

"A plane crash. It wasn't an accident. The NTSB says it was a bomb in the luggage, supposedly put there by a disgruntled former employee. It's always comforting to know your next flight is only as safe as the nearest nut case."

"How long ago?"

"It's been a couple years, but sometimes it feels like only yesterday. You might remember the PSA flight that went down south of Hollister with no survivors. Not even enough pieces left to positively identify all the victims."

"I do remember. The guy still had his airline ID so they let him into the baggage area. I'll bet everyone involved with the investigation was all over you looking for answers you didn't have. You recognize cops because you've spent a lot of time with them at all levels."

Paul laughed softly. "Yes, I've spent my share of time with the police, the NTSB, the FBI, the ATF, and just about every other agency you can name. I don't know what happened. They don't know what happened. And while I'd like to put it behind me, the fact they keep coming up with more things to ask me is like having a chain on my ankle keeping me from getting on with my life."

"Do they think you were involved?"

"They tell me no, but you'd have to ask them what they really think. All I know is my wife, my baby, my partner, my best friend, and my life got blown away! I didn't do it! I don't know anything! I'm tired of being treated like a clever deceiver with visions of grandeur about total ownership of the company and wealth from the life insurance on the two most important people in my life! I've had enough! I came here to find some peace and instead it looks like I'm right in the middle of another damned investigation! One more investigator shows up on my doorstep to question me when I haven't done anything! All I've done is clean up this cabin and meet a nice lady who likes to run on the beach, paint, and share some of her time with me. I'm not a killer, I'm not a spy, and I'm not a drug dealer. I'm just Paul McAfee! Citizen! Taxpayer! What more do you need to know? Did I spend the evening with Jean? Yes! Did we sleep together? None of your damn business! Is there anything else you want to know?" Paul's voice had risen, his face had moved to within an inch of John's, his fists were clenched at his sides, and his eyes blazed with a fury which would have intimidated most men.

John used every ounce of will power to maintain his stoic composure in the face of the rage pouring out of Paul. "Mr. McAfee, I'm investigating a possible murder. It may have happened within sight of your cabin last night. I had no knowledge of the personal tragedies of your life before this very moment. I'm not pursuing anything on behalf of the people in LA or in Washington. I'm a local detective trying to solve a local crime. I understand your feelings and I apologize for upsetting you. It was not my intention to do so. I'm not your enemy or your inquisitor. I'm just trying to do a sometimes unpleasant job you and the other taxpayers expect me to do.

Sometimes I have to ask questions people would prefer weren't asked, but I have to ask them anyway. That said, can we get back to my investigation? I'd like for us both to get through this as easily as we can."

Paul took a deep breath and unclenched his fists. "Am I a suspect?"

"Should I suspect you?"

"I think I just answered that question!"

"Yes, I think you did." John spoke in a quiet voice which did not reflect the defensive posture he had mentally taken, or his preparedness for a physical confrontation with this angry man who looked like he could handle himself in a street fight. With great care, John watched the indicators Paul was returning to a less agitated condition. "Mr. McAfee, did you see or hear anything out of the ordinary last night?"

"The out of the ordinary last night is how I spent the evening with a woman who is not my wife and whom I met only a couple days ago. I saw waves full of lights, a painting that could almost swallow me up in its beauty, and I spent the evening listening to the voice of a lovely lady who was happy to talk about nothing of great importance to anyone but the two of us. All out of the ordinary for me. Is that what you wanted to know? Hey look, I'm sorry I shouted at you. The last couple years have been a challenge and I'm a little on edge. I really do need this vacation."

John smiled. "I understand. I bet if I talked to the guys down south, I'd discover they're just as frustrated as you are. A case you can't close and can't make sense out of drives you nuts. This one is already working on providing me transportation to a rubber room."

"I'd like to help you if I could, but I didn't see or hear anything. My mind was on other things."

"She's a pretty lady. Seems like a pleasant distraction after the stress you've been living through."

"She is indeed a pleasant distraction. The problem is, I feel like I'm cheating on my wife, even though she's been dead for two years."

"I have a friend who told me the same thing after his wife died."

"You have a friend?" Paul asked with a twinkle in his eye and a smile.

John returned the smile. "Yeah, I actually have a friend. I have a wife and family too. Last time I looked I was a regular person who happens to carry a badge. There are times when I get stressed out and I have to get away and regain my perspective. Heck, I think you and I could be friends if we gave it a chance."

"You think? Friends are the people you can shoot your mouth off at and they don't stop being your friend because you happened to blow off at them. Thanks."

"No problem. Look, I don't suppose you have a phone yet, and you're probably getting your mail down at the store, but here's my card if you see or hear of anything. Even if you just want to have a beer. Sometimes people see things they don't know are of any importance. Call me any time."

"Thanks detective, and, uh, sorry about going off on you. I usually have better control of myself."

"Call me John. I'll talk with you later."

"Right. I'll, uh, see you later, uh… John."

7.

JEAN CLOSED THE DOOR, RESTORING HER FEELING
of sanctuary. Looking around the room, her anger drained away as memories of the previous evening surrounded her like the warm glow of a scented candle. She could see Paul standing in front of the fireplace gazing raptly at her painting and sitting on the couch, his feet propped on the coffee table while they shared the last of the wine. No dealing with the problems of the world, no talking about the painful experiences of the past, just quiet conversation about the beach, the forest, the birds, or the magic of this corner of the world. She allowed the simple joy they had shared to swallow her anger and once again felt the stirring of emotion. "Don't fumble this time Jeannie," she mumbled softly.

Paul poured a cup of coffee and walked out to the bluff to watch the surf make its ageless assault on the land. He saw John make a fruitless effort to contact his elderly neighbor before tucking a card into her front door. He gave Paul a friendly wave as he left the area. Paul wondered why the detective was unable to make contact with his neighbor. Her absence seemed strange, she usually worked in her yard in the morning.

He heard a soft footfall and felt a hand in the small of his back. He looked to his left into Jean's eyes.

"Is there more coffee in the pot or did you only make one cup?"

Paul felt a flood of happiness. "I guess I could squeeze another cup out of yesterday's grounds. I'll get you a cup."

"I know where to find the pot. I'll get it myself if it's okay with you."

"Sure."

"Want yours warmed up?"

"Since you offered." He handed her his cup.

"Wait right here and enjoy the morning. I'll be right back."

He admired her pleasing shape as she walked to the cabin.

Paul turned when the gravel crunched under her feet a few minutes later. "Here you go. I scraped the bottom of the pot and stirred it in for you. Just chew up any chunks you find. They're good for you, will help wake you up."

"Thanks! I think! I thought I was already awake. I've had a run on the beach and a close encounter with a local gendarme. All before breakfast. Certainly enough to wake me up."

"Nosy bastard visited me too!"

"Hey, don't take it so personal. He's got a tough enough job without being abused for doing what we pay him to do."

"Are you defending him? Maybe you enjoy having a stranger invade your privacy, but I don't."

"I'm not defending him and I don't particularly enjoy being interviewed by the police. I was just trying to make a point. Neither of us has done anything wrong and we shouldn't get mad at him for trying to eliminate us from his list of possible suspects."

"He wanted to know what we were doing last night!"

"What did you tell him?"

"I told him you came for dinner and spent the night ravishing my body. I told him I was barely able to walk this morning and as soon as he got out of my way I was going to go find you so we could pick up where we left off."

"What?" Paul looked at her in stunned amazement.

Jean burst into laughter. "Are you going to tell me the thought never crossed your mind when we were sitting in front of the fire sipping wine and talking without touching?"

"Whoa! Slow down a minute! I told him nothing happened between us but food and conversation! Jesus, Jean, he's gonna wonder which one of us is telling him the truth, or worse yet, he's gonna wonder if either of us is telling the truth!" Panic was suddenly stealing his breath.

Jean's face sparkled with laughter. "Relax! I told him in blunt terms it was none of his business what we were doing. I know he was only doing his job, but he pissed me off!"

"Okay, we both told him the same thing." Paul paused to look deep into Jean's eyes. "And all that stuff about me jumping your bones was to see if you could get me to react, right?"

"You were thinking about it last night weren't you?"

"I'm widowed, not dead. Yes, I thought about it. So where does it leave us?"

"It leaves us both thinking about it."

Paul raised his cup in a toast. "Here's to two minds on the same track."

Jean clinked her cup against Paul's. "Here's to a good morning and staying on track."

Paul sipped his coffee, looked out at the panorama, put his arm around Jean's waist and enjoyed the feelings rising in him as she leaned against him and rested her head against his shoulder. "I almost came back last night to ask you to come watch the lights in the surf with me."

"You should have."

"You would have come?"

"I'm beginning to feel like I'd be willing to go anywhere with you."

"I don't know if I'm ready for a relationship. I haven't been with anyone since Lisa died. I was a faithful husband and in a way I feel like I'm cheating on her."

"I can see how much you loved her and miss her. I'm not sure I'm ready either, but the thought keeps forming and I like the way it feels. Whatever happened before made us who we are today. No matter how bad things have been, I know you're a good man and there aren't enough good guys around for me to let you slip away without trying to see if we can be more than just friendly neighbors. I'm tired of being alone and whatever is tearing at your heart can't be put to rest until you decide to move on with your life. I'd like to help you if I can. I know your wife is dead. I can't bring her back. I don't want to replace her. I just want to find out if there's a place in your heart for me. If there is, I don't want to let it slip through my fingers without at least trying to hold on to it."

Surrendering to an impulse, he kissed the top of her forehead. Jean looked up, put her arms around his neck, and placed a warm kiss on his lips. "Don't treat me like a sister. I'm not into incestuous relationships."

"Believe me when I say I wasn't thinking of you as a sister. I'm an only child." An involuntary shiver shook his body like a limp dishrag.

"Whoa, what's happening? Someone walk on your grave?"

"No. Just my mind warring with memories and loyalties."

Jean tossed the last of her coffee and looked back at him. "One of your most endearing qualities is how much you loved your wife. I've had two husbands who had no reservations about chasing a loose skirt when I was working. Both of them told me boys will be boys, and I think both are still little boys who don't want to grow up. Don't apologize for your feelings and don't apologize for being a responsible adult. I like the man I see."

"I never even considered playing around. The idea is totally foreign to me. I took my vows seriously and I never even thought about stepping outside them. Sure, I had some opportunities, but,"

"A real straight arrow, huh?"

"It's who I am. We had our ups and downs. Heck, nobody agrees on everything all the time, but I never met anyone I was willing to leave home for."

"A succinct way of putting things. I don't think I've ever heard anyone say it quite that way, and it tells me a lot about you. The only way another woman would be part of your life was if Lisa was no longer a part of it."

"I don't suppose if I took your hand and led you into my bedroom you'd follow along without any argument?" Paul said with a mischievous grin.

"Be careful what you wish for."

"How about another cup of coffee? I think there's a pot inside."

"It's at least a step in the right direction."

8.

THE IDENTITY OF THE BODY REMAINED A MYSTERY when John completed his canvass of the subdivision. Even the owner of the store was a dead end. The only lead was the pickup and camper with the conspicuously absent owner. He was parked in the shade near the store going over his notes when Tom stopped alongside and gave him a thumbs down gesture. "Damn! I was hoping it was taking this long because you were getting it done."

"Sorry. I did everything but get down on my knees and beg. He says just because we can't locate the owner of the truck, it doesn't give us reasonable cause to search the vehicle. When he asked how we knew the body and pickup were connected, I told him a witness put them together. It almost worked until he asked if the ID was absolutely certain and I had to tell him the truth. He said the owner could have gone hiking or fishing. Unless we come up with something solid he won't give us a warrant."

"We knew it was a long shot and he's right. We don't have probable cause."

"You do any good with the residents?"

"No. It was like the three monkeys. Nobody saw anything, nobody heard anything, and nobody will say anything. The guy in the second cabin looks like he's capable of carrying the victim out there, but he has a solid alibi because he spent the evening with the honey at the end of the street. I wouldn't mind having her for an alibi myself."

"I thought you were happily married."

"I am, but being happily married doesn't keep me from appreciating a pretty lady with spirit, and believe me, she has some real fire to go with the looks."

"You're talking about Jean Parker."

"I see I'm not the only married man with an eye for pretty ladies. He's only been here a couple days, but she seems to have latched on to him like a barnacle.

"You think they might be working together?"

"I thought about it. They're definitely working on something, but it has nothing to do with a dead body. He's here from LA trying to get over the death of his wife and partner and Mrs. Alexander tells me Parker moved into the end cabin six months ago to get over a bad marriage and a disappointing career. I'm not ready to rule them out as suspects, but there's nothing pointing to them except the fact they're here and he's physically strong enough. She looks like she spends part of her days working on a hard body, but I don't think they're good prospects for committing a murder, if it is a murder. We won't know for sure until the coroner's report is finished."

"Wait a minute. I've been working this like a murder. Didn't you say…?"

"Take it easy. We'll work this like a homicide until Dennis tells us otherwise. If it turns out to be an accident, there's no harm done by our diligence, and if it is a murder, we have a running start on what already looks like a cold trail."

"Cold! Try frigid, maybe arctic, like fading shadows in an arctic fog, because the trail looks pretty faint to me. Except for the truck! Everything we need to ID the victim is probably sitting right in front of us and we can't even get a look at it."

"Everything came back cold, right?"

"Yeah, except,"

"What?"

"The address for the registered owner didn't lead to a drivers license and neither did the R.O.'s name. I know there's something hinky about a beat up body on a new chassis, but I couldn't get a warrant!"

"Okay, let's approach this from a different angle. We don't have a warrant, we have a cold plate, a registered owner with no drivers license, a post office box for an address, no phone or street address, no evidence of vandalism, no cause to believe it's abandoned, so what's left as a legal way to burglarize the beast?"

"What if the guy hasn't paid the rent on the camp site?"

"Suppose he hasn't. Then what?" John enjoyed the way Tom's mind was working.

A sly grin spread across Tom's face. "This is a county park. No pay, no stay, no grace period for payment. No pay means we can tow it. To tow it we have to inventory the contents when we take custody of it. Think it would stand up in court?"

"My, but you have a devious mind. You might make a detective yet. Okay. It's better than what we had, but first we need to know if the rent is paid. You know where we can find the park ranger to check the rent on the space?"

Tom smiled and pointed. "There he is now. Right on schedule."

"It's your idea, so run with it."

"I'm already gone, chief."

John pondered his dilemma. No suspects, no weapon, no identification, no motive, and one dead, naked white male adult with a bashed-in skull. No one saw anything, no one heard anything, and no one was out in the rain last night. All the boxes came up empty on the checklist for building a case or solving a crime. "I know there's something I'm missing!" he muttered. "The old lady thinks the guy on the beach might belong with the pickup, but she's the only one who got a decent look at him. The owner of the camper is like a shadow. I think we've stumbled onto something we weren't supposed to find." John thought about the man who broke him in as a detective. "Yeah, you cranky old fart, you talked to yourself too. You said it helped you figure things out by hearing how it sounded and now I'm doing it too. You also told me never to ignore a hunch or argue with intuition. Well, I have a hunch there's something out of sync with the truck and if the truck is all I have, the truck's what I need to work on."

John saw Tom returning from the shack which served as a park office. Tom was doing all he could do to keep from running, but his smile indicated something good.

"Bingo! We just hit pay dirt. The guy never paid for the space. Technically, it's a trespassing violation and ordinance 56-32497(a) provides for removal and storage at the owner's expense! The ordinance is posted on the window of the office above the box with the registration cards and the slot for the money! We've got our way in!"

"Okay. This sounds great, but let's make sure we cover our ass. Call the judge and get confirmation this constitutes reasonable cause to inventory the truck's contents. He turned us down once, so let's make sure he isn't going to use the search to throw our case down the dumper. Let's dot our I's and cross our T's. You got his phone number handy?"

"Yeah. And there's a land line in the shack. I'll be right back. Keep your fingers crossed!"

"Go for it. I'm going to take a closer look at this critter

while you're making the call. The parking violation at least gives me reasonable cause to inspect the outside."

Inspection of the truck revealed all the lights, reflectors, and lenses were new or nearly new. Many of the body panels were bent and there was a significant amount of road dirt on the vehicle, most of it recent. The rust on the body was real, the paint was old, but his inspection confirmed Tom's observations. The worn and aging appearance was purely cosmetic. The tires, the running gear, the engine, the frame, and the suspension were new or nearly new and all were first class. The original hood release had been disconnected. "Curiouser and curiouser," he mumbled as more and more of the characteristics of the truck dropped outside what he expected.

"Oh, J-o-h-n-n-n" Tom caroled. "Our friendly judge has confirmed, number one, since the vehicle is not legally in the park, and two, we are unable to locate the R.O., the ordinance is clear in its parameters. We can open her up and inventory the contents. Got a can opener?"

"No, and getting in isn't gonna be easy. You were right about things not being what they seem. No door lock pulls in sight, no hood release, and it might even be booby-trapped. I've got a bad feeling about this. Too many pieces don't fit. Any bright ideas?"

"There's a Slim Jim in my patrol car, unless somebody borrowed it while I was on days off."

"Good idea, but I want to take a closer look under this erector set before we try our hand at burglary, auto."

"What are you looking for?"

"I'm not sure. Whatever it is, I'll bet it's clean and new. Everything important on this buggy is less than a year old. Based on the pan and the exhaust system, I don't think the engine was even an engineer's dream when this baby rolled off the assembly line. Here." John handed his notebook to Tom. "Take some notes for me."

"Sure, anywhere in particular?"

"Start with the first fresh page, title it *under the pickup*. God, I love having a secretary, but in the future, could you freshen your make up, shorten your skirt, and for god sake shave your legs?"

"Careful, old man, I'll sic my dog on you."

"No big deal. Somebody told me he used to chase cars."

"So what?"

"He didn't know what to do with the one he caught," John slid under the pickup with a flashlight. "The hidden number is missing from the frame. This is definitely a chop job. Now we have all the probable cause we need. We can tear this one apart. Best part is we did it without violating some poor criminal's civil rights. Everything we looked at is in plain sight. I love it when a plan comes together. Okay. Starting at the front. The engine is recent, clean, no oil leaks, no dents or scratches on the pan. The exhaust is also new, large enough to handle a big block, which this looks to be, oil cooler on the radiator for the engine, oil cooler near the firewall for the late model tranny. Numbers missing from the case. No chrome, no fancy, but this thing looks like it could cruise at a hundred and never even get warm. You getting all this down?"

"Yeah, but my shorthand is a little rusty, let's see, how do you spell hidden number?"

"Are you shittin' me?"

"Gotcha!"

John shifted his position. "Well, looky here. We may have a hidden compartment behind the seat. Whoever built this tank was good. I almost missed it."

"Can you get it open?"

"Don't know and not going to try. I think it's time to call for the boys from Tom Swift's magic lab and Auto Theft."

"Before we tow it?"

"Yeah. There's too much here to risk screwing it up. Like dirty Harry says, a man's gotta know his limitations. I'm a good detective, but I know when to ask for help. Call the cavalry. Tell 'em to drop whatever they're doing and beat feet. We gotta move fast. It's the only lead we've got."

"I'm on it."

"You know, I think you should pay another call on the judge. We've got enough to establish probable cause without a warrant, but let's get one anyway. Tell him about the hidden compartment and the missing ID numbers. It should convince him we're onto something we need to do exactly right."

"I'm already on my way back with the paperwork."

"I'll keep looking while you're gone. Hurry back now, you hear?"

The activity around the pickup was observed with great interest not only by the campground tenants who were hanging back as Tom had requested, but also by an observer who had taken pains to remain anonymous. His planning began to fall apart when the body didn't float out with the tide. He'd barely had time to locate, dismantle and remove the booby traps from the truck before daylight chased him back under cover. Now the cops were subjecting the truck to a complete physical. His chance to dispose of the truck was lost.

9.

THE CRUNCH OF TIRES ON GRAVEL INTERRUPTED

John's efforts to find a pattern in the evidence. Nothing clearly connected the seemingly related pieces, but he knew he'd missed something. It was like a tiny voice trying to point out what he was overlooking, but fading away before he could understand it. He watched Tom approach wearing a large grin, warrant in one hand and cup of coffee in the other.

"I thought you might be ready for a little refreshment to whet your whistle while you read the good news."

"Where's the donuts? You brought coffee, but no donuts? I suppose you dumped a bunch of sugar and cream in here instead."

"Sugar and cream might sweeten your sunny disposition, but it's black. It's hot, it's black, and it's free. There weren't any donuts, so you can either drink it or let me put a cigarette out in it to prevent forest fires."

"You don't smoke. You'd have to go buy a pack, light one, and put it out just to make your point. Since you seem to feel strongly about it, I guess I'll drink it." He took a sip and made a face. "Man, this shit is awful! Where'd you get it?"

"Hey, be nice. It's fresh from the finest unwashed coffee pot in the north county. You've been drinking the thin stuff they serve in town for so long you've lost your taste for real tall trees chain oil. This is the good stuff. It'll put lead in your pencil, grow hair on your chest, and keep you awake for forty miles."

"Yeah, well, I'm already awake, I mow my chest once a month, and if my pencil gets any heavier I won't be able to lift it. On the other hand, your gesture is most thoughtful. Fuck you very much. How much latitude did the old man give us with the warrant?"

"Carte blanche. I told him what we'd found and he had no problem at all. He said the parking violation was good enough, but the hidden compartment and the missing VIN number sealed the deal. Shall we have a look around?"

"The experts should be here in a few minutes." John picked up the radio mike. "Humboldt, fortysix-two".

"Go ahead."

"Do you have an ETA on the lab crew?"

"ETA five minutes."

"I think we should keep our powder dry and let the experts handle things. They get testy about us poisoning their minds with premature conclusions if we start without them. I think I'll just sit back and enjoy this fine cup of, uh, coffee and consider an appropriate punishment for your good deed."

A pair of vehicles entered the campground while they were talking. The first was a customized Chevy pickup driven by the auto theft officer. With its dark red metallic paint, lowered suspension and tinted windows, the truck glistened in the filtered sunlight and looked nothing like a police vehicle. Calvin Snider had built the truck as an undercover vehicle to gain access to the shadowy world of professional car thieves and chop shops. Cal was an interesting character, tattoos from waist and wrist to collarbone, long hair floating over his shoulders in the gentle waves of a natural curl most women envied, and an immaculately groomed beard. His slouch leather hat and sunglasses left only his nose visible. Known as 'Cousin Itt' in the bars and dives frequented by the outlaw bikers and car thieves, Cal was welcomed in places most police officers never saw. The chop shops he discovered never knew he was the source of their demise. His anonymity was carefully protected from the prying eyes of the open courtroom by never making an actual arrest and posting bail without formal arraignment when he was swept up in a raid. Many deputies were unaware he was one of their own. John was surprised to see him risking exposure of his true identity.

The second vehicle was a drab Dodge mini-van bearing a county seal on the door driven by the tech crew.

John greeted Cal with a warm smile. "I'm surprised to see you in your cover car, old friend. What's shakin'?"

"I'm turning over a new leaf. I've been disreputable long enough. I'm tired of hanging with the dirty-necks and low-lifes. It's time to let some new blood into the operation before my cover and my ass both get blown away. I was on my way to get a haircut and a shave when this came in so I canceled the appointment with my personal groomer. I'll just have to make her day tomorrow."

"You're giving up auto theft? You spent so much time and money building your truck and developing the swagger, I thought you were a permanent fixture on the dark side."

"Exactly what I wanted everyone to think. I worked hard to keep up appearances and the department cooperated, but there comes a time when you have to make a move if you want to stay on the right track before you lose sight of why you're one of the good guys. I've accomplished a lot. Now it's time to be able to eat in a nice place, have a beer with my real friends, show up in public with my family and get on with my life."

"Jesus! I know your last bust was tight and you came close to getting nailed, but I never thought you'd cut and run."

"I've been too close too many times. I've had a long lucky streak. I always managed to skate away without getting hurt when things got dicey, but undercover is like any other gamble. Luck runs hot and cold and you have to recognize when it's changing. It's time to cash in my chips and get out of the game."

"So what's next? You going to leave the department?"

"No way. I love being a cop. I'm just changing details. The boss told me I could name my assignment, a reward for my efforts. I'm coming over to the dick bureau."

"A detective? You wanna be a detective? Damn! I can't think of anybody with a better knowledge of the folks we're up against."

"Then I guess you'll enjoy having me around."

"Yeah? Does the boss want me to handle your break in and training?"

"Not exactly. The boss didn't think I'd need much training so he just made me your partner."

"My partner! What about Hank? Christ, he goes on vacation for a week and comes back to discover he's been replaced! Man, I wouldn't want to be the one who has to tell him."

"Hey, be cool. He made rank. The next time you see him he'll be a lieutenant and expect you to snap to attention and salute him."

"No shit! I knew he'd taken the test, but I hadn't seen the promotion list. Son of a gun! Well good for him and for a replacement I get the illustrated man. What did I do to deserve this?"

Cal laughed. "No good deed goes unpunished. I promise

to be a good boy and wear a long sleeve shirt and respectable clothes. I'll even wash my hands after I go to the bathroom and promise not to belch or fart in public."

John filled the technicians in on what they had found and let them read the search warrant. The crew set to work on everything within a thirty foot radius of the camper. Tom, John and Cal feigned patience while the scientists did their work. They were itching to get involved, but knew to stand clear while the crime scene technicians went about their business.

John had an idea for his new partner. "You know Cal, your disreputable look might play to our advantage."

"Ease up on the disreputable shit, partner. I may look like a dirty-neck scrote, but these clothes are clean and so am I! These are my get dressed up and cruise the bars looking for a fight clothes. Show a little respect for a man's threads."

"Ooh and sensitive too!" John leaned closer and sniffed Cal. "Cologne! My, my, what is that fragrance? Eau de Crankcase Drainings, or perhaps Attar of Simoniz?"

"Cute! So what do you want me to do? Anything would be better than hanging around here trying not to develop indigestion from your lame jokes."

John pointed at the bluff. "You see the end cabin, the yellow one?"

"Hard to miss. What about it?"

"A little old lady lives there. I'm sure she was home when I was doing my canvass this morning, but she wouldn't answer the door. I think she knew I was a cop and didn't want to answer any questions. You, on the contrary, don't look like a cop! Maybe she'll answer the door for you."

"And I'm supposed to find out if she saw or heard anything last night? What's to keep her from slamming the door on my nose when I ID myself?"

"Nothing except maybe your big foot getting in the way. Even if it doesn't work, I figure it's worth a try. We gotta wait for these guys anyway. Since you are now a detective, go and detect."

"Yassuh, Mastah Ragsdale, I's be gwine off to talk wiff da nass lady, rat now, juss lak a good boy."

John laughed. "What's all that?"

"You! Giving me orders! Some partner!"

John held his hands clasped in front of his chest, his voice dripping with a mixture of contrition and angst. "Excuse me, Calvin. I meant not to offend. Please allow me to rephrase my request in a manner less likely to cause you to take umbrage. I was unsuccessful in my efforts to talk with the resident of the cabin this morning. While we wait for the lab crew to finish their pursuit of elusive clues, perhaps you might be more effective than I at involving the lady in cordial conversation. It pains me to ask you to handle this distasteful detail, but when I fall on my face, I must rely on my partner to pick me up and dust me off. I have failed miserably and am suffering a terribly wounded ego. Would you please see if you can persuade her to talk with you?"

Cal erupted into an open mouthed grin with a hand extended for a high five, which John slapped with feeling. "Should I walk, or tool up there in my low rider?"

"Take the low rider. It fits your look and validates your attitude. Unless I miss my guess, her curiosity won't let her ignore you if you arrive in your own distinctive style. If she's already off balance it should be easier to tip her over the rest of the way and get her to talk."

Alma Jacobsen was cautious, but incurably curious and obsessed with knowing everything happening whether it was her business or not. The lowered pickup was unusual enough to attract her attention, but her pulse pounded when the long haired, tattooed driver wearing a black leather vest over a Harley-Davidson T-shirt approached her door. The need to open the door completely submerged the resolve she displayed when John tried to contact her. She opened the door before Cal could knock.

"Good morning, Ma'am." Cal said politely.

"Good morning," Alma responded, suddenly overcome with a sense of foreboding. A parade of goose bumps danced over her and adrenaline pumped through her, making her fight to control her breathing. She knew with terrifying certainty she had stepped into a trap with no way to gracefully remove herself from the situation. "Can I help you?"

Cal displayed his ID. "I'm detective Calvin Snider. I'm investigating an incident that occurred last night."

Alma almost failed to show surprise. "You're a detective? The picture on your identification card certainly doesn't look very much like you!"

"True enough, but my mother would be happy to vouch for me. Are you Alma Jacobsen?"

"Yes, I am."

Cal wrote the identifying information in his notebook. "Were you home last night, ma'am?"

"Yes I was."

"Did you see or hear anything unusual?"

"I went to bed early last night. It was cold and rainy and I was tired, so I turned in about half past eight. I didn't notice anything until I saw the crowd on the beach this morning."

"It got your attention?"

"Well of course. Things like that don't happen every day, you know. This is a nice quiet place."

"Did you go see what it was all about?"

"Lord no! I'm an old woman! If I traipsed all the way down there I'd need to have someone help me home. Arthritis, you know. My poor old hips just can't take the abuse. Sometimes they get so sore I'd swear some gremlin was driving railroad spikes into them."

"So you've been here all morning?"

"Why, yes. I worked a little bit in my yard this morning. The weeds pop up so fast it's a never-ending battle, but I enjoy my flowers and having everything all fresh and tidy. With my children grown and gone, my little yard is all I have to mother over."

"Your yard is certainly beautiful. It looks the way all yards should look and so seldom do. Most of us can't find the time or inclination to keep our yards up. I envy you the freedom to spend time with it. I love to garden myself, but it's hard to make the time."

Alma smiled at the compliments and praise. "Thank you. I do like everything to look pretty."

"Thank you, Mrs. Jacobsen. I think that's all I need to ask you. If you happen to think of anything, even if it seems unimportant, would you give me a call at this number?" He handed her a business card.

Alma pushed the screen door open far enough to take the card. "I don't know what I might think of, but I'll call if I do."

"Thank you very much. Have a nice day."

Alma didn't close the door until Cal walked through her gate, her stare like twin lasers on his back.

A thin smile played across John's features as he watched Cal return. Cal's record as an undercover operator was the stuff of legend, but he sure didn't look like a detective. He couldn't even remember how Cal had looked as a crew cut young deputy. Many years of only seeing him occasionally and always in circumstances requiring maintaining a cover had faded the image of a uniformed officer. "Did you manage to schmooze your way in?"

"I talked to her, but I didn't get much. She's too curious not to open the door to someone who looks like me, but she's not real sociable. It's not just that she's uncomfortable talking with the police. There's something else going on. She isn't inclined to talk about whatever she knows and she wants people to believe she's a frail old woman. I don't buy it. She doesn't look frail or arthritic to me. I think she's either hiding something or hiding from something."

"Any idea what it might be?"

"Not really. It's just a feeling. I took her by surprise and she was off balance for a second before she turned on all the controls. I don't think she's a suspect, but, I don't know, it's just a feeling."

"You think we should watch her?"

"Watching her without being seen would be tough. I don't think anything happens she doesn't see, hear, or know about. I checked out her house on the way in and out. Sheer curtains at all the windows, easy to see out, tough to see in. The shrubs are pruned and groomed to look nice and hide nothing when she looks out any of the windows. It all looks innocent, but my suspicious mind says it's by design. She says she didn't join the crowd on the beach this morning because she has arthritis. She wants me to believe it keeps her from being very active, but she looks pretty fit. The place reminds me of the gingerbread house in *Hansel and Gretel*. You know what I mean?"

"Step into my parlor, said the spider to the fly?"

"Yeah. It's all like camouflage and she gives off a bad vibration."

"Grandma, what big eyes you have?"

"There you go, only this is no fairy tale."

"The body is too real and too dead?"

"Exactly."

"Hey John, come take a look at this," Vince Freitas called from under the camper. "This is interesting."

John and Cal knelt to look under the vehicle. "Whatcha got?" John asked.

"Well, you couldn't find the hidden VIN because the frame wasn't built in nineteen seventy-two. Aside from the side rails and the front and rear cross members, this one is strictly custom, one of a kind special."

"And I couldn't find it because?"

"Because the piece it was stamped on isn't on the truck anymore."

"So did you find a new VIN?" Cal asked.

"No. The hidden number disappeared with original cross member and the new pieces were never stamped. DMV says no new VIN was issued for the truck after it was rebuilt. Not unusual and not difficult to register it without one because the paper trail was already established."

"So what's so interesting?" John asked.

"What's interesting is every new piece of the frame conceals a special compartment."

"Mule, you think?"

"I don't think so. So far we haven't found so much as a hint of dope. This wasn't built for toting chemicals. You already noticed the outside is only camouflage. Whatever this was supposed to carry would either have to be waterproof or the compartments would need a watertight seal."

"Can you open that one?" John pointed at a cross member just behind the fuel tank.

"I think so." Vince slid his hands along the surfaces of the frame. "There has to be a release. Otherwise, the guy would have to… yes!" Taking care not to disturb or drop the contents, he lifted away the cover of a compartment about eighteen inches long, five inches high and two inches deep. "My, my, my. Would you look at this!"

The five bundles of hundred dollar bills were wrapped in plastic and taped to the inside of the compartment.

"Nice work Vince," Cal said. "Very nice work. This looks like a prime time to hook up and tow for further study in a more controlled environment, don't you think?"

"Hey detective, you might want to see this," Vince's partner called from the back of the camper.

Frank Zimmerman was looking at the inside of the camper. "Whatever this guy was up to, I don't think fishing was going to occupy much of his time."

The interior of the camper had a stove, refrigerator, and bed, but instead of a table there was an electronics workbench with a soldering station, oscilloscope, multimeter, and magnifying lamp. An array of tools surrounded the bench, each secured for travel. "Quite a set up," Cal mumbled. "If this belongs to the guy on the beach, he's a real pro."

"Past tense," John said. "Gentlemen, we have stepped through the looking glass. Let's seal it up and get it to where you can take it apart in a controlled environment."

"Here comes the tow," Cal said. "I envy you guys getting to dismantle this chariot. You've got to admire the workmanship."

Frank grinned. "Sometimes we just get lucky."

"Cal, what do you think we've stepped in?" John asked.

"Hey man, I just got here and I feel like I've walked into a war zone. There doesn't seem to be any kind of a pattern, either. Do we actually find something different than we expect under every rock we turn over or is it just a figment of my overactive imagination?"

"If it is, then my imagination is caught on the same figment. I don't know about you, but right now I could use a cup of coffee and some brainstorming."

"A beer would be better, but coffee will better serve the proprieties."

Tom had been keeping the curiosity seekers at a distance. With the arrival of the tow truck he had joined the detectives. "Anything more I can do for you, John?"

"As a matter of fact, there is. You can help us drink some coffee and do some brainstorming. Where's the closest coffee pot, and please don't tell me it's the one you tapped for the witch's brew you brought me with the warrant."

"Mrs. Alexander always has coffee brewing. She has a table where we can talk in private that she lets me use when I need a place where I won't be disturbed."

"Perfect. Lead the way."

The table was sheltered from the breeze, the coffee hot and fresh, and they gratefully sagged into the chairs. They sat without speaking for several minutes.

"Tom, you were first on the scene. What are your thoughts and impressions?" John asked.

Tom took out his notebook. "I don't know if it will help, but a few things are bothering me. The dead guy on the beach didn't look like other drowning victims I've seen. I agree he was dead before he went into the water. His melon being smashed helps to support the notion he was murdered, but what happened to his clothes and why were they removed? I also didn't see any scars and marks on the body. Everybody has scars and marks. It's part of growing up and living. This guy looked like he'd just been created. Maybe I missed them, but it struck me as strange."

The detectives looked at each other while Tom was telling them about the absence of visible marks or scars. "Good observation!" they chorused.

"Thanks. It may be nothing, but I felt like I was being watched the whole time I was canvassing the campground. I kept looking around to see who was watching me."

"Well, you did have a pretty fair crowd around you most of the time," John said.

"No. It wasn't someone in the crowd. I knew who they were and how it felt being around them. This was different. I felt like somebody had me under a microscope. You know how your hair stands up when you almost see or hear something? Like you're walking down a dark alley and know the bad guy is hiding where he can see you and you can't see him. This is the first time all day I haven't had the feeling. After so many hours it feels strange not to have my mystery observer any more. Getting back to what bothers me, the truck seemed wrong. Turns out I was right about it. I don't have anything else."

John nodded. "Good observations, especially the one about the absence of scars or marks. You're right, an adult with no marks is unusual, not impossible, but certainly rare. I'm glad to know I'm not the only one who felt like he was being watched. I couldn't identify the source either, but knowing you had the same feeling confirms my suspicions. You've always done a good job when we've worked together and today is no exception. I know you want to make detective and I'll make sure the boss hears about your contribution. It never hurts to have an old fart in your corner when they start choosing who to promote."

"There's one other thing," Tom said. "Nobody got a good look at this guy when he was around the campground, presuming the dead guy and the camper go together. It's a small campground. There's only twenty sites, and half of them are empty. Almost everyone has been here for several days, including the guy with the camper and nobody got a good look at him. He didn't fish. He didn't socialize. He seems like the shadow of a ghost, like he was here without being here. Everybody remembers seeing him, but aside from Mrs. Woodbine, nobody got a good enough look to recognize his face. It's weird. Maybe it's nothing."

"You're a good observer," Cal said. "It looks weird to you now, but when we get to the bottom of this, most of the weird will look reasonable and some of what looked reasonable will look weird. I felt like somebody was watching us too. The obvious candidate wouldn't raise our hackles."

"Alma Jacobsen?" John asked.

"Exactly! An easy answer because of where she lives and because her curiosity won't let her ignore anything. I bet she has a library of information a gossip columnist would kill for, but she's the librarian and we don't have a library card. Way too easy for her to be what's got us looking over our shoulder."

"Maybe I should have talked to her," Tom said. "She's helped me a few times. Once she called in to report a fraternity party getting a bit rowdy and she was worried someone would get hurt. I've made an effort to get to know her a little and she might have talked to me without the problems you guys ran into, but it's too late for me now that you already scared her off."

John smiled at Tom. "I stand properly chastised. I should

have paid more attention when you said you'd spent time learning your beat. You're right, the egg is drying on my face and the opportunity has been lost. Cal, you didn't talk to the other two folks who live up there on the bluff, but neither of them were real open with their answers either, especially the woman down at the far end. She was a little hostile," John laughed.

"Whatsa matter, Johnny, you losing your charm with the ladies?" Cal jabbed.

"She seems to have something going with her new neighbor and I guess she didn't want to talk about it. She was real defensive about how she spent the evening. She's a good lookin' broad, but I don't care who she's sleeping with. I only wanted to know if she saw or heard anything. Spilled milk. Pointless to waste time worrying about what we did wrong. What are your thoughts, Cal?"

"It looks to me like we have a case of mass confusion involving an unidentified body, a pickup and camper equipped for electronic surveillance, an old hermit who doesn't want to talk to either of us, two neighbors who may be dancing the horizontal mambo and don't think it's any of our business, and no witnesses to anything. A pretty good recap?"

"Right on target. Maybe the coroner will give us some help. Let's get back to the office and bring the boss up to speed."

"Me too?" Tom asked.

"You too. You're part of this detail until I send you home." John glanced at his watch. "Time sure flies when you're having fun and we and we still need to finish the paperwork before this day ends. Tomorrow we should have the coroner's preliminary findings. Then we can plan what we need to do the next time we call on our witnesses."

10.

JEAN LIKED FEELING PAUL WATCH HER. SHE
enjoyed the emotions quivering inside her like a trembling
flame eager to burst forth. Suddenly it was as though a chill
had fallen between them. Puzzled, she turned and saw a vacant
stare in his eyes. She set down her cup and walked to where he
stood in the living room. She saw his eyes become alive with
recognition as she approached. "Are you all right?"

"Yeah, I guess so." He took a deep breath and slowly
released it.

"Should I worry when you zone out?"

"It's a major reason for being here. For the last couple years
I find myself checking out in the middle of whatever I'm doing.
Business meetings were a handy vehicle for my excursions. After
a while my people just handled things and told me about it later.
Old memories and grief are a powerful force. I came here to try to
find a better way to handle the bitter memories and start fresh. It
looks like I still have a way to go. Sorry if I worried you."

"Do you want to talk about it or would your prefer to keep
retreating into the shadows whenever the spirit moves you?
Whichever you choose, I'd like to know what to expect so I can
keep you from walking off a cliff. I kind of like having you around."

"Are you sure you want to hear the whole, long, sad story?"

"Sooner or later you have to trust someone with it or you're
never going to make the fresh start you say you want. As I see
it, the first step in starting fresh is unloading the old baggage."

"I've spent two years and thousands of dollars talking to a psychologist and it hasn't helped. What makes you think you can do better? Do you have a magic wand you can wave to make it all go away?"

"No, I don't have a magic wand or anything special except one important thing. I don't see you as a patient who is renting fifty minutes of my distracted attention. I'm not for rent. I don't care how long it takes to tell your story. I'm retired, living on my ill-gotten gains, and I don't want or need your money. I'm here with you because I choose to be here with you. I'm free to walk out any time I want and not come back. If I stay, it's because I want to stay. If I decide to listen it's because I want to listen. I want to know you. I want to know what makes you who you are. I have my own long, sad story to tell when you want to hear it. If you want to talk I'm ready to listen. If you don't want to talk, that's okay too. There's a lot of things we can do besides sifting through the past looking for artifacts among the midden heaps of your memory."

"You want to take a walk in the trees?"

Jean stepped back, and laughed. "Boy, talk about a quick change of direction!"

"I guess. I just feel like I need to look at some tall trees and gather my thoughts." Paul held up his hand like a traffic cop. "Don't say it. Gathering my thoughts is what started this conversation. I need a little perspective. I've always loved trees. I can tell you the story while we walk can't I?"

"Let me go change my shoes and get a jacket. It's cool in the timber." She paused and looked over her shoulder. "I'll be right back."

The sepulchral aura of the redwoods silenced their conversation. The tangy fragrance of decaying leaf mold and rotting logs filled the air with an almost tangible aroma. The forest floor was carpeted with fallen needles, wood sorrel, small white lilies, and scattered shrubbery of azaleas, rhododendrons, huckleberry, salal, and wild currants.

Jean had walked through the big trees many times, but today she was experiencing a new feeling. The forest felt more active, more real, more alive. She watched Paul absorb the peaceful aura and become content. He seemed to be wrapping the forest around him like a warm blanket as he lifted his face into the filtered sunlight and spread his arms to allow the quiet strength of nature to embrace him. She was happy to quietly share the moment while he cleansed his soul.

Two pairs of eyes watched the Mustang leave the cabin. Alma watched through her sheer curtains, Tim from concealment in a cottage whose owners had not returned for the summer. Worry ran rampant in Tim's thoughts. *It's been a tough two years for you and now the cops are all over you. Hang in there, buddy. Things are going to get even more exciting before we get away from here.*

Looking to the campground, he saw the camper being towed away at the head of a caravan of official vehicles. *I know what you'll find when you strip that thing down, but will you understand where it leads? I hope you guys are good. You need to be really good or more people could end up like our friend on the beach.* He looked around the attic he had chosen as a lookout. The space was populated with folded beach chairs, umbrellas, spare bedding, and ice chests. Concealing his presence was critical until he could contact Paul. The bundle of bloodied clothes on the floor was a disposal problem he needed to handle better than he had the body. He stretched out on a chaise lounge pad and closed his eyes.

The old man sat sphinx-like in the shade of an umbrella covered table. Time and sun had tightened and polished his skin to a patina of fine leather, the folds and wrinkles soft edged, but the weight of the gaze he turned on his visitor was as cold and withering as the stare of a cobra. The visitor felt icy perspiration dampen his armpits and soak his shirt.

"Repeat what you said!" the old man growled.

"Our man disappeared. He hasn't reported in since yesterday and I think he may have been eliminated."

"So much for the headlines. Tell me what led you to this conclusion."

"My source says an unidentified body was found on the beach this morning. The cops have been talking to everybody in the area and there's a crew of technicians swarming over his pickup like ants at a picnic."

"You said the body was unidentified?"

"My source says a guy in the campground told him a naked body washed up on the beach and nobody knew who he was until some old broad told the cops he looked like the guy with the camper. They're looking for the owner, but apparently our man's preparations took them down a blind alley, so they're tearing into the truck. From the way they're going after it, they must think they have something."

"Can they trace it to us?"

"I don't think so."

"You don't think so? I didn't ask what you think! What do you know?" The old man had stood and finished the sentence with his nose only and inch from the face of the younger man.

Swallowing his fear and standing much more steady than he felt, the young man ignored the spittle flying into his face with the enraged outburst. "I know he built the truck himself and equipped it do the kind of work he's done for us in the past. I don't know all his sources for parts, but he was told to make absolutely sure it couldn't be connected to us."

"It damn well better be! We don't need any more heat. Especially not from some podunk police department in the middle of bungfuck nowhere."

The older man walked to the edge of the swimming pool. The view from the pool on a clear day was spectacular. Today the blanket of smog in the LA Basin looked thick enough to walk on. "Who we got to send if our guy turns out to be the stiff?"

"The next best guy we have is in Seattle, but he may be out of the business. He was talking about retiring."

"Bullshit! Those guys never retire! They only want more money! Find him! No! Get him! Get him on the job now! The trail is getting cold and he's gonna need to play catch up."

"I'll get right on it. It may take a day or two to find him."

"Then the sooner you start, the sooner he'll be on the job!"

"Yes, sir!" He turned and walked toward the house, glad he had already started the search before coming to make his report. His people should already have a handle on his location. "Sir," he turned toward the old man. "I believe Pisces is available."

The Don's smile was reptilian. "Send Pisces." He settled back on the chaise lounge and stared venomously at his grandson. "That fuckin' slimeball may have dropped out of sight, but I'll run him down if I have to kill his partner, both their families, and everyone else in his life to do it. He's running, but he can't run forever. I will find him! And when I do," the old man nodded slowly, a grim mirthless smile frozen on his lips.

Special Agent in Charge Joe Carpenter leaned back in his chair when Cliff Reilly entered his office. "Good morning,

Cliff. Sorry to drag you in so early, but I'm concerned about Tim Gordon. Have you heard from him recently?"

"Tim's only been in contact twice in the last six months. He refused to tell me where he's gone to ground and he didn't stay on the phone long enough to trace. I don't blame him for being careful after what happened to McAfee's wife, and he knows the Don's looking for him. Tim's a brave guy, but he's not stupid. I'm more worried about Paul than Tim. The Don is almost certain to try to get to Tim through him and I don't know if he has enough experience to handle what the old man might throw at him. He's smart, but he lacks Tim's field experience."

"Does Paul still think Tim is dead?"

"As far as I know he thinks Tim and his wife were both killed in the crash. He's hired a management firm to run the business and gone up north for an extended vacation. The last couple years have been tough for him. His whole world fell apart and he's been trying to regain his balance ever since."

"You know where he is, don't you?"

"Of course we know where he is and we're keeping tabs on him from a distance. Unfortunately, there's no way we can protect him from everybody who's looking for Tim. Protecting him without him knowing we're around isn't easy. He has a sixth sense about someone watching him. He can feel their eyes. We may have gained one small advantage though. Lately he's been distracted by a good looking woman."

"About now he could use a pleasant female distraction, but it doesn't change our problem. We've got to bring Tim in. He's not helping us by hiding out. We need to protect him until we can get this case to trial. Without him we don't have a case."

"I think he followed Paul, but our pigeon hasn't spotted him yet. Those two guys are closer than most brothers.

Wherever Paul goes, Tim will eventually appear. I don't know if they've been in contact since the plane went down, but I'd bet money they're working a plan as we speak."

Joe looked out the tenth floor window and thought for a moment. "We need to drop a net over this case. A plane full of innocent victims is bad enough. The longer it takes to pull the pieces together, the greater the danger to Paul and everyone who comes in contact with him."

"Yes, sir. I'll start putting together a plan to bring things to a head. We've been on this for case more than five years. We we were almost ready when the plane crash set us back, but we'll nail the bastards anyway. We'll take down the whole bunch. We'll roll up their entire network like a cheap carpet!"

"Make it happen. We're going to find ourselves wishing we never joined this outfit if we come up empty after the time and budget we've invested."

Joe looked out over the smog-shrouded buildings of downtown LA, thinking about what had begun as a carefully planned, skillfully orchestrated operation to bring down a major smuggling operation. Tim had proven incredibly resourceful in learning the names of the players. It had taken more than four years to fill in the chart and to organize a plan to dismantle the network. Then some mental case blew an airplane out of the sky and a bonehead bureaucrat at NSA painted a target on Tim, sending the prime player under ground and derailing the whole scheme. *Sometimes the best laid plans aren't enough. Right now some old fashioned good luck would be a welcome visitor.*

11.

"HUMBOLDT, FORTYSIX-TWO."

"Go ahead."

"Please advise the coroner we'd like to observe the autopsy on the John Doe from the lagoon."

"Ten-four. HS-one requests your ETA."

"ETA about thirty."

"He wants to see you as soon as you arrive."

"Fortysix-nine, fortysix-two"

"Go ahead." Tom responded.

"Did you copy the last transmission?"

"Affirmative."

"I expect you should attend. He'll have questions you can answer."

"Sounds like a perfect way to end the day."

"The day's only just begun."

"Fortysix-two adam, fortysix-two."

The radio crackled with Cal Snider's voice. "Go ahead. is this my new call sign?"

"I don't know, but I thought you'd get the idea. We have a command appearance with the boss."

"I'll alert the media. About now you need all the moral support you can get."

The ribbon of highway rolled under John's car as he drove through the bright sunlight of early afternoon. He thought about the evidence they had collected. He knew they had missed something. Failure to recognize evidence was a given in any investigation. Discovering what, where, and who was missed was the challenge. He didn't expect the autopsy to do more than confirm what he already knew. The victim died from a blow to the head. He mentally checked off the missing information as he drove. *Someone stripped the body. Who? No scuffed skin caused by dragging. Who carried the body? Were the footprints washed away by the surf or simply lost in the tracks of other beach goers? Did the victim fall from the bluff or was he clubbed? Who pushed him or clubbed him? Why? Why is the old woman in the end cabin so secretive? What is she hiding? Is she hiding something or just anti-social? Are the two who are making nice with each other involved? How are they involved? Why is she so hostile? Is she embarrassed, feel threatened or paranoid in some other way? He, on the other hand, is cautious, basically cooperative, and protective of the woman. I sure wouldn't want to go through what he has in the past couple years. He seems like a decent enough guy who had life take a dump on him. It looks like he's trying to wash away the past and find something sweet smelling for the future. Who can blame him? But is he what he seems to be? What the hell can I actually tell the boss about this case? No media showed up at the scene. That's unusual. Why didn't I think about it before? Did the Sheriff ask the news people to stay away? No way. Asking the media to stay back is like directing flies to a cow flop. So where were the news vultures? A dead body washed up on the beach is front-page photos and the lead story on the evening news. How come nobody picked it up on their scanners and came to take a look? The boss will want answers. What can I tell him besides what we don't know? What we don't know would fill a book.*

"Damn!" John swore. "This case is a king size hair ball and naturally the boss wants an immediate update. What we need is time to get the autopsy done, get the pickup and camper scoped out and identify the body. We have enough unanswered questions without adding his to the list! Of course, if I was him I'd want to know the details, if only to know how to spin the story for the press."

John hated autopsies and starting the day with one was about as much fun as his scheduled root canal, but it was part of the job and he loved his job. Sporting a freshly shaved face and a haircut, Cal announced he had skipped breakfast in self-defense before watching his first autopsy. Tom was so tickled to be part of the investigation his feet barely touched the floor. John suggested a couple of Valium might be in order. Cal said a pound or two would be a more appropriate dosage. Tom was in a party mood.

Dennis was recording the identification number of the corpse when the trio arrived. "Well, gentlemen, are you ready for another fine day of forensic investigation?" A twinkling grin showed at the corners of his eyes above his surgical mask.

"Nothing like a little long pig butchery to start the day," John replied. "Our young friend here is so excited he brought a six-pack of Bud and a bag of Doritos. Meanwhile, this freshly shorn and shaved varmint is trying to maintain the strain and not embarrass himself."

"First autopsy?"

"First murder investigation, too," Tom replied, "but not the first stiff I've been around. I've never had the chance to watch an autopsy. You gonna weigh all the internal organs and cut off the top of his head so you can examine the brain too?"

Dennis laughed. "Maintain your positive attitude and you'll be fine. It looks like our pale faced friend isn't quite so happy to be here."

"I'm okay, I guess," Cal said. "I look pale because wearing a full beard for five years means my face hasn't seen much sun. Don't let the lack of a tan worry you. I'm ready. I think."

"All right then. Let's get this show on the road."

The first observations confirmed what he had recorded at the beach. Evidence of scavengers attacking the soft tissues was extremely minor, indicating the body was not on the beach or in the ocean very long. Sand in all the body openings indicated the victim was dead when the body came through the surf.

The head injury received careful examination. The blow caused massive damage to the scalp and the underlying bone structure, but the surrounding tissues had not been swollen by broken blood vessels. "It appears death occurred instantaneously from this blow. It also looks like the implement may have been round, but I'll reserve my opinion until I open the scalp. I don't see any wood fragments in the wound, but I won't know until I do microscopic study."

"Do you think he could have busted his melon doing a header off the bluff?" John asked.

"I don't think so. The bluff is what, maybe fifty feet high? Not high enough to cause this sort of damage unless whatever he hit was moving in the opposite direction. There's no sand or grit impacted into the skin like you'd see if this was from a fall and the angle of the blow looks wrong for a fall. I think our friend got caught where he wasn't supposed to be by someone he didn't expect to meet."

"No other possibilities to consider?" Cal asked.

"I'm a long way from finished, but it looks like the blow was delivered from the rear, from the victim's right, and from above the head. The angle of the indentation of the skull points that way. Once I get a look at the whole skull I'll know a lot more, but my experience tells me this guy got the old Alley Oop treatment."

"Dinosaur bone sized club?"

"The modern equivalent."

"Any thoughts what the club might be?"

"From the feel of the fracture pattern, the shape was round, about four, maybe five centimeters in diameter. It had to be heavy to do this much damage and it was delivered with a lot of force."

"You've just eliminated the artist and the little old lady who likes to work in her garden," John said. "But not the guy in the cabin next door. He's in good enough shape to deliver the blow."

Tom threw a questioning look at John. "I thought he had an alibi."

"He does have an alibi and it looks air tight, but his alibi is the same as Jean Parker's, which doesn't eliminate the possibility they conspired to do this together. We only have their word about just meeting each other. His alibi doesn't rule him out as a suspect. Not yet."

A pensive look crossed Tom's face. "He's in the right place at the right time, he has the physical capability, but what's his motive? Why would he want to kill this guy?"

Cal smiled. "A good question we might be able to answer if we knew the identity of our friend here. We could also be wrong about the two women not being strong enough to do this. It seems unlikely, but we can't discard any possibility until the door gets slammed in our face by a preponderance of evidence to the contrary."

Dennis made a Y shaped incision to open the body cavity. Two hours later he concluded the body showed no signs of significant injury aside from the blow to the head and samples filled a neat and orderly array of containers. Most importantly, Dennis was certain the damage to the skull had been made by the impact of a cylindrical object delivered from behind and above the head of the victim. He also confirmed the body had only been in the water a brief time. Absence of water in the lungs ruled out drowning. He found no evidence the body had been dragged over the ground. The scuffs on the skin were minor and resulted from the surf carrying and rolling the body onto the beach. He speculated the body was carried to the water. One question remained on everyone's mind: By whom?

"I knew we missed something," John said as they left the autopsy suite. "A crushing blow to the head scatters blood and tissue. We didn't find anything because we weren't looking for it. We talked to everyone we could find and we gathered up the truck, but we didn't search for the murder scene. There has to be something to mark the location of the killing."

"Maybe," Cal said, "but the rain could have washed it away. Of course if he was killed in one of the cabins, which is possible, the evidence is still there. We just need to find it."

"I searched the campground pretty thoroughly while you were on the beach," Tom said. "Maybe I missed something, but I don't think it was done there."

"Why not?" John and Cal asked in unison.

"It's just a feeling, but I talked to all the people in the campground. Everyone knew of this guy, but nobody had any contact with him. He seemed to be gone a lot of the time, moved like a shadow, and attracted their attention by an absence of the sociability most campers share. Everyone was curious enough to notice to him, but nobody got close to him. If I were going to try to kill a guy everyone had noticed, I'd do it somewhere chances of being seen or heard would be nil. At least that's how I see it."

DAN RAGON

"Good analysis, Tom. Now take your idea a step further. Put yourself in the killer's shoes. Get inside his head if you can. If you weren't going to do him in the campground, where would you choose?"

"I'm kind of thin on ideas, but he had to leave a trail. I know the rain washed everything down, but what if it was done where the rain didn't reach?"

"Exactly! Someplace sheltered from the rain! Inside a building? Inside the burned out trunk of a redwood? Inside a car? It would have to be some place where the killer could get a good swing, but still manage to sneak up on the victim."

Cal looked at his partner with a puzzled expression. "What makes you think the attacker surprised the victim?"

"Remember the angle and direction of the skull fracture? It broke the skull from an inch above the ear to just above the outer orbit of the right eye. The groove was deeper to the front of the head, and it was crushed in and down at about a forty-five degree angle. Think about this, the victim thinks he's alone, then he hears a sound, starts to turn his head to look over his shoulder, and wham! All the lights go out."

Tom nodded. "Sounds good, but couldn't the attack have come from the front?"

"Okay. Let's see if your idea plays out. I come at you from the front and swing a club at you. What do you do?" John stepped in front of Tom and started a threatening swing at Tom's head.

Tom ducked his head, raised his right arm, then stopped and looked up at John. "The only injury is to the head. No defensive injuries! He didn't have time to protect himself!"

Cal stepped in. "Tom, kneel down with your back to me. Keep your eyes ahead until you hear me, then just react."

Tom stayed in a crouch until he heard a sound at his right

rear. He started to spin his head, only to feel Cal's hand bump the right side of his head. "That's how it was done! Just like that!"

John nodded. "I think you're right. It fits the evidence. Now let's look at how it was done. You were standing and Tom was squatted down. Where could that have happened? Inside a building? Maybe. In a burned out tree? Not likely. On the beach? Possibly. Let's suppose this guy is creeping around trying to find the guy who killed him. Where would he be looking?"

"The cabins," said Cal. "But how could what we just figured out work around the cabins?"

"The cabins have pier and post foundations." Tom stated.

"Yes!" John exclaimed.

"I get it!" Cal agreed. "Our victim is creeping around under a cabin, starts to stick his head out and gets his melon popped!"

"Exactly," John said. "Just for argument sake, let's presume our recent arrival from the south was the target of this creepy crawler. I think we need to look under some cabins."

"Your car or mine?" Cal asked.

"Mine. Grab your camera, Tom. We're going to take a little drive."

12.

"JOE CARPENTER, PLEASE."

"May I tell him who's calling?"

"My information is more important than my name."

"Please hold." The receptionist pressed the intercom. "I'm sorry to interrupt, but you have a call from someone who will not identify herself."

"What did the caller say when you asked for a name? Her exact words."

"She said 'my information is more important than my name'."

"Gentlemen, will you please excuse me?" Joe asked the men seated across the desk from him.

When the door closed he picked up the phone. "Joe Carpenter."

"He's here."

"Have you seen him?"

"Trust me, he is definitely here."

"Can you make contact with him?"

"I don't know. There's so much police activity I'm using every trick I know to go unnoticed. I'll be in touch."

A smile spread across his face as he dialed Cliff Reilly.

"Reilly."

"He's there."

"For sure?"

"A little bird just told me."

"Confirmed contact?"

"If she says he's there, he's there"

"I'm on it."

The young man strode purposefully across the garden toward where the old man sat with the morning paper spread in front of him, cup of coffee in his hand.

"Good morning sir!"

"Is it? According to the paper, there ain't much good anywhere in the world."

"The fisherman is in the boat."

"I appreciate you sending the very best."

"I chose poorly the last time. I try not to make the same mistake twice."

"You may not have chosen badly. He may have underestimated the adversary, an expensive mistake for all of us, especially for the one who made it. Have you made certain he can't be traced to us?"

"I've rechecked to make sure all traces have been eliminated."

"Good. Have our friends at the bureau discovered the trail?"

"Not to my knowledge, but they're very clever, they could have an observer we haven't discovered."

"I don't like surprises."

"Yes sir. I'm giving it my complete attention."

"It's difficult to be patient. Gordon has eluded us for more than two years and caused a substantial amount of expense and frustration. It's unfortunate Webster misjudged him. It appears we all may have misjudged him."

"He's extremely resourceful, very smart, and very dangerous. I've advised Pisces of this. I've learned that when dealing with him he will always be a step ahead of me. I know it's difficult to out think a man who's brighter than me."

"Such humility will serve you well if it's sincere. Remember, humility is more than just knowing or saying the proper words. True humility is recognizing and understanding your own limitations."

"Yes sir."

"Good morning."

"Good morning, sir. I won't fail this time!"

13.

PISCES HOPED NO ONE NOTICED HER ARRIVAL IN the pale light of dawn. Perhaps the exhaustion of the long road trip or the placid surroundings and deep pools of darkness lulled her into a false sense of security. Maybe she just didn't want to think her target was observing everything in the area. She would have been deeply chagrined to know she had been identified the moment her car rolled to a stop.

Pisces was a killer. Her job was simple and singular. Dispose of the target, arrive and depart unnoticed. Pisces was expensive, effective, and untraceable. She worked with a simple set of rules. No jobs aimed at capture. Always study the job carefully before accepting it. Never start a job without careful preparation, unhurried deliberation, and a well designed plan. No exceptions!

Pisces had retired, finished with the life forever, until this job. A job she didn't want. A job she didn't need. A job she couldn't refuse. A job she was planning on the fly, studying on the fly, and preparing on the fly. A job violating her rules. For this job she came out of retirement. She didn't have a choice. The peace of her soul depended on this job. So did her life.

The task was simple. Find, capture, and deliver the target to her employer. The difficulty had been clearly explained. The target had managed to evade and eliminate all the skilled people who had attempted his capture. There was also a major complication. The feds were employing their endless resources to capture the target. Complications usually made the job more interesting, more challenging, more demanding, more, fun. The jogger was the key. She breathed deeply to stave off fatigue while she watched him run on the beach. Twenty hours on the road had drained her stamina. Her muscles were leaden, her eyes were sandy, but she was too keyed up to sleep. Sleep could wait. She could deal with fatigue. She used fatigue to sharpen her senses and focus on the job.

Tim recognized this new player as one of the elite of the profession. He knew the old man had pulled out all the stops because Pisces didn't work cheap and Pisces didn't fail. Life had just become a lot more difficult. The cops were sure to be back today to continue their investigation. He needed a new plan. A worried frown creased his features as stared at the cobwebbed rafters above him.

The three officers enjoyed the drive and the opportunity to share their thoughts. The principal outcome of the discussion was unanimous agreement Paul McAfee was key to the case. It wasn't the evidence or his behavior, or because his activities were suspicious. It was the timing of his arrival, followed by the discovery of the body, and the odd circumstances of the murder, a chain of coincidence they could not ignore. They agreed to begin their search in the area of his cabin.

John parked where the road turned to run parallel to the shoreline. They studied the buildings, the street, and the beach as they walked toward Paul's cabin. Tom observed Alma watch them pass while she worked in yard.

John pointed to the cabin across the grassy driveway from Paul's. "That looks like a good place to start."

Tom walked toward the rear of the cabin. "I'll see what

I can find in back." Moments later, his voice rang out. "Hey guys, come take a look at this."

"Find something of interest?" Cal asked.

"Look for yourself." Tom pointed to scars in the dark soil under the cabin.

"It looks like someone has been here recently," John said. "We need to make sure it isn't neighborhood kids." He leaned in to study the disturbed area more closely. "Whoever was under here wasn't a kid. It looks like someone knelt down here. There's a knee print and a toe print too far apart and too deep to be a kid. We need to get the lab boys out here. We'll see what else we can find to heat up the trail while we wait for them."

"I'll get the camera, and call the lab crew," Tom said as he trotted toward the car.

"Cal, if this is our victim, there's no way he could have been bashed in this location. He was a good three feet under the cabin." He shined his flashlight on the ground at a low angle. He swept the light slowly, looking for where the intruder might have crawled under the cabin floor. The track was so slight he didn't see it until the fourth pass over the same spot. "Take a look!" He adjusted the beam to cast a shadow behind the disturbance. "Looks like a track, but how did he get from here to there without making any other tracks?"

"This guy is good," Cal said. "When I was in 'Nam, we had a guy who could move through anything without making a sound or leaving a track. We can probably find his trail, but I think we should let the lab guys do their thing."

"Right. Let's take a look along the side of the cabin. I think he was moving forward under cover of the building."

"I called the lab," Tom announced as he rejoined them. "What do I need to photograph?"

"It's a tough shot, but give it a try." Cal held the light to highlight the disturbance of the soil. "Do what you can with it. It may be too small to show very well. Try to get a good shot we can blow up."

Tom began making a photographic record of the ground under the cabin from a variety of angles.

"Bring your camera over here."

Cal and Tom moved quickly to the north side of the cabin where John waited about two-thirds of the way to the front.

"I think this might be the scene of the murder." John pointed at a small, rough edged spot on the siding of the cabin, "What does this look like to you?"

In a place sheltered from the rain was a red-brown drop of dried fluid with a fiber stuck in it. "Looks like dried blood with a hair stuck in it," Cal observed.

"I think so too. Now look at this." John pointed at the underside of the floor. There were several more spots of the same color on the floor joists and the sub flooring. On the ground, a scuff and one complete footprint were faintly visible. "I bet if we rolled up the sod and sent it to the lab we would find more evidence this is where our mystery guest checked out. Let's wait for the techs. We don't want to contaminate things any more than we have already. Let's see if we can find how he got to the cabin."

Cal glanced at the back of the property and the roof lines of the houses beyond. "These cabins back up to the ones on the other street don't they?"

"Yes they do," Tom replied. "The fence separating them isn't very tall and there are even gates between some of the lots."

"Gates?" John asked. "They have gates between the back yards?"

"Yeah. Families sometimes bought two lots, built cabins on both and put a gate in the fence so they could go back and forth between them. You know, company in the back cabin, family in the ocean front cabin."

Cal smiled. "I've read about the way some of these vacation subdivisions were originally developed. Families would go in together on the property and build a place for everybody to stay. Time sharing the old fashioned way. Let's go look for a gate."

The back fence area was a tangle of tall weeds, berry vines, and discarded pieces of wood, pipe, fence wire, and used lumber sporting rusty nails. John found a small tuft of fibers caught on the weathered top of the fence. Tom photographed it and the broken weeds at the base of the fence. John and Tom were following the faint trail in the grass when Cal stopped them short.

"Hold it, guys! He had company."

Cal pointed at the roof of the shed next to the fence. "Someone came across the fence and onto the roof. You can see where he moved up the roof."

"So we have an intruder followed by an accomplice to stand watch," John suggested.

Cal shook his head. "I don't think so. Standing lookout up there wouldn't be much help at night in the rain. It's too far away to use hand signals. I think we have one following the other and being careful to stay out of sight."

"Could one of the marks on the fence be from the killer carrying the victim away?" Tom asked.

"Nope" Cal said. "The scuffs show the direction of movement is to this side, not the other. We have two people over the fence, but nobody went back out the way they came in."

"So does this clear Paul McAfee as a suspect?" Tom asked.

"Probably as a suspect," John replied. "But I still think he's connected in some way. It looks like the murder happened within a few feet of his cabin so he still may be involved. He's probably not the killer, but there are other possibilities that keep him in the picture."

"Have we taken a look through the yards behind this fence?" Cal asked.

"Not yet," John said. "Are you volunteering?"

"I thought I'd take Tom and have a look around. Four eyes are better than two and he knows the area. You can wait for the lab crew and maybe talk with Mr. McAfee. Sure happened close to his place. What is it, about fifteen feet from his window?"

"Yeah, but he wasn't home."

"At least that's the story he told you the last time you talked with him and his lady friend."

Tom's forehead wrinkled in puzzlement. "You think he may change his story?"

"Not necessarily," Cal replied, "but we have other questions to ask now. By the way, have you seen him this morning?"

John shook his head and smiled.

Cal scanned the yard. "Okay, what did I miss?"

"Where's the blue Mustang?" Tom replied.

Cal noticed the absence of the vehicle and laughed. "Very observant of me. Just proves I'm a good detective."

"Maybe the barber cut off more than his hair," John said. "Sort of like Samson losing his strength when his hair was cut off, except in your case you seem to be losing your peripheral vision and your mind. Keep an eye on him, Tom, I wouldn't want him to get lost."

"Right! C'mon Tom, let's get out of here before he thinks of any more compliments about my appearance or my powers of observation."

Tom grinned at John and trotted off to catch up with the retreating detective.

14.

PAUL DECIDED TO MAKE A LEISURELY TOUR OF THE
coastline to the county seat to check on his car. Frequent
stops to admire the natural beauty and lunch at a restaurant
overlooking Trinidad Bay stretched the journey to almost three
hours. The service manager told him if all went as expected,
the car would be ready by the end of the week.

Paul stopped at the Safeway at the north edge of the city.
He didn't notice the vehicle shadowing his movements from a
half-mile behind, or that the driver joined the shoppers.

The tail on Pisces was extremely cautious. Neither the need
for maintaining close contact or grocery shopping influenced
the observer's actions. As the tiny caravan stretched out over
a distance of more than a mile, he formulated a plan to deal
with this newest threat. The sloppy disposal of the body had
attracted too much attention from the local police. Another
unexplained death would set off fireworks bright enough
to be visible from Pluto. He had misread the situation and
underestimated Mr. Gordon.

Entry through customs had been ridiculously easy. The
counterfeit passport and visa were accepted and stamped
without question by the official after a cursory examination
of his bag. The most aggravating part of the assignment
was the smell of stale cigar smoke in the rental car. Even
after hanging four air fresheners and driving for hours with

the window down, the pervading stench made every breath unpleasant. None of the non-smoking vehicles available were suitably mundane for his purposes. The best suited vehicle was this wretched smelling Ford. If all went well, perhaps his employer would offer him a bonus, perhaps even give him Pisces. He would enjoy the degradation and abasement of such a remarkable subject. A wolfish grin spread across his stoic features when he thought about the exquisite tortures he would inflict before killing her; fitting vengeance for the loss of face she had inflicted in Hong Kong.

Paul arrived to find his driveway blocked by crime scene tape. John Ragsdale and a crew of technicians were intently combing the neighboring property. "Well, this is a pleasant surprise," he mumbled. He parked in front of his cabin, mentally bracing himself for the inevitable conversation with the detective. He opened the trunk and took out his purchases as though there was nothing unusual about a crime scene crew examining his back yard. He heard John's voice before he reached his front door.

"Good afternoon, Mr. McAfee, could I have a few minutes of your time?"

"I'd like to put my food away first if you don't mind."

"No problem. Let me know when you're ready."

"I'll be a few minutes."

He rejoined John five minutes later. "It looks like you've found something."

"Yes, it does. I need to talk to you about the night of the murder again. Try to establish some times a little better."

"I don't know if I can tell you any more than I have already, but go ahead."

"You said you spent the evening with Ms. Parker?"

"A very enjoyable evening. Good food, nice surroundings, pleasant conversation. She made me feel at home."

"I imagine it was a welcome way to start your vacation. You said you weren't paying attention to what was going on outside, but did you see or hear anything at all?"

"Soft music, good wine, and a pretty woman giving me her undivided attention. What do you think I might hear? I was listening to who was in the room with me, the whole world could have blown up outside and I probably wouldn't have noticed it."

"I understand. She's a pretty lady. Is there any way you can give me a better idea what time you came home?"

"Not really. Like I told you, the moon was about the width of a hand above the horizon. That's the best I can give you. I took off my watch the day I arrived and haven't paid much attention to the time since. Time is a terrible tyrant for a businessman. I came here to escape the stress of running a business. If it's light I figure it's daytime and if it's dark it's night."

"I envy you your freedom. Someday maybe I can do the same. Did you see anyone around the place next door when you were coming home?"

"No. I was watching the ocean and the surf. I was fascinated by the lights in the waves. I wasn't looking at anything else. I just kept watching the light show until I walked through the door. I don't remember even looking at the other cabins. My mind and attention were on other things. You know what I mean?"

"Sure. It must be pretty dark between the cabins at night."

"Seems likely. I've never looked."

"Could I take a look inside?"

"I don't suppose you have a warrant?"

"No, I don't, but I'm sure I can get one based on the proximity of what we found next door."

"Help yourself. I have nothing to hide and it'll save you the time and trouble of getting turned down for a warrant."

"You don't think I could get a warrant?"

"I presume the rules of search and seizure are the same here as the rest of the United States, but the easiest way for me to remove myself from the list of suspects is to let you see there's nothing to connect me to your investigation. C'mon in."

John meticulously looked into the closets, cupboards, and rooms. The search proved fruitless, but Paul watched with appreciation as the detective looked at everything and carefully replaced each item the way he had found it. "Well, detective, are you satisfied I'm who I claim to be?"

"I guess what I see is what I get. Thanks for your cooperation. Sometimes it's difficult for people to understand how much of my job is eliminating possibilities."

"The Sherlock Holmes method of criminal investigation?"

"How's that?"

"You remember Sherlock Holmes' theory of investigation. If you eliminate everything possible, what's left is the answer, no matter how improbable the answer might seem."

"You got it."

"Any details you can share?"

"So far I have a dead body. Probable cause of death is a blow to the head. Probable location of death is near the cabin next door. The body was stripped of clothing before it was dumped on the beach. At the time of the murder the guy who lives within fifteen feet of the scene was in close proximity to a pretty neighbor lady. The auto theft crew is dismantling a pickup and camper in an effort to determine who really owns it, where the owner is located, and whether the vehicle is connected to the victim. There are other possibilities, but that's the public headlines."

"I guess it's safe for me to assume there is no probable cause to suspect I am the party or one of the parties responsible for the unfortunate demise of the mystery guest at the morning beach party."

"For the moment."

"In other words, I'm free to go about my business as long as I don't leave town real sudden like?"

"I would be happy for you to settle in and enjoy the company of your neighbor while we proceed with our investigation. I'll let you know if I have more questions."

"I wasn't planning any long trips. How long before I can put my car away? I'm not comfortable leaving it parked on the street."

"We should be done in a couple hours. Thanks again for your cooperation. My visit has been very enlightening."

Paul checked the position of the sun, looked out over the ocean, and inhaled deeply. He reveled in the soft fragrance of the sea, the beach, and the wild flowers. He smiled as he walked to Jean's cabin.

"Hey, detective, what was your victim wearing?"

"Very funny! You know the victim was bare ass!"

"Right, but if the victim's clothes turn up, we can try to match them to this." The lab tech held up a baggy containing a small swatch of material.

John studied the baggy. "Looks like a piece of dark gray nylon."

"I need to get a better look under a scope, but it may be spandex. You know, the stuff they use to make those skin tight exercise suits."

"Where did you find it?"

"It was hanging from a nail under the floor."

"You don't suppose someone working on the cabin might have left it behind, do you?"

"Sure, doesn't everybody wear a spandex suit to crawl around under the house? I know I do. Makes me feel like I'm gettin' a workout. I was thinking maybe tonight I'd slip on some skins and crawl around under the house."

"You're supposed to be smart, not a smart ass. It's reasonable to presume it's from the victim's clothing. Nice color for night work."

"Makes you think the visitor may not have had a personalized invitation, don't it?"

"And the welcoming committee was well and truly annoyed by the appearance of an uninvited guest."

"One might say the guest found the party to be a smashing event."

"You gotta love gallows humor."

"It's the only defense against cynicism and outright despair."

"How much longer do you need to pick this place clean?"

"Another hour or so. We're making a final pass over the grid. There's some serious degradation because of the rain so we need to make sure we get everything without a return trip."

"Good thinking. I think I'll go chase down my partners and see how they're doing." John radioed Cal to meet at the store in fifteen minutes.

15.

JEAN LOVED THE OILY FRAGRANCE OF THE COLORS
on her palette and the open invitation of a blank canvas. She
laid in a background, creating areas of light and dark she
would to overlay in successive layers of translucent color. She
wanted to capture the latticework of brightness and shadow
of sunlight filtering through the trees. The vision was clear in
her mind. She wanted to capture the radiance spilling over and
around Paul as he stood drinking in the peace and solitude
of the primeval environment. The challenge was to capture a
singular moment on canvas in a way others would understand
or appreciate. She didn't care if her emotional connection was
responsible for the way the image flowed from her brush onto
the canvas. She reveled in the pleasure of creating the image.
She closed her eyes and painted what she visualized. Opening
her eyes, she saw how the yellow and gold underlayment
opened the canvas. It was like looking into a pool of light.
"Yes-s-s-s!" she whispered proudly.

A layer of color forming the framework of the painting
followed. She continued by allowing her unencumbered
instinct to guide the brush. When she stopped to allow the
paint to cure in preparation for the next phase it was nearly
three in the afternoon. "Time flies when you're having fun,"
she sighed. The sun was just peeking over the ridge when
she awoke and took her inspiration into the studio. She
hadn't showered or eaten, she simply lost herself in her work.

Exhilarated by the flow of creative energy, she took a bottle of water from the refrigerator and drank deeply.

The previous day had been filled with warmth, caring, and understanding. They had walked for several hours enjoying the emotional impact of the forest. When they returned Paul said he needed some time alone and went to his cabin. She told him she understood, but couldn't help feeling rejected. She understood his need to come to terms with his memories and emotions. She also felt an intense need to share hers with him. He still hadn't told her the details of his personal tragedy. *Don't press too hard,* she counseled herself. *He's trying to start fresh. If you're his starting place you'll both know it. If not, then at least you've made a friend. A lot worse things could happen.* She started for the bathroom, tossing her paint-stained sweatshirt on the floor. She'd slipped it on when she got up and wore only bikini panties under the shirt which hung nearly to her knees. She paused to study herself in the full-length mirror on the bathroom door. Six months of regular exercise and sensible diet had firmed and smoothed her figure in a pleasing way. She wondered what Paul thought about her figure.

Jean was combing her damp hair when she heard the knock on her door. Her heart flew into her throat when she saw Paul standing on her porch looking out at the ocean. She paused halfway across the living room to regain her composure, but the attempt left her more flushed and aroused than she had felt in years.

She opened the door and greeted him with pink cheeks and a bright smile.

"Good afternoon, pretty lady. Might you have a few moments for a bothersome neighbor?" Paul made a sweeping bow.

"Why yes, kind sir," Jean responded in her best imitation

of a southern belle. "I have several moments I could spare you right now. I just washed my hair, but you are most welcome to watch me untangle it."

"I was just thinking how lovely you looked with your rosy cheeks and a mop to rival Medusa."

"Medusa, huh? Aren't you worried about getting snake bit since you haven't turned to stone from the sight of me?"

"Oh, looking at you doesn't turn me to stone. At least not all of me."

Jean turned away to hide her blush.

"I'm sorry. I didn't mean to embarrass you. That was out of line. Maybe I should leave before I make any more inappropriate remarks."

Jean turned to face him, deliberately blocking his path to the door. "Don't even think about leaving. You didn't step out of line and you didn't embarrass me. I like you Paul. I like you a lot. I don't want you to leave. I want you to stay and I'm happy you feel that way about me."

"I'm not really sure how I feel. I get around you and I feel one way and then when I'm alone I feel guilty. I'm a mess. I don't want to spend my life alone, but I haven't learned how to handle all the crazy feelings I get when I'm around you. You make me feel alive again."

"Take your time, Paul. Your wife was a special lady whose memory is precious. We've only known each other a few days, it just feels longer to me. I left a bad marriage, I quit a creatively stifling, financially rewarding job that required me to play by someone else's rules. I may be in a different emotional place than you, but I want to be with you. I want you to know it. Take your time, I'll be here until we find the right time to be together."

Paul took her in his arms and hugged her close to him.

Jean put her arms around him and rested her head against his chest, enjoying the comfort of his embrace. "I like you a lot Jean. I appreciate your understanding."

"We all have a disguise we show the world and the true face we show to a friend."

He rested his cheek on the top of her head. After a few moments he stepped back. "So how have you spent your day? Accomplish anything important, or did you just hang out and reflect on your next project?"

"I spent my day working. I woke up this morning with the sun in my eyes and the inspiration for a painting in my mind. I only stopped working on it an hour ago. I was just getting cleaned up when you arrived."

"Is it going to be as good as the one over the fireplace?"

"I don't know yet. Want to see it?"

"Are you sure you want to show it before it's done? I wouldn't want to spoil it by seeing it too soon."

"Come look, you won't spoil it."

She saw his amazement at the way the light beams streamed across the canvas. Jean expected to hear him say something and started to speak, but the words caught on her tongue. Her work had struck a chord. She gazed at his face and smiled to know he had inspired her to create what he was studying and absorbing.

Finally, he broke out of his reverie. "My god, it's magnificent!"

She laughed. "You think it's magnificent! I'm just getting started, but I appreciate the compliment."

"I'm no expert, but I think you have a very special talent. Your work is full of light and energy that bursts out and fills the room."

"Let me write this down for the brochure for my first show."

"I don't know how you could sell something this special. Wouldn't it be like selling one of your children?"

"Yes and no. I paint because I love to paint. I love the freedom of expression it allows me. Having someone else like it enough to buy it massages a different part of my ego. I like the validation it represents and the compliment it expresses and of course, ego massage is always nicest when accompanied by a large check."

Jean had been brushing her hair while they talked until it was dry and shiny. Paul touched her hair with the back of his hand. "I can think of a few parts of you I might like to rub."

She looked up at him, eyes aglow. Any inhibitions she might have harbored had long since set sail. "We've been dancing around this for the last two days."

He placed his hands on Jean's shoulders and moved them slowly down her arms. Her skin shivered under his touch. "You certainly are direct," he pulled her to him meeting her lips with his own. The swelling of his manhood pressed against her as she returned his kiss. His hands gathered up the thin dress she was wearing and raised it until he was touching her skin. Jean broke away from his kiss and looked dreamily into his eyes. "Why don't we go to the other room where we can bring this to its proper conclusion?"

"Sure, but not if I have to let go of you to manage it."

Turning slowly to put her back to him, she guided his hand up to cup her breast. "This should work, don't you think? If you don't get me someplace I can lie down I'm going to collapse in a puddle."

"Total meltdown?"

"If I don't get these clothes off the outside and you on the inside I may go crazy."

"I've been alone a long time. Let's slow down enough so

we can enjoy this, starting with undressing each other," he said, pulling her dress over her head. He picked her up and carried her into the bedroom and laid her on the rumpled counterpane.

"Wait," she said, "let me do my part too." She unbuttoned his shirt and pulled it over his shoulders. A moment later he stepped out of his pants. The last garments found their way to the floor and Paul slid gently inside her.

16.

TIM WATCHED THROUGH THE LAYERS OF DIRT AND
salt on the glass while the detectives and lab crew combed
the grounds. It took a moment to recognize Cal as a deep
cover operator freshly returned from the dark side. Watching
them trace the sentinel's steps made him glad he had restricted
his movements to stepping stones and concrete walks. He
was impressed by the talent of the young deputy who found
and followed the trail. He mentally warned himself not to
underestimate the abilities of the detectives. He breathed
easier when the group cleared the scene and he shifted his
observations to the campground and watched Pisces pan her
camera across the cabins. She characteristically searched for
her quarry by using video tape photographs taken through a
powerful lens for immediate review and study. Her presence
and the police scouring the area meant he either had to change
location or take her out. He didn't understand why she was
here. Paul was the only one who knew about their relationship
and she was supposed to be retired. An emotional surf of sweet
memories crashed over him.

Gathered at Alexander's store, John reviewed what he
had pieced together. His voice carried to the Eurasian man
wandering through the store. "It looks like we hit the jackpot
for the murder scene. I talked with McAfee again, but he looks

less and less like a suspect. He's smart and glib, but I don't think he's a killer."

"Tom and I found a faint trace of at least one person walking through the yard in back," Cal said. "It looks like whoever it was knew how to cover his tracks and conceal his movement. Tracking him was like playing connect the dots."

"Yeah," Tom piped up eagerly. "There would be a place where he had stood, then another maybe twenty feet away. Only a few bent blades of grass between where he stood for a while."

John nodded. "Sounds like the Special Forces guys I knew. Move a short distance, then pause to look for any sign of discovery. Sometimes not move for a half hour or longer. Very patient, very stealthy, and very deadly."

"Only somebody still managed to sneak up and nail him," Cal said. "If the victim was wearing gray, then the blue fibers we found on the top of the fence were probably left by the killer."

"Okay," Tom said. "Let me see if I follow you guys. I was still wearing Pampers when Viet Nam ended, but it sounds like you think both these guys were trained by the military to move without being seen or heard and to kill silently. I think the idea was to dispose of the body without leaving any way to identify it. Am I correct in thinking this guy is really good?"

"Good?" John said. "Good doesn't give him half the credit he deserves. Silent and deadly! Kill in a crowd without being seen! I also think the killer may be in a totally defensive posture."

Tom's eyes sparkled as the picture came clear to him. "You mean you think the killer hasn't left the area?"

"Now you get it!"

"You may be right," Cal agreed. "We don't have any idea

who the stiff was after. McAfee looks like a prime candidate because of where the stiff got his ticket punched, but we still don't have anything to connect him to the crime. We've talked to everyone in the neighborhood and they all seem to be in the clear. Maybe we missed someone."

"Know who we missed?" John asked.

"Nobody," Tom answered.

"Yes we did," John insisted. "We missed the one person we really need to find."

Tom smiled. "The killer?"

"The killer."

"Any ideas where we should start looking?" Cal inquired.

"He could be watching us right now, maybe even listening in on our conversation. This guy is good. We don't know who he is, where he is, why he killed this guy, or what he'll do next. I talked to the guys at auto theft this morning. They say the pickup and camper are whole new experience. If it belongs to the victim, he was prepared to go to war. Money, weapons, explosives, electronic bugging devices, and booby traps someone disabled before we got there. The damn thing looks like it was built by the CIA."

Tom leaned back in his chair. "What would someone with those qualifications be doing here?"

"Answer that and you'll solve this case." Cal replied.

John struck the table with his fist. "Exactly! We need to think about who would send a professional killer. You also have to wonder if they'll send another."

Tom looked toward the campground. "I wonder if there are any new arrivals? Maybe I should have a look around."

"Go for it. We'll make another pass through the neighborhood and see who else we can talk to. Meet us back here in an hour."

Tom scanned the campground for any changes since his last visit. The red Jeep Cherokee hadn't been in the park the previous day. There was nothing to make it stand out from the crowd. The paint was fading, the tires half worn, and it bore the scars of being driven off-road. Under the brush scrapes and scratches it looked well maintained. The exhaust pipe was clean, no oil had sprayed across the rear panels and it looked like a thousand other Jeeps. He wrote down the Arizona license plate. The campsite was neatly arranged with a dome tent, camp stove, large ice chest, lantern, and a grub box for pots, pans and utensils. Tom saw nothing noteworthy or unusual about the site as he approached, looking for, but not seeing the occupant.

Her uneasiness was not from exhaustion. Someone was watching her. Pisces was accustomed to attracting attention, but her appearance was also her best camouflage because people don't expect a beautiful woman to deliver a death warrant. This wasn't the clandestine glance of a stranger admiring her; the observer knew her. She wasn't ruling out other possibilities, but she was increasingly certain Tim was watching her. She studied each of the cabins visible from the east shore of the lagoon by turning the camera slowly on its tripod.

The long lens brought Tom's face close enough for her to see no lines creased his youthful brow and the small laugh lines at the corners of his eyes were only beginning to form. She assessed him carefully, trying to learn as much as possible from his demeanor and carriage.

Pisces aimed the camera at the south end of the lagoon and watched Tom in her peripheral vision. Through the camera she saw John and Cal leave the store and walk toward the cabins on the bluff. Taking her eye from the viewfinder, she watched Tom approach through the last fifty feet of tall grass.

"Good morning," Tom greeted her.

"Good morning," she replied. She could see he was surprised to discover the person behind the camera was a startlingly pretty woman. Her camouflage patterned billed cap covered all but a small billowing fringe of medium brown hair and her denim jacket and loose fitting pants concealed a sleek athletic figure she had spent years honing into a deceptively powerful weapon.

"I'm Deputy Tom Schroeder," he presented his identification. "Taking pictures for the folks back home?"

"I'm a professional photographer. I'm working on a project I hope to publish soon. I've been gathering material for several years and I plan to edit the final copy when I get home."

"Where's home?"

"Tucson, Arizona."

"You're a long way from home."

"Tucson is a good central location, I travel all over the United States and Mexico."

"Have I seen your work?"

"My by-line can show up in magazines or almost any newspaper if one of my pictures is picked up by the wire services."

"So what's your by-line?"

"A. Rose."

"I've seen it! I could never tell whether the photographer was a man or a woman. So A. Rose is, uh, like a pen name?"

"Gender bias is real, a neutral name opens doors to more markets."

"What's your real name?"

"Margarita Julia Eloisa Rosales."

"Wow, what a mouthful. Is your family from Mexico?"

"My father's family is from Madrid by way of Guadalajara

and Texas. My mother was enamored of the way the Spanish name their children so I got a whole string of names instead of the usual one or two, but she always called me Julie."

"You don't look Mexican."

"The line was pure Spanish until my father decided to marry an American girl from Kansas, making me an all American mutt."

"The bloodlines do get confused."

"I've concluded the primary reason for concerns about lines of heritage is to justify a prejudice or to maintain some social strata. I don't have time for such silliness."

"This's a video camera, isn't it? Are you working on a video production?"

"Yes and no. It's a video camera, but I can make high quality stills from the video frames. I use a still camera most of the time, but today I'm doing background work to get a feel for the location, it's really beautiful."

"It's always been one of my favorite places. Did you arrive this morning?"

"I did." Julie paused, locking Tom's eyes. "Tell me deputy, does the Sheriff's Department greet all new arrivals or am I getting special attention?"

"Oops! Sorry, I should explain. We had an incident here a couple days ago, so everybody's getting closer attention."

"An incident?"

"Dead body on the beach."

Pisces face lit up in a bright smile. "Do I get to be a suspect? I thought maybe you were working up to making a pass at me and now, well, now I'm disappointed."

A blush spread across Tom's face. "No, not really a, uh, suspect, uh, look I'm married, and I, uh, in a case like this we have to make sure we talk to everyone we can. I didn't mean to imply,"

Pisces' smile erupted in tinkling laughter. "Relax. I'm just having some fun. I just got in and it was a long trip. I got delayed at the start and I've been trying to make up for lost time ever since. I'd like to help you, but I really don't know what I can tell you, other than I think I'm really going to like working in such a beautiful place."

"People have been photographing these beaches and forests for more than a hundred years, yet somehow each photograph offers a new perspective, a different play of light and shadow. I think it's because the forest is always growing, changing, moving with the will of the seasons."

Pisces' assessment of Tom altered as she listened to him speak. "I see you have a true appreciation for your surroundings. I like the way you describe things. You have the eye of an artist."

"Thank you, it's easy to talk about something you love." Tom glanced at his watch. "I'd love to stay and talk but since I've already managed to put my foot in my mouth, I think I'll tuck my tail between my legs and slink back to work. I hope your project is a big success. I'll watch for it in the book store."

"With a bit of luck it should be ready for Christmas."

"If you want to get in touch with me, here's my phone number at the office. They can always find me." Tom wrote the number on a page of his notebook and tore it off. "I don't have a business card because I usually work a patrol car. Good luck with your project. Maybe you could send me a card announcing it." He turned and walked toward the campground.

Pisces took a deep breath and turned back to her camera. Someone was looking back at her, but she hadn't been able to identify the observer or his location. If she was being watched her mission was compromised. She\had to either locate the observer or prove the itchy feeling was a matter of exhaustion and nervous tension. Swinging the camera across the water to view the beach, she panned along the length of the sand bar. No one seemed to be taking any notice of her. Perhaps the only person who had noticed her arrival was the deputy. She was a little disappointed he had noticed her. His knowledge of her presence was a stumbling block she would rather have avoided, but there was no point in worrying about it. Their meeting happened because it was his job to notice things. She believed very little escaped his notice.

She panned across the small subdivision. She went down a mental checklist of where to look for an observer. A discreet location with a clear view and no chance of a surprise visit from the owner would be perfect. She searched for any indication of absentee owners. She knew studying the tape frame-by-frame would reveal volumes. She blinked her eyes in an effort to wash away the overwhelming drowsiness, but exhaustion was taking its toll. She folded her tripod and walked toward her camp.

John and Cal awaited Tom at the car.

"See anyone new?" John asked.

"Just a photographer working on a book."

"Anyone we would know?" Cal asked. "Or just another pretty face?"

"I've seen her stuff in magazines. Her by-line is A. Rose."

"By-line?" Cal grinned. "As in 'photo by'?"

"Yeah."

Cal's smile widened, his eyes twinkling in unconcealed amusement. "That's her name? A. Rose? Did you find out anything important, or were you too busy thinking with the little head instead of the big one?"

"Her name is Margarita Julia Eloisa Rosales. She goes by Julie."

John grinned at Cal and held out his hand. "Pay up! I told you he would at least get her name."

Cal handed John a dollar. "All right, he kept his composure long enough to get her name." Then, to Tom, "Did you learn anything important?"

"What is this? You guys had a bet I couldn't do a simple ID interview?"

"Well, Cal's eyes are pretty good. Even from this distance he could tell she was a pretty lady. I stood up for you! I told him even with a stiff dick you'd still have enough blood getting to your brain to ask her name while you were enjoying a mental blow job."

"Thanks. I should tell you both to go fuck yourselves. In fact," Tom punched Cal's shoulder. "Fuck you and your dollar." He delivered John a similar jab. "Fuck you and your mental blow job." He thumbed through his notebook. "Here's what I noticed between drooling and ejaculations. She drives a Jeep Cherokee with Arizona plates. She keeps an organized camp. She's using a studio quality video camera with a long distance zoom lens. If she's watching us now she can probably count the hairs in your five o'clock shadow. She says she's doing background material for a book she's getting ready for print. She says she travels a lot. The Jeep is no virgin and has the scratches to prove it. She isn't wearing a wedding band or any other jewelry. She's about five feet, three inches tall, probably a hundred ten pounds, brown hair, green eyes, graceful hands and fingers, well tended nails without polish. She arrived this morning too road weary to sleep. She's a very pretty lady and if I wasn't married I would probably plead guilty to all the stupid ideas you two imagined in your childish flights of fancy."

"I think he'll do with a little training and experience." John said to Cal.

Cal winked at Tom. "You may be right but let's not tell him. We don't want the big head to swell up the way the little one did."

"May the fleas of a thousand camels and the crabs from a dozen pest ridden whores infest your pubic hair," Tom suggested, drawing laughter from the detectives.

John started the car. "Well girls, enough fun, let's get back to the office and see what the techno-nerds can tell us about the pickup. Maybe their work will have paid off."

Four pairs of eyes followed the car as it disappeared into the trees.

17.

OBNOXIOUS CURIOSITY IS A DESIRABLE TRAIT IN A policeman, but it made controlling access to the pickup and camper a constant challenge. A rear corner of the courthouse garage had been cordoned off with crime scene tape to help control access and for two days they had meticulously dismantled the vehicle while fending off the badge carrying snoops and other curious occupants of the Courthouse.

Vince Freitas grew up on a local dairy ranch where he spent his youth tearing apart farm equipment and reassembling it in better condition than when he started. Trucks, cars, tractors, balers, mowers, manure spreaders, and milk machines were all fair game. By Vince's sixteenth birthday his father had abandoned hope of making him into a dairyman. To celebrate his twenty-fifth birthday, armed with a degree in mechanical engineering from Oregon State, automotive repair credentials from Arizona Institute of Technology and two years experience in George Barris' custom shop, he joined the Sheriff's Department, rolled his toolbox into a corner of the basement and created a new investigative department devoted to all things mechanical and electrical. In five years devoted to this unique specialty, he had investigated hundreds of vehicles, but the battered pickup and camper from the lagoon was a Pandora's box filled with Pandora's boxes like nothing he had seen. Vince had his head inside the engine compartment studying how to access a compartment hidden in a hollow between the inner and outer body panels when he heard Cal's voice.

"Hey sport, is this area closed to everyone who didn't grow up with cow shit between their toes, or can any old portagee stick his nose in?"

Vince raised his head far enough to see Cal, John and Tom standing at the tape looking like dedicated fans reaching out to touch their favorite film star. "Well, looking at you guys, all I see is a mick, a kraut, and a shithead who thinks he can turn respectable with a shave and a haircut. None of you even qualify."

"What if I offer to buy you a beer?" asked Cal.

"It might make a difference, but what about the other two clowns? They'll want to touch everything and contaminate my evidence"

"Don't worry," John replied. "I promise to keep my hands in my pockets and handcuff the kid to my belt to keep him in line."

"Well, if you promise to be good."

Cal ducked under the tape. "Fuck you! You're working our case, so let's see what you've got. Presuming, of course, you've actually got anything!"

"Oh, I got something, all right. I've got so many somethings I'm not sure where to start. You already know the legal papers on the pickup are in order and lead absolutely nowhere. The address on the registration is a lot that's been vacant ever since the house burned down ten years ago and the owner died in the fire. All the heirs are in Europe and are squabbling over the title.

"The truck is a composite. The original frame was modified to suit special needs. So far we've found a bunch of compartments concealed throughout the body and frame. All the components were assembled to look like factory originals. This is a beautiful job."

"What's in the compartments?" John asked.

"So far, the money you already know about, a high tech bow and arrow, a bunch of electronic listening devices, and three complete sets of ID, all of which are dead ends. I also found two more booby traps, both disabled."

"I thought it looked like good work," Cal said. "Anything actually useful to our case?"

"I did come up with some usable partial prints. We sent them to NCIC, but no match so far. Dennis thinks they look like a match for the stiff, so you can probably presume the floater and the driver of this pickup are the same."

"Well, all right!" John exclaimed. "Things are beginning to fit together."

"Yeah, but does this tell us who killed the guy and why?" Tom asked. "So far we still don't know who he is, why he was there, who mashed his melon, or who dumped him in the ocean. We found where he got bashed, and where he came over the fence, but where are his clothes, and what was he up to? If the pieces are fitting together, why am I so damn confused about what the hell is going on?"

John looked at Tom, smiled, then from deep down came a hearty belly laugh. He was joined almost immediately by Vince and Cal. Tom stared tight lipped at the three men. A flush reddened his cheeks, gradually becoming anger as the laughter continued. "All right, you assholes! What's so damn funny? It looks to me like we're all chasing our tails, so how about letting me in on the joke."

"Ah Tommy, me lad." John put his arm around Tom's shoulder and managed to choke out the words through his slowly fading laughter. "In a murder investigation, any time something fits together is cause for celebration. You being frustrated and confused by all the unanswered questions just struck us funny. No matter how much you learn there are always more unanswered questions. Sometimes we just have to take advantage of the wag method of solving the crime."

"The wag method?"

"Yeah, sometimes you have to play a hunch. Take a wild ass guess."

"Wild ass guess, W, A, G. The wag method. Okay, why don't you just take a wild ass guess and tell me what the hell is going on?"

"So, what do you think Cal? Got any wild ass guesses about what might be at the bottom of this pile of crap?"

"Well, how about this for a wag? Victim and vehicle arrived a few days ago. The victim skulks about in search of his prey, whoever it might be. He is deeply engrossed in being a midnight marauder when prey becomes predator and punches his ticket. The object of his attention hauls his body to the beach, peels his duds, and sets him adrift for the undertow and tide to drag him offshore so mother ocean's little creatures can dispose of the evidence. Two things may have happened. The killer is surprised in the process of cleaning up his trail and has to duck for cover before he's able to set the body clearly out to sea. Maybe the body looks like it's being carried out, but the tide or the current brings it back and the surf tosses it on the beach. The timing is tight because the body's lividity indicates it hit the beach within an hour or so after death. What we don't know is how long the stiff survived after the blow to the head. We know the victim was dead when he was tossed into the surf. The killer either split for his hidey hole or left the area. Two days later, enter a famous photographer who immediately begins a video survey of the area. There's nothing necessarily suspicious about her activity, but she's doing her research from a goodly distance with a lens able to find a flea on a shaggy dog at three thousand yards. Is this simply coincidence? I think our victim may be a contractor who underestimated his target. His truck says he wasn't an amateur and probably didn't work cheap. I may be going off the deep end, but I think our case is a pimple on the butt of something really big."

Confusion once again puckered Tom's forehead. "What makes you think so?"

"Mostly a feeling. You have to be paranoid when you work undercover because paranoia keeps you alert and alive. Maybe it's the confusion factor. Maybe it's the lack of evidence to tie things together. Maybe I'm out in left field, but I keep having a premonition we've either brushed up against organized crime or an operation with a well oiled and well financed organization behind it. Take our man on vacation, um, McAfee. What business is he in?"

"He imports computer components," John answered.

"There you go! Imports, smuggling, drugs, organized crime, all go together, don't they?"

"You think Paul McAfee is a smuggler?" asked Tom.

"It's one possibility. His partner went missing a while back didn't he?"

"I followed up on his story," John said. "His wife and his partner were both in the PSA crash a couple years ago. No survivors. The story is some disgruntled ex-employee was pissed at his ex-boss, so he blew the plane out of the sky to get even with the airline. The guy still had his gate pass and walked right onto the ramp with the bomb in a suitcase and loaded it on the airplane. They subsequently tightened up security procedures and tossed the guy in the looney bin, but the passengers and crew are still dead."

"A case of closing the barn door after the horse escapes," Tom said.

"Okay," Cal said. "Let's give McAfee the benefit of the doubt. Let's say his partner is the smuggler. McAfee has no knowledge of said smuggling, but then his partner and wife end up dead in a plane crash. He descends into grief and depression, hires a management firm to run the company, flees here for six months of R & R. Why here? If he wants to escape his troubles, why not go someplace warm and tropical? Why not another country? Why is it, as soon as he arrives, life gets real exciting in a sleepy, out of the way place like the lagoon? Why does it look like he arrived with a contract killer on his heels? A contractor with the bad luck to get his head busted right alongside McAfee's cabin. This many coincidences have an aroma and it sure as hell don't smell like fresh coffee."

"More pungent?" John raised an eyebrow.

"Like a contract hit gone sour. Maybe a killer still in the vicinity, gone to ground, laying low, waiting for the attention to die down so he can melt into the background and disappear. I felt like we were being watched today and not by the sweety with the Sony. I never saw anybody, but I could feel eyes on me. All the hair on my neck was standing straight up."

"What about you Tom? Do I see more confusion on your face, or did you just experience some sort of epiphany?" John asked.

Tom paused several seconds with a faraway look on his face, then spoke softly. "What if McAfee's partner wasn't on the airplane when it crashed? What if he didn't get on the airplane? What if he turned in his boarding pass, but instead of getting on the plane he used the crowd of people saying their good-byes to slip out of line and leave the airport? What if the people he was working for know he's alive and are looking for him? What if they're using Paul McAfee as a stalking horse, believing sooner or later his partner will get in touch with him? What if McAfee's partner is at the lagoon right now? What if he's the one who snuffed the stiff on the beach? And while we're doing all this what-iffing," Tom looked pointedly at Cal. "What if McAfee's partner is not really a bad guy, but an undercover cop?"

Cal, Vince and John paused a moment as Tom's theory sank in. "Oh shit!" they chorused.

18.

JEAN WAS BASKING IN THE GLOW OF THEIR
lovemaking when she felt a tear drop onto her neck. She drew back and Paul rolled onto his back and covered his eyes. Jean watched another tear trickle down the side of his face. "Hey, big fella, the lady is supposed to be teary at a time like this. What gives?"

Paul wiped his eyes. "I was thinking of Lisa. Being with you has stirred up all these crazy emotions. I'm sorry."

Jean was swept up in the tenderness of Paul's emotions. She wondered what it was like to be loved so deeply even death could not sever the bonds of the heart. "You don't need to apologize for how you feel. Feelings aren't good or bad, they just are. We can't control how we feel. We can only learn to live with our feelings."

"It's confusing wanting to be with you when I still miss her so much."

"I don't expect you to stop missing her, but don't feel guilty because you miss her. You are who you are because she's a part of your life. I'm here with you because of who you are and because she's a part of you. She may be gone, but she'll always be welcome with us, I just don't want her to come between us."

"You're making this too easy for me."

"You're tough enough on yourself. I don't need to add to the load."

"I wish you could have known each other. I think you would have been good friends."

"I do know her, she's a part of you." Jean kissed him tenderly and they lay back on the rumpled sheets in each other's arms.

Tim maintained his vigil as the sun made it's long summer journey across the sky. He was happy to see Paul disappear into the end cabin at mid-afternoon. There was still no visible activity around the cottage. He hoped Paul had found some happiness. He worried about the challenge presented by Pisces' arrival. Pisces was never sent to retrieve anyone, she made people disappear. She was one of the best. He knew she wasn't filming pictures to publish. She was doing high-resolution reconnaissance photography. "I didn't need this!" he muttered under his breath. He looked again at the pile of bloody clothing in the corner of the attic. "Speaking of stuff I didn't need, how the hell am I going to get rid of this stuff? You end up on the beach after your little skinny dip, and I end up with your bloody clothes." *Now Julie's looking for me. How do I keep her from finding me? How do I move without her seeing me? C'mon, make it rain, or make it foggy, just give me some cover.* At that moment he saw Pisces walk out into the lowering sunlight.

Pisces stretched her arms, touched her toes, stood with arms extended above her head and twisted from side to side. The nap had helped, but she was still bone tired and decided to take a swim before going back to work.

The top couple feet of the briny water was warm. She felt the weariness drain from her as the water washed over her and her body rhythms increased in response to the exertion. After a hundred yards, she rolled onto her back, breathed deeply and relaxed for the first time in days. Her mind drifted to memories of the times she and Tim had shared. It seemed they always met somewhere far from home. *How did you manage to get yourself in this fix? How do I make you trust me when you know who I am?* Shaking off those thoughts, she set a vigorous pace for the beach.

19.

SHERIFF KERRY WESTON WAS AN IMPRESSIVE figure at six feet four, two hundred thirty-five pounds. Physically intimidating, his steady gaze and confident manner could set people at ease, if they were innocent. In a business suit he looked more like a banker than a cop. He enjoyed the respect and loyalty of the men and women of his command because they knew what he expected. Step over the line and he'd deal with you forthwith. You always knew where you stood with him.

Weston set aside the papers he was reading. "Do you have something new for me on your floater or did you just drop in for coffee and donuts?"

"We need your help, boss," John announced. "Tom's raised a question that could have a bearing on how we handle this case. He'll lay it out for you."

"Well," Tom began. "We were reviewing what we know and what it might mean and I suggested the killer might be a cop. Maybe undercover for the FBI or some other agency."

The chair creaked softly as the Weston leaned back. "Okay, which one of you old salts fostered this off the wall idea?"

"It was my idea," Tom said. "I was speculating about McAfee's partner, who supposedly was killed in the same airline crash as his wife. It just dawned on me, what if the guy never got on the plane? What if someone was looking for him by using McAfee as a compass? It just popped into my head.

What if the guy's a cop? These guys said we needed to ask you to help."

"Do you guys agree with him?"

"Boss," Cal and John spoke together.

"Go ahead Cal," John said.

"Okay. Look, if this guy is a deep undercover operator who's gone to ground, he may try to contact his partner. The bad guys may think if they tie a tail on McAfee his best friend will surface and they can grab him. If he's deep cover for the FBI, CIA, DEA, or some other agency, you can bet they're looking for him too, and aren't gonna tell us about it. Maybe if you could press one of your low friends in high places to confirm or reject the idea we could avoid chasing down a lot of blind alleys, or maybe keep from screwing up somebody's clandestine operation worse than it already may be."

"All right," Weston said. "Let's take a look at your idea. We have a respected businessman who is a deep cover operative. He's in a hot spot and needs to disappear. He doesn't get on the airplane with his partner's wife and the plane is bombed out of the sky, killing everyone on board. Assume the bomb was supposed to kill him and the rest of the passengers just happened to be in the wrong place at the right time. It's a bit of a stretch, but let's go with it anyway. After a couple years his partner comes here for an extended vacation and the bad guys follow him. Within a couple days after McAfee's arrival their man gets himself killed right outside his cabin. McAfee has an airtight alibi, being down the block making nice with his new neighbor. The bad guys know their man on the scene is terminal. McAfee doesn't know anything or at least isn't telling us anything. Neither are any of the neighbors. We have a naked body with a massive skull fracture, a pickup perfect for James Bond, and no positive ID on the victim. For the sake of argument, let's speculate he's one of the bad guys. We have evidence both the stiff and person or persons unknown came over the fence during the night in question. McAfee's not a suspect and neither is the artist because they were busy sharing pheromones when the deed went down. The little old neighbor lady who would rather be left alone is an unlikely suspect because of her age and size. You come up with the notion there is a secret agent in the form of one Tim Gordon who's managed to dodge detection for two years and is trying to make contact with his partner. Add the possibility he may have bumped off the floater to keep him from getting to his old friend. How am I doing so far?"

"I know it sounds kinda, uh, out there," Tom said. "But,"

Weston held up his hand. "Take it easy. I didn't say the notion was without merit. I was just recapping to make sure I understand where your line of thought began and where it may be headed. So I ask again, how am I doing?"

"Pretty much covers it," John said.

"Neither of you old fossils put him up to this did you?"

"No!" John and Cal responded in unison.

"Good. You're absolutely right, Tom, the whole idea sounds crazy." Weston held his hand up again as Tom began to speak. "You also could be right. Knowing you came up with it on your own has made up my mind. I'll pursue this with the feds. In the meantime Cal, I'm assigning you to a new detail."

"I just got started on this case."

"I know, but John doesn't need you and Pete Holland does. I'm putting you and Dutch together, effective tomorrow morning. He's working a homicide down on the South Fork of the Eel."

"What about Mike?"

"You remember he applied for the Police Chief job in Angel's Camp? He resigned today to take the job. Since Mike is moving on to greener pastures, you get teamed with Dutch."

"You're the boss," Cal said.

"Thank you for reaffirming the obvious. My wife is probably the only person in the county who doesn't share your opinion. Now, moving on to another matter. John, what do you think of Tom as a detective?"

"He's shown a lot of good sense and asked a lot of the right questions the past two days. I think he might be ready to apply for the job someday, you know, in maybe four or five years, but I'm really not very excited about trying to train a green, slick armed rookie."

Tom's face turned dark red as he listened. "Thanks a lot," he mumbled under his breath.

Weston turned to Tom. "You were saying?"

"Nothing."

"If it was nothing I wouldn't have heard it. Now what was it?"

"I said, thanks a lot," Tom replied petulantly.

"Well, detective, whatever sort of pissing match you and your new partner deem necessary, how about you take it out of my office."

"Pissing match, new partner, out of the office, detective," Tom mumbled. Suddenly his eyes lit up, his mouth fell open, and he stared at the tall man.

"The promotion list is so fresh it hasn't been posted yet, but the guy in the number one spot has been reassigned, effective immediately, as John Ragsdale's new partner. Congratulations, Tom." Weston shook Tom's hand.

Cal and John congratulated Tom on his promotion.

"Okay, Detective, Junior Grade," John commanded. "As

your first detail, I could use a cup of coffee, so hustle out and make sure it's still hot when you get back with it."

"Oh, I'll make sure it's hot enough to warm you all the way to your heart when I spill it on you. How about you boss?"

"I'll take a rain check. You guys get back to work."

20.

THE GENERATOR DRONED IN THE BACKGROUND AS
Pisces reviewed the videotape. The detailed search, frame by
frame, was mind-numbing, eye-burning drudgery. Meticulously
examining the contents of each frame was exquisite torture,
until a discovery made the process worthwhile.

Patiently rolling the tape forward and backward, noting
locations for closer study, she worked through the footage three
times. Four hours melted away and night rolled across the
landscape, bringing a damp chill to invade her tent. Stepping
outside, she stretched, yawned and checked the fuel tank on the
generator. The generator made her feel vulnerable. The exhaust
had been modified to near silence, but enough sound remained
to mask the approach of an intruder. She shivered uneasily
with the continuing sensation that she was being observed. She
allowed her eyes to achieve full night vision while she walked
around her camp to circulate blood through cramped muscles.
She had studied with an instructor for the blind to learn how
to use her other senses rather than depending upon her sight.
A side benefit was a heightened sense of an observer's attention
focused on her. Trusting her instincts had saved her skin more
than once, but tonight something was different about what she
sensed lurking in the darkness. She was convinced if Tim was
indeed watching, he wasn't the only observer. She felt a curious
comfort in realizing there was more than a single pair of eyes
spying on her. A glance at her watch told her it was already

an hour into a new day. She shut down the video viewer and generator and retired to her cot.

In the surrounding darkness, three pairs of eyes watched the activity in the campsite wink out. The ghostly motion of an animal traveling on two legs vanished into the shadows of the forest.

The Don tossed from side to side, ending up staring at the shadows on the ceiling. Sleep remained an elusive prey, giggling in the corners just beyond his reach. Insomnia wasn't unusual; his sleep patterns had become erratic in his later years. Tonight made it two days with no word from his grandson. When they had last spoken, Pisces was on her way, and it looked like the months of frustration might finally end, but now it had been two days of uncharacteristic silence. Joey knew it was important to report what was happening. He picked up the telephone and punched the speed dial.

Gino grabbed the phone on the second ring, his voice rough with sleep. "Yes?"

"You heard from Joey?"

The voice brought him fully awake. "No, sir."

"What about his girlfriend? She heard anything?"

"No, sir. She called this evening to ask if I knew where Joey was because she hasn't seen him and got the answering machine when she called him."

"Do you think he might have gone up north to check up on Pisces?"

"Possibly, but he didn't say anything to me about it. Did he mention it to you?"

"No. I'd have forbidden it if he had. He's not supposed to put himself at risk. He isn't prepared for it. He isn't ready."

"Yeah, but he's young and he thinks he's invulnerable and

he wants to make his mark. It's a stupid idea, but he might have."

"I remember what it is to be young, and I leaned on him pretty hard about failing to bring Gordon in, but if he gets too close to Pisces he could be in trouble. She'd not look kindly on an intrusion and he's not prepared to deal with her one on one. I don't want his absence to be permanent. Do you think you can find him?"

"Yes, but I don't know how fast. If he gets in her face she's likely to deal with him first and dispose of the evidence afterward."

"You make sure that doesn't happen."

"Yes, sir." The phone clicked in his ear followed by a dial tone. "Well, crap," he muttered.

"What is it honey?" his wife gently rubbed his back.

"Joey's done something dumb and now I gotta go clean things up, again."

"When do you have to leave?"

"If my hunch is right, he's about seven hundred miles north of here and right in the middle of where he doesn't belong. I gotta to get there before it gets very late in the day."

"You want me to help you pack?"

"Sure. I gotta shower and wake up. Where I'm going I need my Levis and sweatshirts. Pack a suit for me just in case, but I think I'll be more worried about staying warm and dry than about looking dapper."

Throwing back the covers, they both stood up and started across the room. Halfway to the bathroom, he felt her hand on his arm and he stopped. She put her arms around his neck and hugged him. "Be careful, honey," she whispered. "I love you."

He hugged her and kissed the top of her head. "I'm always careful. I love you too." He walked into the bathroom, dropping his shorts on the floor as he entered the room. "Oh, yeah," he said leaning through the door, "would you call and charter an airplane for me? Tell them I need to go almost to Oregon. The number's in my Rolodex; Dragonfly Aviation."

She watched him disappear into the bathroom. "Please come home to me," she whispered, trying to ignore the foreboding sense of doom creeping over her like a wintry cloud.

21.

THE BLANKET OF FOG SLITHERED ASHORE,
enveloping the cabins like a feeding amoeba, layering surfaces
with dew, chilling the air and severely limiting visibility. Tim
thanked whatever deity was smiling down on him. About two
and a half hours before the first rays of sunlight would begin
to dispel the gloom, he grabbed the blood stained clothing,
slipped out of the cabin, and headed for the tall timber.

The fog had softened the dried leaves, silencing their voices
as he crossed them, but his passage left a visible trail. He sensed
he was being followed, but he couldn't see his pursuer. He
patiently waited several minutes in the burned out bole of a
redwood tree, but he saw no sign of an adversary in his wake.
A couple miles of forest separated him from where he had
left his car. He needed to talk to Paul, he needed to dispose
of the bloody clothing, and he needed to eat. A hot fire to
cook breakfast would solve two problems. He was sure he'd
left nothing to connect him to the murder, but it was only a
matter of time before the detectives discovered his hideout.
He was certain Pisces would discover his hideout. He needed
a new observation post and he needed to connect with Paul
long enough to set their plans in motion. He exited his hiding
place and drifted silently through the misty shadows.

Tom was playing a hunch. His wife wasn't happy about
him going out on his own in the middle of the night to try

to catch a murderer, but he convinced her not to make a scene. After three hours he was chilled to the bone and still hadn't seen anything happening where they had found the trail to the murder scene. He was stifling a yawn when a shadowy figure emerged and trotted toward the trees. *Don't try to do anything alone,* he told himself as he followed. He found footprints in the dew and slowed his pace. He paused in the shadow of a cabin to plan his next move. He expected his quarry to stop and watch his back trail from concealment in the trees. In a couple hours the sky would pale with dawn, but darkness was on the side of man he was following.

Fifteen chilly minutes later, Tom had worked his way to the edge of the trees, where shadows reduced visibility enough to make continuing unwise. He studied the ground and saw what looked like a print in the leaf mold, but continuing his pursuit felt like a trap waiting to close on him.

Tom marked a salal bush for reference and retraced his steps to the store. "Ten minutes to three," he mused. "He should have slept enough by now."

The phone brought John fully awake before he could snatch the handset from its cradle and growl, "Ragsdale!"

"Rise and shine partner. We got work to do and we're burning daylight while you're napping!"

"It's three o'clock in the damn morning! What the hell can't wait until the rest of the world wakes up?"

"I've been working while you've been getting your beauty sleep and the world will be turning daylight in about an hour and a half. With all due respect for your age, experience, and need for a beauty treatment, I figured it'd take you at least that long to shit, shave, shampoo, shower, and shag your tired old ass up here."

"Jesus Christ! You make detective and you give up sleeping?"

"I had a hunch and so far it's playing out. I may have the found the killer's trail, but I need to follow it in the daylight with someone to cover my own tired ass. As of yesterday, it's your job."

Suddenly Tom had John's full attention. "What you got, kid?"

"I spotted a guy coming out of the vacant cabin behind the murder scene and trailed him to the trees before I let discretion be the better part of valor and broke off the pursuit. I wasn't going to follow him into the timber on a foggy night."

"Have you been there all night?"

"Pretty much. I got to thinking whoever was watching us wasn't going to move until it was dark and visibility was lousy. You told me to put myself in the other guy's shoes and when I saw the fog rolling in, it seemed like a perfect situation. I thought about calling you, but if it was a wild goose chase there was no need for both of us to be cold and tired and frustrated. I took a chance and played my hunch. I got lucky, but I need you to watch my back before I try to follow him any further. The fog is pea soup, so prepare for a slow trip."

John pulled the curtain aside to check the weather. "It's pretty thick here too. I'm on my way as soon as I can saddle up."

"I'll meet you at the store. Mrs. Alexander usually opens her doors about daylight. I'll have fresh coffee and a couple of sinkers to get you going. Dress for work. It looks like we may be going on a hike."

"See you in a little while, and by the way,"

"Yeah?"

"Nice work, partner."

22.

"OAKLAND CENTER, BARON SIX TWO FIVE EIGHT lima alpha."

"Go ahead, lima alpha"

"What are the current conditions at Eureka-Arcata?"

"Eureka-Arcata currently reporting zero-zero, closed to traffic."

"Roger the zero-zero, any forecast when it may open?"

"Unknown. The stratus layer extends from Monterey to Seattle, so it could be a while."

"Roger"

Gino stared at the sea of lights on the floor of the Sacramento-San Joaquin Valley while he listened to the pilot's side of the conversation. To the west the Coast Range mountains formed a boundary wall with the cottony clouds spilling through the passes into the western edge of the great valley. The lights of the San Francisco Bay Area cast a glow through the clouds. "How long before we get to Eureka?"

"Flying time is about an hour, but it could be nine or ten in the morning before the ceiling lifts. It's hard to tell, we may have to lay over somewhere until it clears. How urgent is your meeting?"

"Urgent. Is there anywhere else we can land?"

"There's a VFR runway on the ridge east of Eureka. No fuel, no food, no car rental, but there is a phone."

"Is it big enough for this bird?"

"Plenty of room if it's in the clear."

"So, if we can't land there, do we have enough fuel to make it back to the valley?"

"No sweat. It's only a short hop to Redding, where they're reporting clear."

"What if we go to Redding and I drive the rest of the way?"

"You could, but it's a hundred fifty miles of mountain road from Redding to Arcata. If you're in a hurry, you might as well wait for the fog to lift."

"Okay. Let's go for the ridge runway and see if we get lucky."

"You got it. It's near the outer marker for Eureka-Arcata, we don't even have to go out of our way."

"You think the car rental people will be up when we get there?"

"Gonna try to get someone to pick you up?"

"If they won't come get me I guess I can try to call a cab, or we can wait for the fog to lift."

"Got cash for a big tip?"

"Of course. Cash always works when you need special service, like getting up in the middle of the night to fly someone, right?"

"I do enjoy your phone calls in the middle of the night."

The conversation drifted to fishing and the merits of trout fried over a campfire. The twin engines rumbled a steady tone as the airplane bored a hole through night en route to a ribbon of asphalt perched atop a mountain ridge. In the distance the runway glowed like a precious jewel in the moonlight, an island of welcome, five hundred feet above the clouds.

John strained to see through the swirling mists and talked to himself. "Damn kid! So eager to look good he goes out on an unapproved stakeout! Lucky little shit may have stumbled onto something. I had high hopes, but not this soon!" The entrance to the lagoon suddenly emerged from the gray mist, and he gratefully exited the highway. "You better have a cup of coffee waiting for me or I'm gonna kill you!" he growled as he parked in front of the store.

"That you John?" Tom called from the back of the store.

"Well, it ain't your fairy godmother! Who the hell else would be out at this time of day in this kind of weather?"

"Good morning to you too. It's so nice to see your smiling face so bright and cheery this lovely summer day. C'mon in, there's coffee and donuts so fresh they don't even need to be chewed. Perfect for an old fart like you who probably doesn't have any real teeth left to chew his food."

"Your ass! Where's the coffee?"

Tom pointed toward the pot of fresh brew perched on the warming plate. A large bakery box sat alongside. "They bring in fresh pastry every morning for the fishermen who are too lazy to cook or afraid to wake their wives. Grab what you want and let's talk about what I found."

John sat at the small table and sipped his coffee. "Did you get a good enough look at this mysterious night crawler to to identify him?"

"Nope. Too foggy, too dark, and too far away. But I do know where he came from and where he went into the woods before I decided following him would be stretching my luck into the realm of stupidity. I marked where I saw him last and called for backup."

"Good work." John took another sip of coffee, winced and rubbed his jaw.

"What's up? Burn yourself?"

"No. I chipped a tooth and I've been putting off having

it fixed. Lately it's gotten to be a real pain. I'll be okay. I have a dentist appointment in a couple weeks. Believe it or not, he can't see me any sooner. Look, I appreciate your initiative, but you do realize what you saw may have nothing to do with our case."

"Why else would somebody be creeping around in the middle of the damn night?"

"You were, weren't you?"

"I was on the job!"

"Yes, you were. It still doesn't necessarily mean whoever else is out for a midnight stroll is involved in anything sinister or illegal. Correct me if I'm wrong. Is there a new curfew prohibiting a citizen from being out after dark?"

"I guess it was a pretty dumb idea to stake out the place and call you out before dawn, huh?"

"I didn't say it was dumb, I said it may be unrelated. I also said I appreciate your initiative. As a hot dog maneuver your little midnight adventure might turn out to be a great idea. First we need to see where it leads. Unless one of us has become a professional tracker, there's not much hope of finding his trail through the trees so I suppose we should take a look at the cabin you say he came from, see if we have a reason to get a warrant. Aside from seeing your suspect walk away from the cabin, what do we have in the way of probable cause to believe evidence pertaining to our case might be inside?"

Tom slammed his hand on the table. "Damn! Unless we can come up with a connection, we don't have a right to do anything but look at whatever is in plain sight!"

John watched Tom thrash about with the frustration of finding probable cause when you needed to produce legitimate grounds for a warrant. "Being a detective isn't all sweetness and light, is it? Let's look at what we know. You observed an unidentified person skulking about in the middle of a foggy night in the vicinity of a building whose owners have been absent for the past three months. We know this because we phoned them in Santa Rosa yesterday. Right?"

"Right! We know the owners aren't here and we know they haven't rented the place out so maybe we have a burglary?"

"If we have cause to believe there has been illegal entry we can possibly get a warrant to search. Or, if we have reasonable cause to believe illegal entry has been made, we have a sworn obligation to investigate further regarding such entry!" John winked and smiled.

"Maybe I did all right after all."

"Yeah. Maybe you did all right after all. Are you ready to go take a look or do you need another cup of chain oil to get you moving?"

"It's turning daylight, so I guess we better go to work."

The cabin was two doors down the street from the store. Tom pointed out where he had been standing when he first observed the suspect and where the man had disappeared into the trees. He pointed out the faint tracks across the grass. The trail was fading as more dew condensed, but remained visible if you knew where to look. Backtracking along the fading footprints, they discovered the trail ended at a series of stepping-stones along the south wall of the house leading to a covered rear porch. Other than the tracks leading to the street the layer of dew was pristine.

"It looks like he materialized somewhere along this walkway." John observed.

"He may have stepped off the porch and stayed on the stepping-stones until he made his dash for the trees." Tom shined his flashlight on the porch exposing a single footprint.

"Good observation, Tom. I don't know how fresh the print

is, but I bet it was made since the last storm. It looks like the porch collects wind drift. Did you also notice there are no tracks leading to or from the door?"

"No, there aren't. They stop right under that ceiling hatch."

"Did you bring your camera?"

"It's in my car."

"Good! We need to take some pictures. We can't get to the hatch without walking on these tracks, so let's photograph them before we contaminate our reasonable cause."

"You got it boss!" Tom sprinted away.

"Good work!" John said quietly. "It may be a dead end, but the kid's doing some good work."

The fog was still heavy. Even though the visibility was improving with the burgeoning daylight, Tom's excitement was high and being observed wasn't among his concerns. He gathered up the camera and his spotlight and trotted back to the cabin without noticing the man standing on the store's front porch sipping his coffee as Tom ran past.

"Good thinking," John said. "The more light the better." It took only a few minutes to document the south side of the building and the porch.

The springs on the hatch protested with a rusty squeak when John pulled it down, extending the attached ladder. "Check this out. Someone's been here recently." Tom photographed the clean areas on the otherwise dusty treads.

John craned his neck to see as much of the attic as possible without climbing the stairs. "You know if anybody's up there, the first one to stick his head out could get it taken off."

"Doesn't feel much like a welcome mat, does it?"

"Not exactly, but God hates a coward." He paused when he stepped on the first rung of the ladder. "Tom."

"Yeah?"

"Promise me one thing."

"What?"

"If I stick my head up there and some asshole puts a hole in it, promise me you'll kill the son of a bitch?"

"With pleasure."

John climbed high enough to see into the attic. Shining the spotlight he confirmed the attic was unoccupied. Footprints trailed across the floor, a small area on one window had been rubbed clean, and a lounge pad propped next to the window still showed the imprint of someone sitting on it.

"Someone's been here, but he's gone. C'mon up and take look around. I don't think we need to call the lab crew, but be careful anyway. We may need to send the whiz kids in later."

"I'm right behind you as soon as your butt is no longer blocking the entrance to the cave."

John knelt to peer through the place where the window had been wiped clean. Visibility was restricted by the fog, but he knew the campground would be easily seen from the window. "Good spot to watch the campground. I think whoever was here was interested in what was happening over there."

"How long do you think he hung out here?"

"A day, maybe two. It looks like he took out everything he brought in. Did you find anything?"

"Spider webs and dust. I don't think he was your basic wandering homeless man looking for a place to crash. It may not be a he, but he moved like a man, like an athlete. Smooth, graceful stride, well balanced."

"Remember women can be athletes too. You're probably right about it being a man, but don't let it poison your mind. Let's go have another cup of coffee and talk this over."

John leaned back and sipped his coffee. "Tom, if you were

making off into the tall timber in the darkest part of the night, where would you be going?"

"If I was the guy in the attic? I'd be looking for a new place to lay low."

"Okay, Patrick's Point is only a couple miles. Do you think he might have left some wheels over there?"

"Safe enough place to leave a car, but he would need to register as he went through the gate unless he was a day visitor. They'd just take his money and give him a card to put in the window." His eyes lit up and he snapped his fingers. "The park ranger would notice if a car was still in the park after dark and go looking for the owner. If the owner failed to show, the car would be towed in the morning. If he didn't have an overnight spot, his car wouldn't be there when he came back. Maybe we should go see how many single campers are registered."

"Good idea. There's only one problem."

"What problem?"

"Who are we looking for?"

Tom's excitement withered as suddenly as it had risen. "We really don't know, do we?"

"You tell me. Describe who we're trying to locate."

"So much for another bright idea."

"The curse of the detective. You have an idea just in time to realize it may be a dead end. Most of what we follow up on are dead ends. It's a process of elimination. On the other hand, staying out all night in the fog and drizzle is better than pounding a beat in a patrol car, isn't it?"

"Is it my imagination or are we no closer to solving this case than we were three days ago?"

"We may be further away. The trail begins to get cold after the first forty-eight hours. Forty-eight's come and gone and we're still grasping at straws. We may not be any closer, but we haven't lost the chance to solve the case. Let's take a walk on the beach and start over."

"Do you think we missed something?"

"I'm sure we missed more than one something. The trick is to figure out what we overlooked and what it means."

23.

ELIAS KIMBROUGH DIDN'T LOOK UP FROM THE
daily reports when he reached for the phone. "Federal Bureau of Investigation."

"Good morning, agent Kimbrough. How are things in the wide, wide world of big, bad criminals?"

"Good morning indeed, Kerry, how are you today?" A smile lit up his craggy features. Elias was an all American mutt, born in South Boston to a Japanese/Hawaiian mother and Danish/Scottish/Irish father. Twenty years with the FBI and degrees from Yale and USC had failed to overcome a southy accent. Elias could lose himself in a crowd with his average height, average weight, average looks, but only the most foolish underestimated his intellect.

"Hale and hearty!" Kerry responded. "How about you?"

"Aside from a little arthritis, rather well. How's the family?"

"Too well to be believed. Have you been fishing lately or are you just buying the dead ones at Safeway after you finish a round of golf?"

"Too right! The only fishing I've done lately is fishing my ball out of the creek on the fourth hole yesterday, at which point I was wishing I was wearing my waders. I've seen shallower water hazards than the fairways at high tide at Muni. I know they drained a swamp to build the course, but I don't think the swamp is convinced." He paused to allow the chuckling on the other end of the line to subside. "Look my friend, I'd love to talk about fishing or golf, but am I being overly cynical in thinking you have something less pleasant on your mind?" A sense of foreboding slipped over him. Kerry Weston was a friend both on and off the job, but calls to the office usually meant a situation or event had crossed departmental lines. He didn't need a jurisdictional dispute to start his day or worse yet, have a local investigation cross into an on-going federal matter local law enforcement didn't know about. FBI policy wasn't always in the best interest of local law enforcement, but it was always his job to administer the policy. They shared a mutual respect and mutual frustration when politics dictated what they could do to help each other.

"You know about the dead body we recovered at the lagoon a couple days ago, don't you?"

"Only what I read in the newspapers."

"You and Will Rogers."

"I know a good line when I steal it. You got something we need to know?"

"One of my detectives came up with a theory I need to run by you. I'd like your opinion even if it proves to be just an off the wall idea without real merit. Besides, it would give us a chance to talk outside the office on company time. Got a few minutes to give it a listen?"

"Sure. I get paid to listen to wild theories and other assorted fantasies. It'll make a pleasant diversion from shuffling papers and reading surveillance reports. I'll let you buy me a cup of coffee and a donut."

"Sten's in fifteen?"

"See you there."

Residents might recognize their sheriff, but the FBI Special Agent in Charge was virtually anonymous. He was not an elected official and avoided publication of his picture or his activities. The agency believed the general public had no need to recognize his face to feel safe. If the FBI wanted people to know who he was they would have issued him a uniform.

Weston met frequently with the business community and seeing him talking with a man in a business suit was too commonplace to raise suspicions. Sten's Bakery on the block separating the Courthouse and the Federal Building frequently hosted their meetings. Sten provided a table in a back corner for some privacy.

Weston related Tom's theory of Tim Gordon being alive and an undercover agent for an undetermined agency who had gone to ground because the water he was swimming in had become too hot.

"It's an interesting theory, but what makes you think he's working for us? Presuming he's actually alive."

"From what we've learned from the LAPD, LASO, Pasadena PD, Glendale PD, San Fernando PD, and the third seat in the outhouse, no one knows anything about him beyond the Chamber of Commerce profile for Gormac, Inc. As far as they know, he's just another good citizen with a successful business. The theory may sound like a reach, but when you play it against the evidence the idea becomes more credible. Since none of those agencies offered any enlightenment it leads me to perusing the food chain on the federal side. You have the great good fortune of not only being my friend, but being the most readily accessible link in the chain. What can you tell me?"

"What makes your detective think the report of Gordon's death is bogus? As I recall, the airplane went down with no survivors. The NTSB and the FAA are thorough about identifying passenger remains, although sometimes they aren't able to be absolutely certain they've found everyone. If

Gordon's boarding pass was turned in, why do you think he didn't get on the plane?"

Kerry watched his friend carefully, looking for signs he was dancing to the tune of a cover up. It was mostly a feeling. Something guarded in Elias' speech patterns and careful control of his expression told him he wasn't getting the true story, but knew he needed to play it out as if he was. "You know how once in a while somebody comes up with a crazy idea and the hair on the back of your neck stands on end and gives you a case of the shivers? Well, that's what happened when I heard this theory. They were doing the 'what if' drill when my newest detective popped up with this idea. His partner's been on the job twenty-five years and he says the kid has an instinct for recognizing obscure connections. I don't know if he's chasing shadows, but I wouldn't be doing my job if I didn't back him until we prove he's wrong."

"What does he think Gordon may have been involved in?"

"Don't have a clue. What we have is a naked dead male with a crushed skull. He was clubbed near the cabin Gordon's partner is renting, then stripped and dumped in the ocean. We found the dead guy's pickup in the campground. The truck's a piece of work in itself. It looks like it was designed for a James Bond movie. We still have no clue who the killer might be or a positive ID on the victim. Gordon's partner comes up squeaky clean and his new girl friend, at least we think she's a new girl friend, has a solid alibi. The reclusive and irascible little old lady next door is also in the clear. Generally speaking, a cooling trail is turning icy. We're grabbing at every straw."

"I really wish I could help, but our priorities are federal offenses, usually involving large amounts of money. I'll call the SAC in LA and ask what he knows. I don't know if I can do anything else."

"Well, I figured it was worth a try. I couldn't just ignore it even if it is a wild ass guess. It sounds like the kind of stuff you feds are famous for doing. Besides, you owe me, I bribed you with coffee and a donut."

"Thanks for the coffee. I'll make a call. We need to do this again soon."

"Some time when neither of us is looking for help."

"I'll call you and let you know what I find out."

"Thanks. Give my best to Georgia and the boys. Don't be such a stranger, give me a call the next time you want to play golf. I need an excuse to embarrass myself in public."

24.

PISCES WOKE BONE WEARY AND EXHAUSTED,
something she had seen kept nagging at her in her sleep.
Somewhere in all those frames was the answer, her subconscious
had recognized it. She scrolled forward until she reached the
cabins.

The first cabin on the bluff had three windows facing
toward the lagoon, all curtained and no reason to keep
looking. Moving to the store and it's living quarters she found
nothing special. The second cabin on the street had a small
attic window in the peak of the roof. "Hello." She focused on
a small patch of glass in the lower corner of the bottom pane
and zoomed in, stopping before the image became too grainy.
"You're probably long gone, but now I know where you've been
hiding."

She walked out of the tent and looked at the tract of
cabins. A shadowy outline of the cabin was barely visible
through the fog-filtered sunlight. She shivered involuntarily,
sensing a sinister presence in the misty light.

Joey hunkered in the shadows waiting for Pisces to appear
through the dense fog that softened shapes and filtered colors
to shades of gray. Her tent glowed like soft yellow candlelight.
Uncertainty bordering on panic plagued him. His feet were
getting cold, figuratively as well as literally. It hadn't been easy
to convince Pisces to take this job. She had refused him time

after time, hung up on him twice. Unwilling to accept defeat, he demanded to know why she kept refusing after he offered to triple her fee. She told him she was retired, said she just wanted to be a photographer. She wanted a normal life, she wanted to have a family. She finally agreed to find Tim Gordon, taking the job because it wasn't a termination. He agreed to pay her four times her usual fee and never to call her again. He was confident she would succeed where the others had failed, but he had an overwhelming curiosity to see how she did it and a powerful need to take charge of Tim Gordon as soon as she grabbed him.

He knew shadowing her was a dangerous gamble. If she discovered him he was a dead man. She wouldn't ask questions, she would simply kill him, then contact his grandfather and raise her price in retribution for his interference and breach of honor.

It had seemed so simple before all his plans spun out of control. Now it was a giant mess he had to clean up. His grandfather blamed him for the failure of the first three attempts because Joey had chosen the operators and all had ended up dead while their quarry remained at large. His grandfather's patience was running out. Joey had never seen him so upset. He mentally tamped down his worries and strained to see her camp. He heard a footfall as soft as a leaf striking the ground at the same instant he felt a hand on his shoulder. Joey spun around and would have spoken if Gino hadn't clamped a hand over his mouth. Joey stared into the eyes of his cousin, whose index finger was raised to his lips. Gino gestured in the direction of the highway and led him away. They stopped fifty feet from the highway where their voices would not carry.

"What are you doing here?" Joey whispered.

"My question exactly! When you stopped checking in,

grandfather sent me to keep you from doing something stupid. Again!"

"Doesn't he trust me?"

"It's not a matter of trust! It's a matter of good sense and good business. You don't belong here. Grandfather will be more than a little upset if you get wasted because your bounty hunter caught you following her. You made a good choice hiring her instead of the guy from Seattle, but we all know how dangerous this pet viper can be. If she walked up on your ass the way I just did they'd be measuring you for a toe tag. He sent me to bring you home and leave her to do her job."

"But I'm really in deep shit if she doesn't bring him in!"

"Wake up! You're already up to your eyeballs in shit, so stop trying to make it worse. Let her do what you hired her to do. We know how good she is. She doesn't want you watching her or trying to help her. Just leave her alone! With a little luck, when it's all over maybe you'll be out of deep shit."

"Maybe. The problem is it's only a maybe. I've never seen grandfather so pissed. Three times I've told him I had the problem solved, and three times Gordon disappeared like a puff of smoke along with the people I sent after him. I have to make sure it gets done this time. If I fuck up again I won't have a future."

"If you get in her way you won't have a present. Now c'mon! Let's get out of here before anyone sees us. I need to call grandfather and ask what he wants us to do next. Cross your fingers and hope he doesn't tell me to drown you. Right now I'd really enjoy doing it!"

Tim used the fog to reach the beach without being seen. He had slipped into the brush several times on his way down the switchback trail to see if anyone was following him. The fog muted sounds. It was like being inside a cold wet cotton ball. No one caught up or passed him before he reached the beach and started toward the lagoon. He never felt the trap close around him. Thoughts focused inward, his eyes on the ocean, he didn't notice the shadowy figure rise from behind a driftwood log and drift silently behind him.

"Hello Tim," Pisces purred.

Startled out of his reverie, he spun and came face to face with his deadly pursuer. Tim stared in shock at the lovely woman he knew so well. His mind responded with a rapid survey of his options for escape and survival, but his expression did not betray the panic he was fighting. "Hello Julie. I guess you've found me."

"I guess I have."

"So do I get a chance to get away, or are you going to kill me right now and be done with it?"

"I'm supposed to bring you in."

"Right. Pisces was sent to bring me in. What a hoot! You've never done a rescue or recovery. You're hired to eliminate people. When you show up, someone dies!"

"I took this job because it was to retrieve you. I told them six months ago I was retiring, but Joey chased me down and told me this was a retrieval, not a hit. I turned him down a half a dozen times. I refused the job until he told me it was you."

"And you figured you'd nail me and go out in a blaze of glory. Retire to be a free-lance photo journalist whenever you felt the need for something to break the monotony."

"It's not like that. I don't know what you've gotten yourself into or how the Don is involved. I don't know why he wants you so bad. I took the job because I wanted to keep you from getting hurt and because I wanted to see you again."

"Of course. You wouldn't want anything to happen to

me after all we've been to each other. How big a paycheck did you negotiate? Should I be flattered to know how much I'm worth?"

"That's not fair. You're the one who walked away. No! You ran away when you found out what I did besides take pictures. I wanted to quit as soon as we met, but I had obligations and responsibilities and the people who hire me don't let you quit in the middle of a job. They tend to get upset if you try to quit without finishing the job and when they get upset, you end up dead. I had to finish what I'd started before I could retire. It was my problem and I solved it. It took a few years, but I was out!"

"What happened? You kissed the old man's ass and he let you retire?"

"Not exactly. I told him I wanted to have a family. I told him I didn't have any more anger to burn off and it was time to move on. He's actually pretty decent in his own way. He understood what I was telling him. I always did good work and we didn't owe each other anything. He let me retire and I planned to stay retired until Joey convinced me I was the only one who could bring you in. I only agreed because it was you. I was never able to let you go. I never stopped loving you."

"So what's next? You take me back to LA so the family can work me over trying to make me talk and kill me when they're done? Thanks a lot for all your help! I'm sure they'll treat me real nice before they put a bullet in my ear!"

"I've spent three days trying to think of how to find you and convince the Don to let you go."

"Sounds like a lovely way to pass the lonely hours on the road. Did you come up with any brilliant ideas?"

"No. Whatever you've done, you've got to find a way to make peace with the Don. If you don't, he'll kill Paul, Paul's family, your family, and anyone else remotely connected to you until he gets what he wants. He can make you die very slowly and very painfully, even if you tell him what he wants to know. You're already dead if you can't find some way to settle accounts with him. He thinks you owe him and he doesn't forgive debts. One way or another, he always gets paid, and sooner or later, he always punishes the people he thinks have done him wrong."

"Don't you know what this is about?"

"I never know. I never ask the reason I'm hired. All I want to know is the target and the terms. It keeps me totally uninvolved with anything but doing my job. I didn't ask why they wanted you, I just couldn't say no when I found out it was you. I'd already squeezed him into agreeing to pay me a huge fee before he used your name to close the deal."

"And you always do your job so well."

"You don't have to approve of what I've done with my life. I made those decisions before I met you and without asking your approval. It doesn't matter because neither of us can go back and undo what we've done. I'm not ashamed of what I've done or why I decided to follow my chosen path."

She watched him staring at the surf with his shoulders hunched and hands shoved deep in his pockets. She was surprised to see a raw mixture of confusion and fear in his eyes. After a few moments she placed her hands on his shoulders.

"Why don't you just make an end of it?"

"Make an end of it? What makes you think I want to make an end of it? Do you want to die?"

"You know my chances are zero if you take me back. I won't talk, the Don won't let me walk, and there's nothing you can do about it! Not you! Not me! Definitely not the government pukes who set this whole thing in motion and then crashed it and painted a target on my forehead. I'm already as dead as Paul's wife and baby, I just haven't stopped walking around yet."

Julie slipped her arms around him while he was talking, resting her cheek against his back. "So why are you here?"

"I'm trying to protect Paul. He's already a victim of this mess and probably just as dead as I am. Another dead man walking. I don't think he has any clue how much danger he's in. Jesus, they blew up a whole damned airplane just to get me. They missed me, but managed to kill Lisa and a whole bunch of innocent people who were just trying to get to LA. I thought I got away clean, but the bastards found me anyway. I talked to my FBI contact to try to use the record of my death to get away and instead, one of the bastards leaked word to the Don I was still alive. Meanwhile, Paul loses his wife, his baby, his partner, and God only knows how much of his sanity."

"Why did you kill the guy they sent to pick you up? Did you think killing Webster would help your smoke screen, or were you just trying to buy time?"

"Webster! That's who he was! I thought I recognized him, but I didn't remember his name."

"So why did you kill him? If you recognized him you must have known he wasn't there to kill you."

"I didn't kill him."

"What?"

"I. Did. Not. Kill. Him." Tim spoke slowly, emphasizing each word. "I saw him go over the fence and I followed him, but I didn't kill him. I found him with his skull caved in and barely alive! I never laid a hand on him."

"Who did?"

"I don't know. It was pouring rain and as dark as the inside of a hat. We were both moving slow and quiet. I was only able to see him when he moved. He was a ghostly shadow I could only see because I knew where to look. After he ducked under the cabin I didn't see him again until I found him dying."

Julie moved in front of Tim and gazed into his troubled eyes. "Did you hear anything? Someone hitting him hard enough to crush his skull should have made some noise."

"The cabins are on the bluff above the beach. The surf was up. Think about the sounds around us right now. What do you hear aside from the surf?"

"It's pretty noisy up close, but is it enough to cover the sound of an attack happening a couple hundred feet away?"

"I didn't hear it and I didn't see who killed him. All of which makes for a lousy alibi. He only lasted a few seconds before all the candles went out. There I was with a dead wise guy ten feet from my partner's cabin and no idea who killed him. I'm sure he was trying to find me. He was planning to bug the cabin so he could listen in on Paul. I guess they were hoping I would contact Paul so they could grab us both, kill two birds with one stone."

"What makes you think he was going to bug the cabin?"

"I found a bunch of bugs in his pocket. I don't think he was planning to use them for fish bait. Besides, wasn't electronic surveillance Webster's specialty?"

"It's what he did best. Did you take him to the beach?"

"Guilty as charged. I knew who sent him. I figured he was trying to use Paul to get to me. I knew if I left the body where I found it the cops would believe Paul was involved. I hauled him down to the beach and put him in the water. I thought the tide would carry him out, but it just moved him up the beach and tossed him on the sand. I took his clothes so there would be nothing to discourage the fish from using him for a main course and to make it harder to identify him if anyone found him. Things didn't work out the way I planned. Things didn't work out the way I planned has been my theme song for the last two years."

"You carried him down to the beach? I'm impressed. I didn't know you were so strong."

"I have strong survival instincts. Fear and adrenaline can make a superman out of a ninety-pound weakling. I walked at the edge of the surf where the sand was firm, so it wasn't too bad."

"Okay, let me see if I have this straight. You see this guy sneaking into your partner's back yard in the middle of the night and follow him. By the way, did you see him from the attic window in the house behind Paul's?"

"When did you figure it out?"

"I noticed a clean spot on the window in one of my photographs. One little spot just big enough to peek through in an otherwise dusty, grimy group of window panes. I knew it was your hide out as soon as I saw it. Getting back to the story, you see this guy sneaking around, so you slip out and follow him, right?"

"Right. He was good, tough to follow without being seen, it took a lot of patience to wait for him to move before making my next move."

"Webster was a pro. This is a prime example of why I retired. Sooner or later even a seasoned pro comes up against the unexpected, the unpredictable, someone better or luckier. Anyway, you trail him, and you find him dying. You don't see or hear anyone. He looks familiar and you decide he was sent to find you. No matter who punched his ticket, leaving him where you found him will point the cops at Paul, so you pack him down to the beach, dump the body and dive back into your hidey hole taking Webster's clothing with you."

"Pretty much sums it up."

"So what do we do about Paul?"

"We? You want to help Paul and me get away? What about Joey and the Don?"

"First we have to bring Paul up to speed. He needs to know he's wearing a target even if we don't know who painted it on him or who's trying to hit it. You have a getaway plan don't you?"

"Only takes a phone call to implement it."

"Good. If we can find a way to make your escape plan work maybe we can solve the other little problems too. I'm not sure how we'll manage it, but we've got to try." Julie smiled at Tim the way she had so long ago. "Who knows? We may even discover how you and I can finally be together."

25.

THE DETECTIVES STROLLED ALONG THE BEACH while they struggled to piece together what had occurred between the site of the attack and the location of the body. There were so many missing pieces they could only speculate about the actual sequence of events and speculation was not a chain of evidence. Time was their enemy and time was rapidly slipping through their fingers.

"How far down the beach do you think he carried our John Doe before he dumped him in the water?" Tom asked.

"Dennis called the weight at a hundred eighty-five pounds?"

"About."

"So he's packing a hundred eighty-five pounds of dead weight down the beach in the rain. You're wondering how far he carried him?"

"Yeah. How far do you think he carried him?"

"Why?"

"Do we have any idea about the killer in terms of size, age, physical condition, or anything else?"

"You think if we can figure about how far he carried him we'll least have some idea of the guy's size and strength."

"Exactly. Look. Correct me if I'm wrong, but didn't we decide the body had to be carried because there was no sign of it being dragged across the beach from the trail?"

"Lots of tracks at the end of the trail, but no sign of a body being dragged."

"And there were no scrapes on the body from being dragged?"

"None we can be sure of, no."

"So how far do you think you could carry me down this beach?"

"Not very far, but I'm not as young as I was and not all pumped up on adrenaline from trying to get rid of the evidence of a murder."

"Right, but say you were. How far do you think you could haul my bones?"

John stopped and looked back in the direction they had come. They were about half a mile from the trail. "Would you be able to see the cabins by the time you got this far on a rainy night?"

"You'd be out of sight for sure by the time you got this far."

"Okay, let's presume he came this far before his ass was dragging so bad he needed to dump the stiff and run for cover. Why did the body wash up a half mile down the beach? Could be tide or currents or undertow. Let's presume he tossed the stiff in the surf and watched it drift out. Where does he go? Back to the attic?"

"Maybe. We know someone was hanging out there for a while and it might be our killer. We still haven't tied the two together. We also don't have a motive for the murder."

"You're right. All we've got is the pickup Vince is tearing apart. He's found more sophisticated listening equipment in the camper than Nixon had in the White House and the weapons he found are pretty sophisticated. Anyone who carries an arsenal of specialized weapons and eavesdropping equipment has to be in somebody's files. He didn't learn his trade without spending a little time someplace where they keep a record of intimate details about you."

"Still nothing from the feebies?"

"Don't hold your breath. You know how those assholes are about sharing information. Everything they have is on a need to know basis, and when you ask, they say you don't need to know."

"Do you think my theory about an undercover fed being at the heart of this is dead in the water?"

"No. We can't afford to ignore any possibilities. Until the suits confirm or deny any connection we just keep looking for ways to explain what happened. If we don't get a break pretty soon we're gonna end up with an unsolved case pushed to the file room by the next case. I don't know about you, but I don't want this one left gathering dust. I don't care about getting a conviction. I want to know what went down and why. I hate it when a case gets away from me."

"An unsolved murder can spoil your whole day, right?"

"Laugh it up, greenie. You'll discover the ones that get away keep you awake at night and drive you to the bar at the end of the shift. But getting back to the biscuits and gravy, the killer has to be in pretty good shape to carry a body this far. Maybe he's a runner or does something besides warm a desk chair?"

"You're thinking about our friend from the big city who's currently hanging out with the artist, aren't you?"

"He's still a prime possibility, but I don't think he did it. Besides, she alibied him for the night of the murder."

"Couldn't she be covering for him?"

"Maybe. She was a bit bristly about answering my questions, but that's not unusual. Women don't like to discuss their personal affairs with a strange man."

Tom favored him with a thoughtful glance.

"What?"

"Nothing."

"What?"

"It just struck me funny hearing you refer to yourself as a strange man. There's people in the department who say you're a little odd, but I think it's interesting you share their opinion." Despite his partner's humorless stare, he continued. "You think having a witness or a suspect get bristly with you is normal because you make a habit of pissing people off with your boyish charm?"

"You think I'm losing my perspective and getting cynical?"

"Along with losing your hair and getting fat."

John laughed. "Thanks for the update and the reality check. How about some new ideas? A stiff washes up on the beach and you arrive to find a crowd of gawkers gathered around a naked victim with a mashed skull and virtually no distinguishing marks. How does a guy live over thirty years and not have any distinguishing marks? Not just hardly any marks, but no scars, no moles, no tattoos, nothing! He's got to have the world's best plastic surgeon. I also think this guy is not only known to the feebies, I think he's very well known to them. They just don't want to share with us."

"Shouldn't we be able to track him because he has no marks? Shouldn't absence work as well as presence or am I leaping to what seems like an obvious conclusion?"

"Good idea. Definitely worth follow up, but for now, tell me exactly what you saw when you arrived on the scene."

"You think I forgot something?"

"I don't think you deliberately forgot anything, I think you saw more than you realize and need a little concentration to bring it into focus."

"Okay, I'll run it down again. I got the call and rolled down here and hiked out to the body. There were a bunch of people standing around and the kid and his dad were doing their best to protect the scene. I secured the scene, called for you, and started gathering ID's of the people in the crowd."

"Before you go further, think about the crowd. Did everyone hang around, or did somone leave before you could talk to them?"

Tom's head snapped up. "Do you think our man was here and took off before I got the chance to talk to him?"

"What do you think? Could it have happened?"

"Man, I never even thought about telling everyone to hang around. I was so busy trying to make sure the scene was secure I didn't start asking questions until I had handed out a string of orders about how no one should touch anything. It would have been easy for someone to just walk away without being noticed. I sure as hell wouldn't have tried to chase any one down. Damn, John, I'm sorry."

"No apologies. You can't think of everything and you can't be expected to do the work of more than one person. You did good. Don't worry about it. Believe me, on this job you'll fuck up so many times you'll lose count. Think about this. Did you see anyone in the crowd when you arrived who wasn't there when we were doing the interviews?"

"I don't know."

"Take a minute. Think about the crowd when you arrived and when you started to interview them. Remember exactly who you saw. Was someone missing when you started getting ID's?"

"Geez, two or three people could have wandered off while I was taking care of the body. The kid and his father were the prime witnesses. They were so eager to help I had to keep asking them to wait for me to finish what I had to do first. When I first got here there were ten or twelve people standing around the body, but let me check something." He took out his notebook. "Let's see how many names I have." He counted the number of people he had interviewed. "Nine. Nine hung around long enough to be identified. Nine! I can see the group as I walked up to it because I remember making a mental count so that I wouldn't miss anyone. There were eleven. Eleven!"

"So we have a count. Are you sure you didn't decide not to talk to a couple of the people because everyone said pretty much the same thing?"

"No! I was only getting names and addresses. Most of them showed up because they saw people milling around. All I have is their ID. No interview. So what happened to the other two?"

"Looks like two got away. Can you scratch enough at the edges of your alleged mind to remember what the missing members of the party looked like?"

"Let me think." Tom closed his eyes. "I walked right past one guy. He said good morning and smiled. I never saw him again. The other one was a woman. I never got a look at her face. She had her back turned to me and was standing back a bit from the rest of the group. I remember she looked like the typical elderly woman bundled up for a morning walk on the beach. But the guy," Tom pointed his finger at John. "He stood out in a subtle way. You know how some people don't have to do anything to stand out in a crowd? Well, that's how he was. He was about forty, about my height, loose clothing, jeans, down jacket, make that a dark blue down jacket, hands in his pockets, brown hair, a bit windblown, cheeks a little red like he'd been on the beach for a while, well, fuck me to tears!

The son of a bitch was right under my damn nose and I never even noticed him!"

"You're sure you aren't just fantasizing this guy?"

"No way! I remember him. Big enough to haul your overweight ass a half-mile down the beach and probably never take a deep breath. He's our man!"

"Whoa! Don't let your imagination run away with you. He might have something to do with this and he might not. So far all we know is he was polite when you arrived and was gone before you could get his name. None of which makes him suspicious, let alone a suspect or the killer. What it makes him is a person of interest. Do you think you'd recognize him if you saw him again?"

"Yeah. I think I'd know him if I saw him again."

John took a photograph out of his pocket. "Did he look anything like this?"

Tom looked at the copy of a newspaper photograph. The quality of the photo wasn't terrific, but the face in the photo was familiar. "Who is this guy?"

"Never mind who he is. Does he look like your missing witness?"

"The picture isn't terrific and looks younger, but yeah, this looks like my missing guy. Who the hell is he?"

"This is an LA Times obit photo of a guy who died two years ago in an airline crash."

"He's dead? Wait a minute. McAfee's partner died two years ago in an airplane crash. Are you telling me this is… ?"

"Bingo! Tim Gordon. Could he be alive and well?"

"So my theory may be right?"

"Maybe. Maybe he isn't dead, but being alive isn't a crime. There's no law against not dying, or not revealing your identity to the world, or dropping out of society, or living below the radar. If he's alive it may help explain things, but it still only makes him a person of interest. It doesn't begin to make him a deep cover agent in some clandestine international crime scheme."

"I'll be damned. Tim Gordon. Yeah, this could be my guy on the beach. If he's alive, if he's here, if his partner's here, and if this murder happens as soon as the partner arrives; a lot of ifs but the picture begins to look a lot clearer. Especially if Gordon's been on the run all this time. There's one really important if. If he's running, who's he running from?"

"Good question. A major missing piece. If he's running and if we can figure out who's chasing him we might actually have a clue what's going on."

"Man, is it just because I'm new, or is this case tougher than the average?"

"The interesting ones are always tough, but this one is a bit of a hair puller. Look at the good news. Our stroll on the beach has given us a couple more pieces to add to the puzzle."

"Yeah, it looks like it," Tom paused. "Okay, if this guy is Tim Gordon, what about the little old lady? Who is she? And where did she go? How the hell can we find her when all I saw was her back?"

"What makes you so sure it was a little old lady?"

"Because gray-haired little old men don't generally wear a dress."

"Where can we find someone who fits the general description?"

"Too easy. Alma Jacobsen lives in the corner cabin. Didn't Cal ask her if she was on the beach?"

"Yes. She told him she saw the crowd on the beach, but never went to see what was going on. Said it was none of her business."

"Sounds like her. She can be crusty, but there's nothing within sight or hearing of her cabin she doesn't know about." He looked where the cabins were emerging from the lifting fog. "Damn! It could have been her! I never put it together. Right size, right height, gray hair, house dress, plain old clothes. Characteristic Alma. She'd take a look and fade into the shadows before anyone could notice her or talk to her. She's a hermit, but she sees and hears everything. She watches the area like a guard dog. Yes! It fits! I ought to go corner the old bag and make her tell me what's going on."

John smiled broadly at his eager young partner while he rattled off this litany of frustration and realization. "Slow down! You probably should go talk with the old dear, but not when you're all steamed up over the wild notion she can solve the case for you. You think you might have seen her. Pretty thin grounds for bracing her."

"Even if she wasn't actually there she'll probably know a whole lot. She watches everything. I wonder if she ever sleeps."

"So how do we play this to our advantage? You seem to know the old girl. Will she talk to you?"

"All I can do is try."

"That's what the steer said. Let's mosey back to the store and swallow some more of Mrs. Alexander's finest chain oil. Then you can try to schmooze some info out of our reclusive resident."

"Before we go, take a look across the lagoon."

The fog had lifted enough to make the opposite side of the lagoon visible. "So what am I looking at? I don't see anything unusual."

"Check the photographer's campsite."

John saw the red Jeep and the tent, but no sign of the occupant. "I don't see our petite shutterbug."

"Uh- huh. Where do you think she might be on such a fine soft morning?"

"You have a decidedly suspicious nature my young friend. Don't ever lose it, but don't jump to any conclusions either. She could be somewhere looking for the right light to capture the mood of the place for her new book."

"Sure she could. What if she isn't?"

"She could be in the shitter. You want to trot over there and start checking the stalls? Maybe if you sniff all the seats you can identify which one she used."

"Ha, ha. Your sense of humor is as limp as your dick."

"Your ass is sucking wind, again. Let's go see if we can find a donut and a couple aspirin for this damn tooth. Dentists have to have the best gig in medicine. Nobody ever dies from a toothache, so you can make the patients dance to the office schedule and let them suffer while you play golf. By the time you finally agree to see them, they're willing to pay almost anything to get some relief."

They were half way to the store when John cuffed Tom on the arm. "Take a look!" He nodded toward the campground. "Is he a classic case of being overdressed or is he deliberately trying to attract attention?"

"Who do you suppose he's looking for? He sure as hell isn't dressed for a camp out or a weenie roast."

"You got that right. Do you think we should perhaps inquire how we might assist him?"

"Obviously a lost soul in need of some friendly attention from the local gendarmerie."

"We can't use highway mopery as an excuse to stop and frisk, so lending aid to a citizen in need will have to fill the gap."

"God bless the Supreme Court and their liberal wisdom."

"Fortunately, there are a lot more bright cops in the real

world thinking of ways around the lawyers and the courts than senile political appointees protecting the rights of the criminals."

"We shouldn't gang up on him, so who gets to talk to our mystery guest?"

"You look like shit. Why don't you go get some coffee and clean up a bit while I go make nice with Mr. Doe."

"Mr. Doe may turn into a nasty tempered old buck with a big rack. Watch your ass."

"Thanks for the reminder. I'll see you in a few minutes. Call the office and see if anything is shaking with Vince."

"Will do. See you in a few." Tom fought off the weariness of a sleepless night and a worrisome sense of foreboding by singing softly to himself. "It's a beautiful day in the neighborhood,"

Alma watched the detectives approach the beach trail. Their voices carried clearly through the slightly raised sash. She heard them discussing the difficulty of carrying a body down the incline and the size of the person able to accomplish the task. Their voices faded as they dropped below the top of the bluff. She had not seen her new neighbor since he had gone to visit the artist the previous afternoon. Worse yet, the fog obscured her view of the campground across the lagoon. *There's just no way for me to know where the damn photographer might be!*

The gloom gradually faded as bright patches of sunlight consumed the overcast while Alma watched the detectives walk along the isthmus dividing the ocean surf from the calm waters of the lagoon. Their animated conversation was like watching a poorly edited silent movie. Frustrated by not being able to hear them she swung her gaze to where the Jeep wore a shimmering blanket of dew. The campground appeared mundane until he stepped from behind a tree. He was difficult not to notice, the business suit might as well have been a flashing neon sign. She watched him speak with a young camper carrying a fishing rod and a tackle box. As the boy walked away the man turned and looked across the lagoon at the detectives. A sharp chill scampered across her back. She held her hand over her suddenly racing heart. The last place she had seen him was in the Director's office. "Oh my."

26.

GRAY MORNING LIGHT WAS ERASING THE SHADOWS
when Paul awoke to see Jean sleeping next to him. Trying not
to wake her, he rose and started for the bathroom.

"Good morning," a sleepy voice called to him. "Nice buns."

"Thanks. I was trying not to wake you."

"I'm glad you did." She stretched languorously and arched
her back. "Hurry back".

"Just as soon as I take care of a pressing obligation."

She tossed back the covers and followed him.

Paul was leaning over the sink when Jean slipped her
arms around his waist and pressed herself against him. "Hi
sailor," she said, looking over his shoulder at his reflection in
the mirror.

"Couldn't wait for me?"

"I didn't want you to forget why you're here." She slid
her hand down his belly and across his penis, evoking an
immediate response. "Someone else is waking up."

"He's battered and bruised, but like a good soldier, he
always rises to the occasion."

"So why don't you just march your soldier back to the
parade ground. I'll be right there for some close order drill."
Jean playfully slapped his backside.

Later, Paul lay watching Jean sleep. Although outwardly
peaceful, his mind was a tangle of confusion and conflict. He
had come here to find a fresh start and here he was in bed with

a lovely woman he'd met a few days ago. The sudden shift in his life had thrown him off balance. He sorted through his emotions and realized he was happy for the first time in years. Watching the morning light cast soft shadows across Jean's features, he marveled how unrelated events had brought them together. He was eagerly anticipating whatever would happen next when Jean woke and smiled at him.

"Mmmmm, good morning again"

"A good morning indeed."

"Did you sleep all right?"

"Like a baby, but dinner was a little light. Might I interest you in some breakfast?"

Jean stretched, then laid her arm across his chest and smiled. "We sort of skipped dinner last night didn't we."

"Uh-huh. Living on love is wonderful, but sooner or later the body requires sustenance if it is to possess the strength to continue."

"Without food we might not have enough energy to continue living on love. I could eat a little something myself, like maybe a small horse, medium rare."

"My thought exactly. Garcon, trot in two Shetlands, we'll have breakfast in bed!" Paul raised his hand to the invisible servant.

"So who's cooking this morning?"

"I need a change of clothes. Let's go raid my fridge and see what we can find. Maybe eggs, hash browns, bacon, toast, and coffee."

"Sounds irresistible, but I need a shower."

"I'll wash your back."

Julie and Tim sat on the floor in a corner of Paul's bedroom while they waited for him to return.

"Where do you think he is?"

"I suspect my partner is in the end cabin making whoopee with a local artist."

"How long has he been here?"

"Got here last Friday, so about a week."

"He's either a fast worker or she's an easy lay."

"Look who's talking. How long did you know me before you jumped my bones in Hong Kong?"

"That was different. I knew who you were before we met. Besides, I was well oiled with some very expensive champagne you bought on your expense account."

"Oh, I see. Champagne excuses your assault on my tender sensibilities."

"Maybe I was in love."

"Were you?"

"I still am."

"Then what are you doing sitting here holding my hand instead of schtupping the man of your dreams?"

"He had a headache and you were handy."

"Is he in Phoenix or Tucson?"

"Probably."

"And I was handy."

Julie leaned her head against his shoulder. "I missed my handyman, so I got in my car and drove here as fast as I could."

"And how am I?"

"You're in such deep shit you could fertilize forty acres. There's another problem. I saw Joey trying to watch me without being seen, but he's not not very good at it. I don't think he trusts me."

"So why didn't you just make him disappear?"

"His cousin arrived and dragged him away. I don't think Joey's supposed to be here, but the little snake apparently feels the overwhelming need to check up on me."

"Maybe the old man sent the cousin to protect Joey from having you snap his dishonorable neck."

"It's a good thing he did if that's what's going on. Joey's a miserable little turd with more ego than brains and I might enjoy curing him of his curiosity, but the timing was wrong. I didn't want to attract any more attention, but seeing the boys gave me an idea how to get you away. The little shit broke the terms of the contract and he's given me some leverage, but I can't just grab you and flee. To make this work I have to fulfill the terms of the contract. Once I do, Joey's made it possible for me to force them to let us leave. I have to make it clear nobody messes with me and gets away with it. I intend to get paid in full for doing my job. The Don isn't going to like it, and that suits me right down to the ground. He should have taught his protege the meaning of honor!"

"What about Paul and his friend?"

"I don't know if having all of you disappear at once is a good idea. It could attract attention."

The key turning in the lock ended their conversation. Tim and Julie prepared to defend themselves, but the voices from the other room weren't threatening.

Paul's footsteps echoed as he crossed the living room. "Let me change clothes and then I'll get breakfast started," he said as he walked into the bedroom.

"I'll start a pot of coffee."

"I'll just be a sec-," Paul stopped dead in his tracks halfway into the bedroom. The silence lasted several seconds.

"Hey old buddy, long time no see." Tim walked toward Paul with his arms extended and wrapped him in a bear hug. Several seconds passed before Paul returned the embrace.

Frowning in consternation, Paul pushed back, his hands gripping Tim's shoulders. "Tim! Where in the hell have you been? I thought you were dead! I went to your funeral! What the hell is going on?"

"We have a lot to catch up on," Julie interrupted, "but right now we need to make sure nobody gets killed."

"Julie! What are you doing here?" Paul stepped away from Tim and bumped into Jean. "Sorry, Jean. We have unexpected guests. Meet my partner and his friend Julie."

"Your partner? I thought your partner was dead!"

"To quote Mark Twain, reports of my death are greatly exaggerated," Tim said.

"And once again," Julie interrupted, "this class reunion is very touching, but we need to do two things. Quiet down so we don't attract the attention of the snoop next door and choose a place where we can make plans without being observed. There are a lot of eyes on this cabin. Some very powerful people are looking for Tim. Our boy has well and truly pissed in somebody's corn flakes. We're all at extreme risk of being exterminated by the local authorities, the friends of the Don, or the Potomac bureaucrats whose lives he could ruin. Making Tim vanish is only half the equation. They aren't going to feel like their problem has been solved until both you guys disappear."

Tim appeared deep in thought as he began to speak. "Right. Daylight is our biggest enemy at the moment. Mrs. Peepers next door is our first major stumbling block. Julie and I can get out the way we got in."

"By the way," Paul interrupted, "how did you get in?"

"Easy. We opened the window and crawled through. It's easy to get into the space between the cabins without being seen, but no matter which way we go from there we're out in the open. I'd suggest we hide in the trunk of your car, but I see your current ride is a Mustang convertible. The trunk is barely big enough for a bag of groceries. What do you have in the back seat?"

"Nothing. Do you really think you can get away by just sitting in the back seat like there's nothing happening? Just brazen it out?"

"Not exactly. Jean, do you have a large painting ready to go to the frame shop?"

"I have one too big to fit in my car. What made you think I would have a painting and why is it important for it to be big?"

"I did my homework. Could you tie it over the back seat of the convertible if the top was down?"

"I think so. It's four by five feet. I hadn't figured out how I was going to get it to the frame shop, but with the top down I think we can lay it over the back seat.

"Perfect! Can you get it and bring it back here? Bring it inside like you want to hang it here. After few minutes you guys can load it in the Mustang. Wrap the painting in a blanket and tie it over the back seat where you can watch to make sure it doesn't shift around. Julie and I will curl up under the painting. Once we're in the clear we can bail out and you can go to the frame shop. Naturally you'll want to stop to make sure the painting isn't working loose. When you do we'll get out. Trust me! This will work!"

Paul smiled at Tim. "You always were a schemer, but you've become truly devious in your old age."

"Survival is a masterful instructor in the fine art of deviousness. Right now two things need to happen. You need to change clothes and Jean needs to go get the painting."

Jean shook her head slowly. "I wish I knew what I'm getting into. I feel like maybe I should just go to my cabin and call the Sheriff's Department. I didn't plan on anything like this when I decided I wanted Paul to be my friend. I didn't expect to find myself in the middle of a manhunt. I don't do things like this. I'm really scared."

Julie took Jean's hand. "I promise to explain everything later. Right now we need you to trust us and help us. The net is closing around all of us, including you. We know you walked into this without any warning and without asking to be a part of it. We know you aren't prepared for this. You should be scared. Paul allowed you inside with us because he believes in you and trusts you, otherwise you wouldn't be here. You have all our lives in your hands. You can call the cops. We can't stop you, but we hope you won't. We need you to keep a cool head because it will help us protect you. We'll protect you, Jean, we don't have a choice. If anything happens to you it means it already happened to us. I wish we had the luxury of time to persuade you to jump into this boat, but you and Paul may have already passed a point of no return as far as the people who are looking for Tim are concerned. I can only ask you one simple question and hope you give me the right answer. Will you help us?"

Jean looked at Paul, who smiled and nodded his head, at Tim who also nodded slowly, and then back to Julie. She was making a life changing decision which would bind her to these three people and the cloud of danger swirling around them. She paused to think and realized she didn't need to think about it. "Okay. Count me in, but you've gotta tell me everything. I need to understand what we're doing and I need to be able to contribute more than a painting. Let's get this little skit in motion before I lose my nerve." She started for the door with her voice raised enough to be heard outside. "Let me go get the painting you like so much. I'll be back in a flash!"

"I'll get breakfast started," Paul called after her.

"Great! I'm starved."

"I'll go change clothes," Paul said. "The coffee should be ready in a couple minutes. Keep your voices down so my nosy neighbor doesn't hear you. She's probably working in her front yard and voices carry."

"Gotcha," Tim stood and turned on Paul's portable stereo. The voice of the disk jockey immediately broke the silence of the room. He adjusted the volume high enough to camouflage their conversation. "Something to make life a little more difficult for the ears next door."

"Okay, bright guy, we have a nice breakfast, slip out the side window and lay down in the back seat of his car," Julie said. "They cover us up with the painting, and drive out of here. How can we be sure we aren't going to be followed? I don't want an unwelcome surprise when we get out of the car."

"Shaking a tail could be a problem. Our best hope is for nobody to follow us when we leave. If we get unlucky Paul will need to be creative and lose whoever it might be without being obvious about it."

"I feel like I just stepped into a James Bond movie without the benefit of a script," Paul said. " I'll do my best. Don't be too disappointed if I'm not very good at losing a tail. I'm not sure I would recognize one if I saw it."

"Remember all four of us may not see tomorrow if you don't get the job done. It will stimulate your survival instincts. You always worked well under pressure and survival is a tremendous incentive for inventive thinking. Trust yourself, buddy, if you give your mind free rein you'll come up with a solution. Our lives depend on it."

"When are you going to fill in the blanks about what's been going on for the last couple years?"

"Soon. Right now let's have something to eat and get out of here. Where's Jean? She should be back by now."

At that moment Jean stepped through the door carrying an unframed painting. "All right, I'm here with the painting. What are we doing next? I don't know about you, but I'm pretty nervous. I'm afraid I'm going to say or do something to foul things up. Why can't we just call the cops and ask them to protect us?"

"I wish it was so easy," Tim replied. "I wish we could just stroll down to the store and have a nice little chat with the detectives who are here again this morning. Just lay it all out chapter and verse and get on with our lives like nothing ever happened. Unfortunately, telling them wouldn't solve the problem. Since it isn't an option, let's have some breakfast and talk about how we get out of here. We're not the bad guys. We started out with good intentions and patriotic zeal to do good for our country. Everything was working fine until the people we were working for pulled the plug and painted a target on me. I've been running for two years and I'm tired of it. I know you're scared. We're all scared, only an idiot wouldn't be scared. It took you quite a while to come back with this painting. Who did you call?"

Jean stared at Tim with an expression which began with horror, then changed to distress, and finally the color rose in her cheeks and anger flashed like lightning in her eyes. "You miserable, rotten, ungrateful son of a bitch!" she snarled, her voice just above a whisper. "I put on a sweater and brought a jacket so I wouldn't catch cold riding in a car with the top down and I had to dig the painting out of the stack. I didn't have plans to spend my morning this way so I needed a few minutes to get organized! I'm doing my best to do what you've asked because you're Paul's partner. I don't even know you! What gives you the right to doubt me?"

Tim held up his hands, a smile twinkling in his eyes. "I

had to ask. I won't apologize for asking. I've managed to stay alive this long by being careful who I trust. I trust Paul with my life and I'm about to do the same with you. Be offended, but ask yourself, in my shoes, wouldn't you ask the same question?"

"Don't you think I know enough not to bring in someone we couldn't trust?" Paul said in a tightly controlled voice.

"Don't go getting your knickers in a knot too. We all have to be on the same page or they'll bury us all in a common grave."

Jean grabbed Tim's ear and turned his head until she was gazing directly into his eyes. "Get something straight right now! I'm nobody's doormat! I'm no shrinking violet! If I'm going to risk my life to protect you, you damn well better be risking yours to protect me! I live up to my commitments and I don't back down once I make up my mind! I said I was in! I said I was going to help! If that's not good enough, you can go fuck yourself!"

"You are a formidable lady, Jean Parker. You'll do just fine. I'm glad you're on my side." Tim extended his hand, Jean took it. "It's a pleasure to meet you."

An hour later, Paul pulled the Mustang between the cabins, lowered the top and went inside to get the painting. Tim and Julie went out the bedroom window and clambered into the car. Paul and Jean tied the painting over them.

They drove away under the watchful eye of Alma Jacobsen. The man in the business suit watched the car pass the campground. Completing the ensemble was the alert observation by a tired young detective.

Tom watched John approach the store. Based on the brief time he'd been gone, he presumed the stranger was gone by the time John got there. "How'd you do with our well dressed friend?"

"I missed him and nobody else saw him leave. Another shadowy disappearance."

"Better luck next time, I guess."

"Hope springs eternal."

The five year old Ford Escort went unnoticed by all but Tom. In two years he had never seen Alma Jacobsen leave her cottage before noon. He pointed at Alma's car rolling toward the highway. "Take a look, partner. Where do you think she's going in such a hurry?"

John only saw the rear bumper as the car moved into the trees. "Obviously you think there's something significant about her going somewhere. What's on your alleged mind?"

"This is the first time in two years I've seen her leave the house before noon. Makes it interesting at the least. If you consider McAfee and the artist just left and the old hermit sails out of here before their dust settles, it makes it worthy of notice, if you take my meaning."

"Indeed I do. Shall we give chase? Observe from a discreet distance?"

"Unless you plan to stay here and wait for me to report to you when I get back."

"Then let us be off! The game's afoot."

Unlike the warmth of Southern California, the north coast often remains cool even in the middle of a sunlit summer day. Paul and Jean wore warm jackets zipped snugly against the cold, but their passengers were not so well protected. "How are you guys doing back there? Are you warm enough or should I turn up the heater?"

"We're doing just fine considering the condition of the seating arrangements. I've never felt so honored to sit where people put their feet. Were it not for the company of a beautiful lady to snuggle with I might complain, but I'm actually enjoying it in a Marquis de Sade sort of way. Can you tell if we're being followed?"

"I've been watching the mirrors, but I don't know for sure. A car pulled onto the highway behind us, but how do I know if it's following us? There aren't many off or on ramps and the only choices are which lane to use, so just because someone happened to pull onto the highway behind us doesn't necessarily mean they're following us does it?"

"No, it doesn't. That's the tough part. You'll need to do something to confirm whether we're being followed. We need to get off this road and watch what happens with the rest of the crowd. It won't be proof positive, but it may give you a clue. Why don't you go down to the old highway and make it look like you're taking the scenic tour? You can pull over to look at the scenery like a couple of tourists. If anyone is following us they'll either stop and wait for you to go on, or they'll drive by and re-acquire you later. If they drive by you can get a look at the car and watch for it to show up later in front or behind you. A tail isn't always in the rear."

"No sooner said than done. I think the next off ramp will take us to the old highway. You know this road, Jean, will this one get us there?"

"Yes, but right now I'm more concerned with how we know if someone is following us." Jean looked to the rear as the road scrolled out beneath the car. " I've seen the movies, but what do we do in real life?"

"The movies are pretty much on track with the concept," Tim said. "They just have to make everything fit into one frame. In real life it isn't so obvious because the tail only has to keep you in sight range. The easiest way is to change directions and see if anyone follows."

Jean looked at the off ramp. "Take this road. It goes to a

place where I like to sketch. If we're quick enough, I know a location where we can't be seen from the road. Take a right when you get to the old highway."

"Great!" Paul said, "Now I really feel like we're in a spy movie."

"You may not be far wrong," Tim said quietly. "You guys have to act like there's nothing special about this little excursion. Don't look back any more than you ordinarily would. I'd be surprised if we aren't being followed, so you have to make them believe you're unaware of them. If they think you know you're being followed they'll get even harder to see. At least they will if they know what they're doing."

"Wonderful!" Paul said, as he turned right at the end of the off ramp onto a narrow two lane road bounded by redwoods on both sides. The road turned left two hundred yards ahead, blocking the view of the off ramp shortly after they left the highway. "It's going to be tough to see them from here because the road just took away my view to the rear. I'm gonna try to put another turn between us so they won't know which way we turned on the old road. How far is it to this special spot of yours after we reach the old highway?"

"Not very far. Hang a right, then turn through an opening in the fence. Don't go in too fast. The ground is hard, but it's bumpy."

"I haven't seen any other cars, but I'm not wasting any time." Paul wheeled through the opening in the fence. The car hopped and lurched as he maneuvered his way through the trees.

"Stop! The road ends right here!"

Paul slammed on the brakes and slid to a stop inches from the rotting carcass of an ancient tree. He turned off the engine and glanced around, listening for the sound of a car following them. "This is a great place, all right, only it's a dead end with only one way in and out. We're trapped if anyone figures out where we went. Why do I feel like this wasn't the best choice?"

"Paul." Tim spoke in a patient voice. "Why don't you guys walk around for a while and see if anybody shows up. Wander around looking at the scenery like a couple of young lovers on vacation. If anyone sees you it will look like you don't know anyone is watching. We'll wait until you tell us it's safe to come out. We promise to be good little mice and not make any noise, so stop fretting and get moving!" There was a brief pause before Tim growled. "Do you get the picture?"

Jean glanced at Paul. "He does get testy doesn't he? You know, there's a wonderful trail to the beach and a secluded cove which is absolutely perfect for lying in the sun wearing nothing but a smile. The college kids love it. Let's go for a walk on the beach and give them some privacy to catch up on old times. I'm sure they'll be just fine!"

"What a lovely idea. A nude beach!" Paul leered. "I haven't been to one of those in years. Y'all hang in there, we'll be back in a while," he drawled.

Alma spaced herself about a half mile behind the Mustang. The decision to follow them was gut instinct. Too many unexplained events were invading her environment and her peace of mind was taking flight. Maybe these two were going somewhere or doing something that would help to clear things up. Her mind sorted possibilities as she cruised along in their wake.

The Mustang passed in and out of sight as the highway moved through the timbered landscape. Alma topped a rise and the road stretched out for more than a mile of unrestricted visibility. The Mustang was gone. The next exit was nearly a mile ahead and the last a half-mile behind. She didn't know which they had taken, but both led to the old highway.

Alma stopped on the shoulder where she had a clear view of the next ramp. She needed to think. She didn't know if they were trying to avoid being followed or had just driven down to the old highway to enjoy the scenery. Time was in short supply and every minute widened the gap between her and the Mustang. Panic threatened to overcome her sense of reason, but she drew a blanket of calm over herself and considered her options.

The unmarked car drove past her while she was considering her next move. The younger detective was looking at her as they drove by. "So what are you guys looking for?" she asked aloud. "You were at the store and you had two cars, now you're together and right behind me going down the highway, and there's the guy in the suit who was snooping around the park this morning!" She watched the turn signal activate on the detective's car as it moved toward the exit. The dapper man's car followed the detectives down the ramp. As soon as she was out of their sight she wheeled through the grassy divider and accelerated toward the previous exit.

"I know she recognized us," Tom insisted as they drove down the ramp. "Our eyes locked for a second and I know she recognized me."

"Okay, she spotted us. We're not trying to hide from her are we? I'm not worried about her, where the hell is the Mustang?"

"I think they got off while we were following the hermit. They could be headed south on the old road right now or they could have stopped to look at the scenery. Maybe they needed to stop and warm up. Maybe she wanted to show him the sights."

"Maybe. Or maybe they doubled back on the old road and are headed for the lagoon. Too many options and not enough of us to cover them all. I think we need to backtrack a bit."

"You mean go back to the lagoon?"

"Well, everyone took off when they left. They managed to drag everyone out in the open. With everyone gone they have an open field to do whatever they were planning, if they were planning to do something."

"Right! But," Tom paused.

John waited a few seconds. "So what's blossoming in your fertile imagination now?"

"I was sorting out the possibilities."

"And?"

"There are too many choices."

"Like what?"

"Like who the hell is right behind us?"

John checked the rear view mirror just as a new Ford, driven by the same well dressed man they had seen at the park, rolled to a stop behind them. "I don't know who he is, but I bet him being here isn't a good thing. Ever get the feeling you just stepped off a cliff?"

"That's why I asked who the hell he is."

"Check the license plate when I pull out and let's see who owns the wheels."

"Go whenever you're ready." Tom read the plate aloud and kept saying it until he wrote it down. He requested the registration information from the dispatcher.

The dapper young man swore under his breath when the detectives turned right and drove away. He picked up the small hand held radio and spoke into it.

"Eureka, six alpha delta."

"Go ahead, six alpha delta."

"I just blew it. The detectives will know who I am in a couple minutes. By the time I realized I was too close I couldn't do anything about it."

"Break it off. I'll meet you at the airport coffee shop in thirty."

"Airport in thirty."

The private line on the SAC's phone blinked insistently. "If you will excuse me, gentlemen, we will continue this discussion at a later time." When the door had closed he lifted the receiver. "Yes?"

"They're on the move in his convertible with the top down."

"Not exactly convertible top down weather is it? Or is the sun shining brighter where you are than it is here?"

"It's turning sunny, but it sure isn't warm. They had a large package covering the rear seat."

"Did you say it covered the back seat?"

"Completely. You could hide three or four bodies under it if you take my meaning."

"My thoughts exactly. At least one. Any sign of our recent arrival this morning?"

"I haven't seen her yet, but she's attracted some attention. Some idiot dressed for downtown Frisco showed up this morning. No sign of her anywhere, I haven't seen her since she turned off the lights last night."

"How are the detectives doing this morning?"

"They're working the hell out of this case. If they don't run it to ground, it will only be because someone blocked the evidence or prevented them from finishing the job. The young one is full of piss and vinegar and the old man is quietly as sharp as they come. Don't sell these guys short or presume they're lacking in skills. Between the two of them they don't miss a beat. I'm seeing some of the best investigative work I've ever witnessed. These guys would be standouts in any department. Time is getting away from them and the older guy can feel the case slipping through his fingers. He knows they're losing the war and he doesn't like it. The kid is frustrated and the old man is fighting to control his exasperation."

"Do you think Mr. Gordon was under the package they hauled out this morning?"

"I'd offer five to two he was and ten to one he wasn't alone. My money is on the photographer being with him, too convenient for her to be off the radar this morning."

"You may be right, coincidences usually aren't. Like McAfee and the artist coincidentally deciding to transport their package this morning instead of waiting until it got warmer or the photographer coincidentally not showing her face this morning. Is the tail in place?"

"The donkey left the barn with the wagon in harness."

"Thanks. Hang in there, I'll be in touch."

The SAC gently rocked his chair back and forth while he stared across the tops of the buildings at the bridge over the bay. He deeply regretted not being able to tell Kerry Weston the whole story. He hated knowing the silence demanded by his superiors put Weston's men in jeopardy. "No wonder they call us chicken shit," he sighed.

27.

TIM AND JULIE WERE EDGY, KNOWING A PURSUER
could find the way into the dead end. Both were perspiring in spite of the cool air and the space felt as if it was shrinking around them. They were struggling to maintain their composure when the car door opened.

"Keep low and stay quiet," Paul whispered. "We're going to take some time checking the ties in case anybody's watching. We'll leave both doors open so you can slide out. Stay low until you get to the other side of the log in front of the car. There's a spot in front of the car where you can crawl under."

"Did you see anyone?" Tim asked.

"No. We heard a car go by, but we couldn't identify it through the trees. I think you better play it safe and keep close to the ground."

"Right!" Tim slithered out and knelt to help Julie exit.

Jean spoke softly as she retied the cord securing the painting. She never looked at Tim and Julie, but concentrated her attention on what she was doing. "There's a trail to the beach and another along the top of the cliff that's supposed to go all the way to Patrick's Point. There are a lot of places where you can hide and wait for dark if you need to, or it might be easier to just hang out like a couple of locals on one of the small beaches. You'll have to figure it out. While you're at it, think of a way to get us out of this mess alive."

"Thanks Jean," Julie said. "We'll find a way out of this. We just need a little time." She squeezed Jean's hand, and received a firm grip in response.

"Hang in there guys," Tim said. "We'll be in touch soon. Don't expect a phone call, if they haven't already bugged your phone they will before the day is out. Be careful what you say and who you talk to. We gotta split!" They slipped into the shifting shadows.

"Okay, what's our next stop?" Paul asked.

"Now we arrange to have this framed."

"While we're at it we can check to see if they've fixed my car." Paul started the car. "I don't know what it is about you, but life sure has been exciting since we met."

"Oh yeah, this is more fun than a root canal. Another shot or two of adrenaline and I'll be able to run a two minute mile. Why don't you take the old highway through Trinidad? It joins up with the freeway at Little River and right now I could use a quiet look at some awesome scenery."

"You got it. First star to the right and straight on 'til morning."

Alma exited the freeway on the same off ramp Paul had used. Several minutes had passed since she had seen the Mustang, but there was a trail to the beach nearby and she thought they might have gone there. She turned right and drove slowly down the old highway looking for where a car had turned off the road. The entry to the beach trail looked like it might have been used recently and thick undergrowth blocked her view, but she kept looking as she passed. About a hundred feet later she saw a flash of cobalt blue. "There you are. Going for a walk on the beach?"

Alma parked under the trees a quarter of a mile down the road and grabbed her field glasses. She had to find a place where she could watch the trail. She she didn't even slow down when she tore her jacket crawling through a barb wire fence. She scrambled up on a stump just in time to see Tim and Julie disappear into the heavy vegetation along the top of the bluff and hear the Mustang start.

Alma lowered the field glasses and exhaled. Until then she didn't realize she had been holding her breath. "So you managed to get out of the cabin and now you're doubling back, eh?" she mumbled. "Well, nothing for it but to go back and wait for you to arrive." She took off her jacket and examined the tear. "Damn! I love this jacket! Maybe I'll stitch a logo patch over it."

Alma arrived at her cabin in a state of extreme agitation. She closed the garage doors securely and stomped through the back door, slamming it behind her. Flushed with anger and frustration, she threw her coat and purse on a kitchen chair and walked to the front window to stare out at the ocean. Once she had her breathing under control she picked up the phone and punched the speed dial. It rang once.

"Yes?" The voice was male, the tone flat.

"He's here," she growled. "I need some help. Everyone who ever came in contact with Gordon is here. There are so many assholes swarming over this place if they all farted at once it would blow the planet out of orbit. You need to send me some help! I can't handle this many alone."

"I can't help you. The area is hot and word is out the target is there. Do your job and stay out of my face about what you think you need. Call me to report the target's actual location, or to tell me you have the situation under control. Otherwise, stay off this line!"

The line went dead. Alma held the phone against her chest and stared into a day quickly brightening as the fog evaporated in the warmth of the sun. She felt alone and inadequate, cast into a situation beyond her level of confidence with no hope of assistance. "Thanks for your support!" she mumbled, and hung up.

28.

JOHN STOPPED A HUNDRED FEET FROM THE OLD highway to wait for the information on the car that followed them down the off-ramp. The driver had driven straight to the on-ramp and re-entered the freeway. "I have a suspicion there's an awful lot of cooks trying to stir this kettle of stew, you know what I mean?"

"The kitchen's beginning to feel a little crowded and everyone wants to use a different temperature and their own seasonings. This case keeps getting stranger all the time. Do you have any idea what we've stumbled into?"

"You mean based on my centuries of experience?"

"Yeah, something like that."

"I haven't a clue. The only thing I know for sure is the clock is ticking, the pieces are scattering, and we still don't know who or what we should be chasing or why." Just as he finished his sentence, Paul and Jean drove through the intersection ahead of them. "I also don't have any idea where those two are going or why, but at the moment they're the only lead we have. There seem to be a lot of people interested in where and how they're spending their time, so let's just get in line and see where they lead us."

"Maybe ten minutes since we lost sight of them a mile from here. What do you think they stopped to do?"

"Your guess is as good as mine. They could have stopped to look at the scenery, jump each other's bones, or dump a body.

Who the hell knows? Damn! They could have been dropping off a passenger who was hiding under the damned painting."

"Fortysix-two, Humboldt."

"Go ahead," Tom responded.

"Ready to copy information?"

"Go ahead."

"License plate is registered to the US Government."

"What department?"

"No department listed, only US Government."

"A cold plate owned by the feds. Now what in the hell is that all about?"

John shrugged. "An unmarked fed snooping around in our investigation and no help coming from the local feebies? I think we've got our tail caught in the wringer and someone is trying to drag us through. Let me have the mike."

"Humboldt, fortysix-two."

"Go ahead."

"Will you notify HS1 we were being followed by the car with the cold plate? The guy split when we spotted him. Would you request the boss give us a call?"

"Ten-four."

"I think maybe the boss is about to take the gloves off," John said.

"Sounds terrific, but what can he do if the feds stonewall him?"

"He didn't get to be the boss without making some friends in very high places. He knows how to drill and dynamite stone walls. I think his buddy over at the FBI is about to get an ear full of words suitable for eternal damnation. We'll just take a nice little drive down the coast and keep our eyes on the drop top happy horse to see what pastures it wanders into."

"Fortysix-two, HS1."

"Let me take it." John said. "I need to make sure he turns up the heat. Go ahead HS1."

"John, it sounds like we kicked over a larger hornet's nest than we thought."

"Yeah, it also looks like your friend in the Federal Building is still treating us like mushrooms. Can you get a little cooperation out of him or should I go over there and crank off a couple of rounds next to his ear to get his attention?"

"What's your location?"

"We're southbound on the old highway just north of Little River following the lovers. When they left the lagoon this morning everybody in the place saddled up to follow them, including the hermit."

"Very interesting. And the fed was following you?"

"You got it! Things keep getting stranger and I'd bet my pension the feds are up to their collective bureaucratic asses in it."

"I agree. I think I'll go shake the bush and see what jumps out. You guys stay on McAfee. He's still your only solid lead."

"Ten-four."

"Well, what do you think now?" John asked.

"I'm beginning to feel like a condom."

"You're what?"

"I said I'm beginning to feel like a damned condom. You know, like everybody's fucking with me and all I get to do is catch the drips and get thrown away when they're finished. What I really want to know is just who in the hell is running this case because it sure doesn't look like either of us is in charge of anything but the broom and dustpan."

John chuckled. "Like a condom! You're right! So far all we have is whatever they don't want to keep and don't give a shit what we do with it. Well, I don't know about you, but I'm not real pleased with this particular situation."

"So let's change it!"

"Any good ideas how?"

"Sure. Since they aren't playing by the rules, let's change the rules."

"What about making an arrest stick?"

"No matter who we arrest, this case isn't going to stick anywhere except in our craw. Let's just solve it and be done with it. Forget about making a case because it's never going to hold up in whatever federal kangaroo court catches it. If it ever gets there they'll make a deal to turn somebody into a protected witness with a new identity at taxpayers expense."

"How long have you been on the job?"

"Five years. Why?"

"Because in five years you have developed a level of cynicism which usually takes a longer career to flower. I like it, I like it a lot." He held out his hand palm up. Tom slapped the hand and received a mutual slap in return. "All right then. Let's see where these folks are going, then we'll boogie back to the barn and check in with Vince. We missed something and I want to find out what it is before it gets any later in the day. The more time slips past, the less chance we have of catching anything but a cold. I have another idea."

John picked up the mike and asked the dispatcher to have Cal Snider call him. "Old Cal will find anything we might have missed. Vince is good, but Cal's been hanging out on the wrong side of the law long enough to know what to look for that the guys on the right side aren't devious enough to think of."

"Are you saying Cal isn't exactly a boy scout?"

"Definitely not a boy scout. Most street gangs would be uncomfortable having him as a member."

"Too straight?"

"Too bright! Too smart! Too tough! Too devious! Too strong! Just too damn much!"

"A good guy to have on your side when you need someone to cover your ass?"

"The best!"

"Fortysix-two, fortysix-eleven," the radio crackled.

"Good morning, sunshine!"

"I got your sunshine. What's on your feeble old mind or have you already forgotten why you called?"

"Not nearly enough to be decent. If meaningful thoughts were clothing my poor old mush would be buck naked, which of course explains why I must beg your able assistance, most honored one."

"And what, pray tell, is this special assignment which requires you to address me with the honors to which I am rightfully entitled?"

"Bless me, oh holy one, for I have committed the sins of self-righteousness and gluttony. I most humbly plead your indulgence of this lowly source of degradation, but could you find it in your heart to cast your eyes upon the carriage of our recently departed fellow traveler and through your infinite wisdom perhaps glean what no other might be able to perceive from their position of limited perspective and knowledge?"

"Yea verily, I shall journey forthwith into the bowels of the building and make a fresh observation of the chariot in question and relay my thoughts in regard thereto without further adieu."

"May the greatness of the universe continue to smile with favor upon you, and may your exalted presence be showered with the many blessings of which you are so richly deserving."

Tom burst into laughter. "What a line of crap! Maybe you ought to genuflect and lick his boots the next time you enter his august presence."

"Whatsa matta, don't chew got no sensayuma?"

29.

"I'M CURIOUS, DID THEY HAVE MORE OF THESE convertibles when you picked this one up?"

"This was the only one. The dealer told me they arranged this one because they felt bad about my nearly new car stranding me at the edge of civilization. The guy even gave me a lower rate. Said I'd enjoy being able to look up at the trees, but my mind was on getting here, not playing tourist. It's a nice enough car. Why do you ask?"

"Maybe it's because I've lived here a while, but convertibles are the exception rather than the rule around here. I hadn't thought about it until this morning, but I think I understand why they don't sell many in this neck of the woods."

"I see what you mean."

Jean was shivering in spite of her heavy jacket. The bright morning sun brushing their cheeks with a promise of warmth was overwhelmed by the chill of the air. Her discomfort was compounded by a cold claw of fear holding her in a vice-like grip. She worried her peaceful world might come to a violent and abrupt conclusion. Her emotions swung from wildly excited elation to gut shriveling terror. She had so many unanswered questions. Tim had promised to tell the whole story of his two years in hiding once they were all safe and all Paul would say was how good it was to see Tim. He was more eager to devise a plan for Tim and Julie to escape from the cabin than to learn the details of Tim's life for the past two years. And then there was Julie. Who was she? She claimed to be a freelance photographer and an old friend. Unlike Jean, who was frightened, Julie behaved like a veteran soldier completely focused on defeating a powerful enemy. "I know Tim is your partner, but who is Julie?"

"They met years ago in Hawaii. He was negotiating a contract with one of our suppliers and she was doing a photo shoot. They were close for a while, traveling together when they could and seeing each other when schedules permitted. Then it stopped and he just said things didn't work out and asked me not to press him for details. He said he needed some space. I swallowed my curiosity and respected his wishes. I know he was heartbroken over the break up. He put on a good show of being the strong silent warrior, but for a long time he lived in a shadow of quiet sadness. I'm not sure he ever stopped hurting over her."

"How close is close?"

"He told me he asked her to marry him, but she wasn't ready to be domestic. He tried to be happy with what she was able to give, but I guess it wasn't enough."

"Do you believe she's really a photographer?"

"I've seen her by-line in a lot of places. She is a freelance photographer no matter what else she does, her professional name is A. Rose. We can stop at a book store and pick up one of her books or look through some magazines for her by-line if you like."

"Doesn't it seem a little too coincidental for all this to be happening at the same time in the same place? I don't think I'm being paranoid. She just happens to find Tim on the beach and they show up unannounced in your cabin. Even if they're long lost lovers, how does she manage to attach herself to him so quickly when he's on the run? How can she drop everything she's doing to play a major role in this cloak and dagger routine? Doesn't she have a deadline? Doesn't it all seem a little too convenient? Think about it!"

"I guess I was so excited to see Tim alive I didn't take time to sort out the coincidences. Seeing him is like meeting a ghost. He's my best friend. I'll do whatever I need to do to help him. As for Julie dropping everything to help him, what about you? Aren't you here with me under a similar sort of circumstances?"

"I see what you mean. I understand how you feel, but set your personal feelings aside. Where does it leave us? Someone is trying to kill him and it looks like we're in the line of fire. What are the odds whoever is chasing him is trying to get to him by going through you?"

"I know, I know. The same thought keeps going through my mind and I'm trying not to think about it. I'm trying not to think about how scared I am. I'm scared for you, I'm scared for me, I'm scared for Tim and Julie. I'm scared of what might happen and I'm trying to keep a lid on the urge to do something crazy."

Jean put her hand on Paul's neck. "I know. I'm scared to death the whole world is about to blow up in our faces and there's nothing we can do but wait around like sitting ducks while it does."

"I'm sorry I got you involved in this. I thought Tim was dead and it turns out he's still alive. I came here to gain some perspective on my life. I didn't plan on meeting you, I didn't plan on caring for you so much. I don't want to lose you, but it's not fair to ask you to risk your life to save someone you just met. Whatever I have to do to protect Tim, I can't let anything happen to you."

"I believe you. I know you're loyal to Tim. He's your best friend, but he's not alone either. What about Julie?"

"Julie may be more than she claims to be, I have to agree with you there. Her coincidental appearance seems a little too fortunate. I think she may have a darker side, something sinister lurking in the background. I don't think I'd want to meet her in a dark alley unless I was wearing an invisible shield and had a couple of bodyguards along."

Yes! Exactly what I'm talking about! Something about her seems so, so-"

"Professional?"

"Yes! Professional! But, at the same time she s so tiny, so beautiful, so-"

"Vulnerable?"

"Yes, but, well, no. More like she's the kind of woman who you expect needs someone to, uh,"

"Like she needs a strong man to protect her?"

"Yeah, kinda. No, not exactly. I don't know how to explain it. Something just doesn't seem to gel with what she appears to be. I've only been around her for a couple hours so I don't have anything to go on but my intuition. Maybe she let her guard down because of you and Tim, and maybe it's just a woman thing, but to me she seems more like a praying mantis than a butterfly."

"Now there's a romantic analogy."

"I just think she's more of a predator than a photographer. I spent enough time in the corporate jungle to learn you don't go anywhere unless you're willing to feed on the people who will allow themselves to be used. I know I'd be worried if she entered the competition for a position I was trying to win. She's like a great white shark dressed up to look like an angel fish."

"She's a beautiful lady and definitely no dummy. On the other hand, I've honestly never looked at her from your perspective."

"Pretty will get the boss's attention, especially if he's a middle aged man. I bet she uses her looks to get what she wants because women learn early how to play the pretty card, but she's more than just a pretty face. She's a dangerous opponent. There's a lot more than being pretty and looking vulnerable and being bright making her dangerous. I think she's willing to do what needs to be done without any compunction about who gets hurt when she has a job to do. She's sweet and she's pretty and she's sexy on the surface, but she's stone cold at the center. Most people wouldn't notice until it's too late."

"You make her sound like a hired gun."

"I just had a terrible thought! What if she is? What if she's the one chasing Tim? What if we've just handed him over to her?"

Paul glanced sharply at Jean, then turned his attention back to the road. "Do you think she's here to, damn! Tim could be in real trouble!"

"I don't think so. I think she has a different agenda. She was waiting for us with Tim this morning, so maybe she really is trying to help him. If she wanted to kill him, she's already had the chance and didn't. If she wanted him dead why would she make sure we know she's hooked up with him? No, I think he's safe with her for the same reason I think he would already be dead if it was her plan to kill him. He may actually be safer with her than with anyone else."

Paul measured Jean's comments against his memories of Julie and what he had seen of her mannerisms earlier in the morning. It all seemed to fit. "I hope you're right. Otherwise I'm going to spend the rest of my life blaming myself for whatever happens to him."

A blanket of silence draped itself over them as they retreated into their own thoughts. Neither noticed the passing scenery or the two detectives following discreetly in their wake. Jean finally broke the reverie to direct Paul to a frame shop in downtown Arcata.

The detectives watched them deliver the painting and followed them to where Paul's car was being repaired. They broke off the surveillance and drove to the courthouse to follow up on Cal's inspection of the pickup.

30.

"JOEY, JOEY, WHAT YOU DOING?" HIS VOICE WAS kind and grandfatherly, skillfully hiding his irritation. "What you gonna do if she see you? She's a stone killer. She ain't gonna look kindly on you checking up on her. What you thinking? Huh, what you thinking? Do you ever consider the consequences before you do something?"

Joey hung his head. The old man wasn't supposed to know he was here. Somebody must have ratted on him. Now he was in even deeper shit and needed to find his way out without having to swallow too much of it. "I fucked up with the others, so I was going to watch closer this time and make sure it went right. I thought-"

"Listen to me! I know you fucked up. Webster got caught with his pants down and got his ticket punched. He was one of the best, but he screwed up and made you look bad. He's gone. This time you got nobody to share the blame. This time you sent Pisces. You wanted to watch you shoulda watched the first three and stayed home to watch a ball game this time. You didn't ask if you should follow her. You made this decision all by yourself and you get the blame for it all by yourself. I want you to get back here where you belong. Now! Let me talk to your cousin."

Joey handed the phone to Gino and went to the window to stare out at the misty morning. It felt as if a giant weight had settled on his chest. The old man had chosen him over

Gino to groom for leadership and he kept screwing up. He'd fouled up another chance to prove himself and as usual, Gino was sent to clean things up. Maybe this time he was supposed to clean the fuck up too.

"Yes, sir," Gino said. "I had the pilot lay over. Yes, sir, we should be home in a few hours. Yes, sir, as soon as we arrive. Yes, sir. Thank you, sir."

The path was barely noticeable. Tim missed it and started down the bluff until Julie called him back and they turned north through the brush. They stopped frequently for the first half mile to be sure they weren't followed. They had reached the edge of the timber where an open meadow separated them from where he had left his car in the State Park when he suddenly stopped and dragged Julie behind a patch of brush.

"What is it?" she asked, peering cautiously to see what had alerted him.

"I'm not sure! I saw a flash of light."

"Are you sure it wasn't just a car catching the sun?"

"No! I'm not sure, but I've stayed alive by looking first and assuming later." Tim looked through the branches for the source of the light. "You caught me the first time I let my guard down, so don't ask why I'm so careful." He raised up enough to see across the meadow and smiled grimly. "There he is."

"What do you see?"

"Look just to the left of the big rock in the middle of the meadow."

Julie moved her head until the large rock came into view. A boy stood on top. His mother stood at the base of the rock watching the child and talking to him. "It's just a kid and his mother, what are you, wait a second, I see a guy with field glasses leaning over the top of a car." As she watched, he lowered the glasses. She instantly recognized Joey. "You slimy son of a bitch!"

"Friend of yours?"

"Not exactly."

"What exactly?"

"He hired me to find you."

"How convenient! Now here he is, ready to take delivery. Nice work! Now you can get your money even faster. I'm sure the old man will be pleased, probably give you a bonus for a job well done. A little something extra for your retirement package! I've got to hand it to you! You actually had me believing it!"

"What the hell are you talking about?"

"Great planning on your part. I fell for the whole thing! Walked right into the trap with my eyes wide open, or at least I would have if he'd been patient enough to stay out of sight until you finished closing the trap. Or has it closed already?"

"It's not like that!"

"Then how is it?"

"It's like I told you on the beach. I didn't lie to you. I didn't plan it this way. I didn't expect him to be waiting for us. I didn't set you up! I took this assignment because I wanted to find you, not because I need the money and not so I could turn you over to them. Joey broke the contract. The old man is going to lose this time. I don't need them or their money, I need you."

"Well that sounds real warm and cuddly, but if he's here he also knows where Paul is. If he can get to Paul, he's definitely going to get to me because I won't abandon my best friend."

"Of course he knows where Paul is! I think everybody in the western world knows where Paul is! That's not the point! The point is we can't help Paul if we can't find a way to neutralize the junior wise guy."

"How about I walk out and distract him while you sneak up and put a shiv in his spine?"

"A very attractive idea, but the location is a little too public. Where's your car?"

"It's down the road you can see behind him. Why? Have you thought of a way to handle this problem?"

"If it doesn't work you'll have to handle him on your own, but if you can get him to your car, I can take him out when he gets there. He's not going to kill you. His grandfather wants you alive. You're of no value dead. His grandfather needs whatever you're packing around in your suspicious mind. The old man is in deep trouble with his unforgiving business associates without it. You're essentially a death warrant for the one who delivers your body. Even if the deliveryman happens to be his favorite grandson."

"He the one in training to take over?"

"Yeah. The old man has big plans for him, but the kid's a loose cannon with an ego bigger than his brain. He's screwed up every job he's ever been given. He lacks patience. He also lacks a lot in the way of trust and honor by checking up on me. I should send his head to his grandfather with my resignation stuck in his mouth."

"Truly a pretty picture. I'm sure the old man would be favorably impressed."

"You don't get it! I'm a free agent! Nobody checks up on me! The brat needs an education in manners and professionalism. I'm going to move around him to the left and work my way to your car. Bring him to me. I'm going to broaden his education in a way that will reach even his pea sized brain. Give me five minutes before you make your break across the meadow. He'll follow you and try to stop you. Make sure you bring him to me. I'll teach the little shit to mess with me!" She disappeared into the brush, silent as a fading shadow.

Tim determined a viable route while five minutes stretched out like hours. He wanted to reach his car just as Joey caught up with him. He hoped the kid didn't get trigger happy and screw up the game plan.

He moved through the shadows at the edge of the timber, watching for a moment when Joey's scan was directed away from him. As soon as the large rock was between them he moved toward the center of the meadow in the sight shadow of the rock. When he was closest to his car he walked briskly toward his camp. He was twenty yards from the road when Joey recognized him and called out. Tim instantly broke into a run. He heard the squeal of tires as Joey took up pursuit. The timing was perfect. Tim reached the campsite just as Joey slid to a stop in front of him and leaped from the car brandishing an automatic pistol.

"Hold it right there!" Joey held steady aim at Tim's head.

Tim stopped, locking his eyes on Joey's and raising his hands shoulder high. "What the hell's going on? Are you nuts?"

"Shut up and get in the car."

"What the hell is this? What's going on?"

"Knock off the bullshit, Gordon. You know exactly what's going on. You have an important appointment to keep in LA."

"Hey man, you got the wrong guy."

Joey's voice rose. "I'm not here to play games. I know who you are, so there's no point in trying to hide any longer. Now get in the fucking car!"

Tim needed to buy time for Julie to arrive. "Why are you trying to kidnap me?"

"Don't think of it as a kidnapping. Think of it as a

command appearance." A sharp point in the small of his back accompanied Pisces' voice in his ear.

"Give me the gun or I'll do some frontier surgery on your kidney. And Joey, move real slow. I wouldn't want to cut you open by mistake."

When Joey started to turn his head a sharp jab in his lower back accompanied her hissed instructions. "Don't bother to turn around. Stand real still and hand the gun over your shoulder. Make sure it's hanging from your trigger finger. I wouldn't want you to try anything dumb like shooting back over your shoulder. Things could get messy."

Tim walked around the rear of the car. "Why don't I take the gun so nobody gets nervous? There, I feel better now. Why don't you tell us what you're doing here?"

"I came after you. I've been chasing you for two years. My grandfather wants to talk to you about some unfinished business."

"I suppose he does, but why did you send all those other people if you were going to come yourself? Didn't you think they could handle me? What if one them discovered you were following them so you could grab the glory? Was that your plan all along? Use them to flush me out and then tell them they weren't going to get paid because you did their job for them? Don't you think they might be a little upset with you? Hmm? Did you ever think about that?"

Joey's fear was beginning to show and he was breaking out in a nervous sweat. His voice cracked when he spoke. "I had to do something. You kept getting away. You got away from the best people I could hire. My grandfather expects me to bring you in. He told me-"

Pisces spoke quietly and added a few more ounces of pressure to the blade she held against Joey's back. "What do you think he'd say if I just sent him an identifiable part and tossed the rest of you in the ocean like happened to Webster? Of course I'd make sure your body wouldn't come back in with the tide."

"I think maybe we should take him somewhere less public," Tim suggested.

"Good idea. Did you have somewhere in mind?"

"I know the perfect spot. Let's take his car. I don't think anyone will connect it to us. Why don't you sit in back with the boy wonder while I take us where no one will hear him scream."

Pisces could tell Joey was past being nervous. It was apparent his emotions had fled past scared to terrified. Trapped by his own bad decisions, he got into the back seat. Pisces sat behind Tim and watched a tsunami of panic overwhelm Joey as he fought to keep tears from welling up in his eyes and his bowel constricted.

Pisces stared coldly at him. "Try not to soil yourself, Junior. You smell bad enough already. Fear has a stink all its own and you smell scared."

Tim didn't care about the car he'd abandoned at the State Park. He'd stolen it in Salinas and sooner or later someone was bound to find it. He glanced around the interior of the car he was driving. "This buggy looks like it spends more time parked than driving. Did you steal somebody's airport car?"

"Th-th-the c-c-c-car rental p-p-places w-w-were all c-c-c-closed and I needed a c-c-c-car."

"The good news is whoever owns it probably won't miss it for a while. The bad news is it's probably going to smell really bad when they do find it. Damn, did you shit yourself?"

"Y-y-yes." Joey stammered, as tears leaked down his cheeks.

31.

"HEY PORT, DID YOU FIND ANYTHING NEW, OR ARE
you just treating this buggy like your personal erector set?"

Vince Freitas looked up as Cal ducked under the crime scene tape. He waited for Cal to survey the piles of parts surrounding the pickup before he answered. "You know, the batmobile handle really fits this crate. I found a built-in GPS system and a mobile phone with enough power to blow life into any dead spot on the planet. The thing is so strong he needed a remote antenna to keep from poaching his eggs when he talked on the damn thing. Take a look." Vince handed him a phone the size of a cigarette pack.

"Anything else of interest?"

"The list is long and distinguished."

"Like the number of asses you had to kiss to get this cushy little job?"

"Oh, much longer. Take a look at this." He handed Cal a yellow legal pad with an inventory several pages long of the items discovered in the truck.

"Seventeen bugs?"

"You betcha. Seventeen of the cutest little eavesdroppers you ever did see, pick-ups so sensitive you could hear a mouse fart two blocks away."

"And probably all the best listening gear as well, all micro miniature so he could carry it around with him?"

"The whole candy store. All very small, a separate recorder

for each lead, and a master board the size of a notebook computer. This guy was equipped with the absolute best in surveillance equipment, including a miniature microwave horn for those times when you just can't plant a bug. The camper is a high tech audio lab. This whole truck is remarkable testimony to the ingenuity of the criminal mind."

"I thought the feds were the only ones with this level of technology."

"Everything's for sale. The companies who invent and build stuff for the government spend a lot of green on R&D and expect it to turn a handsome profit. Uncle Sam may be their biggest customer, but they'll sell to anyone who has enough money."

"Three cheers for free enterprise. Can you give me the run down on the weapons, or do I have to read the whole unedited list?"

"Besides the bow and arrow, there were a couple of Colt forty-fives, a Glock nine millimeter, a Remington Riot Special complete with double ought buck, a Mac ten machine pistol, a Nam-chuck, a night vision scope suitable for mounting or hand-"

"-and a partridge in a pear tree," Cal sang.

"You got it. The bad guys have all the best equipment, the good guys get whatever doesn't offend the sensibilities of the liberals, and only get to use it after you get shot at, as long as it doesn't violate the civil rights of the criminals."

"Constitutional rights. You know we can't have the downtrodden feel like their rights are being infringed upon. Can you imagine the chaos if the good guys were allowed to shoot first with bigger firepower than the bad guys? Why, they might even consider letting us drive fast cars, imagine a pursuit where you're driving a faster car than the guy you're chasing. Now, there's a wet dream."

"Dream on if you like your panties wet. Speaking of fast, this baby was built not only for looking ugly, but for going real fast. High performance suspension system, nitro boost on a race modified engine, close ratio five speed box, and a two speed rear end with a NASCAR oil cooling system for the engine and the running gear."

"How's the work?"

"Tits, man, absolutely tits. Whoever put this baby together had money to buy the best components and the knowledge and talent to build it right. This is a dream. It's also a living unit, a high speed chase vehicle, and a studio for listening to what people don't want you to hear. Of course, if someone complains about what you hear, you have everything needed to inoculate them with a hot lead injection."

"Sounds like you like it, or at least appreciate it."

"What's not to like? The outside looks like a piece of shit, but it's camouflage cosmetics. This is a thing of beauty. Oh yeah, we found some more pocket change. Total of five compartments full of used twenty's. Thirty-five thousand dollars in cash!"

"Should cover lunch for a while."

"And, to light the candles on the cake, we matched a print."

"John Doe has a name?"

"John Doe has several names and a list of addresses from those times he was a guest in some of the country's finer residences for the criminally inclined. This came in just before you got here." He handed Cal a rap sheet. "Take a look."

"Holy shit!"

"Interesting reading, isn't it."

"I gotta talk to John right now! I'll see you later."

"You're welcome. Feel free to drop in any time, asshole."

"I got your asshole." Cal trotted to the elevator.

"In your dreams, man, in your dreams."

Elevators are never fast and when you're in a hurry they feel absolutely glacial. Cal could have sworn this one had an anchor attached. It seemed to take hours to reach the third floor dispatch center. Cal ran from the car as soon as the door opened and burst through the door of the dispatch center making demands.

"Get me Ragsdale right now!"

The dispatcher was in the process of handling a communication when he came through the door and held up one finger. He skidded to a halt and began pacing the floor.

"Please would be a nice word, Cal," she scolded before she keyed the mike. "Fortysix-two, Humboldt"

"Go ahead"

"What's his twenty?"

"Fortysix-two, what's your ten-twenty?"

"About two minutes from the barn."

"Tell him to meet me at the batmobile as soon as he comes off the street."

"Detective Snyder requests you report to the vehicle inspection area as soon as possible."

"We'll be right there."

"Sounds like you have just about enough time to catch the elevator and get down there. Something big going down?"

"Maybe too big." Cal ran to the stairs. He could be in the basement before the creaky damn elevator got to the second floor.

Tom stifled a yawn. "What do you think that's all about?"

"Your guess is as good as mine, but it sounds like Cal found something we need to see right away."

"To the bat cave!"

"Capes and cowls, boy wonder!" John and Tom were still laughing when they saw Cal sprint from the stairs.

Cal didn't wait for John to get out of the car. He yanked the door open and shoved the printout into his hands. "Look at this!"

The rap sheet on Noah Stephen Graham was a gold mine. Two nicknames were the most important of the string of aliases. *Cracker* was a prison tattoo on his right biceps, *Webster* decorated the left shoulder. The background information showed he had a bachelor's degree from Michigan State and Masters Degrees from University of Washington and New Mexico State.

"Chemical Engineering, Electronic Engineering, Mechanical Engineering, what was this guy, some sort of genius?" Tom asked.

Cal laughed. "Surprised to find a bad guy with an education?"

"Not at all. Hell, anybody can go to college, but this guy had enough degrees to make an honest living anywhere he wanted to go."

"Sure he did," Cal agreed. "Enough knowledge to be an expert in clandestine surveillance, bomb construction, and automobile design. Enough to do all the stuff we've found in this truck. He did a hitch in Uncle Sam's Army where they taught him all kinds of nasty tricks. He had enough knowledge and experience to mercenary himself to the highest bidder. Looks like he was a real pro until he met someone who had no respect for the brilliance of his mind."

"One conviction for credit card fraud, did one year of a three year sentence, and got kicked on good behavior. One year at Felony U to make the right friends and he was right back in business with a well healed client," John remarked.

"Yeah, but who's the client?" asked Tom.

"Kids ask the damnedest questions don't they," Cal commented.

John looked up from the papers and smiled. "Well let's see if we can fill in some of the blanks. The sheet shows he was suspected of being connected to organized crime. Where do we look next? LA? Las Vegas? San Francisco? Or is he part of an eastern family? Did a year at Lompoc. Who do you think he might meet there?"

"Presuming he got connected there, euphemistically speaking," Cal interjected.

John decided not to respond to the double meaning. "Presuming. Okay, the chances are pretty good he made friends with some folks from the LA crowd while he was there. Lompoc is the usual play pen for the LA crowd when they're awarded public accommodations."

"And McAfee and his partner are from LA." Tom said.

"Good thinking. You're beginning to see why our fine feathered friend here is so excited. Pieces are beginning to fit together. Cal, can you check with Lompoc and see if any members of the LA crowd were in the population while our friend was at camp?"

"Sure. Don't you think we need to confirm this is our man? I mean this looks real good, but it's only a partial print, and the face and the description aren't what you'd call an exact match. The guy may have had a couple tattoos removed, but look at the face. It doesn't match our guy."

"You're right. Let's not get ahead of ourselves. We'll work on confirming the identity while you run down who was on campus with him at Felony U."

"Wait a minute. If I'm gonna jump back into this case, I gotta get the okay from the powers that be to abandon what we've been working on. It's one thing to take a quick look at the batmobile, but Dutch and I are on another case. I can't just drop it to play with you guys."

"So why haven't you already done it?" John asked. "Maybe you and your partner can catch a ride on this gravy train and help us solve a really interesting crime. I heard your suspect suffered an overwhelming case of remorse and turned himself in. Take his statement, let the DA plead him out, case closed. Finito! No effort at all. This, on the other hand, is a real mystery, an enigma enclosed in a puzzle, a bone you can really sink your teeth into. How can you resist the opportunity to do something worthy of your passion for criminal investigation?"

"Sit and spin. I'll see what I can do. You take a look at what the peerless portagee found and I'll catch up with you at the medical examiner's office."

Tom stared out the windshield. "You know, something is bothering me."

"What's troubling you now, bunky?"

"When we ran background on McAfee he came up Mr. Clean. Absolutely spotless, not even a parking ticket. Then he comes here for a vacation and the whole world blows up around him, but nothing seems to connect to him. Even if we may have a mob connection for the guy with the batmobile, there still isn't anything to tie McAfee to our victim except proximity to the crime scene. I think I saw his partner on the beach. In fact, I'm sure I saw his partner, but that doesn't help much, because all the official records say Tim Gordon is dead. Do we have even a single clue about why this is going on?"

"As usual, your summary is succinct, correct even. So what's bothering you?"

"I feel like a flounder flopping around in the bottom of the boat. We keep diddling around with all this stuff and we still don't know shit about the reason behind this chain of events. If you can call it a chain. It looks more like a bunch of missing links."

"So how would you suggest we find those missing links? Any bold new ideas?"

"Hey, I'm the new kid on the block. What am I supposed to know about being a detective? I'm just stumbling along hoping I don't step on my dick and give myself a fresh circumcision. Not to mention I didn't get any sleep last night and I'm beginning to feel like an intravenous injection of caffeine would only put me to sleep."

"Don't look at me for sympathy. I was laying there happily dreaming about calling in cock-locked in bed. Next thing I know, you're rousting me from my slumbers and dragging me out to the great northwest puddle to go on a scavenger hunt. You'll get over it. Let's go see what Vinnie uncovered. After that, we'll try to see what we can squeeze out of the office coffee pot and review where we are after this latest excursion. We gotta get it written down and see what dots connect."

Vince was waiting patiently at the front of the disassembled vehicle with a clipboard. "Jesus, Tom, you look like you been run over by a truck. I know being a detective has certain privileges, but don't you think shaving should be part of your daily grooming? If you ran out of blades I'll be happy to run over to the 7-11 and pick some up for you."

"Your sincere constructive criticism is deeply appreciated, fuck you very much! You got anything new and interesting or are you just having fun playing hot wheels at company expense?"

32.

THE STINK OF FEAR LEAKED OUT OF JOEY WITH AN
aroma of ripening cheese. The silence of his captors only served
to increase his pulse and respiration. Tim drove at the speed
limit, strangely implacable, yet the one time Joey caught his
eyes in the rear view mirror Tim's reptilian gaze made his
skin crawl. His imagination ran in crazy circles whenever he
focused his thinking on the uncertain future lurking in the
shadows of his imagination. A brief glimpse of Pisces in his
peripheral vision told him anger was not the driving force
behind her expression. He had wanted to show his grandfather
he was worthy of confidence and trust. Now, he just hoped to
survive long enough to apologize for his foolishness. And then
there was Gino. Gino had been sent to bring him home. He
should have waited for the fog to lift and flown home, but he
couldn't resist his compulsion to make sure Pisces did the job.
He'd landed Gino in deep shit, too.

Pisces broke the silence. "Do you feel like your time is
getting short? Sort of like you stepped into the trash compactor
on the Death Star and C3PO and R2D2 are on the Millennium
Falcon and can't shut the damn thing down before it turns you
into a block of shit?"

Her smile was completely devoid of warmth, like the
expression of a cat toying with a mouse just before snack
time. "Wh-wh-what are y-y-y-you g-g-gonna d-d-do?" Joey
stammered.

"W-w-well, T-T-Tim, wh-wh-what do you th-th-think w-w-we s-s-s-should d-d-do?"

"The first thing we need to do is get him out of the car before he shits his pants again. Man that's foul."

Pisces sniffed the air. "I guess I turned off my nose and concentrated on the stuff coming through the window. It's probably worse from where you are than back here with the fresh air in my face. He's definitely in need of a shower at the very least." Rain splattered the windshield. "Looks like a cold one would be the easiest."

Joey felt the car slow as they approached an opening between two redwood trees. "Here we are," Tim said. "A couple more minutes and we'll get poopy pants into the fresh air before one or both of us pass out from the stench."

"Good!" Pisces turned to Joey. "I'll give you some free advice. You don't have the heart, the stomach, the nerves, or the brains for this game. You need to choose a different career. Something quiet and unexciting like, oh, maybe tax accounting. Tax accounting would be good. The family can always use somebody to cook the books. Don't you think so, Tim?"

"I don't know. If he ever got audited, the IRS would have him bent over and his pants down so quick he wouldn't even get a chance to lubricate before they ripped him a new aperture."

"You give a whole new definition to the term Brownie Hawkeye."

"Ah, here we are. Home at last." He stopped next to a large redwood with a narrow arched opening into a burned out bole. "All ashore who's going ashore. We need to have a little conference." Tim stepped from the car and then walked around to open the door and pull the seat forward for Joey to exit. Pisces followed immediately in his wake. "Step into my parlor." Tim indicated the opening into the tree. Joey ducked his head and stepped down into a roughly circular space about twelve feet high and eight feet in diameter.

"Why don't you find a place to sit over there?" She directed Joey to a place directly across from the arched opening. "Isn't this cozy!"

"Cozy and dry and the smell of charcoal and rotting wood make a wonderful air freshener," Tim said. "Almost anything is more pleasant than our fragrant friend. But enough niceties. Tell us why we shouldn't make you disappear."

A small light came on in Joey's eyes like a glimmer of sunlight through a cloudy sky. Hope sprang full grown in his mind and his voice was elated. "You mean you're not gonna kill me?"

Tim smiled. "Maybe, maybe not. It depends on whether or not you have the right answers."

"Speak for yourself, Tim. The little shit really pissed me off. First he talks me out of retirement and then he follows me! He followed me! He didn't trust me to do my job! Nobody follows me and gets away with it! I'd enjoy watching him squirm while the life trickles out of him."

"I know, he's a miserable excuse for a human being and his absence from the population wouldn't make much of a ripple in the greater scheme of things. On the other hand, given the circumstances and his grandfather's affection for him, he might be a useful bargaining chip."

"I'd rather use the little vermin for fertilizer. Nobody would ever find him out here if we didn't lead them to the spot and show them where to dig."

"I agree the idea has merit, but maybe we should use him first for leverage with the old man. For some inexplicable reason the old fart has strong feelings for the kid. Maybe I was wrong thinking he was the kind who would eat his own children. I'd hate to think we tossed away a perfectly good hostage when we could have traded him for something of real value. What the heck, using him as a bargaining chip doesn't mean you can't punish him."

"You're right. If I play my cards right, the old man might even hire me to take him on a vacation like the one he designed for you on PSA. I could have the pleasure of disposing of the little bastard and get paid for it too. It'd be like having my cake and eating it too. Ooooh! I like the way you think!"

"You mean the old man had the airplane blown out of the sky? Lisa and all those people dead? I always thought,"

Pisces' hand rapidly covered Tim's mouth before he could finish the sentence. "I know what you thought. Save it for another time. We've got work to do. Some of it may be wet. Keep your focus on the present to make sure we'll have plenty of time later to deal with the past."

Tim started breathing again and nodded his head. "So tell me, junior wise guy, what can you do to help me? So far everything you touch seems to be like everything you eat. It all turns to shit. Speaking of which, did you shit your pants again? Man, you smell bad!"

Joey hung his head. "Yes."

"Well, for Jesus Christ! Come outside and clean yourself up!" Tim walked outside. Joey followed with Pisces far enough behind to avoid the worst of the smell. A few more embarrassing moments and Joey's soiled underwear lay buried under several inches of leaf mold. They returned to the shelter of the tree.

"So what do you think you can do to convince your grandfather to let me walk away?" Tim asked.

"My grandfather sent my cousin after me so I wouldn't

get in her way and get vanished. He don't want me to die, I'm his favorite grandson. Someday he wants me to take over the family business. He's grooming me, he's-"

Tim held up his hand to stop the rapidly accelerating flow of words. "I don't give a shit how much he loves you, or which way he wants you to comb your hair, or which way you pucker your lips to kiss his ass. I want to know if you can convince him to forget me and my partner and our families. You're of no use to me if you can't."

"I've got it!" he cried out excitedly. "If you let me go, I'll tell him I made a deal with you in exchange for your life. He's a man of honor! If I tell him I made a deal, he'll honor it! You just have to let me go."

Pisces chuckled. "Sure thing. We just let you run home so you can tell the old man to leave us alone, and he's so tickled to have you back in one piece he just forgets the whole thing. I suppose he forgets to pay me too."

"I'll pay you myself! Just let me go."

"No." Tim said. "I think it's gonna take a bit more than your word to convince him of the error of his ways and make him forget me. Where did you ditch your cousin?"

"I ditched him at the airport. I don't know where he is now. He's probably looking for me."

"Do you know this cousin by sight?" Tim asked Pisces.

"Gino? Sure. About the same size as this one, five years older with a full time job sweeping up what this one screws up. Gino's a bright guy. I never understood why the old man dotes on this dumb shit when he's got another grandson with more brains in his little finger than this one has in his whole body."

"It's pointless to try to understand the way people treat their children. I really have only one question. Do you think you can find him?"

"The search area should be relatively small. He knows brain trust here was trying to find me. I'll just go back to my camp and scoop him up. Shouldn't be a problem."

"Gino's smart. He's not just gonna roll over and play dead for you."

Pisces patted Joey on the shoulder. "I have an advantage. He doesn't know I'm looking for him. The trap will be too easy to spring." She handed Tim the gun. "Here, you keep this one. I have another in my car."

Tim kissed her on the forehead. "Hurry home, you know how I worry when you stay out after dark."

33.

PETE HOLLAND ALWAYS HUNG A SPECIAL MONIKER
on his partners, so Cal had no prayer of escaping a nickname.
While his own nickname was a reiteration of his name, the
handles he gave others were often obscure, and frequently
less kind. Having commented how Cal had more war paint
than a Paris whore, he immediately nicknamed him Irma
after Irma la Duce. Cal knew Dutch chose truly demeaning
names for people he liked and respected the most. The men
were born a week and fifty miles apart and grew up following
different paths. While Cal had been up to his elbows in greasy
parts in the Auto Shop at Arcata High, Dutch was immersed
in Chemistry and Physics at Fortuna. The Army sent Cal to
Viet Nam while Dutch acquired a degree in Mathematics and
spent four years in the reserves. Dutch was the department's
statistical analyst and the first deputy with a personal computer
on his desk, the machine programmed to search criminal
information data bases available through the Internet and
NCIC. Others occasionally used it when Dutch was in the
field, but it was clearly understood the boss purchased it for
Dutch and it was his baby.

Dutch was chasing a lead through the San Francisco Police
Department records when Cal entered the bull pen. "Good
morning, sunshine," he greeted Cal. "Whatcha up to so early
in the day?"

"The boss just assigned us to help John and Tom with their murder investigation."

"You mean the floater at the lagoon?"

"The very same. How much do you know about it?"

"Just the office scuttlebutt and what you've told me. Do you know what we need to work on?"

Cal handed him the case file. "Here's what we have so far. It needs to go back to the boss when you're done. You play catch up while I chase some background on our stiff."

"You got an ID?"

"Not a hundred per cent certain, but a real good hit. Here's a copy of the guy's sheet. As soon as I get things rolling we'll go talk to the medical examiner."

Dutch opened the file and began reading. A minute later he let out a low whistle. "Hey Irma, you know who this guy is?"

Cal held up one finger. "Good morning, this is detective Calvin Snider in Humboldt County, I need some assistance with an investigation involving one of your former guests." Cal filled the watch officer in on what they were looking for while Dutch listened to the conversation with undivided attention.

Cal hung up. "Now, what were you trying to tell me?"

"Do you know who this guy is?"

"If we did we wouldn't be chasing all over the country for a complete ID. Do you know this scrote?"

"Only as Webster. He picked up the name in the army. He's smart as hell, absolutely brilliant with listening devices and explosives. How come it took so long to figure out who he is?"

"One picture is so much better than a lot of words. Let us retire to the catacombs for a visit with the resident ghoul. It will answer a multitude of queries."

"A multitude?"

"A veritable plethora of enlightenment awaits in the shadowy depths. Let us be off without further adieu."

"I think you're letting the nickname get to you. Keep your skirt down and your panties up, it's so much more dignified."

"But so much less exciting."

Dennis O'Malley was sitting at his desk with a cup of coffee and a donut when Cal and Dutch arrived. On his desk was a series of eight by ten inch close up photographs of the subject from the lagoon. He glanced up as the detectives entered. "Well, look what the cat dragged in. What're you guys up to this morning? I heard you'd beaten a confession out of your suspect after he turned himself in, just to make sure he wouldn't get cold feet and change his mind before he entered a plea."

Dutch stared coldly at the medical examiner, formulating an appropriate remark, but Cal was quicker to respond. "Guilty as charged. We heard you had a fresh pot of coffee and enough fat pills to harden the arteries of the whole department and didn't want you to face the task of eating them all by yourself. We just got dragged in on Ragsdale's floater. I guess he and the kid can't handle it alone so they asked us to show them the way home."

"Called in the varsity!" Dutch announced.

"More like calling the janitor to mop up," Dennis remarked. "You guys get anything back from NCIC?"

"Actually, yes. We've got a possible ID on the stiff, but there's a lot of pieces that don't fit."

"I know what you mean. I was just taking another look at these pictures. This is the first time I've seen or heard of a guy over thirty with no marks or scars and finger prints so badly hashed you can barely get enough valid points to make a confirmed match. It looks like he burned his hands and they scarred over, but that doesn't jive with the absence of identifying marks everywhere else."

"He probably had a high priced plastic surgeon give him a make over," Dutch suggested.

"That's why I was taking another look at these pictures. It looks like he had at least one tattoo removed and some skin grafts done. Whoever did the work is really good."

"What about the face," Cal asked. "Do you think he's had a Michael Jackson?"

"You mean change the nose, the eyes, the size of the lips, extract a little here, add a little there, make me look beautiful?"

"Sure, why not? In your case it could only be an improvement. Why not this guy?"

"I think you're right. The pictures are good, but another look at the body will probably be more enlightening." Dennis stood up just as John and Tom stepped through the door.

"Top of the marnin' ya old sod," Dennis greeted John.

"Aye, and a fine marnin' it's lookin' to be," John replied.

"Not to be disparagin' o' yer appearance, but you look a mite like a rag what's been played with by a pup."

"An astute observation laddie, but this young buck here got me oot und aboot well afore the sun peaked over the hill and he hasn't given an old man a chance to catch up 'is breathing."

Dennis noticed Tom and also looked worn out. "So tell me, Tommy, was it a fine young filly you had the old feller chasin', or was it honest detective work what had you out so far ye could'na shave proper afore comin' to the orifice?"

"I had a bright idea that didn't work out quite the way I expected, but may have gotten us closer to an answer. On the other hand, maybe it only added confusion to the whole mess."

"Curiouser and curiouser, eh?"

"Thank you, Lewis Carroll."

"Hey, I know a good line when I steal it."

"Dennis, why don't you go locate our mystery guest and help him find a seat out here where we can all take a look at him," John said. "We're going to raid your coffee pot. I need some caffeine to keep me going."

Equipped with full cups and fortified with donuts, they got down to business. Cal and Dutch weren't surprised John asked Tom to update them. Tom only needed five minutes to run down what they knew and what wasn't clear. Dennis was ready by the time he finished.

Dennis began with the right bicep where the rap sheet showed a tattoo. After adjusting the light to various angles he found an area which he marked with a pen, taking care to outline the color changes in the skin using small dots. The finished shape was a match for the photo on the rap sheet. Dennis stepped back to view his handiwork. "Well, what do you guys think?"

John remained skeptical. "Yeah, it looks good, but before we start celebrating let's try to match more than one tat. This guy's sheet shows a lot more identifying marks than one tattoo."

Two hours later they were convinced the man on the table was the mafia soldier known as Webster.

"Well, at least we know who he is," John said. "How are you doing on tracing his buddies at club felony, Cal?"

"I made a call. Maybe we'll have some answers when we get back upstairs."

"Okay. Looks like we're done here. Thanks, Dennis, I'll tell the boss to put something extra in your pay envelope this week."

"I'll be most gratified to receive the benefits of yer munificence, milord. Are ye sure ye'll not be needin' me further this day?"

"'Tis for certain I am, laddie, 'tis for certain."

34.

PISCES STEERED INTO THE TREES A HALF MILE
north of the entrance to the lagoon and turned off the motor.
She left the keys in the ignition and wiped every exposed
surface inside the car and the exterior areas where recent
contact showed on the unwashed surface. Satisfied she had
erased or smudged any fingerprints, she walked into the
timber. She entered the campground like a tourist returning
from a leisurely stroll and went directly to her campsite. Several
people were pleased to see her return; none were campers.

She studied her camp with great care as she approached.
The sun had burned away the last of the fog and was shining
brightly through the branches, sprinkling the ground with a
lacy array of light and shadow. It provided excellent camouflage,
but a bit of luck and the attentiveness born of experience gave
her an advantage. She might not have noticed the man sitting
in her tent if not for a splash of sunlight bouncing off the face
of his watch and casting a momentary pattern of light on the
inside surface of the tent. She retrieved a small automatic pistol
from a compartment concealed inside the front bumper of
her car and clipped the holstered pistol into her waistband at
the small of her back as she walked to the tent. A quick check
confirmed her suspicions. The flap was zipped shut leaving two
inches open. A small design flaw made it impossible to zip the
last two inches of the door flap from inside the tent.

She opened the tent and stepped inside as though she didn't expect to find anyone waiting for her.

Gino smiled thinly. "Good morning."

"Hey, Gino, what brings you to this neck of the woods?"

The smile didn't flicker and his eyes remained emotionless. "An intentional pun I'm sure, but you never do anything without carefully planning every move, even when it's a bubbly greeting. You know why I'm here, so cut the crap. Where's Joey?"

She considered playing him, but he'd made himself too easy to find; not a good time to dance with him. He obviously had his grandfather's foot planted firmly on his neck. "Not far. You want to see him?"

Gino stood up, ducking his head to clear the top of the tent. "Is he alive?"

"He was the last time I saw him, but God only knows what the dumb shit might have done to get himself killed in my absence."

"Killing him would be a mistake. Grandfather dotes on the kid and would think unkindly of anyone who might cause his favorite grandson to expire at an early age."

"He might even think badly of the keeper for not taking better care of his pet terrier."

"This isn't about me."

"Don't you ever get tired of sweeping up behind the miserable little shit?"

"We each have our cross to bear."

"So what's in it for me if I give you back your brain dead cousin?"

"I can't speak for grandfather, but I'm sure he'll be grateful to you for being considerate of his feelings."

"Do you think I could ransom the brat for a large favor or two?"

"I don't know, he doesn't like anyone having leverage on him. Holding the kid for ransom would be a dangerous game, the old man is notorious for carrying a grudge. I heard a story about an unfortunate individual who learned about payback twenty years after he stepped on the old man's toes. I don't think you want to be looking over your shoulder wondering what he'll do to settle a debt."

"You carrying a cell phone that can get out from here?"

"Yeah, what you got in mind?"

"Call your grandfather. I want to talk to him." She watched like a moray eel waiting for a reef fish to swim too close as Gino dialed the unlisted number and waited while it rang ten times before being picked up.

"Yeah?"

"Good morning sir, it's Gino."

"You got him?"

"Not yet. I have someone who would like to speak with you."

"Let me talk to him"

Gino handed her the phone and sat down.

"It's me. What's with siccing your attack dogs on me? You know I work alone. I don't have partners. I don't have helpers. I don't have observers. I deliver the work as agreed without having some lame brained, dipshit asshole looking over my shoulder. I don't deserve this, and I'm not going to put up with it!"

"I apologize for the manner in which my grandson has conducted himself, it was not my wish for him to do this. Have I not always treated you well?"

"Past history doesn't even begin to make up for this. He's compromised my entire operation. You know how I protect myself from this kind of foolishness, I don't offer second chances to anyone who steps on my toes. We've had a working relationship for many years and always treated each other honorably. Because of our history, I wanted you to know my intentions before I eliminated the problem. I'm prepared to start with the one sitting in front of me." As she spoke she slid the pistol from her waistband and pointed it at the center of Gino's forehead, watching his eyes blaze for a fraction of a second before returning to an emotionless stare.

"It pains me to hear such anger in your voice, what can I do to ease your unhappiness?"

She knew not to trust him, but needed to press her advantage. "I don't think you have anything I want. I took this job as a favor for an old friend. I'm distressed to learn you've grown too old and too soft to control your soldiers. I'm also disappointed I have to make an example of these two, but it's just business. As you've told me, business is business. Sometimes you win, sometimes you lose. It's all part of doing business. It looks like our business is finished."

"Wait! Don't hang up! What do I need to do to protect my grandchildren?"

Pisces paused for several heartbeats, feeling the tension build on the other end of the connection before she spoke. "You have four hours. I'll meet you at the airport. Don't be late!" She removed the battery and tossed the pieces of the phone on the cot.

"I think we're about to discover how far the old man will go to save your sorry ass. Unless he's on time and does exactly what he's told, the sand in your hourglass will run out."

"So what are we going to do for the next four hours?"

"To start with, take your gun out of the holster with two fingers and hand it to me. Be careful. If I even think you're about to try something, I'll give you a major headache."

Gino pulled his jacket open with his left hand and gingerly lifted the Glock from the holster and handed it to her. She stuck the weapon in her pocket. "Thank you. What else are you packing?"

"Nothing. My plan was to gather up Joey and go back. I was supposed to keep him from getting in your way. I don't know anything about this operation, I was supposed to bring him home before you killed him for interfering with you."

"You seem to have managed to well and truly foul up your assignment, haven't you? What happened? I thought you had better sense."

"You know I didn't have to wait for you to come into the tent. I didn't have to sit here and let you get the drop on me, I could have just followed you to him, killed you, killed him, and taken Gordon back. I could have blamed you for killing Joey and looked like a hero, but I didn't. I showed you respect and let you walk in here and take me without resistance. Does this sound like the way I usually do things?"

She thought about what she knew of Gino. "So what do you want in return for this respect?"

"Let me take Joey home. I won't let him get away this time. You finish your job, we pay you, and you retire."

"Not good enough. I need a quid pro quo. I need some serious vig to sweeten things or there won't be any deal."

"I figured you would, but you can't blame me for trying."

"No, you had to try. You can honestly say you made a sincere effort. You had breakfast yet?"

"No, and since you mention it, I'm hungry."

"Fine, but if you think I'm cooking for you, you've lost what little sense you had. You can buy breakfast and we'll get some take out for me and my crew. You can put it on your expense account. I'll even let you drive my car."

35.

ALMA SMILED WHEN PISCES EMERGED FROM THE
trees and walked toward her camp. "Where have you been since
yesterday, and what kind of mischief have you been up to?"
She muttered as she adjusted the field glasses to sharpen the
image and observed every move until Pisces disappeared into
the tent. A few minutes later a man exited the tent followed
by Pisces. He walked to the Jeep and got behind the wheel.
She had never met Gino, but his photo was on the chart of
the LA organization in the director's office. A worried frown
pinched Alma's face when she lowered the field glasses. "What
an interesting visitor!"

For the second time in one day, she ran to her car and
followed a vehicle leaving the lagoon. By the time she reached
the highway she had lost sight of her quarry. She did a mental
coin toss and accelerated south. She hoped to catch sight
of the Jeep as she crested the hill where a straight stretch
provided an unobstructed view. The car growled in protest at
Alma's demands, but after a moment the engine note steadied
and the car accelerated smoothly to eighty miles per hour.
Nearly five miles of growing apprehension rolled by before
she was convinced she was going the wrong way. She wheeled
through the grassy median and sped north with anger and
frustration taxing her emotions. She nearly missed seeing the
Jeep parked alongside the café in Orick. She parked with it in

her mirror, defiantly ignoring the impulse to do anything but wait impatiently.

Gino couldn't decide whether to be scared, nervous, or resigned to the worst. Pisces was impossible to read. Her face gave away nothing, her voice was absolutely cold, and those incredible green eyes were at one moment warm and friendly, the next icy and ruthless. Her reputation was frightening. She made people vanish like smoke on the wind. When she finished an assignment the target no longer existed. Gino believed he had become a target and was straining to control his emotions. He couldn't have felt more vulnerable if she had strapped a pound of C4 to his chest.

"Turn left up there," she said.

"Turn left where? I don't see a road."

"Slow down and take a left into the trees just past the end of that log. You'll see a dirt road."

The track leading into the trees didn't look like much of a road to Gino, but he made the turn and drove slowly into the trees. The highway disappeared behind him and his sense of impending doom grew as he drove deeper into the timber.

"Stop here. Get out and walk around to this side."

Gino did as he was told, keeping his hands away from his sides. "We're going to the tree with the hole at the bottom."

Gino had trouble seeing anything except Joey when he first entered the shadowy space. "Go sit with your cousin," Pisces told him. "We'll decide what to do with you in a minute."

Tim spoke from the darkness. "Nice to see you again. It's so nice of you to bring a young man for dinner. He is for dinner, isn't he? I don't know about you, but I'm feeling the need to feed. It would also be nice to secure these two. Standing guard makes it tough to watch my back."

"I have a solution." She went to the Jeep and brought back a bundle of heavy duty cable ties. "These should do the job."

"Joey, stand up and put your hands behind your back. Cross them at the wrist." Pisces quickly secured his hands while Tim did the same with Gino. They seated the men back to back, bound them together at the elbows and secured their ankles. "Now we can have a leisurely lunch surrounded by the beauty of nature. By then it will be time for me to collect the old man."

She took two takeout trays and two drink cups out of the car. "I fed Gino and brought food for us. You're looking a bit thin in the skin. Cousin Dipshit I don't feed."

"Fear and adrenaline will do wonders for your waistline. Eating becomes a real luxury when you're always looking over your shoulder and it doesn't exactly improve your digestion when you do get the chance to eat."

"I know you're tired of running, but you need to stay out of sight a little longer. Those two shouldn't be any trouble. I don't think anyone followed us, but you still need a defensible location. Let our guests fend for themselves, if they don't turn out to be our ticket out, we'll just have to find another way. It's time for me to go meet the old man. Once I have him alone, I'll see what kind of a deal I can make. At the moment we have some leverage and I plan to squeeze him for everything I can. The only flaw in my plan is if he doesn't consider the lives of those two worth buying. If he doesn't, we'll have to dump all their bodies where they'll never be found. We need to hope for the best and cope with the rest." Pisces hugged him. "Take care. Find a spot where you can stay out of sight and still see anybody trying to sneak up on you. I should be back in a couple of hours. If I'm not back in four hours it means I'm probably not coming back. Do what needs to be done with the boys and go to ground. Get word to Paul through Jean, her number should be in the phone book. Protect yourself!"

"I love you too." Tim took her face in his hands and kissed her lightly. "Come back soon."

Tim set off for a location where he could see without being seen.

The voices were too soft for Alma to understand and the breeze rustling the tree tops didn't help. She'd crept close enough to see the Jeep, but she couldn't see who was talking. She worried they would notice her if she got any closer. Tim Gordon had stayed alive by remaining alert for two years, meaning she couldn't count on him lowering his guard if his was one of the voices. She hunkered down behind a mossy log and strained to hear more than scattered fragments of words.

When she heard the Jeep start, she raised up enough to see the top of the vehicle moving toward the highway. Once again she faced two choices. She could stay here and try to see who was talking to the photographer or she could follow her. She could hear the Jeep jockeying to enter the highway. She gathered her feet under her and fled through the trees.

She dashed down the hill leaping over logs, dodging bushes and rocks in a manner uncharacteristic of a woman of an age of disintegrating bones and arthritic disabilities. She leaped into her car and nearly twisted off the key in her eagerness to start the engine. She roared onto the highway with the tires screaming, the engine howled in protest and she swore at the performance of the car, cursing the engineers who designed it. She eased the pressure on the throttle when the speedometer reached eighty miles per hour and tried to relax. She couldn't allow herself to panic even though her mind waged a war of uncertainty over her decision to follow the Jeep. Confused thoughts swarmed in her mind. Years of planning and manipulation were spinning out of control, even her car was overheating. She pounded the steering wheel in frustration.

She crested a rise to discover the Jeep about five hundred feet ahead of her. The photographer was the sole occupant. A flood of questions filled her mind. She took a satellite telephone from the glove box and pressed a programmed number.

Climbing to a rocky outcrop, Tim carefully surveyed the area. As he watched the Jeep begin to turn around he saw a flash of movement in the trees. The notion an animal had been spooked quickly evaporated when he caught sight of the fast moving figure. All he could see were brief flashes of clothing and what looked like gray hair. Something tickled a momentary hint of recognition before disappearing like a dying echo. He pondered the identity problem for a few minutes before returning his focus to the surrounding area, imprinting each feature in his mind.

36.

THE COFFEE TASTED REALLY GOOD AND LUNCH WAS
long overdue for John and Tom. The conversation drifted from
where the fish were biting to how badly the Giants were playing
since the All-Star break. The three older detectives were taking
a break from talking or thinking about the case. Tom's mind
was on a different track and their voices faded to a background
drone while the case raced around in his head like a swarm of
moths beating themselves against a light bulb. One thought
just wouldn't go away. "Hey guys, I hate to break up the party,
but something keeps bothering me."

"What is it this time, Watson?" John asked. "Did you
sleuth out who's gonna pay for lunch?"

"No, I know I'm going to get stuck with the tab. What
keeps getting in my face is Paul McAfee. I know he's got a
solid alibi, no apparent motive, no priors, he's a new arrival
and nothing points to him being the perpetrator, so why do
I keep bumping into him every time I see a new angle? This
morning we followed him and the artist all the way to Eureka.
I'm positive I saw his supposedly dead partner on the beach
where we found the body. We know the stiff is a mafia soldier
connected to an LA crime family. Gormac is an LA based
import business. It seems like there are too many coincidences
not to be a pattern I'm not seeing. Is it because I'm new, or am
I crazy too?"

"Well, being crazy is a distinct possibility," Dutch

commented. "On the other hand, in addition to five fingers and a wart, you may actually be onto something. Where do you see this pattern going? Do you think you know who mashed the victim's melon?"

"I think we missed something with McAfee. For example, why is the hermit so interested in him? She hasn't been out of her place before two o'clock in the afternoon for the past two years, but today she shags out after McAfee and, uh, uh, the artist, uh, Parker! And why was a fed following us when we were following the hermit? If McAfee isn't the killer, why do circumstances and situations keep pointing in his direction? How long do we let him keep running around before we do something?"

"Ah, I see what you're thinking," Cal leaned back and stroked his chin. "Maybe vee should interrogate him," he said in a comic imitation of a member of the Gestapo. "Perhaps vee poot heem een zee vindowless room, ja? Und vee feed heem castor oil und not let heem go potty. Vee chermanz haf vaze to mek you tok!" he growled and slammed his hand down on the table. Cal waited for the laughter to subside. "Seriously though, we don't have probable cause to arrest him. What do you think we would learn if we picked him up and squeezed him, aside from the name of his lawyer?"

"Or, considering another angle," John interjected. "Do you think he might lead us to the killer, or killers, if we maintain a low profile and keep an eye on him?"

"I don't want to throw cold water on your ideas," Dutch chimed in. "I just joined this little party, but it sounds to me like you've already focused your attention on one guy as the prime suspect. Maybe you've missed something obvious, something not connected to him, one important detail illuminating the path to the actual killer. It sounds like the only thing making this guy of interest is his proximity to the murder scene. He sure as hell hasn't confessed. I hate to belabor the obvious, but what you have so far isn't enough to make even a hint of a case. What else you got?"

Tom's gaze held Dutch's for several seconds, neither man blinking or speaking. A small smile slid across Tom's face. "A. Rose."

Dutch's face pinched in a puzzled frown. "A rose?"

Cal could not contain his exasperation. "No, not a rose, dip shit! A. Rose, the professional photographer at the park with eyes like emeralds and a hard body to hold them up."

"A. Rose. Why does the name sound familiar?"

"Because unless you've been on another planet, or not read a magazine or newspaper in the last five years, you've seen her by-line on photographs."

"She's here?"

Cal leaned over and put his nose about an inch from his partner's. "Hello! Earth to Dutch! It's time to join the party."

"Well, fuck you and the pinto pony you rode up on! Not everybody has been here since the beginning of the movie. It looks to me like the junior G-man here may be closer to solving this case than either of you tired old turds, so how about you quit getting in his face and pay attention to what he's saying." Dutch turned to Tom. "So what are you thinking, kid?"

"I'm wondering if she's connected to McAfee. She shows up a couple days after the fact supposedly to take pictures of the lagoon. She's using a lens long enough to count the ticks on a deer at a thousand yards, which is probably what you'd expect for nature photography, but she wasn't shooting nature when I talked to her. She was photographing the cabins and she had an unrestricted view of the attic window in the cabin behind McAfee's."

"And we know someone had been hanging out there," John said. "You saw someone come from there and shag off into the woods in the fog last night which led us to discover someone had been in the attic. Unfortunately, what you could see in the dark was less than enough to identify who it was beyond recognizing he moved like a man rather than a woman."

"Okay, so sue me for not positioning myself better. Getting back to where I was, she was taking pictures of the cabins. Did you see her this morning when we were hanging around waiting for things to happen or when you strolled over to talk with the Brooks Brothers model?"

"Nope. Of course failing to see her may not be significant. We were there early in the morning and she may have been up late. We know she just finished a long road trip. Maybe she was catching up on her beauty sleep. Sorry. I can't attach anything ominous to not seeing her, too many reasonable explanations."

"I didn't see her either. I saw her car, but I didn't see her. From my point of view, it's one more coincidence to add to the pile. I don't think she was there, I don't think I would have missed her if she was there."

"What's your home phone number?" Cal asked.

"Why do you want to know?"

"I want to call your wife and let her know you're wandering around with a stiff dick when you think about staking out a foxy photographer. I think she deserves to know what you were really doing last night when you told her you were working a stakeout."

"Thank you very much! You're a detective. There's a record of it around here somewhere. Go dig it up. Now do you have anything constructive to add to the conversation, or do you just want to fill the air with more verbal vomit?"

Cal smiled at John. "Jesus, for a slick arm rookie detective he has a real attitude. Have you been feedin' him those *old salt* pills again?" Once again, Cal succeeded in breaking the tension with a joke. The laughter was still echoing through the restaurant when their lunch arrived. "Truth be told, Tom, what you're suggesting is a bit of a stretch, but stretching is good. Maybe we need to stretch our thinking a bit and see what fresh fruit we can pluck. I've got a contact in the south I'll call when we get back to the office. There may be a link we don't know about. Sometimes you just need to plant the right seed for an idea to grow into something."

"Thanks. It can't hurt even if it doesn't go anywhere. By the way, how do you think the boss is doing with the feebies, John?"

"I got a suspicion the chair may be feeling a little warm under our local fed. The boss knows how to apply the heat. I bet he's using all of his experience to apply an open flame to the gonads of our favorite fumbling bureaucratic idiot."

Cal glanced at his watch. "Hmm, one-thirty. You think he's managed to spoil the SAC's lunch or maybe irritate his ulcer for him?"

"I'd like to think that by the time the boss is done with him he'll need a hemorrhoid pillow the size of a truck tire."

Dutch grinned wide. "Ooh, what a pretty picture! Those guys are always around to suck up the glory after someone else does the dirty work, or to look good for the cameras after they make a mess for someone else to clean up. And, of course, they're always so helpful when you need information from their computer system. My favorite response from those guys is the famous *need to know* classification. If it isn't on the wanted poster, you don't *need to know*."

"I've been on the job for five years and I still haven't heard anyone say anything good about the feebies except the news media. I grew up thinking those guys were the best in the world. I'm still waiting to see proof. Do they ever get it right?"

"Policy prevents them from being good street cops," John replied. "In fairness, they do a good job on white collar crime and interstate stuff. We don't usually get involved with the crimes they handle and they have a ton of useful information in their computer data banks when you can pry it loose. The problem is they don't tell the locals when they have an undercover operation going. If we stumble over one of the slime balls they've turned as an informant we end up with a lot of wasted time. Their typical response is to tell us it's an FBI operation and they'll call us if they need us. Some of their people may not be arrogant assholes, but I'd be hard pressed to think of one who isn't."

Tom got a look in his eyes all three of the older detectives were beginning to recognize as an intuitive leap. "What now, Tommy? What did you just connect?" Cal asked.

"I don't know if it's a connection or just an idea, sort of a continuation of my original idea."

"You mean like McAfee's partner being an undercover?"

"Think about what John just said. The feebies don't tell us anything about their operations. Gormac's operation is international, they have business contacts all over the world. He could be DEA, CIA, NSA or some obscure alphabet agency we've never heard about. What if he is? What if he was a mole in this LA family and somebody busted his cover? Take it a step further. What if all the people we keep running into are a part of a clandestine operation designed to take down an international ring?" Tom looked around at the others. "What if I've been reading too many spy novels?"

Silence held for a few moments while they digested Tom's idea. Dutch was the first to speak. "You came up with this undercover cop wrinkle a couple days ago. What's come of it so far?"

"Nothing. The boss's first chat with the SAC went nowhere. No surprise there. Still, if there was no substance to my idea, why was a fed following us this morning, and why was he driving a car with a cold plate not attached to any specific agency? The longer this kettle of fish stays on the stove the smellier it gets."

"I've been talking to all my street sources, but nobody in my snitch net knows anything," John remarked. "This case is like a remote island in an empty ocean. Nothing fits. Nothing connects. There's a whole flock of people interested, but nobody wants to share information. It sure smells like a fed undercover party."

"Right," Tom said. "A party we aren't invited to attend. So far our efforts to crash it have gotten us close enough to hear the music, smell the food, and press our noses up against the windows to watch the dancers. Unfortunately, we didn't get invited in. If we're lucky they may let us wash the dishes, sweep the floor, and carry out the garbage."

"You mean like a stiff who had the bad manners to wash up on our beach?" Dutch asked.

"Exactly, my man." Cal looked at Tom with a contemplative expression. "I think the old man has a point. A couple years ago I rubbed up against a feebee operation with the same feel. I think we ought to run this past the boss again. He may be able to shed some light on things."

John looked around the group. "Well if you guys are feeling replete, let's get back to the house and see what the old man has been able to do for us." He handed the check to Tom. "This is for you."

"Thanks, you can leave a tip."

The Sheriff was unavailable so they returned to the squad room. John and Tom had created a chart of the facts and their relationships. They edited the information daily to include deductions and inferences they had drawn. The display included photographs and a USGS map. They were studying the information and making sure Cal and Dutch knew what had been accomplished prior to their becoming actively involved in the case.

Cal stared intently at the chart. "Alma Jacobsen," he mumbled.

"What's that?" Tom asked.

"The old hermit," Cal mused. "Does anything happen she doesn't see or hear?"

"Probably not," Tom replied. "She doesn't talk about it much. It took some time for me to build a speaking relationship with the old girl, but she's proven to be a reliable source for the last year. I think she's lonely and watching other people fills some inner need. It's kind of funny, on the one hand, she watches everything and everybody like a hawk, on the other, she's incredibly discreet, really close-mouthed. She doesn't gossip about anything, she treats the information like a savings account. It's like the more she has salted away, the better she feels about herself. But if she tells you something, you can rely on it being gospel. The trick is getting her to let go of it."

Cal nodded, his attention focused on the chart. "Does she live alone or does somebody else hang out there sometimes?"

"You mean like a boyfriend?" John chuckled.

"No, not a boyfriend! Not that she couldn't have one. I'm sure you've discovered it doesn't grow shut when a woman gets older. I wasn't talking about her sex life, I was thinking she might have a son, or a daughter, or maybe some grandchildren, visit from time to time. Maybe she does have a boyfriend. I don't know, it was just a thought. I'm just looking for a rational way to weave the loose threads into a sensible tapestry."

John wrote *roommate/family/friend?* under Alma's name. "We've been thinking of the hermit as a recluse with no family or friends. So far you're the only one who has talked with her. What made you think she might have a social life we've overlooked?"

"I was thinking about the inside of her house, at least what I could see of it. I can't put my finger what it was, but, I don't know, it seemed like she wasn't the only one living there. The front room had a grandmotherly sort atmosphere, but there was a, uh, a younger feel about it too. One of those little contradictions the kind that nags at your mind until it finally scratches it's way to the surface. It's just like this damn chart! It's a jig saw puzzle whose pieces don't fit. You know what I mean?"

"Irma gets the same feeling every time he goes home," Dutch said. "Makes him wonder what the little lady does to fill up her, uh, shall we say, uh, days, while he's out fighting crime."

Cal took a backhand swipe at his partner and finished with a raised middle finger under Dutch's nose.

Dutch ducked and laughed. "Seriously though, he does have a point. Tom, you know her better than the rest of us. Does she have family or friends who occasionally visit?"

"Anything's possible, but I've never seen any visitors and she's never mentioned anyone. Which doesn't mean nobody's been there. I've never been inside her house. She always comes outside to talk with me or I catch her working in the yard, so I can't confirm what Cal might have seen. I know you guys are on the trail of something, but my mind kept going straight when you took the last couple of turns. How about you clue me in."

John spoke first. "I think I see where Cal's going. Suppose she has a visitor. She's doing her usual neighborhood watch and sees the victim come over the back fence. She sends her friend out the front where he can conceal his movement. He sees the victim move across the yard and duck under the neighbor cabin. He moves to the corner of the McAfee cabin and when the poor schmuck starts to look out from under he does his best Babe Ruth on the guy's noggin." Tom listened to the offered scenario, shaking his head and frowning. "You don't like the idea," John said. "What's wrong?"

"Why!"

"That's what I just asked you."

"No, you old fart! Why would somebody want to sneak around and bash the creep in the head? The accepted methodology when discovering a prowler is to phone and ask us to check it out! Why sneak out in the middle of the night in the pouring rain for batting practice? It doesn't make sense! Besides, if it was somebody being a good citizen and protecting the neighborhood from midnight marauders, why not report it? It wouldn't be the first time somebody got some lumps in that sort of situation! This time the prowler gets lumped, then hauled off and dumped, and everybody's polishing their halo. No! I don't' buy it! Even if what you say is what happened, I still want to know why!"

"Oh, why," John said sarcastically. "You are so damn picky! Picky, picky, picky. You're still looking for a motive! Is that what's troubling you?"

Tom laughed. "It would certainly be nice to have a motive. Something to explain what Webster was doing and why it upset someone enough to make him dead. Whoever laid the wood to him had a reason for busting his lights out. Webster had a solid professional reputation, so it follows that another professional, or someone good enough to be a professional, outwitted him. Maybe I am being picky! I still think it would be a lot easier to find the killer if we knew why he or she wanted Webster dead!"

"Don't you just hate it when somebody shines the cold light of rationality on your speculations?" Dutch asked. "But let's not toss the idea out yet, even it seems weak. Write it down as a possible until we can find something to prove otherwise."

"There he goes using the old Sherlock Holmes approach again," said Cal.

"Sherlock Holmes?" Tom asked.

"Yeah. You know, the way old Sherlock solved crimes. Once you've determined everything that couldn't happen, whatever remains is what did happen, no matter how implausible it may seem. The challenge is trying to eliminate all the possibilities. Sherlock had it easy. Doyle conveniently told the story so everything he needed to rule out could be ruled out. This is real life and real life doesn't usually cooperate with our plans."

"John Lennon said life is what happens while you're making plans," Dutch offered.

"I saw that on your computer," Cal said.

"It's my screen saver. Helps me keep my perspective."

"Speaking of your magic window, have you got anything new on it we can use?" John asked.

"Only some background on Webster. I'll have everything on your chart entered in my data base by tomorrow. I'm still a little behind the curve, but I'll be up to speed by morning. Maybe I'll even find something to illuminate Tom's elusive motive."

"Sure, just toss the evidence into the mixer and watch

it spit out the answer," Tom said. "Crime fighting in the electronic age. If we had a way to get your computer to talk to all the other law enforcement computers we'd save a lot of time. Who knows how many bad guys we could catch if we only knew we were supposed to be looking for them." Tom yawned and looked at the chart. "Okay, since you guys think I know the hermit and have a relationship with her, how about I drop in on her on my way home and see if she'll tell me anything. I need a ride back to my car, Dutch. If you can take me back to the lagoon, John can go visit with the boss and Cal can chase after his friends in the south. Maybe they've uncovered something we can use. I feel like this case is about to break wide open, I just don't know when, where, or how. All I can think to do is keep rooting around like a blind pig hoping to turn up a truffle. I'll go make nice with the hermit and see if she'll talk to me. I honestly don't think she's going to be very cooperative after letting your partner sneak up on her, but I'm willing to try. I'm going to head for home from there. I need a shower and some sleep."

"Sounds like a plan," Dutch said.

"Good idea," John added. "I'll see you in the morning when we've both had a chance to catch up on our rest. I don't need any more early morning wake up calls. It'll be just fine if you meet me here tomorrow morning at eight."

Tom snapped to attention and saluted. "Yes sir! See you tomorrow morning, sir! Who knows? Maybe I'll get lucky with the old girl."

"Now there's a pretty picture!" the other detectives chorused.

37.

KERRY WESTON WAS FAMOUS FOR HIS CALM
demeanor and controlled response to difficult situations, an
image reflected in the way his deputies strived to emulate him.
Elias knew his friend's legendary composure had lost the war
with his temper the moment he strode into the office. He knew
what was coming and braced for the coming assault.

"I understand your bosses think I don't need to know
jack shit about what you and your people do around here,"
Kerry began in a controlled tone of voice. "I honestly don't
give a damn who's kissing who's ass in Washington, but this
is my county! When you set up surveillance on my detectives,
I damn well need to know what's going on!" Weston's voice
became a snarl. "These men are my responsibility! I don't give
a diddly shit what your superiors in Washington told you to
do! If your men interfere in one of our investigations, or put
my officers at risk by not sharing information, I will use every
scintilla of political suck I own on Capital Hill to embarrass
you and your precious bureau and force you to support, assist,
and cooperate with my department in any way I say!"

"C'mon, Kerry, you know I don't make policy. The word
comes down to me. I can't tell you anything without clearance
from higher up."

"Oh yeah? Just following orders bullshit ain't gonna get
you off the hook this time! You need to pick up the phone and
get those orders changed. I've got a dead mafia soldier and

you guys know who he is, where he's been, what tooth paste he prefers, and the color of the hash marks on his skivvies! It's only logical to assume that if you know so much about him, then you also knew he was setting up shop in my county, and chose not to share the information with me. I bet you've been watching every move he's made with somebody from another office to make sure we wouldn't recognize him. My senior detective says the agent following them was a stranger. He knows all your local agents, so I want to know what a strange federal agent is doing tiptoeing around inside our investigation. I didn't just fall off the goddamned carrot wagon, I know what goes on behind the scenes with your witness protection programs, and federal snitches, and undercover drug buys, and all the other shit I don't have a need to know until one of your operations goes tits up. Then you call my department to clean up the mess so you federal golden boys don't get egg on your face or dirt under your fingernails! I've had enough of being kept in the dark while you feed me bullshit! It's time for you to shine some light on the subject. You really don't want me to walk out of here without a complete rundown on this situation, and I mean everything! I want everything relating to this case, or peripherally touching the people involved in this case. If I leave without it, your agents won't be able to fart without one of my deputies being there to write them a ticket for a violation of the clean air act."

"Look, old friend, this thing is a lot bigger than a dead soldier washing up on the beach."

"No shit, Sherlock! In case you hadn't noticed, I figured that out before I walked in here. So let's cut the crap! Every passing hour puts my men further from solving this crime, an unsolved crime with no effect on your department, but one that will make us look like we're not doing the job we're hired to do. I'm sick and tired of this dance. I want the truth, and I want it now!"

Elias leaned back in his chair, maintaining eye contact with the man leaning angrily across his desk. When he spoke it was in a carefully controlled voice. "You've got to be very discreet with what I'm going to tell you. You can't give it to the press and you can't tell anyone I gave you the information. I already made the call. I was supposed to try to stonewall you, but that isn't going to work, so here's what's been dumped on your doorstep."

"Is this like somebody leaving bag of dog shit burning on your front porch and ringing the doorbell so you can stomp it out?"

"An incredibly apt analogy. I hope you're not wearing your good shoes because this case is pretty ripe. Here's the story. A few years ago, Tim Gordon was approached by a big time operator in the orient about smuggling counterfeit computer chips into the country in his containers of legitimate computer components. Gordon was trained as a Special Forces operator by the Army and he saw a chance to do something for his country. He told the smuggler he'd give him an answer when he made his next trip. He got word to the CIA and NSA through his unit commander in the reserves, and we set up a joint operation using Gordon as point man. The objective was to bring down the operator in the orient along with his organized crime connections in LA. Gordon was really good. We ran him successfully for three years. He gave us names, dates, and enough connections to map out the whole operation with the exception of the big man in the Chinese government who was pulling the strings. He had it narrowed down to a few possibles and it looked like a couple more months would be all he needed to confirm the top guy.

We were almost there! Enter a boneheaded new bureaucrat on the hill with visions of cost savings glory. Suddenly the whole operation was shelved."

"Leaving Gordon swinging in the breeze?"

"Worse. The bureaucrat made sure a mafia mole in our LA office got wind of who Gordon was and spilled it to his boss. We know who the mole is because we've been using him to feed bogus stuff to the mob for years, but the new guy on the hill made sure the information was leaked and the mole did what he's paid to do. The bureaucrat basically put out a contract on Tim Gordon."

"Can't you protect him?"

"My boss told me his boss decided to sacrifice Gordon. The guys in charge decided it was better to let the bad guys kill him, rather to than risk having him around to tell tales. He knows too much about too many powerful people in too many sensitive places. The situation has the Maalox flowing freely. Tim Gordon's disappearance is critical in avoiding an international incident."

"Why doesn't the CIA take him out? Don't they do their own wet work any more?"

"You want the official line, or, never mind, it doesn't matter. Washington wants him to go down at the hands of the bad guys so we can keep our skirts clean. This thing stinks so bad it makes me sick, but my hands are tied. I can't do anything until something makes it my unquestioned purview. I'm not even supposed to know what I just told you. The SAC in LA who was running Gordon is an old friend from the academy and we went fishing a while back. You know what I mean?"

"So Tom was right. There's an undercover out there who's had his cover deliberately blown so the guys he was trying to take down can take him down instead. Unfortunately for all the people planning his demise, he's turned out to be quicker, smarter, and a damn sight luckier than anybody who's been sent to kill him. How incredibly inconvenient. I'm curious. Is this one of those bureaucratic debacles involving ten federal agencies where the right hand and the left have no idea what the other is doing?"

"Pretty much. I can't overtly help you. I've told you what you can't officially know and all I can do is try to answer any questions you have about any evidence you've got. I really don't know any more to tell you."

"At least you've removed some of the confusion. You still haven't told me who the hell was following my detectives this morning!"

"Good question. Give me the plate and I'll try to find out. I may get shut out too, this runs real deep in some very high channels. I'll try, I really will."

"Just don't treat us like mushrooms. We're not bulletproof. You know as well as I do cops are always at a disadvantage when it comes to protecting themselves. Not knowing who or what you're facing causes too many short careers. The bad guys always have the advantage and they know how to work together for mutual benefit. It's like the Indians against the US Army. Whenever the Indians gathered together into a united fighting force, they kicked the shit out of the Army. Unfortunately, they all had their own agendas and didn't work together most of the time. Just like us." They exchanged a few banal pleasantries as they walked to the door.

Weston went on his way mentally sorting through what he had learned. Lost in thought, he stepped off the curb against the light and was almost run over by an emerald green Thunderbird. The car's horn blasted him out of his reverie. He glimpsed the startled expressions on the faces of the driver and passenger as he jumped back out of the car's path.

Paul leaned on the horn and stood on the brakes at virtually the same instant the man stepped into the cross walk. In the adrenaline fueled slow motion nature of such events, he confirmed the traffic light was green. Then the man was back on the curb and they were rolling safely through the intersection.

"Holy crap!"

"Certainly enough to get your heart started," Jean commented.

"Or make it come to an abrupt halt. I don't think he even knew what he was doing until I honked at him. He looked completely lost in thought."

"I'm glad you didn't hit him. Running over a pedestrian can spoil your whole day."

"So much for the good news. The bad news is I think I need a change of underwear. Do you see a men's clothing store anywhere close by?"

"I guess it explains the aroma."

Paul wiggled around in the seat. "I don't think I need a change yet, but I'm certainly ready to flee civilization and get back to the quiet of the beach."

"Even the beach hasn't exactly been the picture of quiet lately. What are we going to do about Tim and Julie? We managed to sneak them out of the cabin this morning, but what do we do now? What are they doing right now? I have another painting being framed, you're driving your own car again, but as far as I can see, we still don't really know what's going on."

"Too true. Julie isn't exactly what I expected and Tim has

changed in the past two years. I guess two years of ducking and running is bound to have an effect. Tim was always full of fire and confidence, like he could conquer the world. Mostly he was a lot of fun. He would walk into a room and everybody's spirits would rise. I know the happy spirit is still in there, but he's put it away until he can stop running. So far all we've done to help is smuggle him out of the cabin. I'm waiting to see what he needs next. He seems pretty adept at staying alive when a bunch of people are trying to kill him. As improbable as his story may sound, I have to believe him until something comes along to change my mind. I love him like a brother, I'd believe him and trust him even if no one else in the world would. He's what being best friends is about."

A quiet contentment settled over them as they crossed the bridge north of the city. Glittering jewels of sunlight danced across the rippled surface of the bay and splashed twinkling highlights into the car. They were blissfully unaware of the white Toyota a few hundred yards in their wake.

38.

TIM CONTINUED HIS SURVEILLANCE OF THE FOREST as the breeze freshened and the sun moved past the meridian. The rustling movement of the treetops, ordinarily a soothing white noise, camouflaged all but the loudest sounds, leaving him uneasily dependent on sight. Clouds drifted on the afternoon breeze and lost control of their burden in a heavy rain. He weighed the advantage of high ground against the ease of defending the hollow tree. There was only one narrow entrance and anyone entering would not be able to see much until their eyes adjusted to the interior gloom. A momentary advantage would be all he needed. It was not only dry, there was the possibility his captives might get loose. Tim was soaked to the skin when he ducked into the shelter of the tree.

Whether through good luck or the survival habits of a seasoned professional, Pisces immediately noticed the car appear behind her and maintain constant separation. Not knowing if her suspicion was valid, or a figment of paranoid imagination, she exited the highway near the mouth of a river. A mile south the land rose steeply to the bluff where the airport was located. She had given the old man four hours and she was a half-hour early. She wanted to arrive at the airport just as he exited the terminal, and stopping gave her the chance to photograph the car following her and a few minutes to refine her plans. She took a series of pictures of the Escort as it passed her location. The car exited the highway at the foot of the bluff and continued south on the frontage road. She lost sight of it behind the willows separating the road from a series of salt water ponds. Pisces wondered if her uneasiness was from coincidence or paranoia. Coincidence may not be threatening, paranoia kept you alive.

Pisces let her mind wander while she drove to the airport through drizzling rain. The chain of events carrying her to this place at this time seemed the stuff of novels and movies. Choices and opportunities most young women would shy away from had attracted her to a career of permanently solving problems for people. *Paris in the spring. Unpredictable weather, bright blossoms, sidewalk cafes, and the light. In all the world I have never seen another place where the light is pink. I was so innocent when I arrived with my one year scholarship to study with Phillipe at the Sorbonne. Phillipe. Phillipe the artist, Phillipe the philosopher. Phillipe, my first serious lover. Phillipe who introduced me to the excitement and adventure of ending lives. What a strange life he seduced me into. No, that's not fair. He didn't seduce me into the life. He only swung the door open far enough for me to run through it as if I had found the Holy Grail. Twenty years ago. Five years before Phillipe was killed. Ten years before I met Tim Gordon. Twenty years ago when youthful anger still burned bright enough to fuel my passion for the work. Too many years have passed to keep the anger alive. Anything that burns so hot eventually runs out of fuel. Too many years of living two lives. This is the last time I walk this path. This time I'm not doing it to free myself from my idealistic anger. This time I'm doing it to free myself from the life. I want the freedom to enjoy feeling young before I forget what it's like to be young. I want to be free to surrender to being in love. I want to be free.*

The Don slumped unhappily in the large leather seat of the executive jet as it raced across the late afternoon sky. The luxury of the airplane was the kind of comfort he had come to expect. Comfort didn't enter his brooding thoughts or soften his anger. He was flying to the north coast because the order of things was badly out of order. His grandsons had lost control of the situation. He considered what he should do when he met Pisces. She was always extremely efficient in carrying out her assignments. She was very bright and at the moment she was in control of him. He detested being in someone else's control or debt. She put him in her debt by keeping Joey alive and now she had Gino too. Business always has a cost, but to sacrifice two of his grandchildren over this fiasco was too high a price. *Maybe I would have handled things differently when I was younger. Perhaps I should do things the old way. Time is so precious to me now; time and the children I love. I can see my life coming to an end. If I were younger there would be time to bring other children into the world. But being forced to deal with Pisces on her terms doesn't mean I have to make it easy for her. I know she doesn't intend to make things easy for me. She will undoubtedly prove to be very difficult.*

The pilot taxied to the parking area through the cool, wind-driven rain of a summer storm born in the gulf of Alaska and fed by the warm waters of the Japanese current, a typical weather pattern that kept the region green.

He accepted an umbrella from the co-pilot and walked to the terminal building. Pisces scanned the area to confirm he was alone. She put the Jeep in gear and stopped at the curb as he stepped onto the sidewalk. The car sagged briefly as he settled in the front seat, collapsed the umbrella and closed the door. She watched the rear view mirror as she drove toward the nearby town.

"I had a shadow on the way here. I want to see if anyone takes an interest in us."

He looked into the side view mirror. "What kind of car?"

"A Ford Escort, blue, about ten years old. So far no one has left the airport behind us and I didn't see the car in the parking lot. The last time I saw it was just north of here. I got off the highway and let it go by. I'm not even sure it was a tail. It could have been a coincidence."

"A little caution's not a bad thing."

"A little caution is why you're here. Actually, a lot of caution. I don't see much caution on your part by letting me take you away from your watchdogs. Since when do you go anywhere without an escort? Even if I did tell you to come alone."

"I trust you to behave with honor." His soft rumbling voice seemed to begin in the vicinity of his navel and echoed through his chest like a kettle drum.

"Since when do you trust anyone?"

"Such cynicism is unattractive in a lovely young woman. You gotta let an old man believe in something, don't you? You've always been reliable. This is a sad situation. You're unhappy and so am I. You asked me to come. I am here. You have something you want to discuss with me. I will hear what you got to say. You said you want to do some business."

"Business is why you're here. Your putz of a grandson doesn't understand how I do business. I work alone. I do things my way and nobody checks up on my work. He decided I should have an audience without even knowing how to be discreet about it. Neither does the cousin you always saddle with cleaning up behind him. Those two couldn't sneak up on a deaf, blind mute."

"Forgive them, Bella, they're just trying to make an old man happy. Joey don't mean to make you angry, he just wants to make me happy. Is this such a bad thing? Trying to make an old man happy?"

"I don't really give a shit if you're happy or not at this point. Here's where we stand. Our original agreement is complete. I located Tim Gordon and he's with your pet cousins right now. I've done my job. I don't have to deliver him to you in LA because the bonehead twins showed up on my doorstep. As soon as Tim Gordon and those two were in the same place at the same time my job was done. You owe me the balance on the contract. I want the money now."

"Bella, Bella, you don't got to be so angry. Of course your job is done. Of course you'll get your money. But what about Tim Gordon? You say he is with my grandsons, but you are holding my grandsons hostage. Of course I will pay you. And then will I have Tim Gordon?"

"You make a call and transfer the money. When I confirm the transfer is complete we'll talk about Tim Gordon. We need to make a new agreement. Those are the criteria. It's up to you. No money, no talk. No talk, no new agreement. No new agreement, no Tim Gordon. Very simple. Don't make the mistake of underestimating me again. You will agree to my terms or there will be no more business between us and no cousins to kiss your ass!"

"Such hard words from such a beautiful girl. How can I get the money done at such a late hour? The banks are closed."

An icy smile slid across Pisces' face, sharpening the edge of her voice. "The banks are never closed for their special customers. You know who to call to get the job done, the time of day is irrelevant. Don't try to stall. Make the call. We'll talk after I confirm the transfer. Oh yeah, as a little added incentive, the clock is running. If I don't show up by the agreed time, the boys are history. Understand one thing clearly. I don't plan to show up until the money business is complete and we have a new agreement." Pisces steered into a grocery store parking lot and stopped alongside the building. "There's a phone! Get it done if you want to see your grandsons."

39.

DUTCH WHEELED THE BLAZER OUT OF THE
courthouse garage, darted into traffic, and caught a green
light as he turned onto the highway that ran through the center
of the city, but the light at the next intersection was red. He
glanced at Tom, who was rubbing his eyes and yawning. "Not
planning to be anti-social and go to sleep, are you?"

"No. I'm just a little tired from staying up all night and
dancing with shadows all day. I've reached the point where I
don't actually feel sleepy. Another hour or so and I'll have to
reset my body clock before I can go to sleep. A few years ago I
did a seventy-two hour stretch and it took me three days to get
back to a normal sleep pattern. After the first thirty-six hours
I'm just tired, not sleepy."

"Well, tell me more about this case, it'll help keep you
alert. Start with everything you know about the old lady you
call the hermit."

"Alma Jacobsen?"

"Yeah. The little old lady you plan to pester before you go
home and bore your wife with your snoring."

"I really don't know very much about her."

"So tell me what you do know. I might notice something
you've overlooked. We don't want to ignore the forest while
we're studying the trees."

"Okay, here's the chronology. She bought her cabin about
two years ago. Mrs. Alexander let me know there was a new

resident. She always tells me when anything changes around the neighborhood. I stopped by to introduce myself and let her know how to reach me if she had any problems. She was a bit aloof, like most people are when you first approach them in uniform. We talked about her new home, what she planned to do with the yard, the great view, you know, the usual welcome to the neighborhood."

"Who's Mrs. Alexander?"

"She and her husband own the store at the lagoon. He works in Arcata and she runs the place. Mrs. A enjoys running the store even if it isn't a big money operation. She says it earns enough to keep them comfortable when her husband retires. She's usually one of the first people to meet new arrivals because they drop in to see what she sells and to arrange for a post office box. She grew up working in her grandfather's country store, back when the local ranchers showed up once a month for staples and to catch up on the news. She says she learned about listening to people and how to get them to talk from him. She's a good listener and a great observer, makes her a good resource. Anyway, I stopped in one morning for coffee and conversation and she told me there was a new owner in the end cabin. And, let me think, yeah! She said the new owner was an older woman who didn't talk much, didn't ask much, didn't buy much, and didn't leave the house very often. How did she put it? She said Alma Jacobsen acted like she didn't really want to be friendly and something about the way she went about being unsociable was strange."

"Strange how?"

"I'm trying to remember how she put it. It was sort of an odd observation. The kind you don't necessarily remember and can't quite forget? What was it? Let me think. Yeah! She said Alma acted like she was trying to lose herself or hide from her past life. I know, it's common enough for people to move here to get away from what they think is the real world, but Mrs. A said Alma said something about wanting to hide in plain sight so no one would pay any attention to her."

"Do you know what she might have asked the hermit to foster the comment?"

"I'm not sure. I didn't take much notice of it at the time. We were just talking. I was mostly just making note of a new resident in the cabins in terms of patrolling the area. Knowing who lives where, their normal living patterns, all the stuff that helps you recognize when something is amiss. I was still new to the post, still learning my beat. I was mostly trying to make sure I could do my job, not doing a background check. You know what I mean?"

"See no evil, hear no evil? Of course I know what you mean. Don't look too close or you may discover a reason to do more than the job you've been assigned."

"No, that's not what I mean. There wasn't reason to suspect anything. Everybody makes strange comments from time to time and for all I knew Mrs. A may have heard it wrong."

"Does she hear things wrong a lot of the time or only when you don't want to pay attention to what she's saying?"

"Are you trying to piss me off or just checking to see if I'm really awake?"

"Hey, take it easy, Ace. We all have to learn how to listen. I'll bet right this minute is the first time you've even wondered if the hermit might be something other than what she seems. Am I right?"

"You may be right. I'd forgotten the conversation entirely until you asked. Maybe I should be talking to Mrs. A instead of the hermit. There might be something else she's noticed in the last two years. At worst, we'll accomplish a cup of coffee. Who knows? She always has some new gossip or observations."

"Sounds like there's some unfinished business you need to clean up. I'll tag along. Four ears are better than two, one alert brain better than none."

"I admit my brain's a bit fuzzy around the edges, but I'm not sure yours dropped onto the assembly line."

Dutch offered up a glassy eyed stare. "A while back, I asked my mother if I could look to make sure nothing had been left behind because folks kept suggesting the same thing. She patted me on the head and sent me on my way with a comment about some gray wormy looking stuff the midwife found in the placenta. I figured she was just being difficult, because I don't know nothin' about no placenta. Ma could be testy sometimes. She went and died last year so I guess I'll never know."

The conversation drifted to personal interests and family. The time passed easily as the highway rumbled beneath them. Neither noticed the red Jeep parked at Moonstone beach or the Escort momentarily visible as it pulled off the road at the foot of the bluff.

Dutch parked in front of the store alongside a white Toyota. Nothing about the car drew their attention as they trotted up onto the porch. They also didn't pay any attention to the man perusing fishing lures and visiting with Mrs. Alexander about the best choice for catching steelhead. An unfamiliar fisherman at the lagoon was about as unusual as the fog. They got coffee and sat outside on the covered patio while they waited to talk to Mrs. Alexander.

The coffee restored some of Tom's flagging energy while they reviewed the events of the past few days.

"What made you decide to stake this place out last night? There had to be a reason you expected something to happen.

I know what it's like to be the new detective trying to impress everyone, but a solo stakeout on a murder suspect ranks somewhere between a stroke of genius and incredible stupidity. I don't think you're stupid, so what made you do it?"

"I had a hunch."

Dutch leaned across the table. "Okay! Here's the facts of life. Sooner or later you'll have to explain why you played your hunch and why you had it in the first place. Hunches don't appear out of thin air. Hunches are intuitive responses to stimulae constantly being cataloged and sorted by your subconscious mind. Whether or not this ever goes to court, I can guarantee you the man who promoted you will want an explanation and justification for your actions. Newton's law of motion applies here. For every action there is an equal and opposite reaction. Since you'll eventually need to have an answer you might as well figure it out while it's still fresh in your mind. Two months from now you won't even be able to guess at the reason behind it and a year from now you may not even remember you had a hunch. Now, retrace what you were doing and tell me what made you think something important was about to go down."

Dutch watched Tom begin to bristle and then realize he wasn't trying to make him feel stupid or picking on the new kid on the squad. They were working a case together and he was trying to use Tom's thoughts and observations to link the disjointed pieces into a coherent whole.

"We'd finished dinner and the kids were watching the Disney Channel. Sue and I were talking about the case. I know we're not supposed to discuss this shit with our wives, but she's curious and she's smart and she asks good questions. She helps me to see things from a different perspective, so we were talking about it. I was trying to tie all this crap together, and it dawned on me how we might have overlooked something obvious because it was too familiar. Sometimes, the best place to run after a crime is not to run at all. We'd combed the neighborhood looking for the killer's trail. I thought maybe whoever killed our man on the beach might not have left a trail because he was still hanging around. Take a look at the facts. Fact: the body was only in the water a short time. Fact: this time of the year night lasts about six or eight hours. Fact: we've been all over the campground and the subdivision like a flock of chickens scratching for bugs. Fact: we've talked to everyone in the area and come up with zip. Fact: I saw a guy in the crowd when I arrived who wasn't around when I was trying to get names. Fact: the guy I saw looks like Tim Gordon. When I added it all up, I thought the killer might be laying low, waiting for the right conditions to make a clean getaway. I thought the obvious place to hunker down and hide would be in one of the vacant cabins. We hadn't searched any of them, so we could have missed him. I noticed the fog start to roll in at my place about eight o'clock and realized it would be perfect conditions for somebody trying to sneak away in the dark. So I staked the place out."

"Why choose the store for a lookout point?"

"From the front of the store you can see the street in back of the ocean front cabins. There wasn't any way I could watch both roads and the bluff road seemed like a bad bet. Only three of the cabins are occupied and there isn't any easy way out of there without being seen. The only way to get to the beach is down the trail. The trail's visible from the store and there's no real cover on the beach once you get there. I tried to think like somebody trying to get away without getting caught. If it was me, I'd take the street through the back cabins, where there's more people and less chance of calling attention to myself, and head for the trees. There's always someone walking around the neighborhood on this side, so someone on the street wouldn't raise any suspicions. You know, hide in plain sight? So, I decided I'd watch and see what happened. I got lucky."

"Nothing wrong with dumb luck, sometimes it's the best we can hope for; luck and the inherent stupidity of the perpetrator. I've noticed luck favors people who work hard to be in the right place at the right time. Luck or not, unless you had taken the initiative to be where you could see him make his move we wouldn't be sitting here talking about it. I admire your logic. The beach or the trees are the logical choices for an escape route and the trees are the closest real cover. The woods on a foggy night gives the runner a huge advantage over the pursuer. Just duck off the trail and ambush the pursuer when he comes along."

"Which is why I decided not to follow him into the trees. It looked like a good way to join the ranks of the cranially challenged. If he mashed one guy's melon he sure wouldn't hesitate to do mine. I know the bad guys make mistakes, but so far this perp hasn't shown any signs of being stupid or making mistakes. I think he's an intelligent guy who isn't going to do anything to make our job easier."

"No argument here. It looks like we've got to sharpen our wits if we expect to catch him. The good news is everybody leaves a trail of some kind. The trick is finding it."

"I lost the trail when he went into the trees and I got cold feet about following him."

"Some people might call you chicken shit, but I'm not one of them and neither is your partner. He's pretty impressed with what you did." Dutch saw the question in Tom's eyes and answered before it was asked. "Don't expect a pat on the back. He was impressed enough to tell us you did something special.

You're doing good. Your instincts are good and your reasoning is solid. Don't get overconfident and don't start building walls around your imagination. We need all the creative thinking we can churn up to find this guy. Who knows? Maybe the trail we're trying to find is right here in the store."

Tom looked into the store and saw the customer was paying for his purchases and wrapping up his conversation with Mrs. Alexander. He walked to the door and asked her to come to talk with them. The bell on the front door clattered as it closed.

Mrs. Alexander paused to get a cup of coffee on her way to the patio. She was a tall, large boned woman who had thickened in her middle years. Tom had once described her as having a handsome face and a bubbly personality. They had become friends during the two years he had lived and worked in the area. She set her cup down and stretched like a cat just getting up from a nap, inhaling a deep breath of the cool air. Her shoulder length hair was more gray than brown, thick in texture with a natural wave.

"I bet you drove all the boys crazy," Dutch said.

She winked at him. "I still do, honey, just ask Tommy, he knows all about my string of admirers. What do you fellas have on your minds today? Tom looks like he needs an energy transfusion to bring him back to life. Didn't I see you hanging out in front of my store last night?"

"Yeah. I'm glad you didn't come out to talk to me. It would have blown my cover. We're still trying to get a lead on who left the body on the beach and I was staking out the neighborhood last night."

"Are you getting closer?"

"I'm not sure. Maybe you can help us. You see or hear about most of what happens around here don't you?"

"Didn't your mother teach you it's bad manners to accuse a lady of being a snoopy old gossip? Even if she is, it's extremely ill mannered to say it to her face."

"I didn't mean, I just,"

"Relax. If you weren't so tired and trying so hard to impress the guys you're working with you wouldn't apologize. You're right. What I don't see or hear someone tells me. Everyone expects me to have the inside scoop. Call me gossip central. What's on your mind?"

Dutch spoke before Tom could get his voice back in proper working order. "What do you know about Alma Jacobsen?"

"Our resident recluse? Not much. She keeps pretty much to herself. She sure takes good care of her place though. I've never seen the property look so prim and proper. Makes my yard look unloved, but it's nice to see hers so well kept. People always say it looks like a seaside cottage out of a children's book. I bite my tongue instead of saying right out of Hansel and Gretel. She has a right to her privacy without being accused of being the wicked witch."

Tom smiled. "Nice footwork. Now spill. People can't crap around here without you knowing what color it is and how bad it smells."

She laughed. "I do hear my share of the local dirt. There's just not much to tell. She showed up a couple years ago. She stopped in to visit about the beach and lagoon. We talked about recipes and babies and what it's like being old enough to be truly unappreciated. Next thing I know she's bought the end cabin. The best view anywhere in the place and nobody around here even thought it was for sale. It really upset some of the local folks when they didn't get a chance to grab it. A lot of the folks who have places here in the back would like to move up to the top of the bluff, but the last two cabins have gone to outsiders. Both about the same time too. In fact, they were sold at almost exactly the same time. It was kinda funny too!"

"What's so strange about two places selling at about the same time? Is there some rule against it?" Dutch asked.

"No, no. Of course there's no rule against it. It just didn't fit the normal pattern. Things around here are generally pretty quiet and predictable. Properties don't sell very often and when they do, it usually follows the same pattern. The owners tell us when they want to sell before they tell anyone else. Visitors are always asking what it costs to own a place here and if anything might be for sale. For a while we kept a list of folks who said they were interested in buying. We thought we could pick up a little change on a referral, but the list got so long so fast it turned into a joke. There was no way we could tell one person without hurting someone else's feelings, so we gave up on the idea. Better to not tell anyone and make them all wish you had than to tell one and irritate the rest. We don't really need the money anyway. Getting back to what I was saying, both places sold about the same time to total strangers without any mention to me or anybody else that they were for sale."

"Do you remember who moved in first?" Dutch asked.

"Oh, yes. I'll always remember Mrs. Jacobsen coming into the store and grumbling about how the damn hippy artist who was moving in at the end of the street kept driving by her house and stirring up the dust so it blew all over her clean porch. Hell, how much dust do you think you could kick up on that weedy patch of gravel up there? I remember telling my husband about it and having a good laugh about the old harridan making such a big fuss over it. Here she is, new to the neighborhood herself, and all she can do is complain about how her neighbor is using the street in front of her house. Like she had another choice! I mean, there's only one way in and out. You know? All the same," Mrs. Alexander was giggling. "There she was, stomping up and down and making a scene in the middle of my store. 'I came here for peace and quiet and the first thing you know some hippy artist freak moves in next door and turns the street into a racetrack! What is she doing that she needs to drive back and forth, in and out, up and down, dust flying everywhere, kicking gravel into my flowers! I oughta call the cops!' I gave her your phone number, Tom, and I swear to God I even managed to keep a straight face while I was doing it. Then she looked around and noticed there were four or five people in the store, got red in the face, and left. She hasn't been back in the store much since."

Tom was laughing at the comical imitation of Alma Jacobsen, which Mrs. Alexander had obviously performed before. His weariness withered with the laughter. "How often does she come into the store?"

"Not very often. Old folks don't buy much anyway and in her case it seems like emergencies only. Maybe once a month if she runs out of something she can't buy cheaper in town, or maybe she doesn't want to make the drive. She never has much to say. She just comes in, gets what she wants, pays me, and goes on her way. I consider myself lucky if she says hello or thank you. Not like there's anything wrong with that! Folks are entitled to keep their own counsel."

"What about her mail?"

"She picks up her mail once a week or so, but there's outside access, so I don't have to be here and I don't really see much of folks who come for their mail. I only know she's been here because the mail box is empty."

"How old do you think she is?"

"I don't know, probably about my age, sixties or so."

"Is she on Social Security?"

"That's a good question. I've never seen a Social Security check in her mail, of course she could have direct deposit."

Suddenly a thought leaped through the foggy edges of Tom's mind. "Wait a minute. I thought the artist moved here about six months ago!"

"Yes, she moved here as a full time resident six months ago, but she bought the place two years ago."

"Are you sure?"

"I think so. You can check the tax records to confirm it, but it was at almost the exact same time the recluse moved here. Like I say, it registers because it was unusual for two properties to be sold at the same time to total strangers. It was really unexpected because the Gentry's, who owned the place Jean Parker bought, had been talking about how they were going to keep the place in the family and make it a part of a trust for their grandchildren. Then out of the blue they sell the place and Jean is the new owner. She was an absentee owner for a year and a half. We have a lot of absentee owners who only show up occasionally so I never thought anything of it."

Tom had a far off look in his eyes. Then he raised his right hand, extending his index finger. "All these coincidences make me think there are too many coincidences for the coincidences to be coincidental."

Dutch and Mrs. Alexander shared a puzzled look. "Huh?" they chorused.

Tom stood and walked to the edge of the patio, looking through the rain at the cabins on the bluff. "Two years ago. Everything started two years ago. Two years of circumstances, situations and events, all ending up on our doorstep. Two years ago McAfee's wife is killed. Two years ago McAfee's partner is reportedly killed on the same flight as McAfee's wife. Two years ago both of these houses sell without any of the locals knowing the properties were for sale. Two years ago. What the fuck happened two years ago?" Suddenly Tom spun around to Mrs. Alexander. "Sorry."

She waved a hand. "It's all right. I appreciate the consideration, but fuck's become just another word in polite conversation and it's completely lost its shock value when it's scribbled on a wall."

"Two years ago," Dutch mused. "You may have just lamped on the trail we've been looking for."

"Maybe so," Tom replied. "I also don't think the guy we found on the beach is necessarily an important player. I think he was supposed to disappear and when he didn't, it was like someone opening an unknown door into a dark room. We charged in like a bunch of moths drawn to a light and my eyes are just beginning to adjust. We've got to find out what happened two years ago, starting with Mr. McAfee."

Dutch leaned back. "You think he didn't tell us everything he knows?"

Mrs. Alexander checked the store when the bell on the door tinkled. "My public is calling. I'll be inside if you need me for anything else."

"Thanks," Tom said. "You've been a big help." He turned back to Dutch. "I'm not sure it's a matter of not telling us everything he knows. I think he knows something he doesn't know he knows."

"Do you always talk this way, or am I just having trouble trying to follow what you're saying?"

"Stay with me on this. We didn't know what questions to ask. He answered everything we asked him about the stiff on the beach. The problem is we didn't know to ask him for details about what went on two years ago. If we had, he might have been a lot more help. He might not know he has information we need because he doesn't know the events are related. In other words, he doesn't know what he knows."

"I get it. So how do you want to proceed? It's your case, I'm just here to back you up."

"First, we need to talk to John. He's probably home by now. He told me he didn't want any early wake up calls, but the sun is still up, so he should still be awake. Let's use the phone in her office."

John Ragsdale and Cal Snider listened with amused interest while Weston described his meeting with the SAC. They were delighted to learn Tom's hunch about an undercover agent left out in the cold was confirmed.

A deep chill suddenly ran down John's spine. "Oh shit! Tom and Dutch are just about to stick their noses into a hornet's nest without knowing what they're up against." He reached out and grabbed the phone and dialed the direct connection to dispatch. "Contact Tom Schroeder immediately and have him call in." Realizing Tom was in his or Dutch's personal car, he told the dispatcher to disregard the call.

"Why'd you cancel the call?" Weston asked.

"No radio. Dutch took him back to the lagoon because he left his car parked at the store."

"And there's a chance they may have been followed by someone with no aversion to disposing of a cop who's getting too close for comfort."

Cal ran for the door with John on his heels. "We gotta hit the road chief! We've got some fast traveling to do!"

Tom was dialing the phone when he heard the bell on the front door and John urgently asking Mrs. Alexander if she had seen the two detectives. Seconds later John filled the door of the small office. He slid to a stop before trying to squeeze his bulk into the closet sized space already filled to overflowing by Tom and Dutch. "Jeez, you really know how to make an entrance!" Tom laughed. "What's up? I thought you were on your way to dreamland."

"I'm glad we found you. Let's go outside and we'll fill you in. Is the coffee still hot?"

"Hot and strong. Just right for a cold day," Dutch said as he shouldered his way past the new arrivals. "You guys get something to drink while I go drain the bilges."

"Yeah, me too," Tom said. "We'll bring you up to speed in a minute."

"He's going to bring us up to speed," Cal said. "Aren't we just tickled pink we charged all the way up here in time to get in on his little game of follow the leader."

"Much as I hate to admit it, he's been ahead of us most of the way and it sounds like they learned something important. Let's coffee up and find a couple of comfortable chairs."

Heavy rain was falling when the four detectives gathered on the patio. The rain cooled the air and left it smelling clean and freshly washed. "Who wants to go first?" Tom asked.

"Let me start with what brought us here in such a big damn hurry," John said. "The boss got the feebies to confirm your hunch. Tim Gordon is an undercover federal operative. He was a civilian assisting the feds until the operation got canceled by a newly appointed bureaucrat trying to whittle away at his department budget. Just to make sure his skirts remained unsoiled and insure complete deniability, he made sure Tim Gordon was left swinging in the breeze for the bad guys to use for target practice. He would be listed officially as killed in the line of duty and our budding bureaucrat would have complete deniability to go along with his astute budget management. Everyone would shed a tear for poor Tim and the matter would be closed. Unfortunately, Gordon refuses to die, making a major headache for the big dog at the head of the bureaucratic trough. He's managed to slip the noose every time anyone gets close to him. Now everybody on both sides wants him because he's become a major liability for everyone involved, especially the illustrious doofus who decided he was expendable. So the good guys and the bad guys are chasing and Gordon is running. By now he has to be feeling like Custer at the Little Big Horn waiting for all the Indians in the world to ride down on him."

"And all this went down about two years ago, right?" Tom said.

"I told you he was ahead of us, didn't I?" John said. "So how did you figure out it all started a couple years ago?"

Dutch spoke before Tom could answer. "I thought we should talk to the store owner because Tom said she was gossip central. She told us the hermit and the artist both bought their houses at about the same time, but the artist didn't move in until about six months ago. You'd love the way she tells the story about the hermit getting upset to have a hippy artist for a neighbor. While we were laughing at her story Tom pops up with this two year connection. The chronology turned a lot of the possibilities into probabilities. We didn't have a solid handle on the thread connecting them until you showed up."

"Like two years ago a PSA flight gets bombed out of the sky, McAfee's wife is killed and Gordon supposedly dies in the same crash. Two years ago we have a major shuffle in the Washington bureaucracy. Two years ago the hermit shows up. Stuff like that all tying together?" John asked.

"Right," Tom said. "When did you figure it out?"

"While we were hot footing it up here to try to catch you

guys before you stuck your face into a hornet's nest. Everything started to come together. You just confirmed my suspicion the coincidences are all related. So what else have you come up with?"

Tom clapped his partner on the shoulder. "Well, I'm glad to see your brain hasn't gotten as limp as some other parts of your anatomy. I was beginning to think I was gonna have to solve this all by myself. Right now I have a bunch of unanswered questions. Who we are really dealing with has to be our first priority. Let's look at what's right in front of us. Who is Alma Jacobsen? Who is Jean Parker? What do they have to do with Paul McAfee aside from watching him and screwing him respectively? Another little item I just remembered. McAfee told us it took him six months to get his act together enough to come up here to sort things out. Jean Parker arrived as a permanent fixture a year and a half after she bought her place. McAfee and Parker are both from the same area of LA. They worked about a mile apart, they lived about a mile apart, they've both been working and living there for at least five years. Now they both end up here and take up with each other. I think I see the hand of the master in the orchestration and arrangement of the music, if you take my meaning."

"You got a legal pad in your car, Tom?" John asked.

"They sell paper here. Be right back." He dashed into the store and could be heard telling Mrs. Alexander he was taking one of the newsprint drawing pads and he'd pay for it later. As he laid out the information they knew in a chronology covering two years a pattern began to emerge. Even without any of the details about Tim Gordon's clandestine operation, the vague trail of events began to look like a four lane highway.

40.

THE CRACKLING FIRE CAST A WARM GLOW OVER
Jean's living room. Paul and Jean had been too tense to enjoy lunch at the restaurant overlooking the fishing harbor in Eureka. They had just pushed the food around on their plates while incomplete sentences evaporated above the table. Their attempt at conversation was limited to short groups of words about unimportant matters of no real interest to either of them. Efforts to paint a happy face on Tim's sudden reappearance were fruitless. They were uncomfortable talking where they might be overheard. They gave up on lunch and returned to the lagoon, the trip made in silence, holding hands as if contact with each other would somehow make the uncertainty and fear disappear. It didn't work. Unspoken worry hung thick in the air and the fire failed to abate the gloom shrouding their thoughts.

The tension was finally too much for Jean. "What are we going to do?"

"I don't know. I guess we have to wait for Tim to tell us what to do next."

"The man who was killed was looking for you, wasn't he?"

"It kind of looks like it, but we'll probably never know for sure. He's not talking and whoever hired him isn't likely to tell us. I'm still in shock from walking into the house this morning and finding Tim and Julie. They didn't say much about what's going on. Every time we brought up the subject they told us to concentrate on helping them escape and wait for them to explain later. I finally quit trying because it was obvious they weren't going to discuss it. Tim can be like that. He never wanted to talk about his two years in the Army either. He'd only say he had a great time and never got to use what they taught him because the war ended. I still don't know what they trained him to do."

"Do you think he was Special Forces?"

"He'd have to tell you. Over the years it seemed like he enjoyed the air of mystery it gave him. I've seen him play people by indicating he was involved in something special during the war. He can make himself mysteriously attractive without revealing any details and actually induce a sort of hero worship. People seem to think by being near him something special might rub off. Tim was our front man because he was really good at it. It suited his personality. I stayed home and took care of the management nuts and bolts while he chased all over the planet buying and selling product. His job was locating suppliers and marketing our products. My job was stocking, shipping, and keeping the financials in order. It played to both of our strengths. The company needed both of us. I turned everything over to a management company because I couldn't do both jobs. I don't have a clue how to do what he did so incredibly well. Even with our strong customer base the growth pattern was stunted without Tim out there pressing the flesh. The reason for this retreat was to decide whether to sell the company and move on to something new, go back and hire someone to do Tim's job, or just leave it in the hands of the management company and retire. I thought one of those options would sort of rise up and push the others aside. Now it looks like there may be a fourth choice."

"Okay, Tim's not dead after all, so your situation has

changed. Maybe you'd like to go back to the way things were. I honestly don't think it's a realistic option. Too much has happened. You can't go back! There's no back to go to! It's not just Tim suddenly materializing. It also isn't Tim asking you to start thinking and acting like James Bond. It isn't some guy getting killed in your front yard. It's all those things and none of them. The bottom line is clear. Whatever choices you thought you had are no longer relevant. It looks like somebody else is calling the tune and all you can do is dance to it." Jean leaned in close to his face. "Is that what's troubling you bunky?"

"You have a marvelously lyrical grasp of the obvious, Ms. Parker. Since it looks like you're on a roll, what do you suggest we should do about it?"

A sudden animated change came over Jean, the inner fire she had drawn upon to become a successful businesswoman burst into full flame. "Tell you what we're gonna do!" She stood up and assumed the pose of a pitchman. "We're gonna make some decisions! We're gonna make some love! We're gonna have some dinner! We're gonna let your partner do what he has to do and when he gets it out of his system, we're gonna decide what to do next! We may go left, we may go right, we may jump off a cliff. Now, take your choice! What do you want to do first? Eat, make love, or perhaps you'd prefer to go jump off a cliff? There's one right outside. Make up your mind! What's it going to be? Feed me, fuck me, or fly me?"

41.

THE CAR SHIFTED AS THE OLD MAN DUCKED IN OUT
of the rain. "It is done. The money is in your account."

Pisces removed a cellular telephone from the console and entered a speed dial code. She listened to the phone connect, entered a code, then entered a longer set of numbers, listened, and returned the phone to the console. "Thank you. I would have been terribly disappointed if you had lied to me. And so would you." She pulled out of the parking lot.

He maintained a stoic façade. Outwardly he appeared calm, inside his heart was racing. He could smell himself sweating, but his voice remained calm. "This is just doing business. Joey hired you. You did your job. I paid you as we agreed. I am grieved you don't trust me."

"The only thing you're grieved about is me not buying your story! I trust you to do just one thing! I trust you to have me killed if you live long enough to give the order. Let's be clear about what's going to happen. This is a matter of honor. You failed to behave honorably. I called you on it and you can't let anyone know it happened. You've always operated this way. Your problem is I caught you at it and have you in a compromising position. You can't let the situation go unremedied. You never have before and there's no reason to believe you plan to start now."

"You think you understand me so well. It is true you have

me at a disadvantage. You have my grandsons and you have me and we are unprotected."

"I don't believe for one second you're unprotected. I know someone's out there keeping an eye on us. The only protection I have is to hold you to your honor. I intend to wrap your omerta so tight around your head it will cut off the top of your skull if you try to remove it."

The old man smiled. "I didn't know you held such influence. How did you come to possess such power?"

"This isn't a matter of power, this is a matter of honor. You know I freelanced for people besides you and your family."

"It is a freedom I permitted you."

"You permitted it for the same reason the others did. You needed me and I wouldn't work under any other conditions. I have always treated you with honor. I treat all my clients with honor, which is precisely the reason your family's breach of honor cannot go unrecognized and unpunished. Honor is honor, business is business, and the only way to protect myself is to make it clearly known any breach of honor will never go unrewarded."

"Making threats against my family will only bring swift retribution."

"I'm not threatening you or your family. I'm not threatening anyone. I'm telling you how you will make and keep an honorable agreement with me or you will pay with your life. You will die an old man's death without honor and without respect. You will die alone and no one will even care because everything you stand for will have been lost for all time."

The old man chuckled. "You talk like a soldier, not like a beautiful woman. What makes you believe I'd permit such a promise to be kept? With a nod of my head I could make you disappear."

"You're too late. It's already done. The word is out. If I disappear or stop publishing my work, if I cannot be reached, if anything prevents me from living a normal life, it will be presumed you have dishonored our agreement and tried to cover it up. Even the church will excommunicate you. The arrangements have been made. It's a done deal. The only way to keep what you have is to do what I tell you to do and make sure nothing happens to me. It also means you have to make sure I don't decide to suddenly drop out of sight. If I fail to appear regularly and to answer my phone regularly, you're dead. My life is in your hands and you have to keep me alive. Capisce?"

He understood he had no immediate way to escape. This willowy creature had practiced her arts for every crime family on the planet for nearly two decades and she was playing her network of clients to her advantage. Another day he might find a way out, but today she controlled the game. Patience was a powerful weapon and Pisces had been very patient. She had waited patiently and sprung the trap when Joey screwed up. She had Joey. She had Gino. She had him. Sad words would be spoken over wine about how lack of honor had cost them their lives if they disappeared. Rosaries would be said and tears would be shed, but all would understand this was the way of things. No retribution would be brought. She had been very careful, very clever, and very thorough in her preparations. She had used the unwritten rules to write his death warrant. Given enough time there was a chance she might trip over her own clever feet. Given enough time anything could happen. The old man sighed. "All right. Exactly what do you want?"

Sagging gray clouds delivered moisture gathered from the sea as steady rain. The needles of the redwoods captured raindrops and combined them, forming larger drops until they grew heavy enough to regain their freedom and splash through lower limbs on their journey to the ground. The rain penetrating the canopy danced on the ground in small drops. The collected water falling from the trees hit hard enough to dent a hard hat. Tim was soaked to the skin by the combined deluge. His passage through the soggy undergrowth reminded him of the Army's jungle survival training. He had been young and physically prepared when he acquired mental toughness and stoic endurance in their merciless school, but the intervening years had eroded his preparedness. Being cold, wet, and miserable dulled his senses instead of sharpening them. *Don't look back. The youth bank has been overdrawn. You have to depend more on your brain and less on your brawn. Clear your mind... think!*

Joey and Gino struggled into a sitting position when Tim entered the shelter of the tree and pressed his back against the charred inner surface. The cousins had been unable to free themselves. Tim was neither surprised by their attempts nor the futility of their efforts. Cable ties resist cutting, even with a sharp knife. Tim waited for his eyes to adjust to the dim light, studying his captives as they came more clearly into view. The uncertainty in their eyes increased while he stared silently at them. No voices competed with the sounds of the rain and the wind. Nearly a minute passed before all three men realized they were holding their breath.

Tim warily assessed the cousins. Joey displayed the berserk resolve of a cornered animal ready to try a life or death assault on his captor at the first opportunity, a dangerous enemy whose threat of physical violence was tempered by a shadow of fear he struggled to hide. Joey was a one dimensional threat easily monitored and controlled. Gino represented the greater danger. Wary, thoughtful, observant, coldly in control of his emotions, Gino would instantly take advantage of any weakness or momentary lapse of focus on the part of his opponent. Tim was confident he could deal with either man one on one, but together they represented a serious problem if they regained their freedom. He watched Joey's rage slowly take control of his thinking. His rage was a weakness Tim believed he could use to disable or disarm him. *If things go south, pop Joey immediately and focus on Gino. Joey's ego will make him charge in. Gino will circle and look for an opening while Joey distracts me. Get rid of the distraction quickly and I'm on even ground with Gino. I'm ready now. I can kill them both if I have to. If Julie wasn't using these two clowns as leverage it might be better to simply bury the evidence. Too late! Don't even go there! That bell already rang. We've planned the work, so keep your mind on what you're doing and work the plan!*

Gino's nostrils tingled at the sharp odor of anger and fear being emitted by his cousin. He forced his attention away from Joey and focused on his captor. He studied the way Tim protected himself by taking a position to guard both the door and his prisoners. Gino respected Tim as an extremely intelligent adversary. He had kept the organization off balance for two years, moving like a puff of smoke through every trap set for him, but something had broken the pattern this time. Instead of disappearing like a ghost, he had turned the tables and sprung a trap of his own. Pisces was bringing the old man from the airport so they could be ransomed for Tim's freedom. He was surprised she had changed sides. He didn't know if it was retaliation for Joey following her or if it had been her agenda from the start. Gino smiled slyly as an idea formed in his mind. "Got you right where she wants you, doesn't she?" He watched Tim take several seconds to consider the implications of the question.

"You think so?"

Gino laughed. "She's got you squeezed so tight into a corner I can't believe it. The great Tim Gordon, a magician when it comes to escaping traps is standing around waiting for my grandfather to arrive. For two years we've tried every trick, every trap, every devious swindle we could devise, and you brushed them off like so much lint. Look at you now, standing in the rain and waiting! Waiting! After all this time, we finally discover your weakness. Who'd have thought it would turn out to be a foxy bit of wool who plays with cameras and dispenses death."

"You think I'm cornered? What sort of a corner would that be?"

"Think about it. You didn't stay alive this long without being able to figure it out."

Gino saw doubt flash across Tim's eyes before vanishing behind a curtain of cold professionalism, a brief flicker telling him he'd scored. Gino considered saying more, but much as he might enjoy driving the knife deeper and giving it a little twist, he remained silent, letting the fires of doubt feed on Tim's paranoia.

Tim was alive because of an innate sense of who to trust and what to believe. Julie had always been his blind spot. He forced himself to walk away from their relationship when he learned her real profession. The conscious choice to remove himself from her life didn't mean he could forget her. He wondered if his judgment was flawed by his feelings for her. Could she be coldly professional enough to play on his weakness to set him in the jaws of a trap? He needed to clear his head. He exited the tree and moved into the timber, melting into the undergrowth like a shadow fading into the night.

Luck plays a major role in the success or failure of any venture. While fortune's fickle frolics might be entertaining to an uninvolved observer watching it's lighthearted dance among Alma's failed efforts, the star of the performance was not amused. Chest heaving, she reached the top of a tall dune only to discover the Jeep had vanished. "Shit! I can't catch a damned break! Now what do I do?" Alma raised her face into the wind and waited for her breathing to return to normal. "The game isn't over," she muttered. "The players are still at the table. Deal me in." She slid down the face of the dune and drove to the parking lot where she had last seen the Jeep. She walked out onto the sand and gazed across the mouth of the river at the southern end of the rocky seacoast. Scanning toward the east, she didn't recognize Paul's Thunderbird as it drove by nor did she take note of the white Toyota a half-mile behind it. Minutes slipped by while she analyzed her situation. and considered the best options for achieving her goal. The clock ran out on her mental gymnastics when she saw the red Jeep approaching from the south. She watched the vehicle with intense interest as it drove by carrying two occupants. The photographer was driving and Alma immediately knew what do next. Whatever stops or detours the Jeep might make along the way, the final destination would be in the trees north of the lagoon. Maybe her luck was changing.

42.

TOM WAS IN THE MIDST OF LISTING FACTS AND
suppositions when he spoke to Cal. "Have you heard from your
friends at Felony U.?"

"Not yet. We bugged out when we got the information
on Gordon and I didn't even look to see if I had any messages.
What's on your mind?"

"What I've been thinking all along. We've stepped into
something a lot more complicated than a new version of body
surfing. If we just had some idea what or who is behind this
fiasco we'd be a lot closer to knowing the best way to handle
it. I feel like someone's out there having a wonderful time
watching us chase our tails while the game goes on without us.
Maybe I'm new and I'm not used to feeling like a mushroom,
but I for damn sure don't have to like it or accept it!"

"Good!' John exclaimed. "Since you're mad as hell and
you're not going to take it anymore, where do you think we
should start?"

"Paul McAfee," Cal said. "He's where we should start.
Whether he knows it or not, he's definitely involved. Every
time we turn something up he's right there with his halo
shining bright."

"Along with his girlfriend and the hermit," Dutch added.
"The hermit doesn't miss anything, but she hasn't told us
squat."

"Don't forget A. Rose," Tom offered.

John nodded. "Yes, let's not forget A. Rose, the latest arrival in this little soiree. I think she's involved too, but I haven't been able to figure out how or why. And of course, let's not forget the feds, they look like they're up to their collective assholes in our case and of course it's something we don't need to know."

"Ah yes," Dutch mused. "The feds' collective assholes. Couldn't have described the collection more succinctly myself. And now, for a hundred grand and a year's supply of pizza and beer, which feds are we talking about?"

Tom looked up from his notes. "How many feds could be involved?"

This brought on a renewed chorus of smiles and laughter. "Oh, let's see," John replied. "FBI, CIA, NSC, NSA, DEA, ATF."

"And don't forget the FDA, USDA, State Department." Cal added.

"And there's always-" Dutch began.

Tom raised his hands in surrender. "Okay! I get the picture! And of course none of these collective assholes talk to each other and have even less inclination to talk to a bunch of local beat pounders, right?"

"All that and a buck will buy you a cup of bad coffee," John counseled. "Chasing after things we would like to have and can't is a waste of time. Let's forget what we don't have and can't find out and work with what we do have. Do we know where McAfee is right now?"

Dutch jumped out of his chair waving his arms. "I got a great idea. Let's all go around the corner to his cabin and see if he's at home and if he isn't there,"

"We go check the end cabin to see if anyone's home," Tom added.

"Wait a minute," John cautioned. "We can't all go charging up to his place and confront him like some board of inquisition, especially if he's hanging out with his friendly neighbor. She was a little stand-offish the last time I talked to her and she might still be feeling less than cooperative. Let's not burn down the house trying to light a candle to see what's inside."

"Good point," Cal said. "Why don't you and Tom see if you can locate McAfee and his friend while Dutch and I take a crack at the hermit. She hasn't met him yet, so maybe we can catch her off guard again. If she ain't around, we'll just peruse the premises for anything of passing interest. We promise not to poke our noses anywhere we can't justify as crime scene follow up."

"We certainly wouldn't want to disturb any blatant evidence or tread on the rights of a felon, so we'll be real careful to only bend the law, not make a double pretzel out of it," Dutch said.

"Good enough. Let's take a crack at it and meet back here when we're done." John stood, stretched, and watched Tom do the same. "Just think Tom, this was your idea."

"I'm humbly grateful for your sincere appreciation of my talents. Feel free to sit on your thumb and rotate. What do you want me to do with this list?"

"Hang on to it until we get back. On second thought, let me look at it on the way. It may help direct our line of questioning."

"We'll look it over after we talk to the hermit," Cal said. "Just leave it in your car and we'll pick it up if we finish before you do."

Mrs. Alexander was waiting on a customer when they walked through the store. "Should I assume you'll be back for more coffee?"

"Safe bet Mrs. A," Tom responded. "And you know, maybe some stew would be real nice for dinner, too. Something full bodied and hearty to restore our energy, but only if it's not too much trouble."

She smiled broadly, eyes twinkling with merriment. "No trouble at all, Tom, I'll just call your wife and have her get it ready for you. Will all of you be dining at your house tonight, or will it just be yourself? You know, so she knows how much to fix and how many places to set."

"Oh, for sure, tell her I invited the whole watch. She'll be so tickled to have company for dinner it'll make her day. Better than me showing up with a dozen roses."

The detectives raised their collars against the cool summer rain as they exited the store. No one noticed the white Toyota was no longer parked in front of the store or that the Jeep was parked at the photographer's campsite.

43.

ALMA STEERED INTO THE TREES FIVE HUNDRED
feet north of where she had seen the Jeep enter the forest
earlier in the day. She took a padded aluminum case from
under the seat and laid it open. A small automatic pistol with a
twelve inch barrel and collapsible shoulder stock nestled in the
pockets of the case. She assembled the weapon and attached a
starlight telescopic sight before she affixed an eight inch long
sound and flash suppressor. A fifteen round clip filled the pistol
grip to complete the assembly. She worked the action to load
a round into the firing chamber, set the safety, removed the
clip, and added a cartridge to replace the one chambered. It
was an extremely effective tool at distances up to seventy-five
yards in the hands of a trained shooter. The final detail was a
sling clipped to a ring mounted above the grip on the left side.
She hung the sling over her right shoulder before slipping her
arm back into the sleeve and concealing the weapon within
her jacket.

She pulled the hood over her head and fastened the
drawstring beneath her chin. The dark green jacket would
help her blend into the colors of the forest, but her face shone
like a full moon against the dark color of her clothing. Even if
the rain would soon compromise its effectiveness, dirt was the
only makeup available and it would have to do.

She chose a landmark to guide on before moving quietly
into the forest. Though progress was slow, she knew silent

movement was her ally. She paused frequently to scan the forest for threat. Tim Gordon had become a genuine pain in the ass, a bona fide survivor. She expected to find him here and well armed. She sank to the ground with her back against the rough bark of a fallen tree.

She had been trained to avoid confrontation if she didn't know what she was about to encounter. She knew Gino was probably here with one or more street soldiers, not to mention Tim. She was supposed to take charge of the situation and resolve it, but she didn't know how to manage it alone. Alma's pulse rose steadily as she wrestled with indecision. Nervous perspiration saturated her clothes. She took a long slow breath to calm her thoughts. *Okay, you're not ready to confront anyone, you're up against bad odds, you don't know what you're walking into, and you're expected to do it anyway. I don't care about orders handed down from the comfort of an office three thousand miles away, I'm not about to stroll in like a Sunday visitor just because some idiot on the banks of the Potomac tells me to. Tim will shoot first and apologize later. I need to find a place to watch and see what happens. You can't plan an attack without good intel unless you plan to fail. Same old story, you don't plan to fail, but you can sure as hell fail to plan! Time to sneak and peek. Shoot and loot later!*

Collected moisture fell steadily and wind rustled the tops of the trees, deafening her to small sounds. The deep shadows helped to conceal her, but she still felt dangerously exposed. She had the prickly feeling she was being watched. She hunkered more deeply into the depression alongside the rotting log and struggled to control her emotions. The rustle of wind in the trees and the splashing of rain were the only sounds she could clearly identify. She remained still, only moving her eyes over everything in her field of vision while the chill of fear seeped into her bones. Suddenly she felt the barrel of a gun pressed firmly against the back of her head.

"Moving would be a very bad idea," he said softly. "I might feel threatened and squeeze one off."

It was a voice she had been waiting two years to hear. "How are you, Tim?"

A chill vibrated down his spine and cold sweat leaked from his arm pits. This was not what he expected. In the past this had always been the friendly voice of a valued support system. Two years of defensive paranoia made him weigh the reliability of the feeling of relief. So many lies had been laid in his path he wasn't sure who to trust. "Raise your hands slowly and lace your fingers behind your head." He pressed the gun hard against her skull. "And make sure you move slowly. You wouldn't want me to get the wrong impression." When she moved to comply Tim pulled the gun away from her head and shifted his position atop the log. "Sit up and lean back against the log. Keep your hands where they are."

Alma did as she was told. Tim slid off the log and squatted three feet in front of her. The voice was right, the face was wrong. Still, something about it was familiar. "Jesus, Marnee, what have they done to you? And what the hell are you doing here? I thought you were office staff. Since when do you do field work?" He kept the gun pointed squarely at her chest.

"A bit of plastic surgery that can be undone when the time comes to look like myself again. Gives me a sweet grandmotherly look, don't you think?"

"They must have aged you thirty years! What the hell is going on?"

"Why don't you put down the gun and we'll talk about it. We've known each other too long for you not to trust me."

The gun remained steady as full recognition of who he had captured dawned on him. He pulled the hood off her head. "Alma Jacobsen! You're Alma Jacobsen? What the hell are you doing posing as a nosy little old lady? And don't give me any crap about lowering my gun. You assholes painted a target on me and hung me out to dry. Now you turn up right next door to Paul. You probably manipulated that little scenario too. You probably even arranged for Jean Parker to hit on him so she could stroke him into helping you find me. You sleazy bastards don't give a shit who you hurt as long as you look good for the budget committee!"

"You're right about arranging things so Paul would come here, but the artist wasn't part of the plan. She's a wild card. It really pissed me off when she put the make on him. I had everything planned around convincing the couple who owned the end cabin to put it up for lease. Instead they sold it to her and changed the whole picture. We don't know anything about her and don't have any leverage on her. She didn't even move here until six months ago. I was forced to manipulate the availability of the place next door to mine so Paul could rent it. It's no picnic with everybody knowing what everybody else is doing in the neighborhood, either. We had to pay off the owners and pray nobody caught wind of what we were doing. Paul arrived and before I could even make contact with him, the lovely Ms. Parker was in his face doing the lonely divorcee dance. It pissed me off at first, but then it looked like she might prove to be an unexpected asset. Sort of like the way Paul turned out to be an unexpected asset when it came to hiding our operation in your books."

"I'm so happy you're pleased with his work. From personal experience I'd say it means he's about to discover what it's like to live on the run. Too bad he hasn't had the advantage of being trained to protect himself from people who want to eliminate him. Great plan! You guys are truly unbelievable!"

"We just want you to come in so we can debrief you and find out what went wrong in Taiwan. Nobody wants you or Paul to get hurt. We don't want you dead! We'll protect you!"

"Debrief me? Right! Peel off my shorts and install a new aperture. Did the new Director suddenly have an attack of conscience, or does he think he can salve his conscience by tossing me a bone? Maybe some sort of witness protection arrangement? Hasn't he figured out I'm not quite as stupid as he thought? We wouldn't be having this conversation if I was. He can take his bone and shove it up his ass! I've got nothing to say to any of you guys! You people must think I'm some sort of an idiot. He painted a bulls-eye on my back and pointed me out to the shooters. Too bad it didn't work out the way he hoped. Now he's worried word might slip out about the way you took care of me. It would make all those other poor schmucks who trust you start looking over their shoulders. Maybe stop being quite so helpful. Maybe stop being so patriotic. Maybe start worrying about how long it will be before you make them a bulls eye in the shooting gallery. So now you want to make nice, you want to let bygones be bygones, you want to be friends, you want me to come home like a good little dog! Rollover so you can scratch my belly before you slit me from crotch to eyeball with dull letter opener! Fat chance! The last time I trusted you I damn near got killed. And it was only the first time. I called for help and discovered I had been declared a deniable resource. I was supposed to disappear at the hands of one of the slime balls you guys asked me to set up for you. Sorry I didn't oblige. As for me coming in out of the cold to cooperate with you and make the Director look like a hero, I have three words. Go fuck yourself!"

"Tim, I know things didn't work out the way you expected. We really do want to protect you. We just have to be very quiet about it."

"Oh, sure, you're going to quietly protect me. Silence me is more like it. Take me a hundred miles off shore and toss me into the water to see if I can swim back before hypothermia kills me. Perfect way to protect me from the bad guys and protect the Director from what I could do by dropping a few comments in the right ears. Protection my ass!"

"Dammit, you're not listening to me! I'm supposed to protect your ass, your partner's ass, and now because of her unexpected involvement, the firm female ass your partner's been patting for the last week."

"Of course you are! First you guys toss me to the wolves, then when I outsmart them, you drag my partner into it to sucker me in for you. Damn if it didn't almost work. This is just one more spook scenario designed to take me out. I should just pop a cap on you and be done with it."

"Tim, please listen to me, I want to help,"

"Stop! I'm done listening. Stand up, we're going to take a little hike. I've got a couple friends who will probably enjoy your company. They want to take me back for debriefing too. Maybe they'll settle for yours because I've decided to keep my briefs firmly in place."

She began to move her hands from the back of her head as she stood. Tim halted her immediately. "Hang on, sweetheart, it looks like you've developed a new boob in a strange location." He patted her right side, immediately detecting the weapon. He swung her up against a tree, pinning her hands behind her head as he slid his gun up under her chin.

"Tim! Stop!"

Tim's voice was a violent growl. "Shut up! Keep your

hands where they are and don't even think about moving. Don't even breathe. He grabbed the zipper of the jacket and slid it down to expose the gun. He ejected the clip. "Slip the rig off your shoulder and hand it to me." He slipped the sling over his shoulder and made her lay face down on the ground. He completed his search with one knee planted in the small of her back. The search was thorough and with total disregard for any discomfort or embarrassment as he probed her clothing and body for weapons. She offered no resistance and made no complaints. He found and removed an additional clip from her bra. When he finished he dragged her to her feet.

"Tim,"

"Don't say anything. Just put your jacket on and walk where I say. If you're a good girl, I may let you live."

He directed her into the hollow tree and pushed her as she entered. The shove compromised her balance and she bumped firmly into the opposite side before she could regain control. Joey and Gino were not surprised when Tim bound her hands and feet before sitting her opposite them.

"Hey! Are we gonna have a party or are you just collecting strays?" Joey asked. "What I want to know is who wants to go first? Hey Gino, you ever fuck an old broad?" A glance from Tim silenced his chatter.

"I'm putting all my rotten eggs in one basket. Maybe you should think about what you do with a rotten egg. Rotten eggs smell bad and when you crack them open they give off a flammable gas. Might not be a bad solution. Who's gonna notice a fire inside a burned out tree? It's nice and dry in here too. It should heat up real fast and burn real hot." He noticed Joey's face contort with renewed fear. "Got a match, wise ass?"

"Shut the fuck up!" Gino snarled.

Tim left the prisoners with their own thoughts. He moved

like a phantom through the dripping foliage to new location from which to survey his small domain. He wondered what new surprises awaited him. He resisted the urge to see danger in every moving leaf or shifting shadow. He checked the weapon he had taken from Marnee and arranged it for rapid deployment after testing the motion to bring it up ready to fire. He had been introduced to the weapon at Fort Benning and appreciated the years of improved technology.

44.

JOHN WAITED FOR A RESPONSE TO HIS KNOCK.
"This place looks as vacant as the handicapped parking stalls at the golf course."

"His car's gone too," Tom observed.

They stepped off the porch into the teeth of an intensifying storm. John settled into the driver's seat. "Let's go see what's cooking at the artist's studio."

"I noticed a T-bird parked alongside her cabin when we stopped here."

"Your point being?"

"She drives a Mazda RX-7. I would surmise her visitor is likely our absent tenant."

"I thought McAfee drove a Mustang."

"Absolutely accurate. What you failed to recall is he was driving a Hertz Mustang. He owns a T-bird."

"Yeah?"

"Yep! Like a good little boy, I checked DMV and learned he owns a T-bird. Ergo, the T-bird now parked conveniently next to his main squeeze is probably his personal ride."

"Excellent work. Such initiative and deductive reasoning should be its own reward, but in the interest of follow up and good police work let us go forth and detect the validity of your presumption. One never knows what manner of skullduggery might reveal itself."

John studied the cottage as he drove the short distance.

Smoke came from the chimney and light glowed in the front window. Tom confirmed the license on the T-bird matched the records on Paul's car. Jean Parker's Mazda was visible in the small garage in the rear.

"Looks like the gang's all here," Tom said.

"Sure does. Of course one wouldn't expect them to be strolling on the beach in this crud." Rain hammered the windows, pinging against the glass like hail stones. "Okay, both of them are here. She wasn't very cooperative the first time I talked to her and he may be a major player in this little drama, so we might have to schmooze them into talking to us. We need to find out what happened two years ago and what brought them here. It doesn't look like we can talk to them separately, so watch for any indication they're telling us a story they've prepared for the occasion. I'll take the lead, you take notes and speak up if you think of something I've missed. We want to tag team them without playing good cop/bad cop. Keep things conversational and non-confrontational. We need information. We don't want to get tossed out before we have a chance to learn anything. We won't get to ask everything we need to and I know we won't think of everything we need to ask. We'll just have to come back and try again. Play it cool, be professional and businesslike. They'll expect me to be in charge because I'm older. If we're lucky you may get the chance to blindside them with some unexpected questions. Make sure you listen for what they aren't saying. Body language will tell us more than what they say. You ready?"

"I hear the music. I'll try not to step on your toes as I dance on by."

John's knock immediately resulted in movement and muffled voices. Jean opened the door with Paul standing a few feet behind her. "Hello detective, can I help you?"

"I hope so. We've made some progress on the case, but there are some things I thought you might be able to help us clear up. This is my partner, Tom Schroeder, may we come in?"

"I don't know if I can be of much help, but please come inside so I can close the door and keep the weather out."

"Good afternoon detective," Paul shook John's hand. "Paul McAfee," he said shaking Tom's hand. "Would you like me to leave so you can talk with Jean alone?"

"No, Paul," Jean said firmly. "I want you to stay. I have nothing to say you shouldn't hear."

"We'd like you to stay, too," John agreed. "We wanted to talk with both of you. What we need most is some background information. We have uncovered some, shall we say, coincidental similarities. Perhaps you can help us understand them. Would it be all right if we sit down? We've just pulled an all-nighter and a comfortable chair would feel really good."

"I'm sorry," Jean said. "Where are my manners? My mother would be horrified. Please, sit here in front of the fire and get warm. You look cold and wet as well as worn out."

"Thanks," Tom said, "it almost feels like winter out there today."

Everyone found places to sit. Jean and Paul together on the couch, John and Tom in chairs at each end of the couch facing them.

"Are you getting close to catching the killer?" Paul asked.

"We're not ready to arrest anyone yet. That's part of the reason we're here to talk with you," John replied.

"Are we among your list of suspects?"

"In all honesty, we haven't been able to clearly eliminate you from the list of possible suspects."

"Paul, maybe we should have an attorney before we talk to them."

Tom leaned forward and spoke gently. "Ms. Parker, you aren't obligated to answer any of our questions, but you could help remove yourself from the list of possible suspects if you can help us confirm you have no involvement aside from living near where the crime occurred."

"I don't have to answer anything I don't want to?"

"You can choose not to answer any question or you can answer all our questions or you can ask us to leave before we ask you anything. It's your right, but wouldn't you like to help us find who killed the man if you can?"

"Well, yes, I suppose I would, as long as I can decide not to answer a question if I think it's none of your business."

"How about you Paul?" John asked. "Do you understand you don't have to answer either?"

"No problem. You bump into something I don't want to talk about I'll tell you so."

"Fair enough. Shall we get started?"

"Would you like some coffee?" Jean asked.

John recognized the offer as Jean's way of taking charge of the situation and overcoming the feeling of being invaded. "Coffee would be real nice, if it's not any trouble."

"It's no trouble at all. It will only take a minute."

John focused on Paul. "When did your partner die? Wasn't it a couple years ago?"

"Yes. He and my wife were supposed to catch the same flight home from San Francisco because our company airplane was in the shop for an annual inspection. Turned out to be bad luck all the way around. The inspection took longer than expected, an FAA required upgrade had to be done, one of the mechanics was sick, basically it turned into an expensive nightmare. Our airplane was only the beginning of our misfortunes. The flight was bombed out of the sky. There weren't any survivors." Paul's voice grew shaky and quiet on the last sentence. He stared quietly into the fire for a few moments.

John waited until Paul turned to face him again. "Is there any chance your partner might not have gotten on the airplane?"

Paul looked warily at the detective. "What are you talking about? The NTSB listed Tim and Lisa among the dead. You probably know more about it than I do. I presume you checked the records of the accident."

"We pulled a copy of the NTSB report and the FBI files as well. Four passengers were never positively identified from the remains at the crash site. Your partner was one of the four who remain unconfirmed. Maybe I've been a detective so long almost everything looks suspicious to me, but I wondered if there was any chance he might have missed the plane."

"It's been two years. Don't you think I would have heard from him if he was still alive? I talked to him and Lisa just before they were scheduled to board. He told me they should be home in about an hour and a half. I was at the airport when they asked anyone waiting for the flight to come to the VIP lounge. They told us the flight had disappeared off the radar and there were reports the plane had crashed. The investigators and the airline told me their records showed Tim and Lisa boarded the airplane."

John paused a moment to give Paul a chance to control the emotions playing across his face. "Did you say they both called you?"

"They were both on the same flight. Lisa called to let me know when to meet them before she put Tim on the line. The next thing I knew the plane had crashed and they were, they were, gone."

"I know this is difficult to talk about and I apologize for

having to ask. I'm truly sorry for your loss. I wish I didn't have to ask these questions, but a lot of apparently unrelated events occurred about the same time and all of them seem to point at you. Please don't misunderstand what I'm saying. I'm not accusing you of anything. As far as we know you're simply a victim of circumstances."

Jean returned from the kitchen at that moment. "Coffee should be ready in a few minutes. What sort of things started a couple of years ago?"

"I'm glad you asked. When did you buy this cabin?"

"About two years ago." Paul turned a quizzical look toward her.

"Do you remember the PSA crash a couple years ago?" John asked.

"Yes. I remember thinking I was glad I wasn't flying that day. I've probably taken the same flight a couple dozen times in the past five years. I was nervous about flying anywhere for a while afterward, but that isn't what you asked me is it? I bought this place a few weeks after the airplane crash."

"Did you buy this house with plans to move here or to use it for vacations?"

"I honestly don't remember exactly what I was thinking at the time. I just fell in love with the place and wanted to own it. I decided to move here about a year ago, but I didn't actually move in until six months ago. I had to finalize a divorce from my husband and another from my career. Both took a little time."

"Did you buy your husband out of the property?"

"I paid for it with money I had from my first divorce and my grandmother's estate, and it was excluded from the settlement. He didn't want the place and agreed not to put any claims on it. He told me I could have it clear of the divorce so

I'd have somewhere to go to hide from my personal demons. One of my ex-husband's finer qualities is the uncanny ability to do something nice and then slap your face with it."

"Was it a friendly divorce?"

"Isn't that an oxymoron?"

The men chuckled and Jean smiled.

"Never had the experience, myself," John said. "I think you're probably right. Even the people who claim to have managed a friendly divorce seem to have an undercurrent of bitterness when they talk about it."

"It's hard to deal with. You have this incredible feeling of having failed miserably at the most important thing you've ever done. Failing twice doesn't make it feel like any less of a disaster. My divorce doesn't have anything to do with your investigation does it?"

"I don't think so, but it's difficult to know what's actually pertinent and important, so we try to gather all the information we can and sift it out afterward. Sometimes the key is some small bit of otherwise unrelated information shining a light on what we're looking for. Criminal investigation is best described as eliminating possibilities. Moving on, when did you two meet each other?"

"The day I arrived," Paul smiled wistfully. "I was wrestling with the busted screen door on my cabin when she accosted me and insisted on invading my life." Paul put an arm around her shoulders. "She's such a pushy broad."

"Who're you calling a broad? I resent that remark!" She smiled sweetly at Paul. "Actually he's right. I kind of barged in and took over his life. It seemed like the right thing to do at the time. So far I haven't had any reason to regret it."

John smiled. "Its nice to see you're happy with each other. Would you tell me again what brought you here, Paul?"

"I needed to get away from running the business. I needed some time and distance. Tim was dead, Lisa was dead, and our baby was gone. She was pregnant. The business was beating me down. I was so depressed I knew I had to do something or the business was going to go under. I couldn't run it alone and the people who work for Gormac deserve the security of a well managed company. They helped us become successful and shouldn't have to suffer hardship or risk their careers because of my incompetence. Maybe I just didn't believe I should try to run it alone. Whatever the case, the company was going in the wrong direction and I couldn't sit around and watch it collapse because of my personal feelings of inadequacy and grief. So, I hired a firm to run things and took some time off. This seemed like a nice place to get my feet back on the ground."

"There's a whole world of places you could have gone. Why here? Why not someplace more tropical?"

"One of my neighbors told me about this location. She has a friend who stayed in the campground and fell in love with the place. She told my neighbor there were some cabins here and something might be available for lease. Next thing I know, my neighbor marches into my office with the name and phone number of the people who own the cabin. I took a look at the pictures her friend had given her and decided if any place was a change from the city and the business this had to be it. I leased the place for six months. I left word at the office to come find me if they needed me because I wouldn't be checking in. I turned off my cell phone. If I need to use a phone I can go to the store or borrow Jean's. Mrs. Alexander said she was happy to take any messages and pass them along. She's a real sweetheart. No one's called so far. I guess the world isn't going to fall off its axis without me there to keep it spinning.

With a little luck the management company will do a better job than I did and I won't ever have to go back. I like it here."

"It's not a bad place to live. I know I've always been partial to it. Can you tell me a little about your partner?"

"I can tell you a lot about Tim. He was my best friend. We grew up together, shared an apartment when we were in college, he was my best man, he was my business partner. He's the closest thing to a brother I'll ever have. I know a lot about him. I just don't know if I can tell you what you want to know."

"What do you mean?"

"When Tim and Lisa were killed the FBI showed up at my office and questioned me about Tim's activities in the orient. I know what I told them didn't really answer their questions, at least not in the way they hoped. I'm not sure what they were looking for and they didn't try to help me understand. They just asked their questions and asked me to contact them if I thought of anything that might be of use to them. I know they were looking for something they didn't get from me. I also got a call from a company I didn't recognize asking about Tim's last trip and whether his brief case or luggage had been retrieved. Nothing was returned to me by the airline or anyone else. Tim and Lisa walked onto the airplane and just, well, disappeared." Grief painted his face with deeply shadowed lines. A single tear trickled down his cheek. "I had to use photographs for their funerals." His voice cracked. The soft crackling of the fire was the only sound in the room for a few moments.

Tom waited until he was sure Paul had regained control of his emotions. "I'm sorry we have to ask you to relive this. You said you didn't recognize the name of the company who called about Tim's briefcase. Do you remember the name of the company?"

"Sorry. I wish I did. I was so busy trying to run the company and deal with their deaths I didn't pay much attention to the guy who called. I gave up trying to remember anything. For a while I sort of wandered around in a fog. My staff took care of things and watched me to make sure I didn't endanger myself. My secretary and her family probably did the most to help me find my way back to reality, but I never made it all the way back to where I'd been. I still get lost in thought and lose pieces of time and events. I honestly don't know how many things slipped through my memory in the last two years. When I realized I wasn't able to handle things myself, I hired people to take over and came here. Sorry I can't help more. I wasn't planning on being part of a murder investigation."

John had a question for Jean. "Why did you buy this place if you hadn't decided to move here?"

John watched her consider her answer. The nervous hostility John had encountered during their first conversation was absent. She spoke in a clear and steady voice. "It was purely an impulse. I was getting ready to come up here to organize an advertising campaign for a bicycle rack company in Eureka when a friend suggested I come see the lagoon and Redwood National Park. She told me about the beach and the cabins and insisted I had to make time to see it. She said the view from the top of the bluff was too spectacular to believe. I met with the company and presented my concept for an advertising campaign. They really liked my ideas. After we hammered out the financial details and set a production schedule, I drove up here to scout filming locations. Bicycle people are outdoor types and I planned to use the rustic scenery to show off the advantages of the company's product line. I was exploring locations when I found this cottage. I was standing at the top of the bluff looking at the beach when the owners came home. Like a typical inconsiderate tourist, I'd parked my car blocking their driveway. We started talking, they invited me in, we had coffee, and I asked about buying one of the cabins. They offered to sell me this one, we settled on a price, and I wrote them a check."

"Really?" John asked. "Just like that? They quoted you a price and you wrote them a check? No agent, no negotiations, no appraiser to make sure you weren't getting taken to the cleaners? You just wrote them a check? The decision seems too fast, a bit out of character. I know this was a personal purchase, but it still doesn't seem to fit with the way I'd expect you to do things. Am I wrong?"

"No. Actually it was completely out of character for me to make a major decision so fast. It was the first of a lot of changes in the way I do things. All my life I've been methodical and logical and taken time to think out and research every decision. I've missed out on a lot of opportunities by over-thinking, over-analyzing, and obsessively searching out all the possible options. I know it saved me from making some bad decisions along the way, but there's no sense of freedom when every decision is coldly calculated. You never quite get past feeling indecisive when everything you do has to balance some rational scale. Such careful planning always left me wondering what I forgot to check, or what I might have missed in my research. It took me a long time to realize you never get all the information you need. The reality is you need to make your decisions based on the best knowledge you have at the time. Worrying whether a decision is right or wrong is irrelevant. Think of it as paralysis by analysis. Buying this property was a turning point for me. I walked into this house and I could see myself living here with my studio in there and the ocean out there and it just felt right. I didn't think about the money, or when I would move here, or how I would use it. I just knew

I wanted it to be mine. It changed my life when I made the decision to buy this place."

"What made you decide to change? Was there some particular event?"

"I don't think so, I just went with my feelings, trusted my first reaction. It felt like the right thing to do. Everything in my personal life was a shambles. I decided to do something just because it felt good. I saw a bumper sticker on a beat up van over in the campground that said *If it feels good, do it.* I guess the thought was running around in my mind at the time. It felt really good. It felt wonderful. So I did it. It may be the best decision I've ever made."

"How so?"

"Because it set me free."

"Free in what way?"

"Free to stop chasing someone else's dreams. Free to stop marching to someone else's drummer. Free to do what I wanted to do with my life. Free to stop questioning my decisions and my motives. Free to move forward with my head high. Free to be content to take whatever life hands me and enjoy it. Free to,"

"Free to find yourself?" John smiled.

Jean chuckled. "Yeah. Free to discover who I am. I never really thought of it as finding myself, but it's as good a description as any. I spent years banging my head against the board room door until they finally let me be a visitor in their private club. Once I got there, I found out all the hard work and sacrifice had taken me to a place I didn't really want to be. Nothing was good except the money. I didn't like the work. I didn't like the corporate politics. I felt like I was wasting my life. I felt like the most important part of my job was to make the people above me on the food chain feel good."

John checked his notes from their earlier conversation,

looking for where Jean had worked. "Did you ever have any business dealings with Paul's company? Perhaps an ad campaign?"

"I don't think so."

"We never hired anyone to do an ad campaign" Paul said. "Tim was so effective at locating and developing markets our biggest problem was finding ways to satisfy product demand. He was phenomenal at generating business and finding suppliers."

"You didn't work at selling your company's products?" Tom asked.

"In the beginning we both knocked on a lot of doors, but my strength was in orchestrating the internal operations of the company, not in convincing customers to buy from us. It's what made us such a good team. Tim was the front man everyone wanted to meet. My job was to make certain the company didn't burn down while he was out setting the market on fire. The fortunes of the business began to falter without him to keep the outside world looking to us for components. Don't misunderstand me, we weren't in financial trouble or in danger of not making payroll. There was money in the bank. The company was still strong! I simply refused to ignore the writing on the wall. I recognized that I was the problem! I solved the problem the way I was taught in college. I replaced me!"

"Did you consider changing the way you did business instead of handing it off to a management company? Maybe try some advertising?" John asked.

"I thought about advertising. I knew the kind of volume we always managed without it. I also knew I wasn't a good sales and marketing manager. The most important revelation was when I realized my heart wasn't in the business anymore. There was the real crux of the problem. You can't run a successful business unless your heart is in it. I needed to make a sound business decision to protect and preserve the company. I located a highly respected firm to take over the operation. It took a few months for them to learn the details of the business and get things growing again. I bailed as soon as they had the operation humming."

"So," Tom said, "you both came here hoping to find yourself and found each other?"

"Yeah, I guess so," they chorused.

Jean stood. "I think the coffee is ready. Anyone need sugar or cream?"

"Both for me," Tom answered.

"I'll be right back."

"Paul," John asked, "did you know the man who was found on the beach?"

"I don't even know what he looked like."

John handed him a photo. "This was taken at the morgue. Does he look familiar?"

Paul studied the picture carefully. "No. Definitely not familiar."

"Any idea why he might have been in your yard?"

"None I can think of. I've given it a lot of thought, but I can't imagine what he would be doing there. There's no reason to break in. I don't have anything worth stealing. I don't know what he might expect to find if he was planning to break in."

"What about something to do with your business?" Tom asked.

Paul considered the question for a moment. "I don't think so. I contracted with the management company for the next year with an automatic extension for the next five if they perform as agreed. The only way I can take back control or exert any influence is if they fail to operate the company successfully or do something illegal. I don't see where anyone could gain anything by coming at me. At least not for a year or more."

"How long did you know Tim Gordon before you went into business together?"

"Forever. We grew up together. We played ball together, chased girls together, you know, all the usual stuff. I was best man at his wedding, he was best man at mine. We were like brothers." Paul paused, looking down at the floor. Then slowly he raised his head and looked directly into Tom's eyes. "He was my best friend." His voice choked with emotion.

Once again silence invaded the conversation for a brief period. "We ran a routine background check on Tim," John said. "He was in the Army during the last months of the Viet Nam war. Did he go to Nam?"

"No. I guess he was scheduled to go, but he never went."

"Do you know where he was stationed?"

"Jeez, I don't really know. His letters had APO addresses and after basic he never told me anything specific. He was still in the Reserve when we started the business and when his hitch ran out five years ago he didn't re-enlist. The Reserve might be able to tell you more. He never talked much about what he did in the Reserves, he just joked about it giving him a chance to play soldier once a month and play with a lot of expensive toys."

"Were you in the service?"

"No. I graduated a year after Tim and managed to avoid the lottery. I went to work right out of college and hoped he would come home in one piece."

"Did he volunteer or was he drafted?"

"Drafted. I came home from school one day and found him sitting there half way through a case of beer. He told me he'd gotten his marching papers. That's how he put it. He graduated the last week of May. He was in boot camp in June. Two years later he was home. Same old happy go lucky Tim."

"He never talked about what he did in the Army?" John asked.

"Not really. When anyone asked he'd change the subject. He used to say the Army was a bad place to take a vacation. He said the liberty towns were interesting places to visit, but he wouldn't want to live there."

John laughed. "I've seen some of those liberty towns. Didn't it seem strange he didn't want to talk about those two years of his life? Wouldn't he tell his best friend about it? Especially when he stayed in the Reserves for another what, six or eight years?"

"A lot of guys came home from the war just wanting to move on and not remember. I thought he wanted to put it behind him and get on with his life. You know how Nam vets are. Some are chest beating proud and go around crowing about what they did in country. Others snivel and whine about how our country doesn't appreciate the sacrifices they made. Most just want to get on with their lives. Tim caught a job with Big Blue in sales and marketing and blasted off into new territory."

"You said you were his best man," Tom said. "Our background check showed he was single."

"Divorced. He and Darlene were only married a couple years. He was traveling all the time and she was working for Lockheed. Pretty soon they were going in different directions. She was offered a position with Martin Marietta in Atlanta. She wanted to go. The marriage became a casualty. Look, I know you're just doing background, but why all this interest in Tim?"

Jean returned with the coffee before John could answer.

A few minutes were spent getting everyone settled with a cup of the fresh brew before they picked up the interview again.

"I understand your confusion about our interest in your partner. It's important to know about your partner because you were so close. We don't know if there's any relationship between you and the man who was killed near your cabin. The only way to confirm or discredit any possible connection is to ask a lot of questions. Some of our questions pry into uncomfortable places. I apologize for the intrusion. Our job is to look at all the possibilities."

"I was listening from the kitchen," Jean said. "I get the impression you think Tim is still alive. Is that what this is about?"

"We don't know if he's alive or not," John replied. "He was never positively confirmed as being among the victims of the crash. We know he was supposed to be aboard. We know he turned in his boarding pass. What we don't know is if he actually got on the airplane. It may not mean anything. We still have to consider the possibility."

"So you think there's a connection between the guy who was killed and our company?" Paul asked.

"We know your company is an importer and we know the victim may have been involved in a similar sort of venture. What we don't know is where it leads us. We're just trying to shine a little light on the shadows," Tom said.

"Then I guess you've identified the body since the last time we talked," Paul said.

"We have a positive ID and it raises a lot of new questions," John replied.

Paul leaned forward, resting his elbows on his knees. "Have we helped fill in some of the gaps for you?"

"You've given us a better idea about the chronology of

events and you've helped with some important background information,"

"So are we free to go about our plans?"

John closed his notebook. "Yes. Thank you for your cooperation. I know it wasn't easy to talk about this. You've both been very helpful. Would you give us a call if you think of anything,?"

Tom put his notebook in his pocket. "Thanks for the coffee. It really hit the spot."

Jean closed the door and leaned back against it. She stared intently into Paul's eyes. "I think that went rather well. Now are you finally going to tell me what's really going on?"

"I wish I could."

"Do you mean you don't really know, or do you mean you can't tell me what you know?"

"It means I wish I could tell you what I know."

A chilling sense of foreboding slowly draped over her. She was uneasy about the way he ended the conversation with the detectives. She knew there was a lot he wasn't telling her. It felt like her choices were to let things play out or send him away. Her heart caught in her chest at the thought of sending him away. She believed she only had one choice. "Okay. You can't or won't tell me, yet. So what do we do?"

Paul sat on the couch and stared into the fire. She sat beside him. He put his arm around her shoulder and pulled her close. She tucked her feet up and leaned her head on his shoulder. The cozy warmth of the crackling fire failed to melt the icicle of dread in the pit of her stomach.

45.

JOHN TURNED OFF THE ENGINE. "SO, WHAT'S YOUR take on those two?"

"I think we just witnessed an academy award performance. Sweet little domestic scene, polite conversation, lots of easily verifiable information, nothing of any real use to us, and the interview ended by the interviewee in a very professional manner."

"Don't forget, he's a successful businessman, a professional administrator, accustomed to managing a staff. He knows how to control the direction of a conversation and how to close a meeting. Giving orders and having them followed is familiar territory for him."

"I agree with your assessment, but I think there's a lot more. I have a lot more questions about their suppliers and customers. It might be important to know how many containers they import from the orient every year."

"No argument here. I was working in the same direction when we got derailed."

"I thought you might be. I think he did too. I think you were about to enter territory he didn't want to discuss and the best way to avoid the subject was to end the interview, which he did with great skill. Why didn't you press him harder instead of tucking your tail between your legs and walking away?"

"Circumstances dictate when to push and when to walk away. There's a thousand different ways to handle an interview.

Sometimes you press hard and back a suspect into a corner until he surrenders. Sometimes you pretend to be able to prove more than you can in the hope of getting a confession. When you're on a fishing expedition you have to keep the conversation as non-confrontational as possible and watch their body language, especially when you're on the other guy's turf. I agree, there's important information we didn't get to talk about. What we did get out of our visit is solid confirmation we need to watch Paul McAfee. It's also obvious that if we lean on him, he's going to be quietly defensive and shape his answers to lead us anywhere except where we want to go. He's a very shrewd fellow. He has clear limitations on what he'll say and what he'll do. We can't interrogate him unless we arrest him. If we arrest him he'll immediately request his lawyer and we still won't be able to question him and we won't get any more second chances. We still don't have probable cause to arrest him, only a nagging hunch he's somehow involved. The last time I studied up on the subject, a hunch is not considered probable cause. All we can do is wait and watch. Patient observation is our best hope of unraveling this hair ball."

"You ever see the cartoon of the two buzzards perched on a snag? The caption reads *Patience my ass, I'm gonna kill something*. I felt like one of those birds while we were enjoying our coffee service. I kept my mouth shut and let you handle things, but it looked like those two were as nervous as a long tailed cat in a room full of rocking chairs. Their masterful performance felt slightly off key. Absolute courtesy and cooperation, not a hint of the aggressively defensive behavior she showed before. It looked too carefully orchestrated. I'm convinced there's a nasty secret in there and we're outside with our nose shoved up against a dirty window trying to see what's happening inside. You know what I mean?"

"I know exactly what you mean. I'm also aware that what we know, what we suspect, and what we can prove are a long way apart. Unfortunately, there's no law requiring them to cooperate any more than they have. We need to ask the right questions in the right context to get the right answers because without the right answers we'll never know what's really happening." John stared vacantly through the windshield. "I know what you mean about wanting to make something happen, but like it or not, we've gotta play by the rules and the bad guys don't have any rules."

"Another of life's little injustices?"

"Who said life was just? Maybe Dutch and Cal will turn something up. Who knows? They might actually get something useful out of the hermit."

"Hope springs eternal, but frankly, I'll be surprised if they do. Alma Jacobsen is a reluctant resource for me and I've spent months getting to know her and giving her the chance to get comfortable with me. The first six months was like visiting my grandma's grave. I'd talk and get a polite nod or a wave in return. She's kind of bristly even after you get to know her, so I don't think they'll get much. You think we should go see how they're doing, maybe give them a hand?"

"No. Let them do their own thing. We've already been there, done that, and come up empty. Let's leave them alone and not do anything to influence their thinking. We need their objective observations and deductions. You never know what a fresh set of eyes will notice. Let's go get some coffee and wait to see what they bring back from their fact finding mission."

"Speaking of fishing trips, there's another pond I think we should be trolling across."

"Yeah?"

"We know Tim Gordon is alive, unless the feebies are

yanking our chain. Let's presume they're being straight for a change. It makes it easier to determine what we know. We know Gormac was acting as a cutout for a computer chip smuggling operation. The feebies say the boys were dealing with an LA crime family, but the Chinese Triads and Japanese Yakusa control the orient. I think this case involves some very nasty people who are into drugs, illegal immigrants, industrial counterfeiting, and who knows what else. According to what I've read, the Triads in Southern California make the Mafia and the Latino street gangs look like a kindergarten class when it comes to being ruthless. Dealing with those people is a dangerous game. I don't think Gordon and McAfee decided to do this strictly out of patriotic zeal. There has to be a money trail. Smuggling is always about money, so it follows that Gordon and McAfee must have been pulling down some serious coin to make their act believable. I don't believe for a second they gave it all to Uncle Sam, which poses another important question. Where's the money?"

"Good point. But how do we ask McAfee about it? How do we make him believe we know he and his partner have been getting rich off the government's undercover operation? We need to sic Dutch on the problem. He's our computer and finance guru. Maybe he can get us some details on the scope of their activity. I know ICE has been fighting a losing war on illegal immigration from China, and the DEA has had no success slowing down the flow of white powder, but what I know about the Triads and Yakusa you could put in your eye and it wouldn't hurt you. How about you?"

"I know about enough to be dangerous. I know the Triads have been around for a long time. I know they've controlled Kowloon since the British established the Hong Kong Crown

Colony. I know they're absolutely ruthless. I know they hate the communists and just about any other form of government they can't control. I know you can get out of China and come to the United States if you have enough money to pay the Triads and the snakeheads. If you don't, you can sell yourself to them as an indentured servant to pay for the passage. If you indenture yourself, you owe them your life and your loyalty as well as most of what you earn working in their sweat shops, or doing whatever criminal activity they tell you to do until your debt is paid. Prostitution, gambling, extortion, protection, and murder for hire are all in their bag of tricks. If it's illegal, the Triads will be involved. Like I said, I know enough to be dangerous. I know if we're about to go nose to nose with a Triad we're in deep doo-doo. If you toss in the Yakusa, we need to look up to see bottom."

"If you're right, and I'm not saying you're not, we need to start watching our backs a lot more closely. We also need to start watching for a lot more players in this game. There's one thing you can absolutely count on."

"What's that?"

"None of the bad guys are going to show up wearing a three piece suit and driving an unmarked government car. Let's go have some coffee and wait to see what Sigfreid and Roy turn up."

Dutch and Cal walked to Alma Jacobsen's cabin. Dutch wanted a better look at the lagoon side of the house and to watch for activity. It sounded like a good plan, but the weather proved distracting.

Cal tugged his collar tighter around his neck to reduce the amount of cold water running down his back. "Don'tcha just love sunny California?"

"Think of it as a cold shower. Something to help you focus on the important things."

"Thanks for the detour into the gestalt. Take a look at the placement of the house on the lot. Notice how the windows provide an unrestricted view to the west and north and a pretty clear shot to the east. You can see almost the entire lagoon, most of the campground, and most of the beach. You couldn't build a better lookout. The only thing needed to make it perfect is a three story tower with a solarium at the top."

"Perfect for our reclusive neighborhood snoop. It also looks like nobody's home. No lights, no smoke from the chimney, no television in the background and no little old lady puttering in her yard."

"Maybe too quiet," Cal mumbled. "What the hell. Let's knock on the door and see if anyone answers."

The gate swung open on well oiled hinges. Dutch admired the immaculate condition of the yard. "Looks like she spends time keeping things up. I haven't been up here on the bluff in four or five years. The last time I was here this place looked like most vacation cottages. Now it looks like the cover of Home and Garden."

"She's been here a couple years and obviously likes to work in her yard. I guess she's out here every morning unless the weather is bad. Shows too. I don't have the time or the inclination and I can't afford to hire a professional gardener to keep my yard this nice."

"Join the club. I do my yard chores because they need doing, not because I love pulling weeds and mowing the lawn. This looks like gardening is her passion."

There was no response to Cal's knock. "I guess she's out. Let's take a look around and see if anything jumps out at us."

They walked along the north wall of the cabin on a meandering stepping stone path.

"Do you suppose she locked her garage?" Dutch asked.

There was a door at the rear corner of the garage. "Maybe we should try the back door first," Cal suggested.

"Not much hope there, partner. Check out the lock and hasp. I don't think our local hermit is very trusting. Let's try the garage doors." As they rounded the front of the garage Dutch knew their luck had taken a turn for the better. The lock hanging in the hasp wasn't secured. "The musical question is whether an unsecured lock is an invitation to enter and have a look about. What's your opinion, Holmes?"

"I think we should test the reliability of the security measures." Cal bumped the lock with his elbow, knocking it to the ground. "Oh my," he put his hand to his cheek and displayed an open mouthed expression. "It looks like a person or persons unknown may have gained unlawful entry to this building. We would be remiss in our duty as minions of the law were we to fail to confirm whether or not anything has been purloined."

Dutch put on a solemn expression. "Your honor, the purpose of the investigation was to ascertain whether the property of the resident was safe or had perhaps fallen prey to an evil doer. Do you think we should swing both doors wide so if anyone's inside they'll be instantly exposed in strong light?"

"Excellent idea. You take the one on the right and I'll take what's left. Ready? On three. Three!" They swung the doors wide exposing a vacant single car garage with no access door in the rear. The walls were clean except for a single shelf at the rear which held a bucket filled with car wash supplies. The building was otherwise empty. "Looks like the other door leads to a storage room. Too bad it's locked."

"Terribly unfortunate. There's obviously nothing in here. Let's check the other side of this shack."

They closed the doors and replaced the lock the way they had found it. Behind the garage they found a small vegetable garden as immaculately weed free as the rest of the yard.

"Look in the dictionary for vegetable garden and you'll see a picture of this," Dutch said. "The old crone lives for her garden."

"For sure." Cal's attention was focused on the east wall of the garage.

"What are you looking at?"

"Maybe nothing. Something doesn't look right." He approached the corner of the building. Dutch followed, trying to see what had captured Cal's attention. The wall appeared to be an unbroken surface of weathered wood with a recent coat of paint. What Cal had seen or sensed was nearly invisible. There was a slightly warped plank a little offset from the one next to it. Cal leaned down to look through a small knothole. "Well looky here," he mumbled.

"What have you got?"

Cal put his index finger into the knothole. There was a barely audible click, and he swung open a narrow panel extending the full height of the siding. It stopped against the ends of the roof joists, creating an opening too small for either detective, but enough to provide a clear view of the room. The space was about four by six feet with a plywood floor a foot above ground level. The walls and ceiling were finished with plywood and painted a glossy beige. The room was immaculate. A shelf along the interior wall held a computer and several other electronic devices. A door occupied most of the far wall.

"So what do you suppose this is all about?" Cal asked.

"Could be a lot of perfectly legal explanations. She may be a writer who likes to work in isolated surroundings or she could be a ham radio operator. The computer looks similar to mine and the rest looks like high tech communications gear. Maybe she's a stock trader and this's how she gets her real time quotes. There are a thousand legitimate reasons for this secret room to go along with whatever our suspicious imaginations can dream up as probable cause for a more thorough search, and all of them persuade against issuing a warrant. Maybe she just likes to play with expensive electronic toys."

"Sure. It explains why this room is secured like a secret vault. How much you wanna bet the other door is invisible from the outside and opens with an electric solenoid like this one? I know it isn't the door with the hasp we saw from the other side because this room isn't as long as the width of the garage. I bet you have to dodge a bunch tools and step over a lawn mower to reach the door."

"A logical presumption, but unless we can come up with some reason to believe a crime's been committed, she's still a good citizen who's entitled to her privacy. We may have stumbled on this little hideaway, but there's nothing illegal about owning a computer or this other stuff. Even if the local judge gave us a warrant we'd never get anything into court unless we could connect it to a crime. Just because the owner is a recluse who keeps her toys locked up in a clean room doesn't give us probable cause to suspect a crime has been committed. There isn't a DA or Judge in the county who would be able to keep a straight face while they turned us down."

"First a belly laugh then an in-depth discussion regarding the need for a brain implant for wasting their time. On the other hand, it is an interesting discovery."

"Indeed it is. Interesting, but not necessarily helpful. It

doesn't matter if we think it's a little odd, this country was founded to protect a person's right to be an oddball. If being odd was illegal you'd be doing a life sentence."

"Every organization requires a resident oddball and I take great pride in filling the obligatory position." Cal pushed the door until he heard it click into place. "Besides, working with you feels like a life sentence." They walked out of the yard and returned to the store.

The rain had retreated to a half-hearted drizzle when the four detectives gathered at the back of the store with fresh cups of coffee. Cal sipped the dark brew and spoke to John. "You'll never guess what we found. It opens up a whole new realm of possibilities, including the possibility there is absolutely nothing useful in what we found. Useful or not, it's definitely interesting."

"Are you planning to share this bit of gossip with us perchance? I'm too damn tired to play twenty questions."

A devilish grin splashed across Cal's face. "I suppose I could make you to try to guess what we found, but you'd probably strain your moldy old gray matter in the process. We discovered a small room at the back of the hermit's garage with a computer and what looks like a bunch of sophisticated communications gear. It all looks pretty much state of the art, and as far as we know, totally innocent. There's no law against owning a computer and a rack of electronic gear. The question is why put it out in the garage instead of inside the house?"

"You never know where people will put things like computers," Tom answered. "I have a friend who built a special room in the attic so he could keep it all to himself. I know another guy who turned a storage closet in the garage into a computer room. It's not unusual to find a computer tucked away in some tiny little cubbyhole with barely enough room to sit in front of it. People are funny about their computers and where they put them. What you're describing doesn't even rank as unusual. Her cottage is small. Maybe she didn't want it taking up living space, or maybe she wanted it in a clean room."

Dutch nodded. "You may be right, but something felt, I dunno, kinda sinister. You'd never notice the room if you didn't know it was there. It looks like it's supposed to be a secret."

"How'd you happen to tumble onto this secret hiding place if it was so well concealed?" John asked.

"It wasn't anything specific," Cal said. "Something about the wall just jumped out at me. The siding didn't look like it fit the way it should. It may have shifted or warped in the weather after it was built. Even when I'd seen it, it was still hard to see. You know what I mean?"

"Like your brain, too small to mention?" John offered.

"I got your small brain hanging. If you're so damn smart, how come you didn't notice it? Look, we found the stuff, whether or not it means anything. Maybe when the old broad comes home you can ply her with Geritol until she confesses to whatever nefarious scheme she's cooked up with her magic boxes. What did you guys get from the other two?"

"Not much," John replied. "Nothing to tie them to anything. Nothing to explain anything. Just an absolute certainty McAfee knows a lot more than he's telling us. He's very adept at directing and ending a conversation. He claims his partner was the lead man for their business and he was basically the administrative and bookkeeping side of things. I think whatever his partner may or may not have done for the business, Paul McAfee was firmly in control. If Tim Gordon was the heart, I think Paul McAfee was the brains."

"What about his girlfriend, the artist?" Dutch asked.

"There's nothing to indicate she isn't exactly what she seems to be. At first blush it looks like there's a possible connection in terms of the timing of the purchase of those two cabins, but the trail's a dead end. The purchases coincidentally happened in the same chronology as a lot of events involving Gordon and McAfee, but coincidence is all we can find. Beyond the chain of events beginning a couple years ago we've got doodly squat except her relationship with McAfee. He's not telling us anything important, she doesn't know anything important, the hermit owns a computer and has it stashed in a secret compartment behind her garage. It's all real interesting, but it still leads exactly nowhere. I don't know about you guys, but I've had just about all this outstanding entertainment I can stand for the time being. Let's pack it in and pick it up in the morning. Maybe this time I'll actually get some uninterrupted sleep."

46.

PISCES PARKED WHERE THE CAR WAS CONCEALED
from passing traffic. Though the rain had stopped, the green
canopy continued to shed drops. "We'll walk from here. I don't
think this clunker can make it where we have to go and you
look like you could use the exercise."

"It's unkind to make sport of an old man's frailties. I wasn't
born old. It happens to everyone who lives long enough."

"Old or young, we walk from here. Leave the umbrella."

He looked at the unpaved track leading into the trees, then
looked at his clothes and particularly his custom made Italian
loafers. "You expect me to slog off into the woods dressed like
this?"

"I expect you to do what I tell you. If you're worried about
ruining your shoes or your Italian wool suit, you can take them
off and leave them in the car, but you'll be a lot warmer if you
keep them on. Quit your bellyaching and move it."

He started up the track trying to step where the ground
looked most solid. "You're much too hard for such a lovely
young woman." His tone was soothing, persuasive, spoken as
if to a beloved child. "You should find a nice man and make
pretty babies instead of wandering like a gypsy."

Pisces trailed about six feet behind as he made his way
up the slope, listening to his breathing gradually becoming
labored. "You can stop and rest if you get short of breath."

He stopped and looked back at her. "I get short of breath walking to the john. How far do we gotta go?"

"As far as it takes to get where we're going. Stop if you need to catch your breath. We'll keep going until we get there. Capisce?"

"Si, signorina," he sighed and continued plodding up the muddy track, large drops splattering off him as he went. The cold was making his joints ache and hardening his resolve to extract satisfaction for her treachery. *Joey is a screw-up, and he deserves to be reprimanded for his failure to act in good faith, but not until I punish the treacherous turncoat who has taken my money and imprisoned my grandsons! We'll see whose honor squeezes who! Where is she taking me?*

Pisces' nerves tingled with a sense of being watched, a feeling too strong to ignore. The staccato drumming of the water falling from the trees combined with the rush of the wind through the tree tops to conceal any sounds which might expose the presence of the old man's bodyguards. She hoped her uneasiness was because Tim was watching and not because a trap was closing on them. Something just felt wrong. The tree where they had left the cousins was in sight and she still hadn't seen Tim.

It took several minutes and several more stops to reach the hollow tree. The Don was only a few feet from the entrance when they were halted by a quiet voice.

"That's far enough!"

The sensation she had endured as they climbed the hill was trying to force her into a panic, but she summoned control of her breathing before speaking. "What do you want me to do?"

"Tie him up with the others and come back out. Please don't try anything foolish."

While she was securing the old man she noticed an older woman was now imprisoned with the two young hoods. No one spoke as she completed her task and stepped outside.

She felt the barrel of a gun touch her behind her left ear. "Far enough. Don't look around. You know I'm here and I'm ready to use this. Walk up the hill. I'll be right behind you. Before you go anywhere put your hands on top of your head and lace your fingers together." The man had a strange accent, a mixture of an oriental language and the King's English. She remembered hearing this particular lilt when she was in Hong Kong, but even with the origin of its owner narrowed, it offered no clue to his identity.

As she raised her arms, the pistol holstered on her belt was quickly removed by her captor. She walked up the hill toward a large rock with her captor silently in train. She focused her thinking on how to disarm her captor. *I can't count on Tim to help me, he may have already been taken out. I need to handle this on my own.*

The identity of her captor remained a mystery while she rapidly considered and discarded ways to regain control of the situation. The loss of her gun didn't really disarm her if she could get close enough. Her captor was apparently aware of this and stayed far enough away to prevent her from using her martial arts skills, yet close enough to respond quickly if she attempted to bolt. Sensei's instructions echoed in her mind. *'Your mind is your most powerful weapon. Never allow the situation to rob you of the ability to think clearly. Patience and clear thinking will deliver victory where physical strength cannot prevail.'* She studied the slope of the ground, the position of the trees and the large rock they were approaching. She was at the mercy of her captor. He could instantly end her life by shooting her in the back of the head. His failure to do so at the first opportunity meant the game wasn't over. She expected to be interrogated or even tortured. Interrogation meant prolonged contact with her captor and the possibility he would become overconfident and less vigilant. She kept her face an immobile mask and plotted her retaliation.

Tim watched Pisces approach with the Don. He was about to rise from his position when an unexpected visitor captured her. He quickly stopped cursing his failure and worked on how to deal with the new circumstance. He followed silently as her captor herded her up the hill. The newcomer was obviously a professional. He wore sturdy denim clothing and moved gracefully over the uneven ground without exertion or sound. Tim considered the possibilities. *A new player has entered the game, and he is about to reveal himself as this guy's puppet master.*

In spite of his vigilance Tim nearly missed seeing the second man move from cover. He froze when he realized a limb was moving against the wind. The man stepped from behind the large rock and stopped six feet in front of Pisces.

A wry smile crept across Tim's face. Thomas Hartley was traditional colonial British, born and raised in Hong Kong, educated in the best schools, possessed of the worst of British colonial arrogance, and completely lacking in ethics and morality. He spoke like a member of Parliament and thought like a Triad. He was their contact for the counterfeit computer chips being smuggled into the United States. It was an elegant way of laundering the credibility of the chips and the money used to purchase them. The money had been huge until Tim was compromised and Paul shut down the pipeline. Thomas also knew about Tim's relationship with Julie.

"Well, well, how nice to see you, my dear," Thomas said politely. "I was so hoping we would meet again. It was so good of you to round up all the others and put them in one basket. The only ones missing are the boys from California who were so helpful for so long. Whatever have you done with them?"

"How good of you to inquire. The boys were fine the last time I saw them. I'll be sure to tell them you asked after them and wish them well."

"Yes, I suppose I do wish them well. At least for the time being. Perhaps you could tell me where I might find the lads, I should like to discuss some sort of redress with them. Their defection has been most inconvenient."

"If you're here, you already know where to find Paul, so why are you asking me?"

"Paul. Such a serious young man. Always tending to the financials and the profits. No heart for the front lines. Quite useful in many ways, but such a bother with insisting the numbers match up."

"Did he make it difficult for you to short the shipments and the payments?"

"Theirs was the best of all my pipelines. They had such good connections in the industry and especially with customs. On the negative side of the ledger they were so much more trouble to deal with because Paul simply didn't understand the way business is done in the orient. He didn't have any appreciation of the squeeze. He was so incredibly American when I explained it was a part of doing business. He insisted if I wanted to pay a squeeze it was my problem and not to make my problems his problems. In spite of the unpleasantness, I do rather miss the chaps. It's been difficult to find another reliable courier."

"Don't you mean it's been impossible to find another courier?"

"Yes, I suppose it has. It has placed me in a somewhat awkward position with my suppliers."

"I see. They insist you buy what you contracted for whether you smuggle it into the US or not? How terribly inconvenient for you. Is that why you came here personally? You usually insist on handling everything from within the boundaries of the colony, keeping yourself at arms length from the dirty work."

"Ordinarily my preferred practice. Circumstances, however, have ordained I take a more, shall we say, active position. Since no one has been able to capture our wayward butterfly, I took it upon myself to make a personal effort to pop a net over him before he could take flight again."

"You mean the Triad is leaning on you so hard you had to do something to fix things." Pisces smiled. "If you can't cure this little problem you're going to suffer the consequences of their dissatisfaction."

"An indelicate way of putting it, but essentially accurate. The atmosphere has become quite stifling at home. It seemed a breath of fresh air might be therapeutic. So, here I am in the colonies, searching for my carrier pigeon who seems determined to fly the coop."

"My, my, how elegantly stated. And what do you plan to do when you find him? Invite him to join you for squab under glass and champagne?"

"I'm sure you recall the story of the goose that laid the golden eggs. I certainly wouldn't have gone to so much effort to find him if he were more useful dead than alive. As displeased as I am with his defection, I need him alive and operating his glorious pipeline."

"I see your problem. You're truly screwed if you can't rebuild things, an embarrassing liability without Tim. How incredibly inconvenient."

"Cute. Now what do you suppose we ought to do to draw our little rabbit out of the bush? The little tea party you have going down the hill tells me you've already located our friend. Only the question of what you've done with him remains. Are you going to be cooperative, or should I have my associate take a hand in persuading you? He's terribly good with his hands."

"To coin a rather quaint colonial phrase, why don't you go fuck yourself?"

"Crude. Kwan, perhaps you can provide a small demonstration of what she can expect if she chooses to be stubborn."

Kwan drove his fist into her right kidney, driving her to her knees and was preparing to deliver another blow when his head erupted in a geyser of red and his lifeless body slumped to the ground.

Thomas heard the chuffing sound of the silenced gun and the accompanying ratchet of the weapon chambering another round. "You really need to hire better help," Tim said as he stepped from behind a tree. "Or perhaps you should handle things for yourself. Then again, I don't think you have the stomach for the dirty work. It's much easier to order someone else to do your dirty laundry than to take care of it yourself. I don't share your delicate sensibilities about getting dirt under my fingernails. I'm particularly fond of maiming men who abuse women. Why don't you put your hands behind your head and settle down on your knees. There's a good fellow."

Thomas did as he was told. "Very good, Tim. You seem to have gained the upper hand."

"I never lost it. I was only waiting for your arrogance to overwhelm your good sense. It didn't take very long. Are you okay, Julie?"

She stretched her back and massaged her kidney. "I'm going to have a nice bruise, but he was good. He only did enough to get my attention and maybe make me piss blood for a few days."

"It looked like Thomas already had your attention before he tugged on his dog's leash. What do you think we should do with his lordship?"

Julie looked at the hollow tree. "Toss him in the same barrel as the others. This one too." She nudged Kwan's body with her foot.

"I agree. Thomas, old chap, would you mind terribly carting your man down there for us? The lady is feeling a mite under the weather and I really must maintain my preparedness to shoot you if you should take a notion to be uncooperative."

Julie stayed near Tim, watching Thomas struggle to maintain his footing as he carried Kwan's body. Tim hadn't wanted her in front of him where she might block his view of Thomas and he also didn't want her behind him. "Is something bothering you?" she asked.

"You mean aside from what we're going to do with all these people? Maybe because I just killed a man? Maybe because ever since you showed up the whole world seems to know how to find me. Yes, something's bothering me! There's a lot bothering me, so I'm playing my cards close to the vest until I see which sides the players are on."

She studied his profile. It was the same face she had fallen in love with many years ago, but there was no softness in it at the moment. Something had happened in her absence and she needed to regain his trust. "I brought you here, and I brought the Don and his boys to you as prisoners, not the other way around. I'm on your side. It should be obvious I didn't lead this slime and his pal to you and I sure as hell didn't tell them anything. So what's going on?"

"How about we table this discussion until we get this turd into the bowl with the rest of the shit. Then we can talk about things."

Alma watched the Don study the other prisoners. His grandsons returned his gaze with expressions of shame. He shook his head in disgust and turned his attention to her. "I know why we're here. Why are you?"

She recognized him from a photograph taken years earlier. He looked older and more frail than she expected, but his appearance didn't soften the steely expression in his eyes. "It's a long, boring story."

A hint of a smile lifted a corner of the old man's mouth. "So you think we got somewhere else we're going real soon? A long, boring story might be entertaining."

"Let's just say I work for the competition."

"Ah. The competition. What are we competing for?"

"We both want the same thing."

"Um. We both want Tim Gordon's head on a platter. I kinda wanted him with an apple in his mouth, an elegantly appropriate way to prepare a treacherous pig, don't you think?"

"I had other, less pleasant ideas, something very slow and very painful. Too bad he has us both at a disadvantage."

"For the moment. Given a bit of patience and a little luck all things can change." He leaned his head back and closed his eyes. "It's been a long day." Moments later his snores echoed through the small chamber.

Tension crackled like static electricity among the captives. Kwan's body demonstrated Tim's willingness to be ruthless. Each one knew the next cooling body might be their own. There was no conversation, only a rising temperature in the tiny space as the living bodies emitted an increasingly sour odor of nervous perspiration the tangy fragrance of the primeval forest could not camouflage.

Tim and Julie chose a location where they could observe the makeshift prison and its surrounding approaches. Julie waited for Tim to give voice to his thoughts, but he betrayed nothing of the emotional turmoil seething inside him.

"Do you suppose the locals would be indignant if Kwan happened to wash up on their beach?" she asked.

Tim said nothing for almost a minute. She couldn't look away. She felt like his gaze had pierced her body and stuck her in place like an insect in a display case. "I think I need to do a better job of litter disposal than the last time. The question is how many bodies need to vanish?" He paused a beat. "And whether yours should be one of them."

Everything suddenly became clear. The cousins had managed to plant a suspicion in Tim's mind, a suspicion he might not want to believe, but couldn't afford to ignore. It would explain why he had watched her like an enemy when they were herding Thomas to the tree.

Tim's voice was cold. "So what's really going on? Who are you really working for and when are you planning to turn me over to them?"

Julie breathed slow and deep while she considered her answer. "My work for the family is finished. I've been paid.

I'm permanently retired. As a freelance photojournalist I can sell my work to anyone I choose. Or I can choose to disappear. I've got enough money to live comfortably anywhere I want. I have no obligation or commitment to turn you over to anyone and I don't intend to help anyone kill you. The only people I'm working for are you and me. I'm hoping we can live without constantly looking over our shoulder to see who might be closing in on us. I'd like to go somewhere quiet with you and maybe have a family."

"Nice speech. Nicely designed to push all the right buttons and work your way back inside my defenses. I've managed to stay alive by not trusting anyone to take care of me because if I'm the only one looking out for me, I'm the only one I have to look after. Why should I believe you're retiring from your lucrative career as a hired gun?"

"I only took this job because I hoped I could find a way for us to have a chance to be together. My job was to find you and bring you in alive. I did it. I just didn't do it the way they expected. You can believe what you want and think whatever you like. You will anyway. Just remember one important fact while you're thinking. I painted a target on my back so I could stand here arguing with you while you try to decide who you can trust besides Paul. I presume you still trust Paul, which means you're going to have to trust his new girl friend too. You have to kill me, or trust me, because it's the only way you'll ever know I'm not still hunting you."

The expression in his eyes softened slightly. "Paul has already paid too high a price for our friendship. Lisa died because of me."

"Maybe she did and maybe she didn't. You didn't answer my question."

"I know I didn't."

"Fine! Don't answer it. Here's something else for you to chew on. How deeply is Paul involved in this whole affair? I mean, you guys are best buddies, business partners, partners in crime too, maybe. This didn't start a couple years ago. It crashed a couple of years ago. You always told me Paul made the money go all the right places. You said all you had to do was schmooze and beguile the world into letting Paul make money for you. He seems so innocent, such a lost lamb," Julie's eyes suddenly grew wide. "Holy shit! I get it! You were the big horse on the fast track, but Paul was the jockey! He's not only in on it, he's been in on it from the start and he's still working all the angles. You set up the deals for Paul to operate. Man, you two have the whole world fooled. What an operation! You guys have been stashing the loot and Paul knows where all the money is buried. Paul doesn't need you, you need him. Sweet Jesus! Nobody ever saw it! Everybody thinks you're the man in charge and all the time it's your partner! I gotta take my hat off to you. You guys are really slick! What's really going on? Did Paul do my predecessor the way you just did Kwan, or did you do him and blow the disposal?"

"Neither! We didn't do him. He wasn't part of the plans. His unfortunate and untimely demise is a major pain in the ass. We sure as hell don't need all the attention we're getting from the local police when we're trying to get away. They're watching every move Paul makes because of where the asshole got wasted. The plan was to escape attention and quietly disappear. Instead, Paul's standing in the middle of the damn spotlight at center stage. Great plan, don't you think?" Tim paused to scan the surrounding area. "When did you figure out what we were doing?"

"You mean with the counterfeit computer chip imports?"

"Yeah."

"Do you remember the time we met in Canton?"

"When you were on your way to Tibet for the feature you were doing on the Dalai Lama?"

"Yes. It all began to make sense to me. One of my contacts had dropped a comment about an importer who was quietly smuggling their stock into the US. I knew he was into bogus computer chips and you were a chip importer. I asked a couple of innocuous questions and suddenly all the pieces dropped into place. My biggest concern was that you were fronting the operation for the mob. I worked for those people and I didn't want you for an assignment."

"Did you know the other half of the picture?"

"You mean the feds?"

"Uh-huh."

"About a year later I was in Manila and saw you sitting in a sidewalk restaurant with a young woman. I took a couple shots with a long lens. I thought it would be fun to surprise you with them, just to show you how hard it would be to keep me from knowing what you were doing. I wasn't sure I recognized who you were with until I developed the film. Then I was puzzled."

"Puzzled about what?"

"What an electronic component importer was doing with the Special Assistant to the Director of the NSA. I could see how you could get tangled up with the family because the organization is always looking for legitimate business people to launder their activities. Ordinary greed and opportunistic business practices can explain that, but you're smuggling for the family, and having lunch with the Special Assistant to the Director of the NSA in a café in Manila. What the hell does the NSA have to do with this deal?"

"Now we're getting to the real question! Are Paul and I just a couple of yuppies willing to take a few chances to make a big win and scamper off into the great unwashed nations to live off our ill gotten gains, or are we men of honor and morality? Or maybe we're out there in the shadowy world doing our patriotic best to help our government build a case against the legendary bad guys and coincidentally getting filthy rich along the way? If we are, then how'd we manage to get into the spot we're in and how'd we keep it covered up for so long? Isn't that what you really want to know?"

The realization of the true danger of her situation settled over Julie like the cold wet air of the forest. The rest of the pieces suddenly fell into place. "Something happened a couple years ago to make the whole thing blow up in your face. All the plans evaporated. All the escape routes were cut off and someone turned you into a target. Paul was the pipeline they knew would ultimately lead to you. You were supposed to disappear with Paul's wife when the plane went down, but you never got on the airplane. Why didn't you take Lisa with you?"

"Timing. I got a call on my cell phone as we were boarding. I had to come back out of the jetway to take the call. I had to walk to the side of the terminal to get a clear connection. I don't know who called me. He told me the plane was going down and I needed to get lost and hung up. I thought it was somebody's sick idea of a joke. I looked around for who might be the source of the call and saw a couple of family enforcers walking toward the gate. I had to make a decision. If I went after Lisa we'd never get off the plane and out of the terminal. Whether or not the caller was giving me the straight stuff, I figured the Don wanted to talk to me, so I split. Lisa and a lot of other people weren't so lucky. The whole world thinks it was a mental case who dusted the airplane. He did. He confessed. The security tapes show him entering the gate and at the cargo hold. I'm certain he planted the explosives for somebody else.

He was pissed about getting fired and wanted to get back at the airline, but the guy only had one oar in the water. I don't think he had any idea how to build a sophisticated explosive device. Someone used the poor goofy son of a bitch for their own purposes. He was the perfect fall guy. It worked. No one looked any further. It was a great plan. Everyone's happy except the widows and orphans. The NTSB and the FBI have their bomber and the airline gets nailed for wrongful death so the crazy bastard is happy. Everyone who needs to look clean is spotless. A lot of good people died and maybe it's my fault because maybe it was me they were trying to kill. It haunts my thoughts and my dreams."

"So what do you do now? Do you kill me and all the others down there and bury the evidence where it will never be found, or have you decided to trust me after all? Think about it! Have I ever done you dirt?"

"No. Not even on the beach when you had me completely compromised. I want to believe you. I want to believe we can extricate ourselves from this mess and find a place where we can live normally. I just killed a man for hurting you. I didn't even think about it. I saw him hit you and I wanted to kill him. I did it without a thought and I don't regret it. I guess that says something."

"I think it says it all. By the way, where did you get the gun? I left you a pistol and that is definitely not a pistol. It looks like the kind of specialized Glock the spooks use."

"You do know your weapons. I took this off Marnee when I caught her trying to sneak up on me. I don't know what her instructions were, but this is one of those nice little numbers specially designed for the NSA. It's compact, lightweight, and accurate to about a hundred yards. The scope is light enhancing for a clear view in starlight with adjustable settings to match available light. Break it down and you can carry it like any other automatic pistol. It's a nice piece. Ever seen one up close before?"

"Yeah, I've seen one. Most likely the guy I saw using it didn't get it through normal Government Issue. So, wait a minute. Did you say you took it off Marnee? Are we talking about the Marnee who is special assistant to,"

"The very same. Little Miss Manila of the NSA."

"I'm confused. The woman in Manila was thirty something! The woman down there is sixty something. Are you telling me she's the same person?"

"Amazing what they can do with plastic isn't it."

"I've seen some of the best makeup in Hollywood up close and nothing looks as real as she does. So which look is real and which is the disguise?"

"Plastic surgery, not theatrical prostheses. Real skin, real wrinkles, real changes to age her. Everything except the hair. It needs to be bleached and dyed regularly to keep up appearances. Think about all the effort and consider the reclusive life she's been living. It all begins to make sense."

"The nosy old hermit next door to Paul! It's Marnee! Jesus, how did they manage to get her right next door with the best lookout in the area?"

"Patience, persistence, suggestions, opportunities, diligent effort to manipulate things the way they wanted them to go. I don't know all the details, I only know they're capable of managing almost anything they set out to achieve. The government has lots of time, lots of money, lots of resources, and lots of connections. Hell, they are the connections. They can stack those resources and advantages up on your side of the table or use them to bury you from their side. When they want something there are no limits to what they'll do. When they want complete deniability, they are in total control of all the records, all the reports, all the databases, and all the media. They can make you a hero until they use you up, then turn you into a sacrificial goat and never leave a trail to show they were ever a part of it. All you can do is pray you're quick enough to get away when it happens."

"Okay. I see how you and Paul ended up in the middle of this particular swamp, but what about Jean Parker? Is she just an innocent bystander who coincidentally got involved or is she a part of one of these clandestine scenarios too?"

"She's wrinkle I haven't figured out yet. She wasn't part of the original plan. I have to believe Paul thinks there's an advantage in involving her. It isn't like him to use people. Maybe she'll be the one to bring us down. Maybe he was lonely. Maybe he really likes her. What I saw looked serious."

"It's only been a few days!"

"How long does it take?"

"You're right. Usually it's there at the beginning or it never shows up at all. Falling in love isn't about timing or logic or careful thought. I know how it was for me. So what are we going to do now?"

"I'm not sure. I'm doing my best Indiana Jones and making it up as I go along."

Wind surfed through the tree tops, engulfing them in a wall of white noise. Tim spoke so softly Julie barely heard him. "I have to decide what to do with those people and locate a place to get rid of Kwan's body where it won't be found. I don't expect anyone to come looking for him because he probably hit the beach with counterfeit documents. I'm sure Thomas has already written him off as a casualty of war and is equally interested in making him disappear. Announcing Kwan's death would focus the attention of the authorities on

Thomas. The shadows of obscurity are essential to his survival, but it doesn't solve the problem of what to do with the rest of them. Got any brilliant ideas?"

She had been worrying the problem over in her mind while he talked. "I think we only have a few options. We bury Kwan out here in the trees and he'll probably never be found. It wouldn't be the first time a body vanished around here. A couple years ago some guy confessed to killing a woman and burying her in the redwoods ten years earlier. When they took him to where he said he buried the body everything had grown over and nothing could be found. It had been a long time and he had buried her at night, but he knew enough unpublished specifics to absolutely identify him as the killer. Another option is to just leave them where they are and let them figure out how to get loose. Sooner or later one of them will break out of those ties and once one of them is free, the rest will be loose in minutes. For a really clean break we could bury them all. Maybe the best solution is a combination of all of the above."

"I see we're of a single mind. I keep thinking we need to use the old man to cement our future safety, but I don't think we can trust him. He'll tell us whatever we want to hear while he waits for the opportunity to slip a shiv between our ribs. Our options are limited and I'm going to have to make a decision. So tell me sweetheart, how do you see yourself in this nefarious little scheme?"

"You mean for right now or for tomorrow and the next day?"

"One is kind of dependent on the other isn't it?"

"Very simple. I'm with you. Right beside you to help you find your way, to watch your back, to fill the lonely hours. I've got plenty of money. You're the only thing I still need."

"Then help me decide what to do with our guests."

"We start by having Hartley dispose of his associate. They crashed the party, so let him take out the garbage. Once he's finished his nasty little chore, we let him find his way home or to whatever rock he decides to crawl under. Thomas is an arrogant idiot, but he's not a killer. He probably won't go back to Hong Kong. His future's not real bright if he goes back because he's been working for the Russian mafia the last couple years along with the Triads, making his future look pretty dim no matter where he goes. Let him worry about protecting himself. It should keep him busy enough so we won't have to worry about him.

"Send the NSA operative on her way before she begins to attract attention by not being where she's expected to be at the proper time. If she doesn't report in on schedule it will set off alarms and we'll have even more attention from the suits. Turn her loose with crystal clear instructions. She has to understand you're dead as far as her merry band of bureaucrats are concerned. Getting a bunch of political grunts to close the case shouldn't be a big hurdle. You're supposed to be dead anyway and a closed case looks good on their resume. Leave the old man and the boys to me."

"Sounds simple enough. Once the bad guys are handled we gather up Paul and disappear like so much smoke on the breeze. Work for you?"

"Why not? There's a lot of pleasant places to choose from and between my retirement fund and what you guys managed to stash, I don't think money will be a problem."

"Paul and I are well situated. I hid a small pile in locations outside the reach of the money sentinels in Washington and Paul stuffed even more in places less obvious and more secure. The problem is how to get Paul away safely. He's had spies on him like flies on a cow flop ever since I did my disappearing act. Every time I tried to make contact with him it was a case of out smarting the observers. We spent a couple years putting this together and we still ended up with Marnee on his doorstep and your predecessor dead in his front yard. In spite of our planning we still have the same problem we were trying to solve when we started. How do we escape?"

"I see what you mean about Paul. Paul and Jean from the look of things. What about Jean? Who is she anyway?"

"Another good question. She might be exactly what and who she claims. She could be another layer of the pursuit. Just like you."

"All right, I deserve that. You still have a question in your mind whether I can be trusted or if I'm only going along with things until I can take control and do you dirt. I don't blame you. Paranoia has kept you alive and it's a good habit. I could have taken you out on the beach. I had you cold. You only saw me because I made sure you did. Since then I've had several chances to kill you, kill Paul and Jean, and even to kill the crew tied up over there in the hollow tree. Instead, I'm here talking with you about how to get out of here and not spend the rest of our lives ducking at shadows or running from a pack of mutts howling for our blood. I think it's time you decide what you believe. I can't tell you anything more or do anything more to convince you. You either believe I'm with you or you don't. If you believe me let's get this show on the road. Otherwise use your fancy gun and bury me with Kwan and the rest before you leave. It's up to you. The noose is closing and we only have a short time before it chokes us off."

Tim studied Julie intently as she spoke. Sometimes logic rules your thinking, sometimes you respond on the basis of training and experience, sometimes your response is rooted solely in your emotions. Their relationship had survived years of separation and sporadic contact. Through it all they had remained committed to each other. His emotional attachment won the war. He took her in his arms and hugged her. "Maybe it's finally our turn to be happy. Let's go break up the party and get out of here."

47.

PAUL STARED INTO THE LOW BURNING FIRE. HE hadn't planned on Jean becoming a central player in his life, he had simply discovered the idea of leaving her behind was unacceptable. Unfortunately, Jean didn't know enough about what he and Tim had been doing to ask her to decide whether she was willing to risk her life to be with him. He kept turning the possibilities over in his mind while she sat next to him, her head leaning against his shoulder.

Jean's voice was soft. "I don't know if I should send you away or if it's already too late for me to distance myself from you. Don't you think you owe me the courtesy of telling me if I'm already dead?"

A moment passed before he answered. "You can remove yourself and try to go back to the way things were. I hope no one will try to hurt you if you do. I haven't shared any details, so there's nothing you can tell anyone. It doesn't mean they wouldn't try to make you talk, it only means you can't give them the answers they want. I can't guarantee your safety either way. I know what I want you to do, but that's not the issue. This is your decision. What do you want to do?"

"You really haven't told me anything have you?"

"No, I haven't. Are you really sure you want to know? Or would you rather try to separate yourself from me and all this trouble before you become so deeply entangled you'll never have a chance to be free?"

"Do I have to decide right now?"

He carefully considered his answer. "Yes, I think you do. If you decide not to toss me out, you commit yourself to being part of what Tim and I are doing. Once you're in, you're in to stay. If you stop now, you should be able to take yourself out of it forever. At this point you don't know enough to be a help or a hazard to anyone. As soon as they realize you aren't a reliable source they might leave you alone. They could also decide to dispose of you because you know who they are. This is completely unfair to you, and I apologize for putting you in this situation."

"Did you think about this when we met last week, or did you just figure I looked like an easy romp in the hay, the classic lonely divorcee in need of a man, or was some of what you said real?"

"No matter what I say, I come out looking like a shit heel."

Jean rose and stood in front of the fire. Anger flashed in her eyes. "Maybe you are! Yes, I was lonely, but goddammit, I didn't deserve to get dragged into whatever this is just because I wanted to be your friend! I deserve better and I sure as hell deserve an explanation! I expect to hear your explanation before I decide whether or not to toss you out on your dishonest ass!"

Paul watched her stamping her feet and slashing her hands through the air in frustration. "I deserve that. You're right. You deserve an explanation. So tell me. How much do you want to know? Everything, or just enough to paint a target on your forehead? Right now you don't know enough to be a threat to anyone. As soon as I start telling you the details you can start looking over your shoulder and wondering when a complete stranger will turn out to be your worst nightmare."

Jean had been pacing in front of the fire. She stopped

suddenly. "A target? You, you, you mean like, like, the man they found on the beach?"

"Exactly. You may already qualify. So you need to decide. Do you want to know enough to need to cover up what you know, or do you want to leave it where it is and not know enough to tell anyone anything? You don't need to decide this instant. I'm going back to my cabin. I'm not sure how long I'll be there because I don't know what's going on with Tim and Julie, but I'll be there for a little while at least. Don't take too long. You know how to find me." The door closed behind him.

Paul sat in the bentwood rocker feeling like the walls were closing in on him. Two years of planning and manipulation had failed to successfully resolve the situation threatening their lives and time was running out. They had planned to slip away without leaving even a rippling air current in their wake. So much for the best laid plans. He walked into the kitchen for a drink of water. He paced back and forth across the living room. He went to the bathroom. He returned to the rocking chair. Instead of soothing his nerves the motion of the chair agitated him. He needed to formulate a better plan. He needed some space without interruption from unexpected guests. He needed time and space and neither were to be found within the walls of the cottage. He grabbed his jacket and fled to the beach. The thunder of storm driven surf vibrated the beach as hungry waves gnawed at the edge of the continent. He needed to isolate himself from the storm of events and circumstances, and the natural forces helped put his problems in perspective. Once again he was awestruck by the vista of the tall cliffs and the rocky point to the south. His imagination wandered through the eons of weather that had shaped the land. The patient Pacific Ocean slowly clawed at the land mass, breaking away pieces of rock and soil, grinding them down and casting the finely ground detritus back at the foot of the cliffs, defiantly daring the silent land to halt the progress of the waters.

His thoughts drifted to the chain of events which had brought their lives to the edge of a precipice and was poised to push them over. He had guided Jean to the brink and told her to either jump off with him or go her own way. *Whatever happened to those two wide-eyed dreamers who eagerly set forth to take charge of their destinies and make their mark in the world? Would we have begun this fateful odyssey, or risked our lives if we had known this kind of treachery was a possibility? We were so damned naive. Tim came home from an incredibly successful Hong Kong trip with a story about being asked to smuggle counterfeit computer chips in our shipments. We were young and idealistic so we trotted the story to the Department of State, who sent us to the FBI, who sent us to the CIA, who ultimately connected us to the black ops people at NSA. The NSA, CIA and the FBI used us as a pipeline for tracking the incredibly large amounts of money flowing into the gritty world of organized crime. It was all so heroic, so patriotic, so exciting, and so profitable. We got to keep the money we were paid by the counterfeiters. Our handlers said we needed to keep the money and stash it offshore to prevent being exposed as double agents. The lie had to be consistent and supportable for the scenario to work. The set up was so clean, so clear, so easy to make happen and so easy to keep going while the feds constructed a case and gathered the evidence they needed to shut down the illegal imports and take down the people at the top. At least it seemed easy if you didn't think too much about what you were doing. It was scary in so many exciting ways and the money was unbelievably large. We did everything they asked and got the shaft. We worked hard, we did our job, we followed all their rules. We were almost ready to close the trap when a new man moved into the corner office at the NSA and pruned the project out of the budget. Now bounty hunters from every shadowy corner are waiting for me to lead them to Tim him so they can eliminate us both. Seems like a piss poor idea to ask Jean to grab my hand and jump into this mess along with us, but there's something special about her. Something I don't want to lose. Maybe I should have told her. Maybe I shouldn't have been so blunt. What if she decides to walk away? What will I do if I lose her?*

Lost in thought, he gazed at the ocean, hearing only the voices of nature swirling around him. "Ready to bring down the final curtain?"

It felt like an icicle had been plunged into his heart. He slowly turned and faced a man he hadn't seen in more than three years. Fred Conklin had been married to his mother's best friend until their marriage ended in a bitter divorce. He showed up at Christmas at his mother's home when they were starting Gormac, and introduced them to a man who became one of their major clients. Fred had been a regular visitor to their office until the divorce. Then his appearances gradually became less frequent, until they stopped altogether. "What the hell are you doing here? I haven't seen or heard from you in years."

"Things are not always what they seem. I'm here to finish a job I started a long time ago. When it's done, I can retire in comfort."

"Do I really need to ask what sort of job it might be?"

"Did you ever wonder why you guys were asked to run your shell game?"

For years they had wondered why they were invited to participate in the smuggling activity without being able to nail down the source who had directed the contact to them. Paul suddenly realized the source was the trusted friend he had known since he was a child. "You did this? You sent the guy to ask Tim to make our company his pipeline? We never understood why the Triad singled him out. Tim is too honest to be mistaken for a smuggler. I get the picture now. Was it the same with Washington? We wondered why we got shuffled through the bureaucracy like everyone knew we were coming. You told us to take it to State! Was it you who led us to the front door of NSA? How did you get involved? I thought you were an electrical contractor!"

"Being a contractor makes excellent cover. Anyone can hire you. It's especially useful to quietly develop a reputation for being willing to do any job, no questions asked, and no talk about anything you see or hear. It took a few years before I got any of the big stuff, but eventually I was spending most of my time working for people who operate on the fringes of the law or outside it. My work was never illegal, I just worked for people who were less than reputable. A few comments from my government contacts and I was asked to set up a pipeline for counterfeit computer chips to enter the country. The family would use the operation to launder their funds, and we would be able to track the operation from beginning to end. The old boys from Sicily wanted a way to hold their finger on the pulse of what the Triads and the Russians were shipping through Kowloon and Hong Kong and so did the CIA, FBI, and NSA.

"As usual it was a good news-bad news kind of deal. The bad news was I had to find a legitimate company and romance them into thinking what they were doing was in the national interest. The good news was, if we played everything right, we'd all make a lot of money before the government brought the family down for smuggling, racketeering, tax evasion and whatever else they decided tack onto their laundry list of charges. I set things up so you guys got the job.

"I knew you boys well enough to expect you to jump at the chance to do good for God and country, but your performance was beyond my wildest dreams. Tim turned out to be one of the best field agents anyone has ever seen and you, well, you knew where every particle of product entered and exited your control, and where every penny of revenue accrued. Better yet, if anyone tried to short you, you were in their face snapping at them like a damn pit bull. You didn't give a shit who it was, or whose toes you were standing on while you did it. Man, you drove them bat shit! Everybody underestimated you guys! Tim was flashy. You were quiet. Both of you were smart. You pissed off a lot of people because you were too damn smart. Then the new boss at NSA decided to let the snake out of the cage and dropped a dime on you two years ago. To cover his ass and make himself look like a budget management genius, he made your operation a matter of complete deniability, and invited the bad guys to dispose of you to close the books. I've got to take my hat off to you. Half the bad guys on the planet have been chasing you for two years and still haven't be able to close you out. I don't know how you've managed to stay alive as long as you have, but I'm impressed. Everybody still keeps underestimating you, and you keep right on taking advantage of it."

"I'm so glad to know you're impressed with what we've done and how we're still around to keep impressing you. Let's get back to why you're here. You said you're here to finish the job. What exactly do you mean? A hot lead injection for us and anyone who might have had contact with us? One last job before you retire?"

"It saddens me to see you've become such a cynic. I'm not here to kill you. If I was going to kill you I would have already left you lying face down in the sand. I just want to bring the detail home and ride off into the sunset. You wouldn't happen to know where your partner is right now would you?"

"You expect me to take you to him?"

"No need. I just wanted to know if you knew his whereabouts."

"If you already know where he is, why ask me?"

"Because I need both of you together. I figure if I just exercise a little patience he'll turn up on your doorstep of his own accord. Once he does, maybe he can help me solve some of my problems. Whether or not he will remains to be seen. Only time will tell and only time will bring him back in contact with you. Why don't we go back to your cabin, have a cup of coffee, and see what your lovely neighbor decides to do."

"How did you know?" Paul's eyes widened. "I get it. You bugged both cabins."

"The surveillance was necessary. My partner set up the equipment and handled most of the observation. All I had to do was sit back and monitor what went on. I must say it's been enlightening, if a bit embarrassing at times."

A chilling idea suddenly intruded on Paul's thoughts. "Did you kill that guy? The one they found on the beach?"

"Would it make a difference if I did?"

"It might explain a few things."

"Explanations are not always forthcoming, nor are the answers to all questions necessarily made clear. Let's go have some coffee."

"Thank you, Confucius, but I want an answer! Did you kill the guy they found on the beach?"

"I guess you're entitled to an answer. Webster would have found our stuff and reported it. He would have blown our cover and jeopardized everything we spent so much effort developing. I couldn't let that happen. I was the one who put all the pieces together and kept them running smoothly. It was just business."

"Just business! How do you know he would have found your bugs? It was the middle of the night! He wouldn't have been looking for them would he?"

"His equipment would have picked up feedback from our devices. He would have known about our stuff the instant he activated his own and by checking the signal signatures he would have known the source. Knowing the source would eventually have led him to me. It all comes down to records of your operation still on the NSA computers. Removal was the only viable solution."

"So you killed him and left him where I'd become a prime suspect? How thoughtful of you. You really blew it if you were trying to maintain a low profile! Jesus, are you so arrogant you thought the cops around here were still carrying clubs and spears? Did you honestly believe they wouldn't be smart enough to figure things out?"

"You never would have found out about it and neither would the cops, but I heard someone in the yard behind me right after I did him and I had to duck for cover. Whoever found him hauled him down to the beach and tossed him in the surf. Unfortunately, his attempt to destroy the evidence wasn't successful. The results of his unanticipated intrusion into my midnight sortie has attracted far too much attention."

"Don't you just hate it when someone comes along and catches you with your pants at half mast? And to think you never considered it in your careful planning."

"Go ahead, be sarcastic, asshole! It really made a mess of things. The folks in the marble buildings beside the Potomac are rather uncomfortable knowing the loose cannon they've been trying to spike is still on the loose. Those folks are leaning on the folks I work for to make the problem go away. I'm getting too old for this shit. I used to enjoy the heat. It made me feel alive. Now it just makes me feel vulnerable. With a little luck it will be over soon. Lets go back to your cabin and have some coffee."

48.

THE IDEA TO CHECK THE CAMPGROUND CAME TO Tom as he was about to leave the lagoon, but his tired mind couldn't focus on the exact reason he decided to cruise through the campsites. The Jeep was parked at the photographer's campsite, so he stopped to look in on her. The hood was still warm, but only silence remained when the echoes of his voice faded away. The rain had apparently dampened the spirits of the other campers because the park was deserted except for this one site. It seemed strange not to be able to locate the photographer when the car had so recently returned. On the other hand, many photographs had been taken of the region when it was beginning to clear after a rain and it wouldn't have taken long to walk beyond the range of his voice. There was nothing sinister about her not being in her camp, but a nagging thought kept tugging at his mind and slipping into the shadows when he tried to grasp it. Shrugging off the doubt, he headed home.

Exhaustion clung to Tom like a barnacle. Youthful exuberance wasn't enough to shake off the physical drain of long stressful hours without sleep. He staggered to the bedroom and collapsed on the bed. Susan said dinner would be ready in an hour and he didn't want to disappoint her by not eating with the family. The job put enough strain on the family without missing another dinner. A short nap would recharge his batteries. Sleep, however, eluded him. He lay wide awake with the case playing across his mind's eye like a grainy silent movie. He realized it wasn't just the case keeping him awake. Something he'd seen on the way home kept prodding him, tugging at the corners of his mind every time he began to doze off, but eluding his efforts to identify it. It wasn't the Jeep at the empty camp. It was something he'd seen on the drive home. Something important his weary mind kept bumping into but refused to illuminate. Ravenously starved for rest, sleep wasn't on the menu.

He was talking with his son about Little League when the thought exploded into his consciousness. *What the hell was the hermit's car doing parked a mile north of the bridge?* Then a second observation burst onto center stage. *There were fresh tire tracks on the old skid road near where her car was parked. Should I call John or check it out myself or just wait and call John in the morning?*

"Tom?" Sue wore a puzzled expression.

"Yeah?"

"What's going on? You were talking to Jackie and just stopped in the middle of a sentence and zoned out."

"I just thought of something and I don't know if it's related to the case or not. I know it kept me from going to sleep. I don't know if I should go check it out or wait until tomorrow, or call John, or wind my ass or scratch my watch."

The children snickered and giggled. Sue was less amused. "Nice talk at the dinner table! Maybe I can help you focus on a solution. Forget you haven't slept in a couple days. Forget you're exhausted. Forget you're obsessing about this investigation. Just look at the situation objectively and don't try to rationalize the what's or the why's and trust your instincts. What's your first inclination?"

"Call John and get him here to help me check it out."

"Why are you waiting to call him?"

"What if he wants to wait? He's the lead investigator."

"Problem solved! You can get some sleep. If he says it can wait, it can wait. Call him and let him make the decision! It'll take the monkey off your back."

"You're right. Whatever he decides, at least I won't feel like I'm doing nothing when I should be working the case."

The phone rang twice before John picked it up. "Do you have a sleep disorder?"

"I don't think so. At least I didn't before I started working with you." Tom filled him in on what he had seen. "What do you think we should do?"

John sat on the edge of the bed rubbing his eyes. "Are you sure this is related to the murder?"

"No. I'm not sure it isn't either. I don't know how to handle it and I didn't want to strike off on another solo mission. I had a feeling then and it worked out. I have a feeling about this one too. I can't give you a specific reason. It's kind of like looking at a jigsaw puzzle where a couple of pieces are in the wrong place. It was enough to keep me awake so I didn't think I should ignore it. It's your fault. You told me the most important part of any investigation is not confirming what you know, but recognizing the seemingly unrelated stuff that breaks open the case. Or words to that effect."

"Yeah. Sounds like the sort of stupid remark I'd make when I was trying to impress some youngster with the great wisdom I've gained at the hands of fate. When do you think we should check this out?"

"I don't know. I'm too tired to think straight. I just know if we wait and find out we should have looked sooner I'm gonna feel pretty stupid."

"Stupidity is probably the only thing preventing you from

feeling that way anyhow. Let me take a shower and wake up my tired old body. I'll be there in about an hour and you better have a fresh pot of coffee waiting for me. A fresh cup of coffee is the least you can do for dragging me back out like this."

"The welcome mat is out. See you in a bit."

"Feel better now?" Sue asked.

Tom kissed the woman he met the first day of High School and married a month after they graduated. He was still amazed she had chosen him from the herd of young bucks vying for her attention. He wasn't the best looking or the richest or the smartest. When she accepted his proposal the night of the Senior Prom he knew he was the luckiest man on the planet. "Much better. He'll be here in about an hour. Time enough to finish dinner, take a shower, and make a fresh pot of coffee. Then back to work."

"You really love this stuff, don't you?"

Tom snapped to attention. "Law enforcement is my life!"

"Cops and robbers is more like it. You guys are like a bunch of little boys chasing around with your lights and sirens at all hours of the day and night hoping for the adrenaline rush you get when things turn dangerous. What was it Randy called you the other day? Dickless Tracy?"

"I don't know about the Tracy part, but unless you've been swapping fluids with the milkman these two prove the first part ain't real accurate."

"That was then and this is now. Maybe I should find a friendly milkman, because you're not home often enough to take care of business. When you do come home, you only stay long enough to change your clothes."

"Oh yeah? I need to take a shower and last time I looked there's room enough for two."

"Ooooh. You talked me into it, you silver tongued devil."

49.

THEY BURIED KWAN'S BODY IN A HOLLOW A HALF- mile into the timber where an undercut bank could be collapsed over the remains. They piled leaf mold and dry limbs on the raw earth to finish the job. The shadows of early evening were lengthening when they returned to where Julie stood guard over the prisoners. Tim cut the ties from their ankles and the captives were brought outside.

They were a bedraggled looking bunch; wet, cold, and displaying nervous uncertainty about what would happen next. Tim took tremendous satisfaction in their discomfort. He enjoyed seeing people who had held the power of life and death over him quake and cower when confronted with a similar fate. All except for the old man. His eyes smoldered with anger, resentment, and hate, making it clear he would not honor any deal they struck.

Tim freed Marnee's wrists. "Go home. Tell the Director it's over. Tell him this politically incorrect project is completely dismantled. The news should satisfy his bureaucratic ass right down to the ground. Tell him not to send anyone else looking for me. This is where it ends. I won't be so nice the next time. I won't send the next messenger back alive. Got it?"

Marnee rubbed her wrists. "I understand, but I'm not sure he will."

"You make him understand. Tell the him it's time to follow his own advice. Remember the message he had you deliver to me in Manila? Remember what he said when I told him I wanted out? Tell him the message is being returned with extreme prejudice. Tell him I've spent four years setting it up. All I have to do is say the word and he'll be nothing but a memory. Make sure he understands my threat isn't political smoke and mirrors. He won't be moving on to some cushy consulting job among the government suppliers if I come after him. I'll make him disappear in a way that will force his family to wait seven years to have him declared dead so they can claim his benefits. If he really pisses me off I can make it look like he's still alive every time they try to prove he isn't. The people you've been partying with the past few hours have taught me well. I'll use every dirty trick, every conceivable deceit, every Machiavellian manipulation I can dream up to pay him back if he tries to fuck with me again! It's up to you to make sure he receives the message loud and clear!"

"I'll deliver the message."

"Good! Now hustle your butt out of here and don't look back. If I see your head turn this way I'll apply a bit of Hammurabi's code and strike out the offending eye with this delightful toy you gave me."

Tim stepped back. "Your turn."

Pisces released the Don. "It is time to make an arrangement, a small trade. Call it professional courtesy, a demonstration of respect, an act restoring honor. Joey hired me to locate and deliver Tim Gordon. It's done. He's here and so are you. I've been paid for my services. I'm satisfied with the arrangement, are you?"

"I haven't dealt with Mr. Gordon and his duplicity, but you have done as you agreed, all things considered."

"Good! As long as we're considering things, here's the rest of what we're going to agree on. You see Lieutenant Dipshit over there? I think he followed me to make sure I didn't collect for the job by removing me from the picture after I found Tim. Unfortunately, or fortunately, depending on your point of view, he and Deputy Dawg stepped in something along the way and it stuck to their shoes. I've provided services to you on many occasions. We've always been clear about our responsibilities to each other. I've always understood the penalty if I failed to perform as agreed. I also believe we've been equally clear about the penalty for anyone interfering with me doing my job. Correct?"

"Yes, but he's young. He sometimes forgets himself and don't consider the consequences of what he's doing."

"No kidding! Every time he forgets himself and does something stupid you send Gino to clean up his mess. Joey screws up and you send Gino to make things right. I don't get it. Gino's a smart professional, but you keep holding him back while you attempt to install a brain in Joey. Were you this stupid when you were working your way up?"

"Be cautious what liberties you take. I do not forget an insult. You gotta understand, they're the children of my children."

"I understand, so do those two. You love your grandsons."

"I do. You must forgive an old man's weakness."

"Here's how you earn your forgiveness. We're going to strike a deal and all three of you will agree to honor it. It will be the way I say and there will be no further discussions, negotiations, or future attempts to seek restitution. Capisce?"

"I will agree and so will they. Won't you!"

"Yes, Papa," they chorused.

"Name your terms. We will abide by them."

"The terms are simple. You and the boys are free to go and so are we. No one follows, no one makes any contracts, everything ends. If anyone comes after us all three of you go down. This is a matter of honor, a matter of restoring the honor you have lost. This is not negotiable. Either you agree, or you don't leave here. Understand?"

"I understand, and we agree. Is there more?"

"One small item. You make it known that any attack on Tim, Paul, their families, their employees, their business interests, or me and my family will be considered a personal attack on you and you will deal as harshly with those who have attacked us as you would if they had attacked you. Agreed?"

He looked at Joey and Gino. Both nodded their assent. "Yes. We agree. We make an end of it."

Tim watched the three walk out of sight in the direction of the car Pisces had parked near the highway.

Only Thomas Hartley remained. Tim looked at him and shook his head. "You are one pathetic piece of monkey shit! Still, it's a good thing you were here to witness the agreement with the old man and the boys. Maybe the two of you can find some other dumb bastard to smuggle your shit. Today you leave the way you came, minus one passenger. I don't expect to see or hear from you again. Your problems with the Russians and the Triads isn't my concern. Whatever you do will not involve Paul or me or anyone connected with us. Don't even think about trying to rain on our parade unless you want some of what I promised the Director."

"Well old cock, it was a good run while it lasted." Thomas offered his hand. "No hard feelings?"

Tim took the his hand. "No hard feelings. I'm sure you understand why I never want to see you again. Have a safe trip."

"Yes. I expect it will be an uneventful flight." He walked into the trees.

"I say, old girl," Tim mimicked Hartley's accent. "All things considered it's been a delightful little party we cooked up, don't you think? By the by, do you perhaps know the way back to your camp?"

"I believe I do. It's about two miles from here, but it would be bad form to hitch hike."

"It's entirely too nice a day to be looking for a ride with a stranger. There's so many weirdos out there and hitchhiking can be terribly risky. A couple miles is just a good stretch of the legs. We can use the hike to shed the stress of the past few hours." They set off through the forest hand in hand.

50.

CONKLIN DID A SLOW TURN IN THE CENTER OF THE
room. "A decent enough place in a tacky sort of way."

"It's a nice little place. Given a some TLC it would be rustic cozy instead of vacation tacky. It serves its purpose. Now cut the crap and tell me what you're doing here and exactly how you're responsible for this debacle."

Conklin's smile made the image of a cat playing with a mouse flash across Paul's mind.

"You guys got involved in this debacle, as you call it, about what, maybe seven years ago? A couple years ago a bonehead bureaucrat decided to dispossess the operation and painted a target on you. Fortunately, Mr. Bonehead was informed his decision was ill conceived and unsuccessfully tried to reinstate your position. Unfortunately, both of you had been compromised, and Tim was on the run. Meanwhile, back at the ranch, you were merrily trying to run the company without Tim or the smuggling operation. You not only turned off the pipeline, you streamlined the company and set up a third party to run things so you could scamper off to the north woods to bury the bone with the local talent."

"Thanks for the synopsis of the press release, but you didn't answer my question. I hope you're planning to get to it pretty soon because my patience is wearing thin."

The bentwood rocker squeaked in protest as Conklin settled himself. "You were never patient with the social niceties."

He waved a hand, stopping Paul from responding. "Whatever. Here's a lesson in how things work in the real world. How do you think you got picked for this operation? Somebody had to choose you. Somebody had to set things up so you could make a nice little piece of change in exchange for your services. Tim had some specialized military training, but you had nothing to qualify you for covert operations. You guys were so young and so eager and innocent no one believed you were anything but a couple of ambitious young businessmen. Shit, nobody even dreamed you could be working the inside track for us. It was a perfect cover and it worked beautifully. You didn't even realize nothing ever works unless there's somebody pulling strings to keep it on track. Somebody had to decide when your operation would begin and when it would end, or if it was going to end. Somebody had to be responsible for protecting you, exposing you, and terminating your contract, if or when it became necessary."

Paul was seeing Conklin in a new light, as though the man's image was shifting as he listened to him. The curly dark brown hair had gone gray and the smile wrinkles around the eyes sagged with age. His thickened waist and sagging belly were a faded memory of what had been. The remembered image of the young man who played baseball with them and sat on the patio drinking beer with his father was gone. What had always been a mischievously happy gaze was now malevolent and sinister. Paul measured his visitor physically and had no doubts about his ability to defeat the older man. He watched his old friend die before his eyes, replaced by a repugnant troll who fostered a cold hatred deep in his heart. "And that somebody was you? You're telling me you have that kind of influence? You want me to believe all these years you were playing the part of the successful contractor when you were actually working for the CIA, or the NSA, or ATF, or DEA, or FBI, or whoever is supposed to be in charge?"

Conklin shrugged. "If you think about it, it all makes sense in a Machiavellian way. Did you ever notice how often my company was awarded government contracts? Did you ever think it was strange I never did much work for anyone except the government? Somebody always gets the work when they put out an RFP. It would look suspicious if I bid every job, but I usually ended up the low bidder when I entered the competition. By sharing profits with some friends I never lost a single bid. I always knew what the other bids were before mine hit the table. That's right! I was supposed to do the work, and I was going to get the work, but to keep the books straight and keep everyone's skirts clean, someone always called to tell me my final page was missing and give me a heads up on the low numbers. I just typed in a lower price and got awarded the project. There was always work where my employers needed a permanent listening or viewing post. It's ridiculously easy to cable eavesdropping devices when you're putting in all the other cables. Everything goes into the conduit and looks like it belongs there. There was always the incredible adrenaline rush of doing it right under the noses of people who wouldn't hesitate to dump my body in a ditch if they figured out what I was doing. I bugged the homes and offices of diplomats, business executives, senators and congressmen, remodeled homes for the mafia, and the whole time I was working for the same guys you were. But the best job of all was running you boys. You kids took us places we had never hoped to see and led us to a supply chain that was competing unfairly with our country's companies and whose bogus chips were finding their way into our military equipment. You guys were the pipeline bringing the stuff in and we almost had the complete trail wired, all the evidence we needed to bring it down, until numb nuts decided to blow the whole operation apart. The one constant in this line of work is the arrogant stupidity of the people appointed by politicians to fill decision making positions over operations where they have no knowledge or expertise. Sometimes their politically expedient decisions are a giant brain fart and people get killed. People like Lisa and all those other innocent passengers."

Paul felt like the floor was sinking beneath him. He had accepted the story about the bomb being planted by a disgruntled airline employee and worked his way through the anger and confusion it caused. He had finally managed to compartmentalize his feelings about the misguided soul and believed the entire incident was the action of a man whose mind had escaped the bounds of reality. Anger rose like a volcanic flash. "Are you telling me the government blew her plane out of the sky?"

"Take it easy. I don't know for sure. I'm just speculating. I'm just saying, what if the goof ball is just a fall guy and not the brains behind it. I know the word went out to silence both of you. Marnee had come back from Manila after delivering the Director's message. Her report hit the office grapevine and within twenty-four hours the whole building knew Tim was in trouble. Of course the heat from the media came on so fast after the crash everything had to go low profile. Especially when it was discovered Tim never got on the flight. The best protection you had was Tim being in the wind. Everyone was looking for him, and we knew sooner or later the two of you would turn up in the same place at the same time. A little careful planning, a bit of manipulation of events and voila, here you are, together again! All I need to do is gather you up and finish things."

"And of course heads will roll."

Conklin stood. "Poetically stated, but at this point a final decision hasn't been made. It's not up to me, I'm just the messenger. Say, I haven't eaten all day, you think you could make a couple sandwiches and some coffee? It's kind of a cold day and a cup of coffee would sure help to warm me up."

Paul marveled at the brass of the man he had always called friend. He wondered if he should kill him now or wait for Tim and Julie to join in the fun. Fury boiled with volcanic intensity as the full scope of the deception became clear. He carefully banked his emotions into a slow burning fire. "Sure. The condemned man ate a hearty meal." Conklin leaned against the doorjamb, effectively confining Paul to the limited space of the kitchen.

Jean listened to Paul drive away. Her cabin was warm and cozy, but her safe haven felt cold and lonely. It had become occupied by a deep fear of the future and a petrifying terror of the present that squeezed her heart in an icy grip.

She was engaged in a personal war. Following Paul would set her on a pathway filled with risks she had no obligation to take. She stomped her foot in frustration and spun around to pace the opposite direction. Her mind wrestled with her options. Paul's decisions had put his life and his partner's at stake as well as the future of anyone who shared their life. The only risks she had ever taken were two men she married and then divorced. Both had depended on her to fulfill their lives and support them and their crazy schemes. Neither achieved much success on their own and deeply resented her success.

Paul was already successful. He didn't need her to decide what choices he should make, he was a decision maker. He'd told her his decision. She could join in or be left behind when he moved on with his life and whatever risks it involved. In the brief time she had known him she had seen him grieve deeply for his wife, share his warmth and love with her, and have the strength to walk away, leaving her struggling to make a decision. Years of training kept getting in the way of following the desires of her heart. She knew why Paul wasn't telling her the whole story.

Part of her wanted to grab Paul and follow regardless of the risks. She found something in him she wanted and it was in danger of slipping through her fingers while she fretted and fussed with indecision about a future she didn't want to imagine without him. She wavered between emotion and rationality. Undecided, uncertain, unable to go, not wanting to stay. She looked outside just as Paul started down the beach trail. Questions swarmed her mind like moths beating themselves against a light. *Is he going to the beach to meet Tim? Is he about to walk out of my life as easily as he drifted into it? Can he just walk away? Does he want to walk away? Is he walking away or is he waiting for me to grab his hand and jump into the future with blind faith we will land safely?*

She continued to pace the floor for several minutes before she walked to the edge of the bluff to look for Paul. To the north a couple strolled along the surf line. The wind tossed her hair, making her glad she had slipped on a jacket. To the south Paul walked slowly, looking at the ocean when a man rose from behind a drifted log and approached him. Paul's startled body language was unmistakable. She ran to get her field glasses and stretched out at the edge of the bluff where she could watch without being observed from the beach. Paul's expression confirmed this was an unexpected encounter. The unruffled demeanor he'd displayed for the police was replaced by surprised confusion. The conversation was clearly upsetting him. Watching his reaction to being caught off guard, she couldn't help admiring how he brought himself under control and recovered his stoic professionalism. Jean crawled away from the bluff when they started toward the trail, sprinted to Paul's cabin, and hid in the bedroom closet.

She listened to them talking as they entered the cabin. Her pulse pounded in her ears like a drum chorus and her breath was so ragged it seemed to whistle in her throat. The voices were slightly muffled by the intervening wall and the partially closed door. She willed herself to calmly focus on the conversation.

"Things may not be so bad," Conklin was saying. "After all, I'm not expected to do much. I was told to keep an eye on things and make sure nothing got out of hand. I'm just supposed to watch from the shadows while the crew does their job."

Paul turned from the stove where he had started some bacon frying. "You're supposed to make sure nothing's gotten out of hand? I'd hate to see a situation you think has gotten out of control. Take a look around Mr. Professional Keep an Eye on Things! The local cops would like nothing better than to arrest me for murder, the feds would enjoy giving me a lobotomy, and there's folks hiding in the shadows who think the best place for my head is on a pike. As far as I'm concerned, it's most definitely out of hand!"

Conklin chuckled. "After all this time, you still think this is school yard games where nobody gets hurt and we all stroll off into the sunset to live happily ever after? Come on, you're smarter than that or we never would have picked you for the job. What'd you think was going to happen when you agreed to do this? Did you honestly believe you'd get to keep all the money just because you were doing your patriotic duty? You knew you were smuggling counterfeit chips into the country and making a lot of money doing it. You knew you were rubbing shoulders with the bad guys on both sides of the ocean and working for us at the same time. Double agents are detested and distrusted by the people on both sides. Sooner or later it was bound to come crashing down. Didn't you ever worry about the day it would finally come to a showdown and neither side would want to admit you existed? The folks on the dark side have a simple solution, they don't make any secret about it. Over here on Uncle Sam's side we're a bit more devious, but either way, when push comes to shove, everyone's expendable. Double agents are the most expendable of all."

"Is that what this is? A showdown? Politically correct trade off's? Between who? For what? What's on the table? You aren't going to just toss more than five years of work in the dumper and walk away. Like you say, you're much too devious for anything so uncomplicated. You aren't here to arrest the bad guys either. If you are, I have a pretty good idea where you can find them, but you probably already know where they are, don't you? No, you're not here for a showdown, or to arrest anyone, or any of those noble things we were supposed to be doing to make the world a better place for freedom and democracy. No. You're here to make an embarrassing situation quietly vanish. You hang around, gather us up and make sure we disappear. Tim's easy. Just take him out and nobody's the wiser. The whole world thinks he's dead. Me? I'm another story. Maybe you've got to make it look like an accident. So you use your friendship to walk through the door and gather me up. I've conveniently taken myself out of the real world so nobody will miss me for weeks or even months and by then there won't be any trace of me. How convenient. Very cleverly arranged and manipulated to close up shop and slip away into obscurity. You've probably got a paper trail on the money and a plan to make sure it doesn't go to waste. After all, you're just a contractor and your retirement plan could use a little supplemental funding." Paul paused. "Well, am I right?"

"You're not entirely wrong."

"Not entirely wrong? What's that supposed to mean? I'm on the right track but I haven't included enough people who need to disappear? This isn't LA. You can't just make a bunch of people disappear in a place like this and not have it attract attention. Shit, man, take a look around! The cops are all over this place because of one body. Somebody else turns up dead or missing and those guys are gonna get real serious about finding out how and why. Maybe nobody back home will miss me very soon, but with all the attention I've been getting around here, my disappearance will be noticed." Paul stared through narrowed eyes at the other man. "Jean would notice right away if I was gone, but you've already thought of her, haven't you. You can't do it. Those two detectives would notice right away if we were both gone."

"Are you telling me not to underestimate the local fuzz? Well, I'm not. But I think you're wrong about you and the artist lady going missing being something to arouse suspicion. Your absence would probably convince the local snoop and gossip patrol the two of you have gone off to do some he'ing and she'ing in some exotic location. See, she doesn't make it more difficult, she actually makes it a lot easier. I know you weren't thinking about it when you hooked up with her, but it fits real well with the plans we made for you."

"I think if you presume the local detectives are a couple of dumb door shakers, you're making a serious error in your assessment. The lead detective is the stoic type, but nothing gets by him. He's been chasing bad guys a long time and doesn't waste any motions. He may look slow, but he's as crafty as they come. His partner only acts like he's just carrying water for the old man. He's sharp. I've had the privilege of watching the two of them up close and personal. It's a bit disconcerting because you're not sure what the old one is thinking and the young one's mind is running at full throttle. I know they've already figured out I'm not what I seem. They just haven't been able to put all the pieces together yet."

"High praise for the backwoodsmen. And to what do you attribute your uncanny ability to size up the innate capabilities of these two super sleuths?"

"Think about it. Tim may be the magic man when it comes to making the deals and getting the product, but I didn't run the business without learning to read people. I built a staff of people bright enough to see what was happening, honest enough to understand what we were doing, and the personal integrity to keep their mouths shut. I did a damn good job of choosing the right people. I read people pretty well."

"You didn't read me very well."

"No, I didn't. You were always uncle Fred. Call it familial blindness. I don't have any blinders on when it comes to these guys. They're looking for a killer and I'm still a prime suspect just by being in the vicinity." A thought suddenly surfaced. "It's the perfect set up! All you have to do is make sure they find evidence pointing at me and I'm out of the picture. Off to the slammer for at least seven years. Taking me out once I'm inside is a no risk situation. Just hire a con and I get a shiv between the ribs. Neatly disposed of and no one the wiser. Great plan except for some loose ends."

"You always were a bright kid. I hope you know there's no hard feelings. This is just a job I'm expected to finish. I'm just doing my job and it isn't an easy one."

"Are you quoting Eichmann or Mengele?"

"Dammit, this isn't personal! It's just the way it has to-" Conklin suddenly slumped to the floor at Paul's feet. Jean materialized in the doorway with the fireplace poker held up like a baseball bat.

Paul didn't move for several seconds, looking first at Conklin, then at Jean, then at Conklin and finally back to Jean. "Where did you come from?"

"Is he dead?"

Conklin's chest rose and fell. "No, but when he comes to he's gonna be well and truly pissed. Where did you come from?"

"Turn the heat off under the bacon before it burns and help me tie this guy up instead of worrying about how I got here. I'm here, he isn't dead, and we need to make sure he doesn't wake up and give us any more surprises. Then we can talk about what to do next."

Paul opened a drawer and took out a roll of duct tape. "This'll keep him from running." He tossed her the tape and turned off the stove.

Jean wrapped the tape around Conklin's wrists and ankles, then rolled him over and taped his mouth as well. "That should hold him."

"I see you've made a decision."

51.

WHEN JOHN ARRIVED THE LOW HANGING SUN promised a couple hours before day faded into night. "So is the coffee ready?" he asked when the Tom opened the door.

"Not quite. I thought you'd probably want to sit for a minute and talk."

"To quote an old John Wayne movie, we're burnin' daylight! The shadows are getting long, so pour it in a thermos, or travel cups, or a Ziploc bag. Just bring it along and let's go before we lose whatever small advantage we might have with the sun to illuminate things."

Five minutes later they were looking for where he'd seen Alma's car. "You know this may turn out to be a wild goose chase don't you?" John said as they entered the deep shade of the corridor of trees.

"Absolutely! But it always feels like we're a couple steps behind. Whatever we need to find is always just out of reach, or just around the next turn. It's like chasing the end of a rainbow through an army shadows. Everything keeps moving away or fading in and out. It's frustrating!"

"You'll get used to it. Detectives either learn how not to be frustrated by uncooperative circumstances, or they change careers. We aren't usually about crime prevention. Our job is reassembling enough pieces to discover what happened, why it happened, and who's responsible. What happened is the easy part, identifying who and why can drive you nuts. Most of what we handle is straightforward, people do dumb things and help us catch them. Sometimes we catch a case where we're up against some very smart people who play the game so well we can't pin them down. In case you hadn't noticed, the folks involved in this little soiree are way above average intellect. They know what we're going to do, how we have to go about doing it, and how to make it difficult. I don't enjoy being led around any more than you do, but we don't have any choice. We have to keep following the trail of bread crumbs and hope it leads us home."

"Thanks for the Hansel and Gretel analogy, makes me feel right at home. I have a question though. You've picked my brain for days, you've listened to everything I've said and been real close mouthed about what you think. Isn't it about time to share some of the sage analysis you're so famous for?"

John smiled. "You've finally arrived. You're turning out to be a pretty good partner. But before I tell you what I think, I need to ask one question."

"Ask away."

"Are you planning to let me sleep one of these days?"

"What's the matter? You getting so old and fat you don't have any stamina? Sleep is what you do when there's nothing important to do. C'mon old man, we've got crime to fight, women to love, and dangerous deeds to keep the adrenaline pumping. Do you mean to tell me you'd rather sleep?"

"To quote someone close enough I can reach out and swat his ear, fuck you and the horse you rode up on. Every time I get close enough to my wife to start thinking about why I can still get a stiffy some dickhead drags me out of bed to play cops and robbers. Now where did you see the old lady's car?"

"Slow down, it's just ahead. There!" Tom pointed to the opposite side of the highway. "Looks like she's gone."

John pulled across the highway and stopped facing the northbound traffic. "Are you sure it was her car? A Ford Escort isn't exactly an exotic breed. Ford says it's the most popular car on the planet. How do you know the one you saw belongs to the hermit?"

"Because her car has a ding in the rear bumper covered with a tree hugger bumper sticker and an auto club sticker in the rear window. I know her car!"

"Okay, you know her car. Let's see if we can find out what she was doing here. I'm not sure how, or even if, she fits into the picture, but if this is a professional operation, we probably won't find much. We might not find anything. For all we know she was gathering leaf mold for her garden. Lets keep reality close at hand, even if we're hoping for more. The most important thing is to make sure we don't ignore anything."

They found where the car had been parked, but the leaf mold revealed nothing else. They drove a quarter mile south and stopped across from where the skid road led into the trees. "Someone drove in there recently," John said. We'd best not drive over the tracks and erase whatever the lab can make of them if we need to call them out."

The tracks indicated two different vehicles had been over the road. One with mud and snow lugs and one with highway treads. They found where the highway tires pulled off into a secluded location and came back out on top of the first tracks. The mud and snow tire tracks continued up the skid road.

"You got any idea what we might be walking into?" Tom asked.

"No."

"Does it worry you as much as it worries me?"

"As you so astutely pointed out, we've been one step

behind all along. We've got no back up, a couple pea shooters for protection, and there are more places for the bad guys to hide than you can shake a stick at! Whatever would I have to worry about?"

"I just wanted to make sure I wasn't the only one feeling uneasy. I know this was my idea, but the further we go the less happy I am. Kinda like the night I chased a shadow into the trees. I have the same feeling on the back of my neck."

"More information than I needed, but better than a simple yes. Let's take it slow and keep our heads on a swivel. I'll concentrate on this side, you watch the other, and we both scan front and rear. You ready?"

"I was born ready."

The detectives moved at the unhurried pace learned early in a law enforcement career, scanning all sides and listening for any unusual sounds. The forest didn't make it easy for them. The wind created a background layer of sound punctuated by the songs of birds and the clicks and chirps of insects. Tension heightened their senses to the point where they could hear each other breathing. They stopped twenty-five feet short of the end of the tracks.

John could see the opening in the large tree. "Looks like a goose pen in that tree and it looks like there's been some activity around it," he whispered.

"Sure looks like it. How about we go over the side here and approach from the back to avoid walking into a trap?"

"Good idea. Work your way around to the other side and I'll ease up from this one. You can watch my back when I make a break to the inside. Give me a minute or two to close my eyes and let my pupils adjust so I can see better when I step into the black hole."

"Gotcha. Once I'm in position I'll count to fifty. I'll call out when I finish my count. Wait for a response before you make your move."

"Plan sounds good."

"Plan sounds like a good way to get your head blown off, but it's the best I can come up with. Any improvements you can think of?"

"You mean aside from waiting in the car to see if you come out alive? No. Let's go earn our pay."

They positioned themselves to assault the tree. Tom called out to anyone inside to come out with their hands raised. He called three times with no response. John moved swiftly through the opening with his gun drawn and swept the space for a threat. The tree was empty except for the scattered remains of cable ties littering the ground. "C'mon in, the coast is clear. As usual, we're a day late and a dollar short."

Tom stepped into the bole and looked around. He picked up one of the cable ties and put the ends together, checking the size of the opening. "Plastic handcuffs?"

"Could be. There were a bunch of folks here if it's what they were used for. What are there, eight, ten of 'em?"

"Uh, nine, yeah, total of twelve, five small, five large, two a different size. Hands and feet, maybe something else?"

"Could be. Any ideas?"

"Me? I'm the new kid on the block. What's the old expert make of this?"

"I'm not sure. The only thing linking this to the murder victim is knowing the hermit's car might have been parked at the bottom of the hill when you went by. At best, a really thin connection."

"I know it's thin, but think about it. I saw her car near here. She has a special room with a bunch of high tech stuff in it. She lives right next door to the murder scene. She watches everything. It's thin, but what the hell, thin is all we got."

"Speak for yourself. I ain't been thin in half a life time."

Tom chuckled, then his expression changed and he shivered involuntarily. "What the hell have we stepped in?"

"I don't know. I'm beginning to think we'd be better served if this case just went unsolved and we moved on to other things."

"How come?"

"I'm beginning to believe if we learned the real story we'd also discover we'd become expendable. I don't think these are very nice people we're dealing with and they're just letting us do our thing because we haven't managed to get in their way. As long as we keep fumbling and stumbling back and forth across their trail we don't pose a threat. That could change if we start to get too close. Who knows what they might do? I'm also trying not to think about how many more bodies may litter the trail."

"You think there's more than the guy on the beach?"

"I think we've rubbed up against a bunch of folks who wouldn't think twice about removing a couple of local detectives who got in the way. We weren't supposed to find the body. It wasn't supposed to wash up on the beach. Something went sour and the scene didn't get cleaned up and we stepped into the middle of it. We're chasing all over their tracks and if they get nervous we could disappear and no one would know what happened to us."

"You mean like the guy who tried to show us where he'd buried the body and couldn't find right place? He thought he knew where he'd buried the woman he killed, but we dug around for a week and never found a trace."

"These woods are a great place to dispose of remains. A

shallow grave, a pile of leaf mold, no flies, no odor, no sign of anything, and in a few months the forest floor consumes the remains." John stretched tired muscles. "It looks like the next stop is the hermit's place. As long as we're chasing our tail we might as well keep up the pursuit."

"You telling me a piece of tail is always a good idea even if it happens to be your own?"

John shoved him outside. "Let's go, funny man. Maybe we'll find something new this time."

52.

GINO CONCENTRATED ON DRIVING, SURREPTITIOUSLY
observing his grandfather in the rearview mirror while Joey
huddled nervously in the passenger seat. Turbulent waves of
anger pulsed from their grandfather as they traveled through
the lengthening shadows. He knew it was best to keep quiet.
Sooner or later their grandfather would give voice to his
thoughts and whoever attracted his attention first would be
the recipient of a volatile wave of acidic invective. It was like
sitting on a time bomb. In spite of the cooling evening, he and
Joey perspired heavily, giving the car the stale odor of a locker
room. The angry silence of the wounded lion in the back seat
intensified like a compressed spring struggling to burst free of
its restraints.

The Don brooded in the back seat, the eye of a hurricane
of rage, embarrassment and defeat. "This guy Hartley, you
think he rolled over on us?"

Neither cousin answered right away. Joey finally broke the
silence. "Somebody sure as hell rolled over on us. I think we
should make an example of Hartley, show people they can't
fuck us and get away with it!"

"So you think we ought to make an example of him?" the
voice was soft as velvet.

Joey's confidence swelled. The worry he was taking
his last ride evaporated, leaving a relieved euphoria in it's
wake. *Grandfather has forgiven me, my ideas and opinions*

are of value. He turned to face the old man and nearly swallowed his tongue when his eyes locked onto those of his grandfather. The beginnings of a smile slid off his face so rapidly it seemed to flutter to the floor like an autumn leaf. Unfortunately, he couldn't turn away without offending his grandfather. His shaky voice caught dryly in his mouth. "It looks like the leak came from over there in his front yard. If he isn't the squealer, then he's the contact man. Making an example of him would serve notice we won't put up with any crap."

His grandfather stared coldly without speaking. After several seconds he spoke in a voice dripping with disgust. "You disappoint me. Who, besides Paul Bunyan, is gonna know what we done if we make an example of him up here in the middle of nowhere? You think this is a good example? Just because the canary showed up on his turf don't mean he's the one singing. We bag him instead of the real bird and maybe people think we're too stupid to know what's really going on. Instead of proving we mean business, you got an example of how not to make your point. Turn around and think about it. While you're at it maybe you should try to grow a brain." Joey turned in the seat and watched the road wind its way through the canyon of tall trees.

The old man spoke a few minutes later. "Pull off at the park, Gino. You'n me need to talk."

"Yes, sir."

Uncertainty settled on Gino's heart like a block of ice. He'd known the old man all his life and he'd always been afraid of him. He'd never seen him so angry. There was a chance this little talk would be his grandfatherly way of saying goodbye, payment for his failure to keep the situation under control, punishment for placing the old man in a compromising situation. A glance in the mirror revealed eyes no softer than carbon steel.

"Pull over and stop. We'll take a walk."

"Yes, sir," Gino replied in a shaky whisper.

The car had barely halted when the old man shoved the door open and got out. "Joey, you watch the car." When Gino joined him they walked into the woods. "I got something I need you to take care of."

53.

CONKLIN'S PULSE WAS STRONG. THE BLOW ACROSS the base of his neck had produced unconsciousness and brief paralysis. "I guess he'll live. Where the hell did you come from and what possessed you to hit him?"

"I saw you meet on the beach and it looked like you weren't very happy to see him. You obviously didn't like what he was telling you and were only going along with it because you didn't have any choice. When you started back I came here and hid in the closet." Jean's excited words flew into the room like a swarm of bats escaping from a cave. "I heard everything. I knew he was going to kill you, and me too, so I sneaked up behind him while he was bragging about setting you up. The poker was the only weapon I could find so I hit him with it."

Paul stared incredulously, not sure he was comfortable with what she had done. "Why'd you hit him?"

"He was going to kill you! I couldn't stand around and do nothing! No matter what you've done, I couldn't let him kill you! He was going to kill me too! It didn't matter to him if I don't know anything about what you and Tim have been doing." A smile crept across her face. "I have strong survival instincts."

Paul looked at Conklin again. "You know, if we hadn't been together when the guy was killed, I'd have to wonder if you weren't the one who killed him. But he was hit across the head and you hit my old friend across the base of the neck.

How'd you know where to hit him to stun him?" Conklin groaned softly.

"Self-defense training. A girl can't be too careful. There's bogeymen everywhere, one of those marvelous modern realities. A woman isn't safe on her own. Since the equal rights furor, it isn't cool to ask a man to walk you to your car, so you have to learn how to gain enough advantage to run away and you practice how to run away. You gotta know how to stand and fight well enough to get away. It's important to know how to disable from the rear because with a little luck you can spin an attacker around, hammer him across the right spot and beat a retreat."

"A handy bit of street smarts. What do you think we should do with our friend now that you've invited him to sleep over?"

"I guess it depends on what we're going to do next."

"True enough. The other question,"

"I knew there was another example of the cobbler's art about to clatter to the floor."

"What?"

"The other shoe is about to drop."

"Right. It would be nice to know about the next unplanned event before it enters the room, like who's the next surprise guest who's about to turn up on the doorstep."

"You're perhaps referring to our reclusive neighbor who just came home? I heard her drive in while you and your friend were catching up on old times. I don't think she put her car in the garage. You don't think she's involved in this do you?"

"I don't know who all the players are. All I know is we've got to figure out a way to get out of here." He turned toward Conklin, who was now completely conscious, eyes open wide, but silent behind the tape across his mouth. "Right now, there are so many people watching me I feel like a damned goldfish being eyed by a hungry house cat. To make matters worse, I don't know what Tim and Julie are doing or even if they're still alive."

"Didn't you boys have a contingency plan in case your original plans got derailed?"

"Of course we made contingency plans! We knew Murphy would almost certainly crash our party. We just didn't figure on this kind of a contingency. In light of which, I don't think we should be discussing things where this turd can hear us." He gazed sadly at Conklin. "I thought you were my friend." He took Jean's hand and led her toward the door. "Let's go for a walk."

The cabin crackled and popped in the cool of the gathering evening. Minutes passed slowly while Conklin struggled to fight off the effects of the blow. His neck burned where a painful bruise was swelling under his collar. He felt more than heard the footstep on the porch. He thought it was Paul and Jean returning. He waited for a command rather than rolling over to see who had arrived. His eyes flew open when the realization it wasn't Paul flashed across his foggy synapses. The smell was wrong. The second impact of the fireplace poker brutally drove the backward curving hook through his skull above the orbit of his left eye. Conklin didn't hear the door close behind the departing visitor.

Gino saw Paul and Jean walking north on the beach when he stepped outside. He was turning to go back to the cabin when he saw another couple walking toward them. He was laughing when he dragged a wheelbarrow from under the cabin next door.

He succeeded in reaching the Jeep without attracting attention. The campground was deserted and the tent concealed the Jeep from the beach. He opened the right door and prepared to load Conklin's body. As he picked up the map lying on the seat he noticed a wire hanging just below the dash. Curious, he checked the source. A sinister smile spread across his face.

Gino slid the seat all the way back and loaded Conklin into the front floor with his head and shoulders lying on the seat so the body would only be seen when the door was opened. He grabbed the wheelbarrow and trotted off into the timber, giggling with satisfaction. *Grandfather should be pleased with this solution.*

Marnee seethed with anger. Two years of manipulation and subtle suggestions to bring these people together, and now looked like it was all for nothing. *Unless I can throw a wrinkle or two into the boys' plans.* She parked in the driveway instead of pulling into the garage and went directly to the communications room. She immediately noticed the tiny fiber at the corner of the the escape hatch had been had been broken. She scanned the tidy space for evidence anyone had actually been inside the room or if any of her equipment had been compromised. *Probably the detectives. Too damn big to fit through the skinny little opening and had to settle for a visual study of the room's contents. I bet your curiosity took an interesting hike when you found this.*

The detective's discovery of the small room changed the situation, but before she moved the equipment to defeat a search warrant there was work to do. She perched on the stool and fitted the headset. Paul and Jean's voices immediately filled her ears.

Marnee was trying to decide what to do next when she heard the door open followed by a sound reminiscent of a melon breaking open and the door closing. Her eyes grew large. "Oh my God." She slowly removed the headset, turned the volume control to its lowest setting, and rested her head in her hands. She knew Fred Conklin had retired.

54.

TIM AND JULIE MOVED WITH THE SWIFT,
economical movement of professional soldiers. Julie led the
way while Tim watched their back trail. They paused at the
edge of the highway near the north end of the lagoon before
they scurried across. The northern hundred feet of the sand
bar, depending on the season and the tide, could be a barrier
between the lagoon and the surf, or a spillway joining the two
bodies of water. During summer, the area became a soggy
slurry of seeping water. They were soon strolling down the
beach, a couple out for a walk. They were half way down the
length of the lagoon when Tim saw a couple start down the
trail from the cabins.

"Looks like Paul and Jean. This isn't how we planned to
meet, so either something has gone sour or he decided to come
looking for us. Either way, this is good timing."

"I don't think they're expecting to see us. Looks like they're
having a pretty intense conversation. A lover's quarrel maybe?"

Tim watched as the distance between them shrank,
recognizing the posture and gestures his friend made when
upset or agitated. "Maybe so, but unless somebody changes
directions, we're about to have a close encounter of the third
kind." At that moment, Paul swung his attention to the north,
saw Tim and Julie, and stopped in his tracks.

"Sort of removes all doubt whether they were expecting
to see us," Tim said.

"It sure looks like it. I know he's good at making an entrance, but I think we took him by surprise."

Both couples walked in silence as they closed the distance separating them. Paul and Tim hugged each other warmly.

"Remember Fred Conklin?" Paul asked.

"Yeah, sure, your mom's old friend. The guy who helped us kick start our business and used to stop by for coffee all the time. Everybody called him uncle Fred."

"He was also instrumental in setting up the smuggling operation."

"Conklin? Are you sure?"

"Just sure as I am that he's trussed up on my living room floor right now. He's probably trying to get loose from several wraps of duct tape."

"He's tied up in your cabin? What happened? I mean, how did you find out he was involved in the smuggling?"

"The short track on the long story is he set up our whole operation. He was the primary operator for the NSA and we were a couple patsies who were too naïve to understand what was really going on. All those friendly visits were follow up to make sure we were living up to our side of the bargain. As long as we did everything the way he planned, he and the agency would never come to the surface and nobody would suspect we were playing both sides against the middle. The contractor routine was a smoke screen to conceal his real job: running us. He caught me on the beach and insisted we go back to the cabin to talk. Jean did a Babe Ruth on him with the fireplace poker while he was explaining how he was just finishing his job by making us disappear."

Tim altered his assessment of Jean, realizing it was dangerous to underestimate what she would do in a crunch.

He smiled warmly. "Thanks for looking out for my buddy. It means a lot to me." He turned back to Paul. "This is getting to be more and more like peeling an onion. Lots of layers and the closer you get to the center the more it makes your eyes burn. We need to plan our next move and do it fast. I presume we are a foursome."

Jean smiled at Paul. "Unless he tosses me out with the trash, I'm planning to be with him wherever he goes."

"We're happy for you," Julie said, "but we need to get moving. We extracted an end to the hunt agreement from our pursuers, but I have no faith they'll honor what they agreed to at the point of a gun. The Christianizing effect of that sort of duress fades fast and leaves a bad taste in the mouth. I'm sure they're already plotting their revenge and taking advantage of the head start we gave them."

"Is Conklin really tied up in your cabin?" Tim asked.

"Uh-huh. We needed to decide what to do with him, so we went for a walk to think things through. I didn't want to talk about it where we could be heard. Jean thinks we could try the same method we used to get you guys out, but I'm not convinced we can get away with the same ruse twice."

"I tend to agree. How did he, never mind! We'll talk about it later. How do you think we should get rid of him?"

"I'm not sure. Alma Jacobsen is home again. Maybe we should wait until dark to move him, but even in the dark there's no guarantee she won't have her nose pressed up against the window."

"Alma Jacobsen is actually Marnee."

"Marnee?"

"Imagine my surprise when I realized who she is. She's been watching you and reporting all the sordid details to her boss. She was surgically altered to make her look older. They

447

did a good job, but when you see her up close, you can tell it's her."

"You mean Marnee from,"

"Bull's eye."

"Who's Marnee?" Jean asked.

"It's a long story, but basically, she was our contact at NSA. I haven't spoken with her since the plane crash and now I know why." Paul suddenly thought of something else. The color drained from his face and he spun around to look toward the cabins. "She's probably got bugs all over my cabin and Jean's as well." Another thought burst forth in Paul's mind. "Tim! She's NSA and Conklin's the one who set everything up! They're working together! She knows he's in my cabin and she's got to have enough sophisticated equipment to hear what we're saying right now! She probably bugged Jean's cabin the first time we left to walk on the beach! Damn! Marnee knows everything we've said."

Jean blushed. "You mean she was listening to us when we were,"

"I'm afraid so," Paul said. "Sorry."

"Jesus!" Tim exclaimed. "You're right! She probably has listening devices all over the place and maybe even a parabolic disc aimed at us right now, listening to every word we're saying."

"Can she really do that?" Jean asked incredulously.

"Possibly," Paul said. "They have satellites that can take pictures clear enough to count the leg hairs on a mosquito from three hundred miles in space, listening to us from half a mile away isn't even a challenge."

Tim saw John Ragsdale's unmarked car approaching the bluff. "Looks like someone is getting a return visit from the boys in blue. Be prepared to play it cool."

Paul's face lost it's color again. "Oh shit! How are we going to explain Conklin lying on my floor trussed up like a calf at a rodeo?"

"Brazen it out," Julie advised. "Play dumb! You don't know who he is or how he got there! You went for a walk on the beach. You can bet Conklin isn't going to admit he got taken out by a civilian. Think of the humiliation! Besides, if he starts down that trail, he has to explain what he was doing here in the first place, which will make your detective friends start asking questions Conklin doesn't want to answer. Don't think of him as a problem, Think of him as a partner who doesn't dare rat on you."

Worry danced in Jean's eyes. "What about my fingerprints on the poker? Won't it make them start asking questions?"

Julie smiled. "Your fingerprints are expected to be in the cabin. Relax. It's all going to work out."

"All right. I see what you mean. On the job training for this position has a steep learning curve. I feel like my heart is working overtime and fear is snapping at my heels like a pack of wolves, but the excitement is a rush like I've never experienced."

Julie hugged her, then stepped back keeping her hands on Jean's shoulders. "You're doing fine. Follow Paul's lead and keep asking questions when something bothers you. It will help us keep thinking clearly. The most important thing is to think before you speak, but don't pause so long it makes people think you're formulating an answer. The dance takes some practice, but you're learning fast. Keep your head, and trust your instincts. Female instinct is the most important part of trying to keep the guys off balance and we girls use it all the time, right?"

"I hate to break up this little hen party," Paul interrupted, "but we need to get back to some rather important considerations. Where do we meet up, or where do we call you to make contact after we split up here? We have to go distract the detectives long enough for you two to clear the area. You've got to move fast and we need a place to join up once we get clear."

"We'll be in Manzanillo in a week," Julie said. "Look for us at a cantina called El Iguana Verde. We'll stop in for a drink every day after five for the next two weeks. Then we'll be at the Hotel de Mediterranea in Menorca for a week. The week after we will be at the Frenchman's in New Zealand. Good enough?"

Paul sighed. "It'll have to do."

"What if we don't make contact with you in the next three weeks, how will you find us?" Jean asked.

Tim smiled broadly. "Paul knows what to do."

"Pick off play?"

"Pick off play."

"Good enough," Julie said. "We're going to go break camp as fast as we can, but we can't leave anything behind. It has to look like I've finished what I came to do and moved on. You guys do your best to put the cops to sleep and we'll see you in old Mexico."

Paul looked back toward the cabins. "Yeah, well there might be a problem. I wish the guys in the unmarked car weren't who I know they are, and I sure as hell hope they don't find our friend. Right now, the last thing we need is more questions and more delays. We'll go put on our best dog and pony show. Maybe we'll even tell them we're planning to go someplace warm and tropical, just to see if they have any objections to our leaving town. Good lord willing and the creek don't rise, we'll be doing shooters at the Green Iguana next week."

55.

TOM PARKED AT THE EDGE OF THE BLUFF ACROSS from Paul's cabin. "Did you see what I just saw?"

"You mean the hermit's car sitting in her driveway?"

"Yeah, instead of in the garage. She's so anal about everything being in its place, leaving her car outside attracts attention."

"Do you really know her this well, or are you just blowing smoke up my ass?"

"I've been on this beat for two years. Since nothing much exciting happens, I've spent my time getting to know the people and their personal quirks. A fat, old, over-the-hill, moss-badged detective once told me observation is more about what doesn't look right than what does. Said I should look for what was out of place instead of what was where it was supposed to be. Something about the best laid plans going astray because of some little thing out of place. I paid attention to the old fart and made an effort to learn my area of responsibility. Some people aren't easy to nail down because they go through life bending whichever way the wind blows. This old girl's predictable and fussy. She never leaves her car sitting in the driveway, just like she never leaves the doors to the garage open. She always does things the same way. You can set your watch by her activities, and she's never varied her schedule or her daily activities until today. She's broken the pattern and

I'm wondering what she's up to. Something has her off her feed and it's making my curiosity run wild."

"Okay, you've been paying attention to the little things. What about the artist in the end cabin? You know her too?"

"More or less. She's a lot less regimented in her habits than Alma. She seems to be friendly with the people who visit the area, at least she's polite and cordial. She keeps in shape by running on the beach and she paints really nice landscapes. You saw the one hanging over her fireplace and she's done others just as spectacular. I think the lady shows some serious talent in the way she sees things and puts them on canvas. She apparently managed to pile up a comfortable enough nest egg to live modestly. She'd like to become recognized as an artist and sell her work, but she doesn't need to sell anything to get by. Mrs. A says she was hurt real bad before she moved here."

"Hurt? She doesn't look like she's recovering from an accident or injury."

"Mrs. A says somebody hurt her enough to make her throw away everything she'd worked for and come here to start over. She says she can see it in her eyes, says she looks like a wounded deer."

"Interesting. How much do you learn from Mrs. Alexander?"

"She's gossip central around here and talks to everybody who comes into the store. If it happens in the neighborhood, she can usually tell you how, when, where, what color it is, how deep it is, and how bad it smells. The fact she doesn't know what happened with the body on the beach just proves she's not infallible."

John pointed at Paul's cabin. "Do you see any signs of life around here?"

"Don't see a soul. I know the hermit's car is here so she

must be home, but I haven't seen her look out the window to see what we're doing. Maybe she's just staying out of sight. She's reclusive enough to hide just so we'll leave her alone. McAfee's T-bird is parked in his driveway and there's smoke from the chimney at the Parker place. He's probably down there. Nobody's where we can see them, but trust me, they're all close by. Where should we start? The sun is getting closer to the horizon while we sit here yakking. You're the lead dick, so lead. I'll cover your backside. And if I might make an objective observation, it's a fine looking backside, fills your pants with great abundance."

John made a familiar gesture with his middle finger. "I got your abundance. First, let's take a gander at the beach. McAfee and Parker spend a lot of time down there. It's stopped raining so maybe they went for a stroll."

The detectives stood at the top of the bluff, the breeze riffling their clothing and mussing their hair. Looking north, the sand bar was empty except for the shore birds probing the sand with their long bills and the gulls sailing on the breeze. To the south a few hardy souls at the far end were walking the beach. Tom looked to the north just as Paul and Jean reached the top of the trail from the beach. "Good call, partner. How nice of them to join us."

"Five bucks says they suggest we go to her place," John said.

Tom chuckled. "I may be young, but I'm old enough to know a sucker bet. The fire's burning in her cabin. His place looks cold. I'd bet money he hasn't spent much time there lately except to get a change of clothes. Going to her place also keeps us away from his. We haven't been inside his house since he let you look around."

"An astute observation. He's cleverly innocent in the way

he keeps us out, but that doesn't make the maneuver any less effective."

"Good evening," Tom greeted Paul and Jean. "How was the beach?"

"Cool and breezy," Jean answered. "The fresh air was pleasant after being cooped up all day. We're on our way to warm up over a cup of coffee, would you like to join us?"

"Sounds great!" John replied. "The air is a bit brisk."

The warmth of the cabin was like a grandmother's hug. Paul stirred the fire and added wood while Jean went to make coffee.

"What brings you back?" Paul asked. "If I didn't know better, I'd think you never sleep. No offense, but you two look like you've been rode hard and put away wet."

John spoke before Tom had the chance. "A murder case tends to drain you, so much to do, so little time to accomplish it. After a few days of chasing shadows into blind alleys, you begin to feel a little used up."

"Are you any closer to catching the murderer?" Jean asked as she returned from the kitchen with the coffee. "I just microwaved the leftovers. I'm so cold I didn't want to wait for a fresh pot to brew."

"No problem," Tom assured her. "Cops are notorious for drinking any kind of coffee as long as it's free. Nuked, boiled or burned, as long as it's hot and caffeinated, it's perfect."

John slapped him on the back of the head. "Very gracious, clod. You try to teach them some manners, educate them properly, and what do you get? A constant embarrassment. Please, don't think badly of my young friend, he just don't got no fetchin' up."

"Only yesterday he taught me to stop marking all four wheels of the patrol car and use a bush instead," Tom said.

"He insists one is just messy and the other is good for the environment."

Paul and Jean joined in the laughter while she took a seat near the fire facing the detectives. "So what brings you out at this hour? Did you like my coffee so much you had to drop by for a refill?"

"Ah, the lovely lady has figured us out, Tommy. It's so difficult being a detective. Whoever you call on just knows there's got to be another agenda hidden somewhere under even a friendly conversation."

"One of life's great injustices. Like not being able to choose your relatives from among the sane," Paul said.

"Or your partners," John noted. "But yes, you're right. We didn't come calling just to enjoy your coffee, although it is worthy of an encore."

"Thank you," Jean said.

John looked to Paul. "I'm sure you're tired of us intruding on you, but I hope you understand it's our job. We've been looking into your background because your cabin is so close to the murder scene. You might be more comfortable if we took our conversation down to your cabin."

"Jean can hear anything we have to say."

John studied Paul for a moment while he considered how to direct the conversation. Outwardly Paul was calm and controlled, maybe a little too controlled. John suspected he was hiding something in his cabin. "You're sure you wouldn't feel more comfortable talking in private?"

"Actually, I prefer for Jean to hear anything we have to say. This situation has upset her enough already without leaving her to wonder what you want to talk to me about and it's warm here. My place is about the same temperature as the outside air."

"Okay. The FBI has told us your partner was involved in a deep cover operation. They say some granite headed bureaucrat blew the lid off a couple years ago and left you guys swinging in the breeze. They said it was a classified project. It's the excuse they use when they don't want to share information with us. We know he supposedly died in the same airplane crash as your wife. We also know the FBI has been in contact with him since the crash, so, as the saying goes, rumors of his death seem to be exaggerated. We know he was alive six months ago and on the run from some really nasty folks he had been dancing with at the request of the folks in Washington. The feds have been less than clear about who the bad guys in the posse are, so Tom and I can only hope if we happen to bump into one of them they'll be cool and not hand us our heads before we know who we're up against. All of which leads us back to you and what you know about what your partner was doing." John paused to study Paul's face. Although Paul's expression changed to one of surprise when he announced Tim was alive, Jean's face remained calm almost until the end, when she suddenly showed extreme surprise. "Were you aware of your partner's involvement in this government cloak and dagger operation?"

Paul paused a beat. "Yes, I was. You're sure Tim is alive?"

"Were you an equal participant in the operation?" John deliberately ignored Paul's question.

Paul paused briefly. "No. My plate was already full. Running our company and keeping everyone marching in close order was a full time job. I didn't have any spare time to indulge in some arcane undercover affair. Tim managed to keep the customers coming and the product flowing while he was playing spy games for the government. I'm not as good a juggler or salesman. Hell, just maintaining the level of customer activity after he disappeared was beyond my capabilities. I didn't have the time or skills to handle the legitimate business without Tim, let alone involve myself in some weird spy game. I've always had a pretty solid grasp of my own limitations, but this fiasco managed to spotlight them much more brightly than I like. Nobody likes to have their weaknesses exposed, and believe me, I was exposed! With Tim out of the picture and Lisa gone, I was trying to manage the business, and endure my grief, and still keep everything going like nothing had changed. I was driving myself crazy at high speed. Sometimes you just have to say enough is enough and step away. I came here to put some space between me and the past. I needed to separate myself from the business and the nightmares keeping me awake at night. I needed to come to terms with Lisa and Tim's deaths. I needed to let the wounds heal and the scars fade."

John nodded. "I understand. I've never experienced anything like you have, but I've held more than one friend's hand when their life fell apart. It isn't easy to deal with the death of a loved one. I respect the loyalty you showed your employees by arranging to keep the wheels spinning and their jobs secure. I understand how hard it is for you to talk about these things, but a man is dead. We're expected to learn why. So here comes the next rudely uncomfortable question. You told us your wife was pregnant. How far along was she?"

"Maybe three months. You know how the doctors are. They want you to think they know to the minute, but it's really just educated guess work."

"So she was just beginning to show?"

"Almost. She was maintaining her exercise program and changing it to suit the pregnancy. She hadn't even started to shop for maternity clothes. She looked radiant and happy. It was a beautiful thing." Paul's voice had become tight. "You're sure Tim is alive?"

"Yes. Unfortunately, the FBI hasn't shared any details beyond confirming he didn't die in the airplane crash."

John formed some opinions while he observed Paul and Jean. *He knows where all the bones are buried. He's a damn good actor in the bargain. I don't doubt the emotion he shows when he talks about his wife or the frustration and anger he feels about not being able to run the business alone. The story checks out and it makes sense. She's still a beginner and hasn't learned to cover up as well. Got to give her credit, though, she's managed to move to the center of this game and she knows a lot more than she's telling us. I wonder when he really learned his partner is alive. It sure as hell wasn't in the last fifteen minutes.*

"So you never took part in any of the operations Tim was involved in for the government, or whoever he was working with besides your company?" John continued.

"Nope. The undercover gig was Tim's baby. I just did my best to make sure he had the opportunity to do what he believed was the right thing to do."

"So what was in it for you? I mean, you're doing all this extra work to take care of your partner so he can play spy games. What were you supposed to get in return?"

"I wasn't supposed to get anything. We, our company, were supposed to get the inside track on future business opportunities with several defense contractors."

"So you didn't make any money from this undercover stuff? You were just taking all those risks on the basis of a promise that maybe sometime in the future you'd get the inside track on some big jobs, if they happened to come up, and if you made an attempt to land them?"

"That was the deal."

"Maybe I'm being cynical, and what you're telling me sounds real patriotic, but you're a good businessman, so it's a little hard to believe when you tell me you were doing it on the basis of vague promises of future favors from some highly placed bureaucrat or politician. We both know political promises barely last until the echoes die in the room."

"I know it sounds crazy, and I know it's hard to believe, but Tim had a burning need to do something important for our country. Maybe it was an obsession he picked up in the Army. He was my best friend, he was my partner, and it was really important to him. I didn't have to agree with him. It mattered to him and he mattered to me. I did my best to make sure he had the chance to do what he believed. I figured it was payment enough if all we ever got out of it was the chance for him to feel like he had made an important contribution. The business was flourishing whether we had the promised contracts or not. Tim wanted to do it, so we did it."

"I envy you your friendship. It's a rare blessing. Maybe you can help me with something else. Was one of Tim's contacts a mob family in Los Angeles?"

"I don't know. Tim made sure I was isolated from whoever he was dealing with so I couldn't lead anyone back to them. He thought it was the best way to protect me from the people he was involved with. You know, what you don't know you can't tell."

"You never knew who he was working with or who his contacts were?"

"Nope. I was just ran the business that legitimized what he was doing. The secret operation was Tim's bailiwick."

"So a mob enforcer getting his skull bashed in next to your cabin doesn't make you want to tell us who Tim was dancing with?"

Paul raised his hands palms up in a display of helplessness. "I can't tell you what I don't know. I can't tell you if one of his contacts was a mob family, or if they came after me to try to find Tim, or who killed the guy, or what he was doing here, or why whoever killed him decided to do it here. I honestly don't know. I know it's frustrating for you to need help I can't give you, but I can't tell you what I don't know. Tim set things up to protect me and Gormac. He said my best protection was not knowing anything. He called it compartmentalized deniability."

"When was the last time you saw or heard from your partner?" John asked.

"I talked to him a couple minutes before he was supposed to get on the airplane to fly home with Lisa. Now you tell me he's alive and still working with the FBI, or whatever agency is pulling his strings. I'm stunned and overwhelmed. I'm having trouble wrapping my mind around the idea he's still alive, and maybe on the run from the kind of people I've only read about in novels. It sounds like he needs my help, and I don't know what to do to help him."

Sure you're stunned, John thought. He took note of Jean's tightly controlled outward calm and wondered how real her composure was. "So if Tim Gordon showed up on your doorstep right now you'd be shocked to see him?"

"God, yes! He's my best friend. As far as I know, he's been dead for two years. How do you think I'd react?" Paul stood and paced in front of the fireplace. "Hey Tim, you wanna beer? Whatcha been up to the last couple years while I've been going out of my mind with grief? C'mon detective! Get real!"

"Okay. Fair enough. But look, we have reason to believe this may not be over yet. It looks like some really nasty people are trying to put a final period on the end of the sentence.

The folks who conduct their business in the shadows and back alleys don't consider accounts settled until there's nobody walking around who was connected to it. Whether you like it or not, you're connected to Tim's operation. You know you don't know anything, we know you don't know anything. Unfortunately, those people probably don't care if you don't know anything. Taking care of you is just part of the after job clean up. Try to be cautious around anyone you don't know."

Paul chuckled. "I've been here a couple weeks, so I know maybe five or six people well enough to call them by name and you guys are two of them. You want me to be suspicious of anyone I don't recognize? You'll have to forgive me if I can't spin my head fast enough to see them all."

"I know, it sounds like a dumb idea. I just want you to be aware of the situation and try to act accordingly. We wouldn't want anything to happen to either one of you."

"Thanks for the warning. I'm just not sure how to make use of it."

John stood and Tom followed a heartbeat later. "I guess we don't need to take up any more of your time. Thanks again for the coffee. By the way, you make a great cup of coffee, and if you think of anything,"

"We'll be sure to give you a call," Paul and Jean chorused.

John moved to the door. "We'll show ourselves out. Thanks for the coffee."

They stood in front of the fire as the door closed and listened to the footsteps fade from the porch. "I think that went rather well." Paul said.

"I'm relieved they're finally gone. I was sure they'd hear my teeth chattering and my knees knocking together. I'm glad they didn't ask me anything, because I don't know if I could have kept myself under control. They already seem to know a lot about you."

"They know a lot more than they're telling us. You handled things very well. Saying nothing was the best thing you could do. Those guys aren't dummies. Did you notice the young one sat there taking notes and not saying anything? He was watching us like we were under a microscope. You can bet he knew you were nervous and I was lying. They know I'm involved and they know I can answer any questions they have about who was involved and what link they were in the chain. You remember Ragsdale's comment about me being a good businessman? He was saying he knew I wouldn't do anything without knowing all aspects of what was involved and how big a reward was waiting at the end of the day. On the other hand, they have no reason to believe you know anything. They also know they can't force me to tell them anything. It's got to be a major frustration for them to know they're so close to the answers and have no way to make me give up the information. That's their problem. We have one of our own, and I'm not looking forward to handling it."

"Conklin?"

"Conklin, and Marnee too. If Alma Jacobsen is really Marnee, then she's been listening to everything we've done or said here, or in my cabin. She's been listening in or recording every sound in both places." Paul looked out the front window. "Oh shit!"

"What now?"

"It just dawned on me. If Marnee has been here for two years, then the agency knew our plans and has been two steps ahead of us from the get-go. We've got to move fast."

Jean put her hands on Paul's shoulders and looked into his eyes. "Okay. But we have to know which way to move and how fast to move. Take a breath! Let's not panic. Speed depends on good planning. Right?"

Paul found a calm strength in Jean's eyes. He could see she was using her fear to fuel her calm resolve. "Right! You know, you're showing a real talent for this. You sure you haven't been leading a secret life?"

"Oh yeah, very secret! I'll tell you all about it someday. Something I don't choose to share with Alma, or Marnee, or whatever her name is, listening in. The best place for us to do our planning is somewhere outside her sound studio. Let's take a walk and watch the sunset."

"Great idea. Just for the sake of caution, let's go out the back door. Our friends may still be watching us."

"Gendarme a la locale, mon ami?"

"Oui, oui. I love it when you speak French."

56.

TIM AND JULIE STROLLED ALONG THE SWIMMING
beach at the south edge of the lagoon. "Any chance we actually pulled it off back there?" Tim asked.

"You mean with the old man, or the other two?"

"The Don. Marnee won't do anything until she has new orders. I think she's primarily an observer. Her job was to manipulate things so Paul would be here and I would come looking for him. She's probably supposed to call Washington as soon as she confirms my location and let the disposal crew handle the dirty work. Wet work was Conklin's job, not hers. She had the scenario mapped out and tracking nicely until Webster washed up on the beach. She's been scrambling to recover ever since. Now that we've managed to wreck her little house of cards and spoil her party, she won't move until someone in Washington tugs her leash. Hartley's a wild card, he's in trouble back home and it will go badly for him if he shows up empty handed and without his companion. Always bad form to carry bad news back to the colony. Coming home without the Triad's man could make life short for our Thomas. I think he'll watch what happens from some safe burrow where he's stashed some of his loot. He may surface in a year or two. I don't see him as a threat.

"The old man and the boys are an immediate problem. From their perspective, you're a traitor who stomped a mud hole in their pride, wiped your feet on their honor, and then kicked what little remained of their dignity right up their ass. Paul and I caused a minor irritation when we shut off their cash flow. He could get over that, chalk it up to the cost of doing business, but he ain't too pleased with you, and he isn't likely to ignore the insult and walk away."

"Succinctly put. Do you suppose he might change his mind if I chase him down before he gets on his airplane and humble myself? You know, offer to do public penance for my sins and ask for absolution?"

"You mean promise to say five *Our fathers* and ten *Hale Mary's*? I don't think so, not even if you promised sexual favors to the whole family for the next five years. The only absolution he's interested in involves seeing our heads on a pike at his front gate. He isn't interested in apologies. He's an injured leader who lost control of his command. We didn't steal his money or short his shipments or anything so mundane and explainable as business. We made him look weak and vulnerable. Hell, you proved he's vulnerable. He can't live with knowing it, and he sure as hell can't let us live after we accomplished it. He needs to repair the damage and show the world what happens to anyone foolish enough to cross him."

"I was thinking the same thing. I knew the risk I was taking, but I wasn't sure what I would do until I saw you on the beach. All I could think of was all the years we'd lost and how I'd never stopped loving you. I agree, we aren't home free. What do you think will happen next?"

"I don't know, my crystal ball is a little cloudy. I only know I have a really bad feeling. Things are too quiet. Something is out of place. Do you see anything wrong in your camp?"

Julie studied her campsite. "I think we may be walking into a trap. We let everyone else leave with their wheels while we took the old fashioned mode of travel. They've had time to get ready for us to stroll into their sights. We're definitely at a disadvantage. Using the scope on your shooter to scan things would almost certainly attract attention. My cameras are at the camp, so I can't use a telephoto lens to take a look. We need to get in and get out before people start lighting up the world around us."

Their pace gradually slowed as they talked. Tim stepped behind a tree a hundred feet from Julie's camp. "I'll cover you from here. Pack up and pick me up on the way out. I'll keep an eye out for our friends."

Julie scrutinized everything as she continued to her camp, her nerves tight as a bowstring. The feeling of uneasiness increased as she approached her campsite. The intensity of her internal alarm swelled as the distance shortened. Nothing looked out of place, but the hair on the back of her neck stood at attention and goose bumps paraded across her skin. An unidentified threat lurked in her camp like a moray eel hiding in a reef.

Julie walked into her camp like she was returning from a walk in the forest. Her best defense was to look as though she suspected nothing. Entering the tent could be tricky. She checked the zipper to see if it had been opened in her absence. It didn't look out of place, it just felt wrong. Masking her concern for imminent hazard, she moved the zipper just past top center. Hoping to confuse anyone waiting inside, she went to the Jeep, rested her hand on the fender to feel for movement, and found none.

She turned and burst into the tent, hit the ground and rolled onto her back with her pistol drawn. The tent was empty, but someone had been there. She could feel it. "Calm yourself," she whispered. "Pack it up."

She took quick mental inventory of what she needed to take and what she could leave behind. Even though the equipment could all be replaced, leaving it behind would set off suspicions with the police, a risk she couldn't afford. She had packed and unpacked her equipment a hundred times and everything went into a prearranged location. In a matter of minutes she was bagging up the debris and tossing the bag into the Jeep.

Tim swept the area with the scope, frustrated by the limited field of vision. The light enhancement qualities of the scope worked well in the dark, but poorly in the dappled sunlight. The setting sun made the shadows longer and darker, the bright areas brighter, and helped to conceal his presence, but the other side shared the same advantage. They had almost certainly watched them approach and knew his location. Cold sweat trickled down his spine.

Tim moved toward the road when the engine started and the Jeep began to roll forward. He was fifty feet away when the Jeep exploded. The shock wave tossed him ten feet. He rolled onto his hands and knees, a galaxy of stars dancing in his eyes and the echo of the blast screaming in his ears. He shook his head and blinked, attempting to regain his equilibrium. He felt a gun press against his head before he could stand. "She was such a pretty little thing," Gino's voice penetrated the ringing in his ears. "We'll all miss her. Now, if you would be good enough to accompany me, grandfather has some unfinished business to discuss with you."

The burst of adrenaline at the sound of Gino's voice swept the cobwebs from Tim's brain. The image of the explosion danced blackly in his blurred vision and a trickle of blood ran from his right ear. He choked back the grief swelling in his chest. Grief would have to wait for a time when he could allow the pain of loss to run its course. Rage set his jaw in a grim determination to extract payment for Julie's murder. He blinked to clear his eyes and looked over his shoulder at the man who had recently been his prisoner. Groggy, shaken, his balance uneven, he knew he needed to do as he was told and wait for an opportunity to retaliate. They moved about fifty feet into the seclusion of the trees before Gino disarmed him.

Confused thoughts whirled madly in Tim's mind as he struggled to focus his attention on his situation. Thoughts of Julie and the vision of her Jeep exploding contended with his efforts to devise a way out of his predicament. He knew the Don would be unhappy about recent events, even if he was about to achieve his original goal. *No good deed goes unpunished. All we accomplished by letting these goons go was to give them another chance to kill us. It looks like half the task has been accomplished. What a great way to end the day.* Grief settled coldly on his heart, strengthening his rage and fueling an icy resolve to avenge Julie's murder.

57.

THE DETECTIVES WERE TURNING THE CORNER IN
front of Alma Jacobsen's cabin when they saw and heard
the explosion. The shock wave rocked the vehicle and made
them duck reflexively. They arrived on the scene in less than a
minute, but failed to observe the two men hurrying into the
forest. The blast had scorched the trees around what remained
of the Jeep. Rain still dripped from the trees and combined
with the soggy forest floor to prevent a fire. The smoldering
remains of the car offered little hope of discovering anyone
alive in the wreckage. The blast had blown the doors open and
bulged the top.

"This is the photographer's car," Tom said. "Jesus, she was
such a nice lady."

"They all seem a lot nicer when you think about them after
something like this. What's your preference? You wanna guard
the scene or make the call?"

"You call it in, I'll see what I can do to preserve the scene.
At least I can cover her up, whatever's left of her. Jesus, what a
mess." Tom fought rising nausea as the smell of burnt hair and
flesh mingled with the smell of cordite and wet forest.

People were pouring out of the houses and running toward
the scene. "You've got a crowd coming, so be prepared."

"Like a good scout!" Tom looked at the wreckage of the
car. "You think this is part of our case?"

"Maybe, maybe not. Either way, it looks like we've got another homicide to work. Hope you weren't planning on getting any sleep, because it looks like we're gonna be here a while. Try to find the outer radius of the debris field before it gets too dark. I'll help you string crime scene tape as soon as I finish calling the experts."

John wondered about the coincidence of two murders in the same place a few days apart when he'd ordinarily investigate four or five in a couple years in the whole county. He wondered what might connect a professional photojournalist with a mafia goon. It seemed like a tougher question than who killed the goon. *Twenty years on this job and I still don't understand why people do what they do to each other. What I do understand is how coincidence is very rarely coincidental.*

Jean was locking her back door when the explosion shattered the quiet of the late afternoon. They ran down the street looking for the source of the blast in time to see the detectives reach the scene and the crowd of people scurrying to the source of the disturbance. Excited voices filled the air as residents ran toward the cloud of smoke rising from the campground. It was obvious a red Jeep was the source of the explosion.

"That's Julie's car! We don't have much time! C'mon!" Paul grabbed Jean and dragged her along with him.

They sprinted to his cabin, lunged through the door and skidded to a halt. Where they'd left Conklin lying on the floor there was only a dark pool of drying blood. The silent cabin was empty.

"One of our problems seems to be solved," Jean said. "Whatever happened to him, he's not our worry anymore." She picked up the fireplace poker and studied the end. "I don't know if this was used after we left, but I'm going to wash it anyway."

Paul marveled at Jean's clear headed calm in the face of disaster. "We don't have much time. If you can clean this up, I'll go throw some things in a suitcase. We need to travel light. There's a roll of paper towels and a bottle of cleaner under the sink. We'll burn the towels in your fireplace. Luminol will show the blood if they look for it, but do the best you can." He saw panic, fear, uncertainty, and a flinty resolve in Jean's eyes, all shining from the edge of tears threatening to flow. "Are you going to be all right?"

Jean blinked, looked at the poker in her hand and the blood on the floor, and then met his eyes. "I don't know. I hope so. I think so. I always wondered what it would be like to live an exciting life, to flirt with danger like the heroine in a movie or a novel. I never dreamed of anything like this. I don't know if I'm going to be all right, I'm just going to do what I need to do and hang on for the next turn in this wild ride. Go pack your stuff, I'll get to work on this mess."

Paul gathered up what he would need and made sure the house looked like he was planning to return. He loaded the suitcase in his car and they drove to Jean's cabin.

Paul stopped Jean from getting out of the car. "Wait a second. Conklin may be out of the way and there's no way the cops should think we had anything to do with blowing up Julie's car, but we can't leave yet."

"Why not?"

"Because if we leave right now, it might look like we had something to do with the explosion. Besides, until we know better, we have to presume Tim and Julie are dead. So, let's dispose of the stuff you used to clean the floor and walk down there to see what's going on. We need to look as curious as everyone else in the neighborhood. If we don't show up it will look suspicious. If we leave right now it will look suspicious. For the moment at least, we gotta stay put."

"I see what you mean, but I'm scared. Somebody is killing everyone close to you and it really scares me."

"Me too, honey." He turned off the ignition and looked sorrowfully at her. "I'm trying to get used to the idea they got Tim this time and Julie along with him. I was just getting used to the idea we would be together again and now it's pretty much gone up in smoke. You're all I have left and knowing whoever is doing this is able to get this close to us and never be seen isn't making me feel confident we can get away. Right now we don't seem to have much choice. We have to make sure no one suspects us of knowing Julie and the only way we can convince them is to go down there and join the crowd." Hand in hand, they set off for the campground.

Marnee had just made contact with the agency when the explosion rattled the walls and rained dust and grit on her. She shouted at her contact to hold on and ripped off the headset. She squeezed through the narrow door the detectives had found and peered through an opening in the fence in the direction of the ball of smoke. She recognized the Jeep and dashed back to the communications console. The conversation was brief and the directions were specific. The agency didn't care if she liked what she was told to do or agreed with their decisions, she was expected to execute their orders, with or without backup. She knew screwing up would play into Washington's hands by providing them a handy scapegoat. After seven years living vicariously with Paul and Tim's undercover operation, she had an escape plan ready. She knew where some of the money was buried, all she needed to do was squeeze some of it out of the boys she had always liked.

58.

THEY DISCOVERED ONE BODY IN THE CAR, A GRAY
haired man whose ruined body resembled a charred rag doll
with the stuffing torn out of it. Shreds of clothing and flesh
were splashed like gobs of red mud across the interior of the
vehicle. There was no sign of the petite photographer.

Tom managed about three steps before he vomited. John
patiently waited for his partner to regain his composure. "Don't
feel bad. This is nasty enough to get to anyone."

"I usually have better control, but I've never seen anything
this bad. How many do you have to see before it doesn't make
you puke?"

"Depends. I had to learn to turn off the smell and the
general horror so I could be objective. No matter how many
dead bodies I've retrieved, it's always unpleasant. Good news,
the boss is on his way. Bad news, a delegation from the feebies
and ATF are right on his bumper. Seems this little event is being
taken out of our hands and dropped squarely in the feds' lap."

"Why? They think we can't handle it?"

"It's their purview and provides an opportunity to justify
their existence. Look at it this way, if they want to grab the
glory, let them argue about it among themselves. We'll smile
politely and let them clean things up while we go back to
our case and don't worry about this one. This is a win-win
situation."

"What if they're connected?"

"We still can't keep them out, so let's be good little soldiers and hold the fort until the cavalry arrives."

They didn't notice the white Chevrolet leaving the area while they moved through the crowd asking if anyone had seen the explosion. They were eager to learn the identity of the victim, but their orders were to secure the area, identify any witnesses, and not to touch anything, it was the feds' party. The call for an ambulance was canceled in favor of the Coroner when they found the body. The initial procedures of the investigation filled their time without revealing anything of substance. Tom noticed Paul and Jean at the edge of the crowd and approached them.

"What's going on detective?" Paul asked. "You had just left when we heard an explosion. Was anyone hurt?"

"The explosion involved a Jeep in the campground. Do you recognize the car?"

"I think I've seen it here the last couple days," Paul replied. "I don't know anything else about it."

"I think I might have seen it yesterday," Jean said. "So many cars come and go I can't be sure. I don't pay much attention to what goes on over here. Can't you find out who owns it from the license plates?"

"Identifying the owner isn't difficult. Discovering why it blew up and if the guy inside is the owner is another matter."

Paul frowned. "I came here to get away from the pressures and dangers of the city. It's beginning to look like it's more dangerous here than LA. First the guy on the beach and now this. Is this normal?"

"Thankfully, no," Tom replied. "Look folks, we know where you were when this went down and we've got our hands full. There's really nothing for you to see, so you'd do us a tremendous favor if you just went about your business."

"I don't think I'd want your job right now," Paul said. "We'll leave you to it."

Paul didn't speak until they were a hundred feet away. "It's Julie's car, but it isn't Julie."

"How do you know it isn't, oh, you're right! The detective said the guy hadn't been identified, right? Guy, not girl." A look of distress draped itself across Jean's face like a falling curtain. "Oh my God! It might be Tim."

"I'm hoping it isn't."

Jean stopped. "Maybe it's Conklin. Do you think we could be so lucky?"

"Keep walking. We don't know what happened to Conklin. Blowing up a body would remove any evidence of murder and distract the cops from the real crime scene, which helps us, but if it's Conklin, it raises a lot of questions. Who killed him? Why was he killed? Did the same person who killed him set the bomb, or is there another killer out there stalking us while we're playing hide and seek with Tim and Julie? Maybe we could be lucky enough for it to be Conklin. I just don't know whether it's good luck or bad."

"I was just beginning to feel some hope of getting clear of this and now I'm terrified there's somebody else involved. Who else might be after you?"

Paul walked with his arm around her shoulder and spoke directly into her ear. "I'm not sure how many people are involved. There was a network in Asia connected through us to a network here while we were attached to a network of agencies in Washington; a lot of people you wouldn't take home to meet your mother."

"How reassuring. You're saying there could be somebody behind every tree or window with a score to settle? Wouldn't it be better to just bunker ourselves in a defensible location and tell them to come and get us? We could pick them off one by one like the colonial militia did to the British during the Revolution."

"You know it's not so simple. Our best chance is still to disappear before somebody makes us disappear."

59.

HER EARS WERE RINGING, A NAUSEATING HEADACHE
threatened to send her into a coma, her eyes were full of grit,
blood trickled from her ears and nose, but Pisces was alive,
and alert enough to crawl into the underbrush and watch
Gino herd Tim into the timber. Her escape had been a near
thing. She saw Conklin's body as soon as she opened the door
and suspected the body was supposed to distract her from
the real danger. Wariness born of experience made her search
for and find the explosive device. She recognized the trigger
mechanism as one designed to activate fifteen seconds after the
engine started. There was enough C-4 to destroy the vehicle
plus a deadly radius of thirty feet. She knew leaving it parked
could place innocent bystanders at risk.

She made sure the Jeep was pointed into an open area,
started the engine, put the transmission into gear and dashed
for cover. The blast lifted her off her feet and slammed her
into a tree before she landed in a crumpled heap. *Pain is a good
thing. God! It hurts! Pain means you're alive! The blood running
out of your ears and nose proves your heart is still beating and the
dizzy nauseous headache tells you your brain is really pissed about
being rattled around in its unpadded room.*

Pisces checked for broken bones, but found only bruises
and lacerations to accompany a concussion. She blinked the grit
out of her eyes and followed Gino and Tim. Nausea suddenly
overwhelmed her. She leaned unsteadily against a tree while

her stomach emptied itself. She knew she had to keep moving and not allow the concussion to steal her consciousness.

Tim tripped over a root and caught himself against a tree. His balance was shaky and his head ached, but his vision had cleared and the ringing in his ears was beginning to fade. It was hard to tell if he was hearing the wind in the tree tops or if the sound was his ears protesting the impact of the explosion. Gino followed at enough distance to prevent Tim from trying to disarm him, yet close enough to be able to shoot him if he tried to bolt.

Survival was his paramount concern as they were walked toward the State Park. The events of the past few days seemed like they had happened in another lifetime. He wondered if he would leave the encounter with the old man on his feet. Chances of survival seemed about as good as winning the lottery. Large drops still fell from the trees. The cold water running down his neck helped to revive him as he moved through the undergrowth. He thought he saw a figure paralleling their route in the shadows once. *Has another player had joined the game? Did Gino notice? Screw him, let him watch his own ass.*

The warmth of Jean's cabin wrapped around them like a blanket in stark contrast to the cool ocean breeze that had literally pushed them through the door. Jean spun around in the middle of the room, tears welling up in her eyes. "I'm terrified! I feel like I have no control of anything and no matter what I do, or where I turn, or what I think, the world is closing in like a pack of wolves. People are dying! You and I could be next! We don't even know who may be trying to kill us! You seem so calm and it's all I can do to keep panic at bay and my voice from shaking as hard as my hands and knees! How do you do it? How do you stay calm when the people you love are dying and someone is trying to kill you? How do I just pack my things and leave everything I love to run away with you?"

Paul took her gently in his arms and held her close. "Calm? You think I'm calm?" He leaned his cheek against her head, inhaling the scent of her hair, a mixture of sea air and shampoo. "I'm not calm. My nerves are screaming. Panic is perched on my shoulder and yelling in my ear. I'm getting dizzy trying to look in every direction at once. I only look calm because I've had longer to learn how to maintain the act. We can't afford to panic or let down our guard. We're at war. If we win, we have a long time to be together. If we lose, at least we'll have what we've shared. I'd be worried if you weren't scared. You're scared because you don't know what to expect, or who to expect it from. I'm scared because I know who we're up against and I don't know if we have a good enough escape route to get away. Panic is gnawing away at both of us, but we can't let it win. We have to use it to keep our minds sharp and reactions swift. Panic is like an animal trapped in the headlights of a car. It makes you freeze instead of act. But if you can channel the adrenaline as it rises with the panic, you can use it to protect yourself from the fear causing the panic. Does any of this make sense to you?"

"Yes, it makes sense. I've used the same technique for years when I had to make a presentation to a tough client. I guess I just needed to know I'm not the only one in this particular boat." She took a deep breath. "I love you, Paul. I don't know how, or why, or just when I knew, but I do. Why don't you take care of burning those paper towels while I pack a change of clothes. I really don't need anything more do I?"

"We have to travel light. Keep it to essentials. Take a coat, wear your running shoes, put on a couple layers of clothes. You can take something off if you get too warm. We can presume whatever we've just said has been recorded somewhere, so they'll know we're on the move. They were probably expecting us to run anyway. What the hell, forget the layers. We can buy clothes. It's easier to blend in with the surroundings if you buy the kind of clothes local folks wear. We may be shopping at the Salvation Army for a while, because used stuff is the easiest disguise."

Paul stirred the ashes, letting his thoughts wander. *I'm really going to miss this place, especially her paintings. If it's tough for me, it's got to be devastating for her. She's leaving everything she loves to leap into the unknown with nothing to hold onto but my hand. What have I done to earn such loyalty and trust? Why didn't I just keep my heart locked up and my pants zipped? What was I thinking? I knew this was coming and I dragged her along anyway! Yeah, she invited herself when she laid out Conklin, but she only did it because I'd pushed her into a corner. Now I have to protect her when I don't even know if I can protect myself from the people who blew up Julie's Jeep. Dragging her into this was dumb! But how can I walk away from her? Someday we can come back for her things. Her paintings should be safe. The Sheriff's Department is diligent about patrolling the area and our safety depends on swift flight.*

Paul's reverie was broken by a soft footstep. He turned and discovered Marnee standing at the kitchen door with a gun leveled at him. "Well, well, the reclusive neighbor shows her face. And it used to be such a lovely face. What have they done to you, Marnee?"

"I'm sure Tim already filled you in. They changed my appearance and I'm still not used to seeing it looking out of the mirror at me."

"Can they put you back together, or are you like Humpty-Dumpty?" Jean asked.

Marnee scowled. "Cute. It sounds like you've managed to regain control of yourself. You walked into this with your arms and legs open. I didn't have a choice. This is my job and I'm damn good at it. Like any good soldier, if they tell me to jump my only question is whether I jumped high enough. This look was necessary for me to get close enough to catch the boys. They can do surgery to change me back or even give me a whole new look, better than the original."

"It's amazing what they can do with plastic isn't it?" Paul commented.

"What is this? Are you two planning a comedy tour?"

"Yeah. We thought we'd hit all the hot spots," Paul said. "Vegas, New York, Miami, maybe Cancun. All we want to do is get away from you, and the agency, and the family, and the Triads, and anybody else who wants to yank our leash and shorten our lives. Are you here to take us in or to take us out?"

"You always were direct."

"If you mean I don't play politics, you're right. Politics is for liars and cowards. I already know you're a liar. Are you a coward too?"

"Ooh. Unkind, too. Fred always thought you were a time bomb. He watched you closer than any of our other agents. He said you were the wild card. He thought Tim would be easy to manage, but he misread his tea leaves. Neither of you is particularly tractable. Extremely useful, but not very tractable."

"This is all very polite and I'm sure Paul appreciates the ego massage, but how about we cut through the bullshit! What do you want?"

Marnee looked carefully at Jean. "Do you have any idea what you've stepped into, hot pants?"

Jean answered in a firm, steady voice. "I know that from the day this man arrived, people have been dying. I know this entire dance is because your agency bungled things. It looks like you've spent two years manipulating events and circumstances to get Paul to come here. I presume the purpose was to lure Tim out of hiding. I know you have enough horsepower to sweep this entire mess under the carpet and nail the rug down so nobody will ever learn the truth. How am I doing so far?"

"Very astute. You've solved one dilemma."

"Which is?" Paul growled.

"Whether to turn her loose or gather her up with the rest of the herd."

"You mean until you decide to dispose of her."

"We're all expendable, cannon fodder to be used and disposed of when the time comes. But to answer your question, I've been instructed to detain you, so let's head over to my place and make ourselves comfortable."

"Okay. Do you want to take my car or would you rather walk?" When Marnee glared at him he continued. "Yeah, I suppose we should walk. You probably want us to lead the way."

Paul and Jean walked hand in hand into the lowering light of the dying day.

60.

KERRY WESTON LED THE PARADE, FOLLOWED BY

the FBI, ATF, DEA, NSA, the coroner's wagon, and a white Chevrolet which continued to the store.

"Jesus Christ!" Tom exclaimed. "It looks like a damned invasion."

"Yep! It appears our responsibility for this little shiveree has concluded. From here on this party belongs to the G-men. Be prepared to wait tables for them."

"Will the boss let them take over?"

"He won't have any choice if they pull rank, and trust me, they already pulled rank. He won't like it, but he'll smile and wag his tail like a good little dog. It sucks, but it's the way it is."

"Damn! It may be their purview and they can take over the investigation, but I'm not ready to be a lackey to some suit with a federal ID."

John chuckled. "When rape is inevitable it's better to lay back and enjoy it. They're going to save us a lot of work. Since we don't know if our case is connected to this one, we'll just mosey on our way and let the suits do their thing."

Tom grinned. "I like the way you think. We let them try to figure out who turned the campground into a war zone and concentrate on solving our own case. Yeah! I like it!"

"There's just one thing."

"Yeah?"

"We gotta talk to them about our dead goon if they ask.

They read the papers and they'll probably use that juicy tidbit to do the Texas two-step all over our investigation in an effort to tie the two together. The boss will be asked to turn over all our records and we'll get the bum's rush. Of course it'll take a day or two to make and deliver all those copies, so we probably have about twenty-four hours before our carriage turns into a pumpkin."

"Great! I guess we'll just sleep for a couple days when they get done picking our brains under hot lights."

"Yeah, but an empty head rests so much easier. Here comes the boss. Let's bring him up to speed and prepare to be kicked off the case on the grounds the G-men are more bored than we are."

61.

STARS CONTINUED TO FLICKER AT THE EDGES OF
Julie's vision, a dull roar squealed in her ears, but her balance
was improving. Keeping pace with the two men without
sounding like a stampeding herd was a challenge because they
were following a trail and she was breaking one. She was
concerned Gino's hearing was undamaged while hers was so
badly compromised she didn't know if her efforts to remain
silent were effective or not. Twice she concealed herself when
Tim looked in her direction, but he moved on as if he hadn't
seen her. Gino's attention remained focused on his prisoner.
Apparently her skills were working even if her ears were not.
After a mile she realized where they were going, moved ahead
and picked up a game trail, allowing her to travel quickly and
silently. She found the Don and Joey parked right next to Tim's
car. She took up a post and waited for Tim and Gino to arrive.
She hoped a little more time would help alleviate the effects
of the concussion.

The Don was fuming when Gino and Tim entered the
campsite. Joey moved to a position behind Tim about six feet
from Gino. Tim faced him from the middle of a triangle.

"Mr. Gordon, how kind of you to join us." His warm
demeanor belied the intense rage boiling just below surface.

Tim smiled cordially. "How could I possibly refuse your
gracious invitation."

The Don's eyes widened and his nostrils flared. "You got such a smart mouth. You got a clever remark for every occasion and a knack for turning every disaster into a victory. You make it look like you never make mistakes. You're real smart, real clever. You never do nothing to upset nobody, but nobody's perfect. Everybody screws up sooner or later and you screwed up big time when you decided to stick a knife in me!" he snarled, spittle flying in Tim's face.

Tim stared at the old man without reacting.

"I treated you like family and you betrayed me! You dropped dime on me! You brought down my whole operation! You cost me a lot of money! How could you do that to me? I trusted you!"

Tim spoke quietly. "Oh sure, you trusted me all right. You trusted me just as long as I kept the pipeline open." Tim paused a heartbeat. "But there's a hole in your story. I never told anyone anything. The feds decided to tip over the apple cart and tell the world I was a mole. You lost a few dollars. I lost what passed for a life! I've spent two years playing dead, waiting for you and all the other folks to stop looking for me and let me get on with whatever life I could manage to create. It sure as hell wouldn't have been a very public life, but at least I'd still be alive."

"You're a fucking mole! You're a two faced, lying, low life mole!"

"And when did you discover I was a mole? You're making a lot of noise in front of the gold dust twins, but let's get down to the nitty gritty. Let's talk about when you learned I was a mole. Do you remember the first person who told you I was a mole?"

Chagrin painted the old man's face. "Yeah! I remember!"

"Right. Inconvenient how the truth shines light in

shadowy places you would rather keep dark. When your people approached me to set up our little smuggling operation I told them I'd think about it. A week later, I came to you and told you I was going to set it up because the feds wanted me to do it and to report back to them what you were doing. Remember? I told you what I was going to do and who I was doing it for before we brought in the first shipment. Remember?"

"Yeah. You told me you was going to play both sides of the table. You said you'd always tell me what you were gonna tell them. Until you tore down the entire network! You never warned me so I could cover myself! You pulled the plug and left me looking foolish."

"Yes, we did. The feds decided to cut me loose and make sure someone out there in the wonderful world of no-good-nicks would make me disappear. I was between a rock and a hard place. Shutting down the network was the only way I could protect Paul from you and anyone else who decided we were too much of an embarrassment to have around. My only chance was to create so much chaos I could slip away in the confusion. I didn't have time to spread the word."

"You cost me a lot a money and made me look bad."

"I also made sure the trail couldn't be traced back to you."

"So you say, but my people are still unhappy. They want to know what I'm gonna do to the rat. You know what we do to rats?"

"Of course I know what you do to rats! I also know I didn't rat anything you didn't know before I gave it to the feds. You always had a chance to edit what I gave them. Why don't you just tell your people the whole story? Why don't you explain how you and the rat were feeding disinformation to the disinformation specialists? What's the matter? Are you afraid they'll get suspicious why you were playing things so cozy with the feds? Worried they might start to wonder which side you're on? Maybe start to look at you as the real rat?"

"Yeah. I could tell them. Maybe they'd start to think like you say, but if I was gonna tell them, I shoulda done it when we was just getting started. Now I'd look bad because I didn't. You understand how it is. It's too late to tell them I had the fix in all along. How do I keep the respect of the family if I don't do what's gotta be done? You understand it's a matter of appearances and perceptions. It's just business. If I don't make an example of you it will look like I was in on it and all those suspicions you talked about will be real. I'm an old man. All I have left is the respect of the family. A man who dies without respect is less than nothing."

The Don saw movement behind Gino just as Pisces' blade penetrated his neck and severed his spinal cord. His body was slumping to the ground before Joey could draw his gun. The weapon was barely free of the holster before Pisces had cleared the space separating them and drove the ends of her fingers into his throat. He fell to his knees clutching his throat with both hands, struggling to breathe through the blood pouring down his broken windpipe.

The Don stared in shock at his two grandsons lying on the ground while what should have been a ghost approached him. "But, but, I thought you were,"

"I'm not as dead as I'm supposed to be. As for them," Pisces pointed at the body of Gino and the convulsing form of Joey. "I told you I would hold you to your honor." She leaned forward until her nose was nearly touching the old man's. The fetid odor of fear suddenly filled the air around him as his breath quickened and his face turned ashen. "The price for failure to behave with honor has always been the same in the family. I won't belabor the point you just explained to Tim.

Don't worry. Your debt is paid. They paid it for you. What you tell the family is up to you."

The old man stared over her shoulder at the bodies of his grandsons, thoughts racing through his mind about what he would tell the family. *The family! Their families! I have to go home to their funerals and my own. I misjudged and underestimated these people from the beginning. Machiavelli would have been proud to count this young man and his partner among his lieutenants.* "Are you going to tell me if you only told them what we agreed upon or leave me to wonder if you told them everything including what I told you not to tell them?"

Tim picked up Joey's pistol and was removing the assault weapon from Gino. "I guess you'll just have to wonder. A little knowledge is truly a dangerous thing when the knowledge is only enough to create a storm of doubts and uncertainties. I'm glad she decided to let you live. You deserve to worry and wonder about what I did and I'm certainly going to enjoy knowing you are."

"This is not a good thing."

"You have a choice," Pisces said. "You can let it end here and now, get back on your airplane, go home and tell your people Tim and Paul are dead, or hang around and try to postpone the inevitable. You won't die at our hands. We don't need you dead. We need you to be a scapegoat. You can go home and face the music or you can stick around to see what we do to make your people believe you rolled over on them. I already planted the seeds of doubt with them. Your choice."

The old man stared with sad eyes at his grandsons. The inevitability of his situation crashed around him like a collapsing building. "Perhaps it is best to let it end."

"Then let's load the boys in the car and take them to

the airport," Pisces said. "You did keep the plane waiting, didn't you?"

"Yes. It is waiting. It will be a long, sad journey. Perhaps my last."

"We'll stop along the way so you can let folks know we're off the target list. We wouldn't want a repeat performance of this little scene, would we?"

"It will be as you say."

They loaded the bodies into the back seat so they would look like sleeping passengers to passing motorists. They started for the airport with Julie driving Joey's car and Tim following in his borrowed ride.

62.

KERRY WESTON WASN'T HAPPY, BUT HE DISPLAYED
a professional aspect. "It looks like we've been relieved of
responsibility for this one. The ATF and the FBI say thank you
very much for calling us, now go write some parking tickets
and let the professionals take care of the important work."

John nodded. "We figured as much. It looks like every
agent within a two hundred mile radius has arrived to
investigate what we would handle with two men. It must be
nice to have so much budget and manpower you need seven
men to do the work of one ordinary street cop and pay them
twice as much for the inefficiency. Oh well, we've had this
conversation before. What do you want us to do?"

"The usual. Answer their questions and bug out before
they decide to use you as a traffic cone."

"What about our investigation?" Tom asked.

"It ceased to be ours the minute you called in the bombing.
Get over it. Go back to your case and let the G-men do their
thing."

John scratched his ear. "There may be a small problem."

"What small problem would that be?" Weston asked.

"The owner of the Jeep may be connected to the body on
the beach," Tom answered.

"The connection is mostly a circumstantial hunch," John
added, "but we think there's a good chance they're connected."

Weston paused a moment. "If they ask, tell them,

otherwise, keep your counsel. Unless they invite you to join their little shindig, a possibility I consider to be as likely as you sprouting wings, give them the basics, give them the scene, and boogie. As I recall, you were still looking for a viable suspect to arrest when the fireworks went off. If it turns out the two events are connected, we'll tell them immediately about what we've discovered. Until we have something more than a hunch, the two aren't related."

"You're the boss," John said. "We'll just toss them the keys to the joint and go back to our own little can of worms."

"Excellent. I'm going to go be politically correct and make sure everyone is satisfied I've removed you from the scene before I head for home. It's been a long day."

A short time later, the detectives were seated at the patio table behind the store, a fresh cup of coffee steaming in front of each of them. "This sucks," Tom grouched. "Those assholes couldn't care less what happens with Podunk PD's cases. They never offer to help when we really need it, but blow up one car and they're all over it like ants at a picnic and we have to go scurrying for cover. What a crock of shit!"

"Look at the bright side. There's already lots of work for us to do and we've almost hit the end of the possibilities with our case. Unless something breaks in the next couple days we're going to move on to other things and this case will drift into the shadows and turn cold while we put out new fires."

"I don't want my first homicide investigation to turn into a cold case. I keep thinking the answer is right under our noses. Did you notice the tires on the Jeep were the same tread pattern as the tracks into the trees? And did you notice the photographer's camp was completely gone except for the bits and pieces blown out the windows when the bomb went off? It seems like an awful big coincidence, you know what I mean? Those assholes didn't even ask if I knew any reason the Jeep might have been blown up. They didn't ask me anything except whether or not I'd touched anything. I sure as hell wasn't going to volunteer the information about how the explosion might be connected to our investigation. They can shake those bushes on their own. If they want my help they can kiss my ass."

"Good pick up. Why didn't you tell the boss?"

"Why didn't you?"

John raised an eyebrow. "What makes you think I noticed anything before you told me about it?"

Tom leaned across the table. "You may need glasses to read, your waist may be getting thick, and your butt may be getting broad, but there is damned little I see that you haven't already seen, noted, and filed in the proper pigeon hole for use at a later time. You saw it. You connected it. Why didn't you tell him?"

"Do you think he likes those guys usurping his territory any better than you do? Hell no! The boss is a stand up guy who'll go to the wall for any one of us. You think he likes being told his department isn't qualified to investigate a crime just because it involves an explosive? Give me a break! But, if we don't tell him the connection he isn't required to tell them they have to take over our murder case. See how it works?"

"I get it, but if we don't tell him about the connection until later, how do we tie it together to make our case? The feds have the Jeep. All we have is a tire track with the same tread and I know Goodyear sold more than one set of those tires."

"True enough." John took a small Ziploc bag from his pocket. "But if this sample of dirt from those tires matches the dirt back there in the trees, and if the photos and casts you're going to take of those tracks matches the make, model and size I wrote down off the tires, then wouldn't we have at least a circumstantial connection?"

"You sly old dog! You covered our ass before they arrived. Next you're going to tell me you took photographs of the Jeep and the tires while I was busy keeping the crowd away from the scene."

John took a handful of Polaroid photos from his pocket and tossed them on the table. "You mean like these?"

"Just like these. Don't let it go to your head, but I think I love you."

"It's always nice to be appreciated when you're as old and cold and hard to start as I am. Remember we still don't have a viable suspect. We still don't know what was going on up there in the trees or whether it's connected to the dead guy on the beach, but it seems like coincidences keep piling up."

"No kidding. Coincidentally, the photographer shows up a day after we find the body. Coincidentally, McAfee shows up a week before we find the body. Coincidentally, the killing ground is next to McAfee's cabin. Coincidentally, the hermit lives next door to McAfee. Coincidentally, I saw the hermit's car parked near where we found the tracks of the Jeep. Coincidentally, the photographer's Jeep just got blown to smithereens with an unidentified man in the front seat. Coincidentally, McAfee and his girlfriend showed up to gawk at the scene of the explosion. Coincidentally, I never saw the hermit at the scene. Did you see her anywhere?"

"Now that you mention it, no."

"She's always poking her nose into everything and coincidentally doesn't turn up at the scene of a car bombing that dragged everyone else in the neighborhood out of the woodwork. Coincidentally, it seems like no matter which way

I look at what we know about the body on the beach, Paul McAfee, Jean Parker, and Alma Jacobsen keep rising to the surface. Even though they're always around we haven't found anything to connect them to the murder, except for living where it happened. I'm running out of places to look. Got any ideas what to try next?"

"We still haven't talked to the hermit. As long as we're here, we might as well try again. Maybe you can charm her into telling us something useful."

"You seem to think she likes me better than you."

"I think she knows you better and may be willing to tell you stuff she won't tell me. You said you've been using her as a source didn't you?"

"A reluctant source, but do you think she might tell me what she was doing out tramping around the woods on a rainy day?"

"Can't hurt to ask, can it?"

"Sure can't," Weston said as he stepped through the door. "Mind if I join you?"

"Do you wanna tell him to go peddle his papers?" John asked Tom.

Tom rubbed his jaw, one eye squinted as though deep in thought. "Naw! He'd probably get pissed off and start ordering us around. You know how some people are when they get a little authority. They aren't happy unless they're leaning on somebody who can't lean back."

Weston chuckled. "I had second thoughts about pairing you two, but I'm beginning to think you're a perfect match. Been together, what, a couple days, and neither one of you shows me any respect. John, you're a bad influence."

"Don't blame him, boss," Tom said. "I have as much respect for you as I ever did."

"That's what worries me." Weston joined them at the table. "So where are we on your case?"

"Do you have those notes you've been working on, Tom? A review might be a good idea."

"They're kind of a mess. I need to do a new recap sheet. I have some new ideas about how to arrange some of the pieces."

"He's been thinking again," John explained.

"You haven't succeeded in discouraging this sort of behavior yet have you?"

"I'm sorry, boss. I've tried my best, but he keeps thinking no matter what I do."

Tom offered his partner an extended middle finger. "Fuck you and your discouragement. " He turned to Weston. "And with all due respect to your office and rank, fuck you too."

"Fuck you too, what, detective?" He said with a cold stare.

Tom mentally weighed his next response and decided to just say it and let the chips fall where they might. "Fuck you, too. Sir!"

"Much better! Always remember to show proper respect for the office."

Tom started to laugh and soon all three were laughing. The tension of the day was broken.

Weston sipped his coffee. "Okay, Tommy, lay it out and let's see if we can get a handle on this while we still have the chance. The feds will probably find the circumstantial connection by morning and we'll be asked to get them coffee and donuts while they tap dance all over our investigation."

"It looks like we're seeing the final chapter of a story that started about seven years ago. The feds set up Tim Gordon as a cutout in an operation to smuggle counterfeit computer chips into the country. He was supposed to play both sides and keep the profits as payment."

"Right," Weston said. "CPU chips in particular. Specifically, counterfeit Intel CPU chips. Apparently the counterfeit copies look and act pretty much like the real thing and cost about ten cents on the dollar compared to the price of real Intel chips. A high profit smuggling operation under the banner of a legitimate importer with the advice and consent of the government."

"Okay," Tom continued. "Gordon and McAfee agree to this operation and set out to play the game. Then a couple years ago, instead of using what the boys had learned to take out the bad guys, some bureaucrat without the brains God gave a gnat decides to dump the operation. He not only terminates the operation, he drops dime with the bad guys, telling them Gordon is a double agent, leaving Gordon and McAfee swinging in the breeze with a target on their foreheads.

"Gordon is supposed to catch a flight with McAfee's pregnant wife, but she gets on the plane and he doesn't. The plane goes down south of Hollister with no survivors. The investigation comes up with a bomb in the luggage as the cause of the crash, placed by a disgruntled ex-employee.

"The feebies know Gordon is alive. The rest of the world thinks he's dead. McAfee buries empty caskets for his wife and his partner and then prepares to walk away from the business.

"Within a couple months the hermit and the artist buy the cabins at opposite ends of the street here. Hermit moves in and sets up housekeeping. The artist doesn't move in until about six months ago.

"A couple weeks ago Paul McAfee shows up. Meets and makes friends with the artist.

"A week ago a stiff washes up on the beach. We discover the victim was murdered right outside McAfee's cabin. The victim is a mafia soldier out of LA with a truck that looks like a beater and is equipped like the batmobile.

"McAfee has a solid alibi. He was making small talk with the artist until the wee hours on the night of the murder.

"I see a guy in the crowd on the beach who disappears before I can talk to him. Turns out to be Tim Gordon or a look-alike.

"While I'm doing a bit of survey work I spot someone going from the cabin behind McAfee's toward the timber to the south. We investigate and find where someone's been sitting in the attic of the cabin behind McAfee's, but no luck identifying the trespasser. Whoever it was didn't leave any usable prints.

"The Jeep shows up in the campground. The owner is a well known professional photojournalist. Interestingly enough, she's in the campsite across from where we found the goon's pickup.

"We spot a parade of cars leaving the area a couple days ago. Or was it yesterday? Whatever, since the last time I slept. We join the parade and discover we're being followed by a suit in a federal motor pool vehicle. By the time we check in, do an interim report, and I start for home it's late afternoon. I see the hermit's car at the side of the road just north of the lagoon. I think about it and call the old man. We decide to check it out.

"We go to the location, find a bunch of tracks, a goose pen with a pile of what looks like plastic cuffs. Without a lab scan for skin cells, they're only cable ties, but my hunch says they were used as cuffs.

"We come back here to ask around some more. The hermit isn't answering the door, but we see McAfee and the artist and talk with them. Nothing new there, so we take another stab at the hermit. No answer. We're on our way to the store when the Jeep turns into a cherry bomb."

"McAfee and the artist, of course, have another concrete alibi," Weston observed. "At least I presume you guys are reliable as witnesses to their absence from the scene."

"At this point I'm not sure I'm a reliable witness to anything," Tom said. "It looks like the photographer's Jeep may have been driven into the trees where we found the plastic cuffs. John took some pictures and a soil sample off the tires before the G-men arrived, but they didn't ask and we didn't volunteer anything. We hope the lab will confirm our suspicions.

"That pretty well brings you up to date. We've ID'd the stiff on the beach. We know Tim Gordon is alive. We know he and McAfee are both in the area. We have nothing to tie either of them to the murder."

"What about connecting them to the hermit or the artist before they came here?"

"Nothing solid. Definitely some circumstantial opportunities with the artist," John said. "McAfee and Parker are both from the San Fernando Valley. The hermit's from the south, but not the valley."

"Wait a minute," Tom said, checking his notes. "She moved here from Santa Barbara. Santa Barbara's not very far from the valley. I visited my cousin when he was stationed at Port Hueneme. It was only about forty-five minutes or an hour to either one. We didn't dig very deep on the hermit. Records showed she'd been in Santa Barbara for the last five years so we stopped looking. We don't know where she was before then."

"Yes we do," John took out his note book. "She moved to Santa Barbara from Simi Valley. Where's Simi Valley in relation to the San Fernando Valley?"

"Just over the pass," Tom said. "Wait a minute! McAfee and Gordon grew up in Simi Valley!" Then he shook his head. "But we're talking about a city of a hundred thousand even back in the seventies."

"But is it only a coincidence?"

"Let's see what ties this together," Weston said. "Gordon and McAfee grow up in Simi Valley and move over the hill to the San Fernando Valley. The hermit lives in Simi Valley and moves west to Santa Barbara. The artist lives in the San Fernando Valley for what, ten years, maybe longer before she moves here?"

"Looks like it," Tom agreed.

"But it could all be coincidence," John said. "None of those places are small town America. It's a pretty thin connection."

"It may be thin, but what do you have besides a big pile of circumstantial coincidence thin enough to read a newspaper through?" Weston asked.

"True story," John agreed. "Unless you want to add a very short fuse until someone slams the door on our involvement in this case. I guess it's time to go visit our reclusive groundskeeper and see what she can tell us. Wanna go along for the ride?"

"I'm here. Maybe she'll talk to an authority figure. Or maybe she'll clam up and not even give us the time of day."

Marnee paced back and forth, struggling to remain calm while she waited for instructions. She could see Paul and Jean were quietly enjoying her discomfort. Their placid behavior grated on her frayed nerves.

Suddenly, she stopped pacing, and stared through the sheer drapes at the street. "Damn," she growled through clenched teeth as the detectives came through her gate.

Paul smiled. "This should be interesting, Marnee. How do you want to play it?"

"We're neighbors having a cup of coffee and talking about all the excitement. I bumped into you on your way back from the campground and invited you in to talk about the ruckus because I didn't want to hobble my arthritic old bones down there to see. Got it?"

"Sounds easy enough," Jean said.

"No problem," Paul agreed.

There was a knock at the door. "And remember, my name is Alma Jacobsen." She opened the door and invited the officers to come in and sit down. "Can I get you some coffee?"

They accepted her offer and found places to sit facing Paul and Jean. Weston introduced himself while Marnee went to make a fresh pot of coffee while she listened to the conversation in the living room.

"We didn't expect to find you here, Mr. McAfee," Tom said.

"We ran into Mrs. Jacobsen on our way back from the campground and started talking about the explosion," Paul said. "She invited us in for coffee and we accepted her hospitality. Kind of like strength in numbers. With all the excitement we're all feeling a little, uh, I guess kind of nervous about how safe it is living here."

"I wouldn't think this would be such a big deal to a guy from the city," John said.

"The valley has its problem neighborhoods, like all cities. I'm sure you have one or two around here as well. Where I live it's pretty quiet most of the time. This sort of thing would certainly be cause for excitement and have most folks checking their doors and making sure the dead bolts are all in good working order."

"Car bombings weren't exactly an everyday event where I lived either," Jean added. "What's going on around here? First some guy gets murdered right on our street and now this. I thought this was a quiet place where I could live in peace."

"That's what we're trying to figure out," Weston said. "Murder doesn't happen often enough for us to have a separate division and car bombings are even more rare. The last time we had a car blow up a guy had parked his pickup too close to a stump he was trying to dynamite. Did a fine job on his truck, but still needed a couple more sticks to up-root the stump. I don't have an explanation for this sudden increase in activity, but I can assure you, it bothers me a lot. I usually don't get involved in my detectives' field work, but I was here and my curiosity got the better of me. We hoped to find Mrs. Jacobsen at home, but I'm glad you're here. It gives us a chance to talk with all of you at once."

"The detectives were just talking with us before the car blew up," Paul chuckled. "I guess you could say they're the best confirmation of where we were when it happened. When you need an iron clad alibi, you guys are the best!"

Weston chuckled. "Yes. They told me how they turned out to be your alibi. Just the same, there are some other things you might be able to help us with. You don't mind do you?"

"Nope. Ask away."

"You arrived here, what, a couple weeks ago, Mr. McAfee?"

"Yes. And please call me Paul."

"Thanks. What brought you here? Specifically, here. These cabins aren't exactly highly publicized."

"I was working on taking a break from my business. I didn't know where I was going to go, I only knew I needed to go someplace and regroup. My neighbors brought a newspaper to my office with an article about the coast up here and my secretary brought them in to see me. They thought it would make a nice retreat for me. There was a photograph of the cabins and there was a real estate sign in front of that one." He pointed to the next cabin. "A friend of mine had already been telling me I should come up here, so I guess I was receptive to the idea. Something about a cabin on an ocean bluff appealed to me. Something reclusive and mysterious, with a lighthouse keeper sort of appeal. It seemed like a perfect way to separate myself from the last couple years. I told my secretary to follow up on the location and the cabin in particular because if the place was for sale, maybe the owners would be willing to accept a lease while it was on the market. A deal was struck for a six month lease."

"How do you like it?"

"What's not to like? Great view, great beaches, nice neighbors," he took Jean's hand and smiled at her. "I'm tempted to buy the place. I don't think there's a city kid anywhere who hasn't dreamed about a cabin on the beach and I have the chance to live the dream. There are worse choices."

"No argument here. I grew up here and went to college in the Bay Area. For me the city is a nice place to visit, but I wouldn't want to live there." Weston shifted his attention to Jean.

"Where did you move from, Ms. Parker?"

"Granada Hills."

"Isn't that part of Los Angeles?"

"Yes. North part of the San Fernando Valley."

"What about you Paul?"

"Northridge. My office is in North Hollywood."

"Where did you work, Ms. Parker?"

"Toluca Lake."

"Sounds impressive."

"Not really. It's just across the river from Universal Studios and not too bad a commute. The name is more impressive than the area, even if a lot of the Hollywood crowd live there."

"Doesn't Bob Hope live there?" Tom asked.

"He did for a long time, on Moorpark Ave. He may still live there. I never paid much attention to the entertainers, they're just people with an incredibly precarious high profile career."

"Fame is but a fleeting moment?" Weston said.

"Andy Warhol said everyone gets fifteen minutes," Jean replied. "For some people it just happens again and again or for a longer time. The rest of us hope we'll recognize our fifteen minutes and enjoy it before it's gone."

"You're probably right. Most of us aren't sure when our moment will be and probably don't recognize it until it's already been over for a couple days. Both you and Paul lived and worked in the San Fernando Valley. Did you ever bump into each other before you came here?"

"Have you ever been to the Valley?" Jean asked.

"No," he admitted.

"The San Fernando Valley is several hundred square miles of houses, freeways, businesses, shopping centers, and traffic. About four million people live there. The ease with which you can avoid contact with people is astounding. Almost as astounding as learning Paul's office and mine were only about a mile apart and our homes were within a couple miles of each other. We shopped in the same stores, drove the same streets, went to the same movies, and never met until we came here.

"Its a funny thing about living where there are so many people. You develop a circle of friends and add some new ones from time to time. You tend to work and socialize within a relatively small group. The rest of the time you try to be anonymous and find some privacy. It's like being a face in the crowd. You cherish your anonymity because there's no other way to be alone."

"Sounds like a sad way to live," Weston observed. "All those people rushing around with their own agendas trying to avoid contact with anyone they don't know."

Paul shrugged, "Life's a bitch, then you die."

"I guess our little corner of the world feels pretty comfortable to you."

"It's definitely a far cry from the city."

"Even with all this excitement?"

"I guess this is pretty unusual. Mrs. Alexander says this is the most excitement there's been around here since the big flood."

"Fortunately, yes. Unfortunately, we're having a tough time sorting out the cause and the culprit. We've managed to dig up a lot of information about the victim, but we could really use a break."

"Got yourself a nice pot of beans but nobody's turned up the inevitable rock?" Paul asked.

"Yeah, or the washer in the roll of nickles. I know the detectives talked to you just a little while ago, but is there anything you haven't told us? Sometimes a seemingly unrelated fact or observation turns out to be the key. For instance, do you know this man?" Weston took a photograph from his pocket and handed it to him.

Paul studied a picture taken through a long distance lens and blown up. "No, I don't think so," he said slowly.

"Doesn't look familiar at all?"

"Could be almost anybody I might have seen at some time."

"How about you, Ms. Parker?"

"Sorry, no. Who is he?"

"The victim on the beach. I thought he might have been coming to see you, Paul. It was a long shot."

"If he was coming to see me, it was without invitation and without my knowledge. Maybe he was looking for the owners. Maybe he was interested in buying the place."

Weston shook his head. "They don't know him either and yours was the only inquiry on the property in the past six months. Which is kind of unusual. There's almost always someone in a back cabin who wants to move to the front. You timed things just right. The lack of interest is why they decided to lease the place. It's interesting to know you're thinking about staying because they leased it hoping you would buy it."

While Alma listened to the conversation in the next room through the open doorway a small light blinked on the wall, indicating a message was arriving. There was no way she could slip out and retrieve it with the cops here. She listened carefully, waiting for Weston to ask anything important. The older detective looked like something was bothering him. *I don't think he sees me watching him and Tom looks completely at ease. I wonder if he might be planning something to trip me up. I need to keep my guard up.* She picked up the tray and returned to the living room. "Here's some refreshment for everyone."

Weston held the photograph out to Alma. "Do you know this man?"

She moved to the window where the light was better and held the photo as though looking through bifocals at the face of a man she knew was a collector and enforcer. Her expression divulged no sense of recognition. "Sorry. I've never seen him."

"Are you sure you haven't seen him somewhere, Mrs. Jacobsen?" John asked.

She paused briefly before she shook her head. "I suppose I might have seen him in passing somewhere, but I don't have any idea who he might be. Sorry."

"So none of you have any idea why this man might have been prowling around in the middle of the night?" Tom asked.

Their negative response reminded Alma of the three monkeys: hear no evil, see no evil, speak no evil. *We didn't plan this little Q & A, but as long as we can keep a united front we can escape without setting off too many alarms with this little inquisition.*

"This is what's so difficult," Weston explained. "We've identified the victim, but we don't know why he was here, who attacked him, or why he was attacked. You live where it happened and can't shed any light on the problem either. It's an enigma."

Silence ruled the room for a moment before Jean spoke. "Does the exploding car have something to do with the murder?"

"We're not sure," John answered. "The feds are picking through the debris. If they decide the two incidents are related they'll be doing the same things we are and you'll be answering all these questions again."

"So this is like a dress rehearsal?" Jean asked.

John smiled. "No. This is the process of an investigation. The basic work always needs to be done no matter what agency has the lead. Whenever another agency is required by jurisdictional responsibilities to assume a case in progress, the same process has to be completed. Even if it means going over the same ground someone else already plowed. By the way, have you been home all day?"

"No. Paul and I went into town this morning. We got back a little after one o'clock."

"What about you, Mrs. Jacobsen?" Tom inquired. "Did you go anywhere today?"

"Yes. I was out for a while, looking for things for my garden. You know, an old limb I could use as a trellis for my nasturtiums, maybe a small azalea or a rhodedendrum."

"Did you find what you were looking for?"

"No, but I did manage to get wet and cold. I came home and took a hot bath. It felt so good I didn't really want to get out."

"We're not trained investigators," Paul said, "but if you tell us what we need to look for or think about maybe something will come to mind later. We'd like to help if we can."

Alma understood Paul's remark was an indicator he was about to leave and her mind ran crazy trying to figure out how to keep control of them. *I hope no one saw me react to the picture of Webster, but I'm not sure I covered up quick enough.*

"Maybe it's easier than you think," Weston said. "Something as simple as seeing someone new, or a strange car, anything irregular."

Jean laughed. "How long a list do you want? The campground is almost always filled with visitors, and the tourists from the State Park who walk to this end of the beach come up here to look at the cabins all the time. This may be a little remote, but believe me, it's a far cry from private and even further from unnoticed. New faces, unfamiliar cars, hikers, rock hounds, fishermen, bird watchers, photographers, even the occasional surf bum shows up from time to time. I can't speak for Paul, but trying to sort out something unusual or irregular from the broad selection of unfamiliar faces is beyond my abilities."

"I understand. But even so, looking for someone or something out of the ordinary is something you could do."

"What do you mean by out of the ordinary?" Paul asked. "I'm new here. It all looks pretty much out of the ordinary to me."

"A good question, Maybe I used a poor example. Maybe if you notice anyone who seems to have an unusual interest in the cabins. Taking pictures, wandering around the area, sort of snoopy, maybe."

"Its going to be another long list," Jean said. "Cameras, people walking around your yard, invasion of privacy, are a daily event here. It's amazing how people would be incensed if a stranger just wandered into their yard and started taking pictures, picking the flowers, and peering through the windows of their house, but they assume it's okay to do it here. They even get upset and defensive if you ask them to respect your property and privacy."

"The good news and bad news of the tourist trade, huh? The good news is they come here and leave their money. The bad news is they tend to be a bunch of rude, insensitive jerks."

"I guess if we see anything suspicious or out of place we'll call your detectives and let them know. It sounds like about all we can do." Paul glanced at his watch. He and Jean stood up. "But right now, we have previous plans. If you're finished with us, we really need to go."

"Of course. What about it, John? Do you and Tom have any more questions for Paul and Jean?"

Alma noticed how Paul had been cooperative, friendly, answered all the questions he was asked, and said absolutely nothing important before he diplomatically ended the conversation and extracted himself and Jean from scrutiny. It was frustrating because there was really nothing she could do about it.

"No," John said. "But we would like you to stick around the area for a little while longer."

"Shouldn't be a problem," Paul said. "You know where to find us."

"Do you really have to leave so soon?" Alma complained. "We were just getting to know each other when these gentlemen arrived. Can't you stay a bit longer? I'm sure they're about to leave and we can go on with our chat." Alma moved in front of the door. "Lately I've begun to feel lonely. Getting to know you is really important to me."

Paul extended his hand to her as he approached the door. "I'm sure we'll have lots of time to talk and get to know each other, but right now, we need to go." He released her hand and reached for the doorknob.

Alma put her hand on his arm. "Please stay. We have so much to talk about. I really want to get to know both of you better."

"It will have to be another time. We're supposed to meet some folks in Trinidad who are interested in buying some of Jean's work. I'm sure you understand how important it is for her to establish herself as an artist. We'll talk with you in the next day or two and fill you in on how we did." He opened the door. "Good afternoon, gentlemen," he called out as he shepherded Jean through the door.

Alma stepped back to avoid making a scene. She shivered inwardly as the focus of the detectives' attention settled upon her. Carefully controlling her emotions, she sat primly erect facing her inquisitors, fighting the anger and frustration of knowing Paul and Jean had slithered through her fingers with the help of the men in front of her.

John had noticed small flaws in her story. He also noticed how Paul and Jean seemed to be very cooperative, but Weston hadn't pressed them for anything. It also seemed like they were in no hurry for the detectives to leave. *What sort of game were they playing? You really didn't want us to leave and the hermit can't wait for us to pack our shit and split. She also says she took a bath, but her hair needs to be combed and there's a mud stain on the back of her pants. You'd think she would have put on clean clothes after her bath and taken the time to comb her hair. It even looks like there's a small leaf caught in her hair.* "So how long were you out this afternoon looking for things for your garden?" *They just escaped her clutches and she is well and truly pissed about it,* John thought as he studied the poised countenance she presented to him. *We walked in on a gathering that had nothing to do with neighbors getting to know each other. I'd bet a month's pay those two aren't off to meet with patrons of the arts either.* "I know it's easy to lose track of time when you're visiting Mother Nature, even when it's raining."

Alma settled into the innocent guise of her character and focused her attention on John's question. "Oh, gosh, I'm not sure, about an hour and a half, maybe two hours, I guess. I got caught up in my quest and I wasn't paying much attention to the time." Alma was trapped, caught in a lie, without Paul's skill at ending a conversation. All she could do was keep the lie consistent. "It wasn't raining when I left the house, just the usual collected stuff falling from the trees. When it started to rain I had to hurry back to my car before I drowned."

"Where did you go?"

"I went up into the trees north of the lagoon. You know, up near where the old logging road goes into the trees?"

John's suspicions were confirmed. "You mean the road running past the hollow tree?"

"Yes, that's the one."

"Did you see anyone else?"

"No."

"You didn't see any cars parked near yours?"

"No. As far as I know I was alone, but it's a big forest. I wasn't looking for people, I was hunting for things for my garden."

"Did you see anyone up there around the hollow tree?" Tom asked

"No. I was on the north side of the hill near the creek. I didn't go anywhere near the hollow tree. Did something happen I should know about?"

"No, not really," John said. "We're just trying to check all the possibilities. We found some fresh tire tracks on the old skid road. Where did you park your car? Did you drive into the trees or just pull off the highway and walk?"

"Oh, I was afraid I'd get stuck if I tried to drive into the trees."

"Thank you, Mrs. Jacobsen," Weston and the detectives stood. "We really appreciate your help. And thanks for the coffee."

Alma cursed all the gods of fortune for the way timing of events allowed Paul and Jean to escape. She slipped on a jacket and went out the back door to see what new orders had come from the desk pilots on the Potomac.

63.

THE PHONE WAS RINGING WHEN THEY REACHED
Jean's door. She dashed to grab it before the caller hung up.
"It's for you," she said.

His ear was filled with the background sounds of a cellular
phone in a moving automobile. "Yes?"

"The net is closing," Pisces said.

"Thank you."

"See you soon." The connection was broken, but not before
the scanner in the white Chevrolet picked up the conversation.

Weston leaned back and sipped his coffee. "Neither of
you said much in there, which is fine. A lot can be learned
by watching and listening while someone else conducts an
interview. It felt good to be in the middle of an investigation.
I have a better feel for this case now. Tell me what you saw
and heard."

"Why don't you tell us what you think," Tom asked.

Weston looked at Tom with a growing respect for his
instincts. "Fair enough. You guys have been studying this
cast of characters for a while and could probably use a fresh
perspective. I think Mr. McAfee knows a lot more than he's
telling us. The older woman is a bit of a mystery and she's
definitely not telling us truth. I'm sure you noticed she wasn't
wearing clean clothes after her alleged bath. Something about
her appearance and mannerisms just doesn't ring true either. If

you aren't looking at her when she's talking, she doesn't sound like an elderly woman who's worried about getting her senior citizen discounts."

"Almost like she's in makeup and costume, right?" Tom said.

Suddenly John sat up straight. "Yes! That's what's been bugging me about her! The voice! Her goddamn voice! She looks old, but her voice is young. Or at least a lot younger!"

Weston nodded emphatically. "I think you're right. So what can we do with the information? Does it actually lead us anywhere? What if she's just one of those women whose voice doesn't get older sounding? Take a look at the rest of the package. She's trim, tanned, her mind is sharp, and she doesn't move like an elderly woman on the edge of arthritic pain, no matter what she claims. Maybe she's lucky and the years haven't taken as big a toll on her as the average woman. Maybe she's in a disguise of some kind, but the law doesn't say you can't wear a costume or change your name or have surgery done to change your appearance. If you take all of it and add a buck, Mrs. Alexander will sell you a cup of coffee. What good does it do us in terms of trying to solve this case?"

"Wait a minute!" Tom stood so quickly he knocked over his chair. "If we go back to my original idea this begins to make some sense." Tom paced up and down, talking excitedly. "Gordon is a cutout for some unidentified agency, working to set up the bad guys, using a scheme smuggling counterfeit computer chips until everything gets screwed up and he gets hung out to dry. He's supposed to die quietly in a plane crash along with McAfee's wife, but he slips away. Now everybody on both sides of the operation is trying to catch him. Alma Jacobsen sets up housekeeping here within a few weeks of the crash. Some time passes and McAfee rents the place next door to her. A couple weeks later we have a body on the beach and another in a bombed out Jeep. To add to the confusion, the body in the Jeep doesn't belong to the owner because the petite photographer sure wasn't a fat, gray haired old man. No disguise is that good!

"Boss, how unusual is it for the feds to jump on a case the way they pounced on the car bomb? In my experience they aren't usually eager to chase anything but bank robbers and today they arrived like they were lashed to the bumper of your car."

"An astute observation! It usually takes them a while to respond when we call them. They were on this so fast it's like they were waiting for the call. They couldn't wait to kick us off the case. I kept thinking about it on the way up here, but I chalked it up to being the end of a boring day and a long dry spell for them, especially the bomb squad, things have been pretty quiet for them lately."

"Almost like they knew what they'd find before they got here?" John said.

"Almost. I've long since disposed of any notions about building a better bridge between us and those agencies, but I had a crawly feeling watching them dogging my trail. It makes me nervous knowing you found a connection between your case and the car bomb. I know it's thin, but it's still a thread. Even a thin thread means the incidents might be related."

"Okay," Tom said. "Let me go on with this before I lose track of where I was. I think I saw Tim Gordon in the crowd on the beach, but I didn't get a chance to talk to him. So let's say he's here, and just for good measure, let's presume the photographer is somehow involved. I don't know how, it's just a feeling. Her work lets her move around a lot without attracting undue attention. She's always going to attract attention because of the way she looks, but the photojournalist job would make a great cover for something less reputable.

"Anyway, let's say we've got Gordon, McAfee, Rose, and Jacobsen, maybe even Parker, all involved in this smuggling operation and they all end up here at the same time. How do we prove they're in this together and how do we link them to the murder?"

"Right," John said. "How do they all fit together and how does Jean Parker fit into the story? In case you've forgotten, she bought her place just after the plane crash and she's from the same area as McAfee and Gordon. We've confirmed her divorces, her place of employment, and her University of California degree. Maybe she's just an innocent bystander who got caught up in this affair and can't get loose."

"Or doesn't want to get loose," Weston offered.

"Another possibility," John agreed. "I see the way she and McAfee behave together and it looks real. It still seems like an awful lot of coincidences for it to be coincidental."

"You're right, partner. There's an awful big cloud of smoke for us not to be getting close to a fire. It really pisses me off how McAfee always finds a way to turn off our questions whenever he decides to. The son of a bitch seems to know how to say all the right things, tell us nothing, and then shuffle us off to peddle our papers. And then there's the hermit. She damn sure knows a lot more about what was going on out there in the woods than she's telling us. I was watching her body language. It was subtle, but she was definitely uncomfortable to have us join their little party. I also think she recognized the picture of the dead goon. I can feel it! I can smell it! I can taste it! But there's no way I can see how to get inside their minds and finish it! It pisses me off!"

"A rather bright young fellow, isn't he?" Weston commented.

"Yes, but somewhat emotional. Gets entirely too caught up in his work and tends to forget there's more to life than fighting crime."

"I suppose, in all fairness, we should encourage him to continue in this manner. What do you think?"

"I think trying to discourage him would prove to be a rather fruitless endeavor."

Tom waited patiently until they finished. "So what do you really think? And I mean about what I just said, not the bullshit you've been using to clear your throats."

"Well, I don't know about your partner, but I think you might be onto something. I wish I could tell you how to tie it all together, but I honestly don't know. We got little or nothing important out of our visit with the folks on the bluff. I also think you're right about Jacobsen recognizing the stiff. The reaction flashed in her eyes before she dropped the blinds over it. You're also right about the way McAfee controls a conversation. He lets you take things wherever you want to go, answers whatever you ask with unassailable responses having no real substance. When he's ready to stop talking, he politely stands up, says good-bye and walks away. If Jean Parker hasn't got something going with him, she sure as hell thinks she does. Of course it could all be an act. People can be devious when it comes to protecting themselves. In fact, the more I think about it, the more devious these characters seem to be. Tempus fugit, guys. The clock is ticking and the witching hour approaches. You better hustle if you plan to win this skirmish, because the cavalry is just over the hill and I can hear their horses and bugles."

64.

THE PUFFY EDGE OF THE FOG WAS CROWDING THE
coast when the executive jet lifted from the runway and
folded its landing gear. Air traffic control directed the pilot
to the airway intersection off Pt. Reyes. Two minutes later,
the navigation system was homed in on the way point and the
plane was climbing out over a cottony bank of coastal stratus.
The radar blip representing the aircraft suddenly disappeared
from the Air Traffic Controller's screen a mile south of Cape
Mendocino. The flaming wreckage briefly burned a hole in
the clouds on it's way to a watery grave in a deep ocean valley.

Tim kissed Julie when she got into the car. "Are you ready
to get out of here?"

"The sooner the better. I've had enough excitement for a
while."

Tim headed for the exit from the parking lot without
noticing the white Chevrolet parked alongside an airport
building. "Hopefully, this is the last we'll see of him. I hate to
think the only way to make him stop chasing us is to kill him."

"Only time will tell."

"How did you get away from the Jeep? I thought you were
gone when it blew up. What the hell happened?"

"Somebody left a body in my car. When I leaned in to
check the stiff, I noticed a wire hanging below the dash. Sloppy
work, but it led me to a bomb under the dash. I recognized the

trigger mechanism as one I'd seen in the Middle East. Difficult to disarm and equipped with a fifteen second delay. I never got into the car. I started it up, dropped it into gear and headed for the tall timber. I was barely clear when the blast treated me to a brief flight and a hard landing."

"What body? Who put a body in your car? Who put a bomb in the car? Gino didn't have enough time. I know anything's possible, but it sure sounds like an installation done in a hurry, maybe by someone Gino scared off before the job was complete."

"I don't know where either one came from or who put them there. I was too busy trying to stay alive to worry about it. When my eyes uncrossed I saw Gino taking you away and I followed you. You know what happened next."

"Jesus, first a bomb in the airplane killed Lisa and then a bomb in your car knocks us both for a loop. It looks like the boys from Gormac aren't safe to be around if you favor a long life. I thought I knew all the players in this game, but who the hell is the bomber? It's pretty obvious whoever it is doesn't care about collateral damage as long as the target goes down. Maybe there's no connection between the bomb on the airplane and the bomb in your car, but it seems awfully coincidental. What do you think?"

"Hard to tell. I don't know about you, but I still have a splitting headache and I'm not thinking very clearly. I bet my pupils are still different sizes. I know they don't respond very well to changes in light. If I don't have a concussion I have all the symptoms. Maybe I'll be able to make sense of this once my head's cleared, but right now I don't want to think very hard about anything."

"The first store we come to we'll pick up some Excedrin or Tylenol for both of us. My ears are still fuzzy and my head feels like a three star hangover. We sure as hell can't let our guard down. The car bomb blew up our plans along with your gear and I think Gino had something to do with it. He sure was happy to see the car explode. But where would he have gotten a bomb and where did he get the body and why would he choose a disposal method with such a large signature? My brain is too foggy to think clearly, but it just doesn't make sense!"

"I don't know. I don't think he had time to set the bomb and I don't think the materials to build it were in the car they were driving. I didn't find anything when I checked it before we came to get you. I really don't want to think about it right now. Can we just get the hell out of here and try to figure it out later?"

"You got my vote. Don't conk out on me. We need all our faculties in full operation for a little while longer. Marnee or our English friend could still be hiding in the weeds waiting for us to get complacent."

65.

JEAN WATCHED PAUL'S FACE AS HE HUNG UP THE phone.

"That sounded like Julie. Is everything all right?"

"Everything may be just fine."

"May?"

"Huh?"

"You said everything *may* be just fine."

"I guess I did. You never really know in a situation like this."

"You've been in this kind of situation before?"

"Not exactly, but you always try to plan for the contingencies. Mr. Murphy will usually inject an interesting surprise you don't expect at the least opportune moment with the worst possible results. I think we have things in control for the moment, but I'm not ready to breathe easy just yet."

The room suddenly felt very cold to Jean. She crossed her arms in a classic defensive posture and steeled herself against the impact of the answer she didn't want to hear. "Like me, you mean? An unexpected surprise getting in the way of your carefully laid plans?"

"Yes. Like you. You were not a factor in the original planning."

"So where do I stand? Am I a part of your plans or am I about to be the girl you left behind?" Fear was beginning to fire her temper. She felt like what she had been planning for the last few days was about to vaporize. "Am I going to have an unpleasant driving experience like our friend across the way?"

Paul's unwavering gaze settled on Jean's frightened eyes. "Not if you want to come with me. But we have to leave now! Right this minute! There's no time to pack a suitcase or anything else. I really want you to come with me, but I can't guarantee your safety either way. I can't decide your life for you and I wouldn't presume to do so. If you decide to stay, I'll miss you and always wish you had come with me, but I'd have to learn to live with it because I don't have any other choice if I want to stay alive. The decision is yours. You know what I want. It's your life. It's your choice."

"Master of my own destiny, huh? Just lock the door and leave? Just like that?"

"Just like that."

Jean studied Paul's face for a full minute without speaking. She couldn't imagine what it would be like to look back on her life and know she had passed up her chance to be with him. He wanted her to go with him. He had enough money to establish them in some exotic location or travel anyplace they chose. She looked around at her paintings and the cozy little house she had made her home and realized it would never be warm again without Paul to share it. "Lock the back door while I grab my coat."

"Better to lock the front and go out the back. We'll leave my car here and close the doors on your garage so it looks like we're still here. With luck it'll stall the wolves for the few hours we need to get out of town."

"Okay. Throw the bolt and meet me at the car. If I think about this any longer I may lose my nerve and I don't want to lose my nerve. The car keys are hanging by the back door. Get my car and close things up the way you think they should look."

Marnee watched Jean and Paul drive toward the highway. She had been directed to keep them under surveillance, but not to leave her cottage until she received further instructions. They were leaving and she was hampered by impossible instructions from a handler thousands of miles away. Everything looks fine to the handler sitting in a comfortable office while the field agent sees the objective slipping away by obeying orders. "Screw it!" The door slammed behind her as she ran for her car.

Tom and John were getting into their car when Jean and Paul drove by. "Just can't help wondering where they're going, can you?" Tom said. "My money says they aren't headed for Trinidad to meet with a patron of the arts. Wouldn't you like to be a fly on the roof of their car? I bet you'd learn the answers to a lot of questions. You think we should keep an eye on them? You know, just for the sake of being thorough about our investigative practices. There's no way he can dissemble his way out of the direction they're driving."

"Wouldn't hurt," John said. "Actually helps. If we're following them, the G-men can't get in our face about what we didn't tell them."

"Well, well. There goes the hermit. I'm beginning to get a sense of déjà vu. The same little wagon train rolled out of here the last time we were here. Do you think maybe,"

"She's following them?"

"You guys are getting scary," Weston said. "How long have you been finishing each other's sentences?"

The detectives shrugged. "Talk to you later, boss," they chorused and followed the two cars.

When they reached the highway neither car was in sight. "Turn left!" Tom shouted before they rolled to a stop.

John wheeled into the northbound lanes and pressed the throttle to the floor. "All right, I got the pedal to the metal. Why north instead of south?"

"Because up until now they've always turned south. It figures this time they'll head the other way."

"What kind of logic is that?"

"At least half right logic. There's the hermit's rust mobile. Ease off a bit so we don't run over her."

"An amazing call. How the hell did you do it?"

"Shit man, I figured an old dog like you would know without asking."

"You're right. It makes sense. McAfee made a point of telling us they were headed for Trinidad, maybe hoping we'd look there first and give them a lead on us. As long as I'm driving and you're talking, where are they going and what are they going to do when they get there?"

"I think if we mind our manners we'll witness a gathering of the crowd as they make ready to do a disappearing act. They're either headed for an airport or a harbor because they need to get off the road. Both are available at Crescent City. I don't think we need to look for a boat because a boat is too slow and too easy to catch. Which leaves an airplane. A fast way to put some serious distance on us. All they need is a fast plane, and I have every reason to think they have one because McAfee told us his wife and partner were only on the PSA flight because the company bird was in the shop. We're going to the Crescent City airport."

"Great! It's in the next county and fifty miles outside

our jurisdiction. What are you planning to do if we catch everybody in one place? Make a citizen's arrest?"

"Unless they do something illegal we still don't have reasonable cause to arrest any of them, do we?"

"Right! So cut to the chase. What do think we should do? I'm too tired to do much more than agree with you. Besides, as scary as it is to admit it, you're making sense."

"We hang in there, see where they're going, and call the feebies. It ain't out of their jurisdiction. Even if we can't make the arrest we can at least rub their noses in solving the case for them or, at worst, inform them their pigeons have flown the coop."

"Did I ever tell you you have a devious mind?"

"Is it a problem?"

"Not for me. Only for the poor bastards you get in your sights when you're about to pull something." John paused. "I have a question for you. Now that we have them all rounded up what do we tell the feds to arrest them for?"

"I don't know. Tell them they planted the bomb in the Jeep to cover up what really happened to the guy we found inside it. Tell them we have reason to believe they've been passing funny money, no, that's Secret Service and Treasury. I don't know. I'm making this up as I go along. You're the ancient sage. What do you think?"

"I think it's time to change your diaper because the one you're wearing is full of shit. I think we only have one choice. Follow the trail and see what jumps out of the bushes at us."

"With any luck Tim Gordon will suddenly materialize, arisen from the allegedly dead."

"Rumors of his death have been exaggerated?"

"My thoughts exactly. Hey take a look." Tom pointed into the fading light. "It looks like, yeah it is! The artist's car is up there about a quarter mile in front of the hermit. This keeps getting better all the time."

"You're right. There's just one problem."

"What now?"

"It's hard to tell because there's not many places to turn off, but what if we've just made ourselves the cheese in the sandwich?" John looked in the rear view mirror. "Don't turn around. Use the mirror on the visor to check out the cars behind us."

Tom positioned the visor to reflect the road behind. "So what should I be looking for?"

"One, maybe two cars. The first is a shit brown Ford in the left lane. It hangs the same distance behind us like it's tied on a string. I think there's two people in it."

"Got it! What's the other one?"

"Watch about a quarter mile behind the Ford. There's a white Chevrolet keeping the same speed and distance too. Looks like we've got two in front, two in back, and we, my friend, are the cheese. I know who's in front of us, but who do you suppose is sniffing our exhaust plume?"

Tom stared into the mirror for several minutes while he studied the cars behind them. While other traffic seemed to drift and float in relation to each other, the brown Ford and the white Chevrolet seemed almost locked together. Both occasionally changed lanes, but the distance remained constant. "It definitely looks like a five car caravan. The county line approaches. Should we break it off or hang in and watch what happens?"

"What the hell, we've got nothing to lose, maybe fortune will smile on us and we'll finally get some answers. At the very least we'll have the satisfaction of knowing we took our best shot when we had the chance."

It was only fifteen minutes in the Beechcraft King Air 200 from Brookings to Crescent City. The pilot had spent the last three days waiting for the call. The airport was blessed with a comfortably long runway and an easy approach along the beach. He taxied to the parking area, shut down the engines, and lowered the air stair. He immediately began a pre-flight inspection. The pilot attributed his thousands of hours of incident free flying time to not cutting corners in his pre-flight preparations. Experience had taught him there was always time to prepare as long as you didn't waste the time you had available. Preparations included a licensed nine millimeter Beretta in a shoulder holster. He met Tim when they were in the Army. By the time the pilot retired from the Army, Tim and Paul had achieved a level of success which made it easy for him to convince them to buy the airplane and hire him to fly and manage it. Over the past five years he had accommodated passengers ranging from underworld toughs to congressional aides, but most of the time he flew the boys and as Tim put it, kept their asses out of a sling.

Jean and Paul arrived first and hurried to the airplane. He hadn't expected Marnee to wheel her car onto the ramp and roar across the tarmac toward them. Paul stopped the pilot when he reached for his gun. "Let's see what's on her mind," he said. "Jean, why don't you get on the plane while I handle this."

The next surprise was seeing John and Tom pull into the lot and park alongside Jean's car. "Friends of yours?" the pilot asked.

"Local talent. They're the detectives who've been trying to learn who's responsible for this mess. Luckily, they're outside their jurisdiction. Up here they're just interested citizens, but they still have their radio and their guns. Let's not make them nervous."

"That's fine unless they invite the feds to join the party. Last time I looked this is definitely inside their purview and the one driving up is NSA in a rather good disguise. I think we're already at risk."

Paul watched the detectives get out and lean against the front of their car as Marnee came to a stop alongside the airplane. He turned to the pilot. "How did you recognize, never mind, you can tell me later." Marnee got out and stood at the open door of her car looking toward the detectives.

"So what do you want, Marnee? You want to thumb a ride? I don't think we're going anywhere you want to go."

"No, but it's nice of you to think of the comfort of a old lady. I suppose you're expecting your partner to show up as well?"

Paul looked over her shoulder as the brown Ford stopped alongside Jean's car. He saw Tim start to wave cheerily at the detectives. Paul began to smile, but then he saw the white Chevrolet entering the parking lot as well. He yelled to get Tim's attention, pushed Marnee aside and jumped into her car. He spun the car in the direction of the Chevrolet bearing down on Tim and Julie as they ran for the airplane.

The detectives were still adjusting to Tim's sudden appearance when they realized the driver of the Chevrolet was pointing a machine pistol out the window of the car. Tom shouted "Gun! Gun! Gun!" as he dived for cover. John moved with surprising agility to draw his weapon as he heard the first staccato burst of automatic weapon fire.

Paul had positioned the Escort between the shooter and Tim and Julie just as the driver began to fire. Bullets stitched the side of the car and shattered the side window.

Tom and John couldn't shoot at the driver of the Chevrolet because Tim and Julie were in their line of fire.

Paul floored the accelerator and aimed the Escort at the Chevrolet. He slammed into the left rear, spinning the car violently and making it careen onto two wheels before settling back on all four.

Tim and Julie took advantage of the collision to reach the airplane. The pilot was starting the engines when Tim pushed Julie inside and tossed aside his jacket to free the assault weapon he had taken from Gino's body.

Paul wheeled the Escort back toward the airplane. The crumpled front fender threatened to flatten the tire before he covered the short distance to the airplane.

The detectives broke from cover in opposite directions to put the Chevrolet in a crossfire. The car was handling badly when the driver regained control. The left rear wheel was bent and gas was leaking onto the pavement. Tim fired a short burst from the assault weapon into the radiator and engine and a second burst into the right front tire. The engine screamed a tortured accompaniment to the howling tires as the driver squeezed the last ounces of life from the car as it limped toward the airplane.

Tim calmly drew a bead on the forehead of the driver, but hesitated when he recognized the face behind the wheel. The driver was bringing the machine pistol up to aim at him when John Ragsdale's shot entered the driver's left temple. Paul managed to get a running start for the airstair before the Chevrolet slammed into the rear of the Escort.

Tim grabbed Paul's hand and pulled him into the cabin as the airplane began a fast taxi. Tim pulled the airstair shut and slammed the locking mechanism into place. "Door secure!" he shouted as the pilot increased the taxi speed.

The detectives ran to the Chevrolet, where they found the driver slumped over the steering wheel. The gun had fallen from the driver's hand and lay several feet behind the car. John checked for a pulse and found none. Tom leaned the driver back against the seat and pulled the door open, preparing to start CPR.

"Don't bother," John said, pointing at the exit wound that gaped between the right eye and ear. "She's not coming back. I don't think they are either." The sleek aircraft lifted from the runway and folded its gear.

"It looks like we may not solve this case after all, doesn't it?" Tom said. "I wonder how long it will take to identify her."

66.

Another day and several hours of sleep later, they learned the driver had been identified as Lisa McAfee. More importantly, the questions raised by her sudden appearance were not to remain entirely unanswered. The search of her car revealed the kind of materials used to manufacture the bomb used to destroy the Jeep. The discovery sent a ripple through the records in Washington DC and sent the detectives to the California Medical Facility at Vacaville to talk to the man convicted of planting the bomb in the luggage of the PSA flight.

The detectives were joined for the interview by investigators from the NTSB and the FBI.

The prisoner was a thirty year old male of medium build, dark brown hair and eyebrows like a large caterpillar.

"Mr. Jacobs, I'm John Ragsdale, Humboldt County Sheriff's detective. This is my partner Tom Schroeder, Agent Woods of the FBI and Mr. Peebles of the NTSB. We'd like to talk to you about the crash of PSA Flight 367. Do you remember it?"

Jacobs smiled and shook hands with each of them. "Sure, what do you want to know?"

"Why did you put the bomb on the airplane?"

"The motherfuckers fired me! So I put a bomb on their airplane!"

"How did you learn to build a bomb?"

"Why?"

"We thought you could explain how you built the device and where you got the materials."

"Who cares? It worked!"

"We'd really like to know."

"Will they let me out of here if I tell you?"

"It's not up to us."

"Then why should I tell you?"

"Maybe just to satisfy our curiosity. Do you recognize this woman?" John handed Jacobs a photograph of Lisa McAfee.

"What if I do?"

"Do you?"

"Maybe. Who is she?"

"I hoped you could tell me."

"How would I know?"

"Do you recognize her? Have you ever seen her?"

"Maybe. I seen a lot of people. I can't remember them all."

"Of course not. But do you remember her?"

"Why should I?"

"Maybe she gave you the bomb you put on the airplane."

"Bullshit! That's bullshit! I built it myself! I blew the fucker out of the sky! All those pieces! I did it! They deserved it! They fired me! They deserved to die!"

"They fired you, so you built a bomb and put it on the airplane? You killed a hundred people because they fired you?"

"You damn right! I did it and ain't nobody gonna take credit for it but me! I did it!" Jacobs leaped to his feet. The guards grabbed him by both arms. "I built the bomb! I blew the fucking airplane out of the sky! I killed all those people to prove the sons of bitches shouldn't have fired me!" Jacobs kicked and squirmed and continued shouting obscenities as they removed him from the room and herded him down the hall.

"Well, this looks like a dead end," Woods said.

Peebles stood, shaking his head. "Yeah. It looked like we might have a shot at something, but this looney isn't going to help us. Maybe Lisa McAfee built the bomb, the materials in her car matched what we could identify from the PSA flight. Maybe she built it for him. Maybe she got him to put it on the plane. Maybe they were working together. It makes a nice clean answer and would tie everything up in a neat little package, but I don't think there's any way we'll ever be able to prove it."

"Didn't you say the residue of the explosives from the airplane and the residue from the Jeep were almost identical?" Tom asked.

"Yes, and it looks like the Lear that went down off the coast may be the same as well, but we need more than similar materials to conclude the bombs were built by the same person. C-4 was used in all three cases, but the switches weren't the same, so if it was the same person building them it was someone with serious knowledge of demolition devices. We'll probably never know. This guy sure as hell isn't going to help us, he wants to be the mad bomber, probably gives him street cred in the nut house. It doesn't matter if we think he was her accomplice. We can't prove it. She's dead and he's nuts. Even if he told us she gave him the device and asked him to plant it on the airplane, who would believe him? Would you?"

Tom shook his head. "No. As much as I would like to, I don't think I would."

"What about you guys?" John asked Woods. "Have you found anything more on Lisa McAfee?"

"Whoever she might have been working for slammed the door on us. The records on Lisa McAfee only go back fifteen years, before then she never existed. No birth certificates, no social security numbers, no tax returns, no addresses, no parents, no family. Nothing."

"Another deep cover operator?" Tom asked.

"Maybe. I don't know and I can't find out. Like the guy Conklin, who got blown up in the car. Everything about him says he was an electrical contractor with a long history of government contracts. He was married for more than thirty years to Paul McAfee's mother's best friend. He helped Gordon and McAfee get their business going. We don't have a clue what he was doing at the time of his death and the NSA is a stonewall about him."

"Like we don't have a clue where their airplane went after it took off from Crescent City?" Tom said.

"Right. The tail number you gave us came back to a different aircraft than the one you saw."

"What about the rest of the cast of characters? I managed to trace Alma Jacobsen back about ten years without finding anything out of the ordinary before you guys took over. Did you discover anything interesting?"

"Another dancing shadow, classified." Woods held up his hand to stop Tom from asking the obvious question. "Classified as in 'its none of your business, agent, go chase an embezzler'. It turns out there are more classified blind alleys around this group than you can shake a stick at, including McAfee and Gordon. You can follow their tracks in a steady line from about age ten, but along the way, there are a lot of closed doors when you start digging into the details, and those doors are locked tight. The lid is sealed and there's nothing we can do about it. It looks like the only player in the mix without a watchdog on her past is Jean Parker. Everything about her is an open book up to when she got on the airplane."

"Quite a dance routine they had going with keeping

a legitimate business front out in the public and handling undercover activities in the background for who knows how many agencies in Washington."

"More than a dance routine, deputy," Peebles said. "This was a precision ballet of shadows on a world stage. These guys are really good. When somebody canceled the show and turned up the house lights they just faded into the shadows. I feel sorry for you guys. All the hard work and heavy digging and when you got all done, you still didn't find the gold. At least my investigation had a conclusion, even if it did end up in the looney bin."

John took a deep breath of the warm afternoon air. "Well, Tommy, I guess it's time to go home."

Printed in the United States
By Bookmasters